y:
ce
an

ven-
at it?" questions'

SFX

metal here, usually in the smoulder-
of the next city state the Artemisians have torn
So what more could you want? The next book
ase, Mr Ballantyne . . . There's so much implicit in
the title of this book, which hints at the philosophical
layers underlying but not undermining rip-snorting
robot total war. A thumping good read'   Neal Asher

'Written in a deceptively simple style, *Twisted Metal* is
not only highly readable, but surprisingly thoughtful.
Ballantyne's creation of a world of robots allows him to
focus on the beliefs that we humans have about ourselves from an entertainingly different perspective'

The Times

'Ballantyne's fourth novel is an original work with a distinctive voice. It works not only as a thrilling action adventure, but as a thought experiment exploring free will, independence and totalitarianism' *Guardian*

'An oddly fashioned yet brilliantly written fable that's also a genuinely harrowing read . . . A weird and truly unsettling allegory of genetic inheritance, nationalism, religion and sheer barbaric cruelty of war . . . An affecting, powerful and deeply relevant work of science fiction' *SFX*

'Full blooded fantasy . . . An engaging adventure'
DeathRay

'Edgy, kinetic, and creative' *SciFiNow*

'Ballantyne's slow and steady doling out of facts and scenery builds up a world and ideologies that are worth the read and give you plenty to think about. When you add a hefty dose of action to the mix (which Ballantyne certainly does!) then you have a story that rockets along to a heady finish. Ballantyne has a great time sending opposing robots up against each other and he does this with great panache, leaving no diode un-wrenched in scenes of full on robot warfare'

graemesfantasybookreview.com

BLOOD AND IRON

Tony Ballantyne, who lives in the Manchester area, regularly contributed to magazines such as *Interzone* and *Private Eye* before embarking on his first novel, *Recursion*. *Twisted Metal* was the first novel in his Penrose series and is available in paperback now.

BLOOD
AND IRON

TONY BALLANTYNE

TOR

First published 2010 by Tor

This edition published 2011 by Tor
an imprint of Pan Macmillan, a division of Macmillan Publishers Limited
Pan Macmillan, 20 New Wharf Road, London N1 9RR
Basingstoke and Oxford
Associated companies throughout the world
www.panmacmillan.com

ISBN 978-0-330-47889-2

1 3 5 7 9 8 6 4 2

A CIP catalogue record for this book is available
from the British Library.

Typeset by Ellipsis Books Limited, Glasgow
Printed in the UK by CPI Mackays, Chatham ME5 8TD

Map artwork by Raymond Turvey

For Eric, Chris and Simon

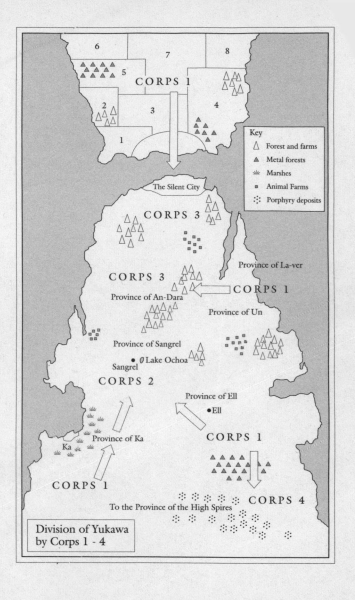

Division of Yukawa
by Corps 1 - 4

Key

△ Forest and farms
▲ Metal forests
⚹ Marshes
▪ Animal Farms
⁘ Porphyry deposits

6
7
8
5
CORPS 1
2
3
4
1

The Silent City

CORPS 3

CORPS 3

Province of La-ver

Province of An-Dara

CORPS 1

Province of Un

Province of Sangrel

Sangrel · Ø Lake Ochoa

CORPS 2

Province of Ell

· Ell

Province of Ka

Ka

CORPS 1

CORPS 1

CORPS 4

To the Province of the High Spires

My God, My God, why have you forsaken me?
I have cried desperately for help
but still it does not come.
During the day I call to you, my God
but you do not answer,
I call at night, but get no rest . . .

From Psalm 22

The Story of Kavan and Karel

This is the story of Kavan and Karel, who fought when they were a thousand miles apart and endured a bitter truce when together.

Both represented their states, though neither was of their states.

At the time of their making, Artemis and Turing City were the two greatest states on the continent of Shull. The robots of Turing City were made to respect themselves and others as individuals; the robots of Artemis were made to place the state above all else. Turing City celebrated the ascendancy of the mind. Its streets and buildings were artfully planned and decorated, its parliament and forges rang to the sound of vigorous debate as the robots discussed the philosophy of their state and others. Artemis City saw no distinction between the twisted metal that formed a robot's mind and any other metal. Its forges rang to the noise of hammers, building the army that was already marching into other states and claiming them for its own. Already the robots of Artemis City were looking beyond Shull and thinking of other continents they could subsume. Some had even dared to think of moving beyond the planet of Penrose itself. Little were they to know that other planets were looking to them.

But that is not part of this story, rather it is part of *Blood and Iron*, the story that follows.

Now, Karel was a child of war. His mother was forced to weave his mind from the metal of an Artemisian soldier. All through the making of the mind, the soldier taunted the mother by asking which philosophy she had chosen to weave, but Liza refused to answer. So Karel grow up surrounded by suspicion, never quite trusted by any robot save Susan, his wife, and that was only because Susan had been woven to love Karel. When Artemis turned its attention towards Turing City, many doubted where Karel's loyalties lay.

Kavan was not made in Artemis, but no one doubted his loyalties. It was said that his mother came from Segre, that she had looked at the way the world was moving and wove the Artemisian philosophy into her son, believing it to be the best route to his survival. If that were true, she wove better than most mothers of Artemis itself. Artemis welcomed all robots who were willing to follow Nyro's way, so Kavan became a member of the Artemisian infantry. He gained status all the time in the eyes of other Artemisians, eventually leading the final push that ensured the fall of the state of Wien. So great was his following by this time that Spoole, first amongst equals of the Generals who led Artemis City, began to regard him as a threat. It was Spoole who ordered Kavan to attack Turing City, reasoning that whether Kavan or Turing City fell, he would rid himself of one of the greatest threats to his leadership.

Kavan succeeded in taking Turing City, and during the battle Karel saw his son killed, his wife taken into slavery and all he believed in destroyed. Karel's mind was removed from his own body and set to driving a diesel engine in support of the Artemisian war effort.

Now all of Shull knew Kavan's name, and Karel hated him. Karel blamed Kavan for the death of his son, the loss of his wife, and his enslavement.

But did Kavan know of Karel? For Karel was still spoken of by many robots, mentioned by some as a traitor who had betrayed Turing City, mentioned by others as the coming mind that was referred to in the almost mythical Book of Robots.

Perhaps Kavan was yet to hear of Karel, but the time was approaching when the two robots would certainly know of each other's existence. When that happened, life on Penrose would change forever.

Here the story of Karel and Kavan fragments into many versions.

All agree that Kavan was sent by Spoole to conquer the kingdoms of northern Shull, for Spoole still feared Kavan, and did not wish him to return to Artemis City at the head of an army.

Artemisian records were second to none, and most survived the coming troubles that were to beset Artemis City, so it is without doubt that Karel travelled north, carrying troops and other materiel to support the invasion.

All of the accounts agree that Karel and Kavan met on the northern coast of Shull and that Karel fought Kavan, but before the outcome could be resolved, circumstances forced them to go their separate ways. It is also agreed that it was on the northern coast that Karel finally understood his own nature. He saw that the anger within him was so powerful he would never accept the world as it was, and would instead try to change it. In this, he was unusual indeed amongst robots, most of whom had their beliefs set when their minds were woven.

The different versions of the stories arise in their recounting of what happened just before they fought, when Karel and Kavan entered an ancient building that stood on an island just off the coast of Shull said to hold the proof of the origins of life on Penrose.

In some stories, the building is said to hold a copy of the Book of Robots, the book that contains the instructions for building the original robot mind.

In other stories, the building is said to contain proof that robots evolved naturally on Penrose.

All these stories agree on only one point.

When Karel and Kavan entered the building, they found the titles of three stories written in metal on the far wall.

The Story of Nicolas the Coward
The Story of the Four Blind Horses
and
The Story of Eric and the Mountain

Ruth Powdermaker, 2141

(For a fuller, though less rigorous and occasionally historically inaccurate retelling of the history of Penrose immediately before the arrival of the human race, see *Twisted Metal* by Tony Ballantyne.)

Merriac's Robots

From all over Shull, trains were converging on Artemis City.

They carried the spoils of war, materials captured by the Artemisian army in its conquest of the continent. Long chains of rolling stock, bumping together, shaking the dust from the coal and ore in the hoppers; rippling the oil and the acid in the brim-filled tankers; rattling the metal plate and wire stacked on the trucks; and unnerving the prisoners crowded together in the locked wagons.

'We're almost there,' said the robot by the door, peering out through the crack. 'I can see the glow from the forges.'

A low hiss of static swept through the tightly packed wagon, the sound of barely restrained fear.

'They say that the Artemisians allow you to enlist in their army!'

'They say that they only destroy the old and the damaged!'

'They say that if you can prove yourself there's always a place for you in Artemis City!'

The tightly packed robots looked at one another for comfort, dark shapes striped in the red light squeezing through cracks in the panelling.

'Not true, I'm afraid,' said the robot by the door.

He was different from the rest of them. They had been

1

herded onto the train at some tiny little city state in northern Shull, just a few forges and fortifications clinging to the side of a hill. They built themselves all in the same manner, tall and thin, of copper and iron. The man by the door was different. A little shorter and stronger, he wove the electromuscle in his arms and legs in a thicker pattern.

'Not true?' said one of the terrified robots. 'But it's got to be! Merriac told us.'

Merriac was their king, or at least, he had been until Artemis had driven its railway line into the valley below the castle and sent three trainfuls of troops to its gate. To the consternation of his subjects, Merriac had surrendered without a shot being fired.

'*Don't worry,*' he had said. '*Artemis will make use of us.*' And Merriac's subjects had listened to him, because they trusted him.

'Merriac said Artemis will make use of us,' said one of them.

'And so it will,' replied the man by the door, 'for this is Artemis City. The city built out of the bodies and minds of robots from across the continent of Shull. Literally.'

There was another low hiss of static, and the man by the door warmed to his theme. 'Once you're through that door they will march you into the disassembly rooms, where you'll be taken apart. Plating in one hopper, electromuscle in the next, cogs and gears in a third. They'll spool the copper wire from your bodies, unscrew your arms and legs and peel away the electromuscle, ready for combing and reweaving. And then they'll lay your bodies on conveyor belts and dismantle your chests and unhook your coils and remove your heads. Last of all, they'll unwind the blue twisted metal of your minds.'

'No!' The sound of static was both pathetic and terrifying.

'But why?' asked one of them. 'Surely we are more use to them as living, moving robots? Why take us apart?'

'Because, above all else, they want your metal. Because Artemis doesn't recognize the difference between the living metal of the mind and the unfused metal of the body. To them you're nothing more than raw material, walking into their forges.'

In the dimness they could just make out his face, smiling grimly.

'Come on, you must have heard of the forges of Artemis! You can see them for miles across the great plain: square, red-brick buildings, topped with grey chimneys belching smoke into the air, filling the sky with black cloud. The broken-up parts of conquered robots go into them, and sheet metal and wire and plate is rolled out.'

'What will they do with our metal?' asked one, timorously.

'Some of you will be used to build more Artemisian soldiers. The wide parade grounds before the military factories shake to the stamp of feet of newly made infantryrobots marching!

'Some of you will go to make more railway lines and engines and trains. The railway system that binds together the continent grows all the time, extending branches and lines to the remotest corners of distant lands!

'And some of you will go to make new buildings. To make new factories and forges in order that Artemis grows still further in strength.'

The wagon swayed. Now yellow bands of light swept across its interior and the robots heard the sound of heavy machinery pounding, clanking, thumping. Iron was being beaten somewhere close by.

They looked at one another in terror.

'But that can't be true. Merriac said we would be safe!'

'Safe?' said the man by the door. 'Doomed more like.' He looked around the frightened faces for a moment. 'Or maybe not. Because all is not yet lost.'

The background noise of static ceased at once.

'Go on . . .'

'Have you heard of Turing City?'

They looked at one another.

'No,' said one.

'Turing City once stood on the southern coast of Shull. It was the last of the great city states of Shull to stand up to Artemis. But now it too is defeated.'

And at that he lowered his voice. '. . . or so it seems. For it is rumoured that deep below the ground, below the broken and shattered ground on which the city once stood, some few robots still shelter. They gather the minds of those captured by the Artemisians, and build them new bodies. Soldiers' bodies. They say that they are building an army that will some day rise up and defeat Artemis City.'

'Could it be true?' asked one of the captured robots, eagerly. Merriac's mistaken words were already forgotten, now they had new hope. The mothers of their kingdom twisted minds that were gullible. Small wonder it had fallen so easily.

'Oh, it's true,' said the man by the door.

'But how do you know this?'

The man raised his voice. 'Because I am not a prisoner, as you are. Or rather, I am a prisoner, but voluntarily so.'

'Why? What do you mean?'

The expectation in the wagon was audible. Metal squeaked as the robots leaned closer to listen.

'Listen, robots. I know a way to escape. I found the route by chance two years ago when I rode this train as you do. I return time and again to lead others to safety.'

'Who are you? You must have great courage!'

'My name is Banjo Macrodocious, and no, I do not have great courage. For I feel no hope or fear.'

'Banjo Macrodocious!' chorused the other robots. They may not have heard of Turing City, but all of them had heard of the robots from the North Kingdom. Twisted to have no sense of self, they were in much demand for dangerous work. Or had been until Artemis had invaded.

'Listen,' said Banjo Macrodocious. 'I work for the resistance of Turing City. I travel these lines, bringing the news to robots of how they may escape. Listen closely, for I know the route to freedom. It is dangerous, but you too may follow me, if you have the courage.'

'We have the courage! Tell us, what should we do?'

Banjo Macrodocious leaned forward a little.

'When the train draws up we will be met by soldiers with guns. They will herd us off this truck into a wide

5

area, lit by lights but surrounded by darkness. There are few guards, and you may be tempted to run. Do not do so! It is a trick! The ground is surrounded by a moat of acid. Fall in and the metal of your mind will quickly burn away, leaving your body lifeless and easier to manipulate. Do not give the Artemisians that satisfaction!'

'We hear you, Banjo Macrodocious. What should we do?'

'Follow the guards' directions. They will march you into the first disassembly area. Do not wait for their mechanics to come to you! Strip apart your own bodies. Tear the plating from your chest and arms and legs, and throw it into the waiting hoppers. Speed is of the essence!'

'But why?'

'Because though the disassembly room will be empty at first, it will fill with more and more robots as this train empties. More Artemisians will enter to aid in the deconstruction. We need to be at the front of the line! The first few minds through are always the ones to be saved: they are taken for storage. It takes time to twist a mind, and the women of Artemis are always behind schedule. Artemis will ensure its store rooms are full before it destroys healthy minds!'

The robots looked from one to another.

'That makes sense, Banjo Macrodocious. What do we do next?'

'Once you have stripped your panelling, form into a line.'

'Okay . . .'

'Take apart the robot in front of you. Remove their

6

electromuscles and drop them on the moving belt to your left. Unship their arms and legs and drop them on the belt to your right, and then lift the body onto the final conveyor belt, and hope that the robot behind will do the same for you.'

'Where will you be, Banjo Macrodocious?'

'I will be at the rear of the line.'

'What if someone does not do the same for you? What if you are left whole?'

'Then I will not make it through.'

A brief hiss of static.

'But what do I care? I who have no sense of self. You robots will survive. Though your minds will be in darkness, you will be safe, in the store rooms. Some of you will be used to drive machinery, some of you may even be used as minds for infantryrobots. But you will be safe, waiting for the call. Waiting for the day that Turing City rises again!'

Although they had never heard of Turing City, they felt a surge of hope at the name. They wanted to live.

They wanted Artemis City to be defeated.

And so the train drew to a halt. The robots waited in tense anticipation, but now a little of the fear had gone. The doors fell open and the sound of a guard was heard, harsh and commanding.

'Outside, all of you!'

The robots dutifully filed out into a wide area lit by floodlights and surrounded by darkness. To their surprise there was only one guard, and he was a pitiful thing, a grey infantryrobot carrying an old weapon. But they weren't fooled. They marched forward in line, into the waiting building.

Inside all was astir, blue-painted Artemisian engineers marched back and forth, sorting through the hoppers of robot parts. Hands and feet and electromuscles of robots from across the continent. Bins filled with blue twisted wire.

The engineers looked on in amazement as the prisoners began to strip themselves down, but then they moved forward and helped them to remove those awkward parts that had stuck together during those long weeks in the wagon without oil or grease.

First the panels, then the electromuscle, then the steel bones; the robots took themselves apart, dropping muscle here and limbs there. The air was filled with the clank of metal, the hum of machinery, the spark of the cutter, the glow of the forge.

The engineers' surprise turned to disbelief as the prisoners lifted each other onto the final conveyor belt. These robots were of an unusual build, but the engineers had disassembled bodies from across the continent. They quickly figured out what to do.

Now all of the robots from the wagon were lying on the conveyor belt, and the blue-painted engineers moved in to remove their minds from their heads. They cracked open the metal skulls and pulled out the blue wire bundles inside, which they tossed into the fires that glowed yellow-red behind them. The blue metal sagged and then melted, running down through the coal to form a hard metal clinker beneath. Soon the fires would be extinguished and the ash and clinker raked away to be re-cycled.

One of the engineers moved to the rear of the line. The last robot from the wagon stood there, watching in amusement.

'I don't know how you get them to do that, Fess,' he said.

The man who pretended to be called Banjo Macro-docious was looking on in wonder.

'Their king had his subjects made to be that gullible. It's how he kept himself in power.'

'Well not any more,' said the engineer briskly. 'He'll be through here himself soon. Artemis will have no use for someone like that.'

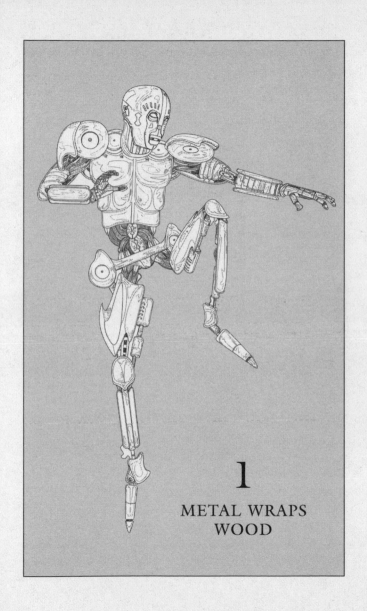

1

METAL WRAPS
WOOD

Wa-Ka-Mo-Do

How beautiful stand the plants in the Emperor's garden.

Wa-Ka-Mo-Do, self-built robot; warrior of Ko of the state of Ekrano in the High Spires; one of the Eleven, displayed none of the wonder he felt at standing here in the heart of the Silent City. His expression was still, for the mothers of Ko believed in this as they knelt to twist the wire that would form the minds of the next generation: that a robot should have the aspect of a warrior, but the soul of a poet.

So Wa-Ka-Mo-Do's body was still and silent. Unlike the other robots here in the Silent City, his panelling was painted. The metal had been dipped in scarlet paint and then left to dry smooth. Gloss paint, polished to a shine, easy to chip, easily damaged in a fight. Did the robots of the Silent City understand that? Did they understand that the chrome beading around the eyes, the mouth, the joints in his arms and legs would easily mark? That keeping himself unscratched was an advertisement of his skill?

The red joints of his fingers and feet would move like beetle backs, but for now he was motionless, blending into brightly coloured surroundings. Seen from a distance he was a collection of fragments, sharp amidst the dappled sunlight, hard blades and glossy red painted metal; mind fixed in contemplation of the poetry arranged before him.

Poems written in the medium of organic life: a folio compiled by the robots whom the Emperor had sent out across the planet Penrose, commanding them to seek beauty in every form, whether it be the glow of iron, pulled hot from the forge, or the curve of the body of some young robot in her newly built adult form.

But the Emperor's vision was wider than this, for he also commanded that his robots look for poetry amongst the lewd profusion of organic life that flourishes in the most unlikely corners of the continents of Yukawa: maybe in the curl of a plant or the arrangement of petals on a flower or the spreading canopy of a tree.

And so those robots, those poets of another age, had travelled the length and breadth of the continent, taking an insect or a seed here, a piece of plating or a cutting there, and had brought them back to be placed in the garden of the Emperor.

And, oh, what vision the Emperor had displayed when he had his stately garden decreed.

A pit, three miles across, long mined of porphyry copper, had been filled with gravel and soil and then surrounded by a wall of burnished iron, bound in brass, inlaid with copper. Stone paths had been laid through the virgin soil, along which robot gardeners walked, sowing seeds, planting roots, watering and weeding, pruning and tending, raising the plants and trees and ferns that were brought to them. Silver insects scuttled across the floor, metal shells flashing brightly. Larger animals paced their gilded cages or pulled disconsolately at feet welded to metal platforms.

In the midst of this, Wa-Ka-Mo-Do finally collected his thoughts and began to walk towards the Silver Circle, the heart of the garden. His iron feet pressed dents into the green turf, his polished scarlet body danced in yellow and gold, the reflections of the cloud of butterflies that burst from the grass with each step. Pollen fell from the scarlet flowers that sprouted in obscene profusion amongst the canopy of the fuchsia trees, it dusted his body, worked its way into his joints and seams to be trapped in the delicate thread of his electromuscle. White pom-poms nodded their heads in the breeze, a stream of pink blossom meandered its lazy way down from the treetops, it wound its way through the golden butterflies, a widening stream of blossom, a river, a wave of pink petals, a tsunami . . .

From the swirl of colour, a figure materialized. A tall robot, clad in intricately worked metal. He had no arms.

Wa-Ka-Mo-Do lowered his head in submission.

The tall robot spoke.

'When you meet the Emperor, don't speak of the world outside of the garden.'

'I thought you were the Emperor,' said Wa-Ka-Mo-Do, looking up.

'No, I am O, his spokesrobot. The Emperor is too busy to attend to all the details of the State of Yukawa. Your audience, however brief, will be sufficient to grant the seal of approval on your mission.'

'So I am still to see the Emperor?' Wa-Ka-Mo-Do could not quite conceal the edge of hope in his voice.

'Yes. The importance of your mission is such that an

audience is necessary. Now, it would be appropriate to remain silent until we are within the Silver Circle. A wise robot would enjoy the delights of the garden.'

And indeed now they were passing two tall trees that seemed to have lifted themselves from the ground, their roots standing in a lily pond, the trunks well clear of the water. Wa-Ka-Mo-Do eyed the two creatures trapped in the cages of roots. One of them reached out a metal hand in supplication, eyes glowing pale green, and Wa-Ka-Mo-Do looked away.

They approached the Silver Circle: a loop of silver filigree that wove its way through the garden in a circle half a mile across. Wa-Ka-Mo-Do could cut easily through it with one of the blades in his hands, but he knew he would be dead even as he approached it. The loop of silver rose up in an arch, flanked by two more robots without arms.

They gazed straight ahead as O led Wa-Ka-Mo-Do past them, into the garden beyond, Wa-Ka-Mo-Do struggling not to betray the excitement he felt at being here.

O turned to him. 'Now we are within the Silver Circle, I will speak freely. You will have heard that Yukawa has been visited by creatures from beyond our shores?'

'I had heard that they come from beyond even our world, my master.'

'You would do well not to speak of such things to the Emperor,' replied the armless robot drily. 'You may also have heard that the visitors are not robots?'

Wa-Ka-Mo-Do said nothing.

'You are wise to remain silent. You learn quickly. So I will tell you that the rumours are true.'

Wa-Ka-Mo-Do paced on. The sound of birds singing from tiny barbed cages covered the increased hum of current in his electromuscles.

'The visitors are animals,' continued O. 'Naturally, this does not worry the Emperor. The Emperor is wise and all powerful, and his rule of the continent of Yukawa is just and proper. Those who perpetuate the myth of the Book of Robots are hunted down and destroyed, because it is beyond doubt that robots evolved here on Penrose. There is no possibility that they were originally constructed by others, for whatever reason. Certainly, we could not have been constructed by animals such as those that are now visiting us.'

'Indeed,' agreed Wa-Ka-Mo-Do, his face devoid of expression.

'Your silence speaks volumes, Wa-Ka-Mo-Do. There are many within the Emperor's court who would feel it odd that one such as yourself, a half-caste from the far south, a near *Tokvah*, should be welcomed at court . . .'

'Ekrano has long been a part of the Empire,' answered Wa-Ka-Mo-Do. 'The right to send eleven warriors to serve the Emperor is a long-cherished tradition.'

'The Eleven have a duty to replace the Emperor if he fails the Empire,' observed O drily. 'The warriors of Ko have done so in the past.'

'A responsibility that has long been remembered in tradition, though rarely in practice,' said Wa-Ka-Mo-Do. 'I hope, rather, that it is remembered here in the Silent City how well the Eleven have served the Emperor.'

'Indeed. And today you will have the chance to prove yourself equal to your predecessors.'

'I hope so.'

Wa-Ka-Mo-Do felt unnerved by the armless robot. It was known by all that the Emperor had no arms, this way others must serve him. But Wa-Ka-Mo-Do hadn't realized that others within the Silent City also went armless. Oddly, even though he was trained in the arts of war, even though his arms and legs contained tempered blades, hard and sharp, it was he who felt at a disadvantage. But what could this robot do to harm him?

'It pleases the Emperor to deal with the animals, Wa-Ka-Mo-Do,' continued O. 'He has established trading areas in designated parts of the Empire. Whilst, naturally, the animals do not have the same grasp of culture or society as the Empire, it amuses the Emperor to speak with them, to trade examples of their technology and thus to educate them in our ways.'

'The Emperor is indeed generous.'

'He is indeed. He has established an Embassy for the animals in the city of Sangrel. You are to travel there as his Special Commander.'

'Commander of Sangrel? That is indeed an honour!'

'A warrior may rejoice at such an honour, Wa-Ka-Mo-Do, for in Sangrel he may prove himself worthy of the Emperor's trust in upholding the ways of the Empire. For the Emperor could not lose face by having his subjects attack the animals through a mistaken sense of grievance. A feeling that, perhaps, the interests of the Emperor's subjects have been placed below those of the animals.'

Now Wa-Ka-Mo-Do began to understand the nature

of his mission. He needed to be diplomatic in his questioning.

'I'm sure that it is inconceivable that the Emperor's subjects would shame him so. But, my master, suppose that such a circumstance was to arise?'

'Then I am sure that the Commander of Sangrel would make it plain that, in the long run, all favours granted to the animals would be repaid tenfold by them to the Empire.'

The armless robot smiled as he spoke these words.

'Of course,' said Wa-Ka-Mo-Do. 'But suppose, for example, that some robots found themselves driven from land that they and their family had occupied for many generations. Suppose that they found themselves in the grip of an unreasonable desire for reparations and found themselves, unjustly of course, in conflict with the Emperor's appointed officials. What course would the Commander of Sangrel be wise to adopt in such a case?'

O smiled.

'You are wise in the manners of court, Wa-Ka-Mo-Do, despite your origin. You ask my advice, as is right in these circumstances. I would say that it would be appropriate, if not desirable, for the Commander to destroy all those robots, and their families, and their villages, as an expression of the sorrow of the Emperor, and his wish to demonstrate his authority.'

'I understand,' replied Wa-Ka-Mo-Do, and, true to his mother's weave, his face betrayed no expression of the discomfort he felt at these words.

'And let me say furthermore, Wa-Ka-Mo-Do,' continued O, 'that I'm sure the Emperor would wish the

same attention to be paid to those who were to perpetuate the myth that our creators have returned to rule us.
The idea is, of course, ridiculous.'

'Of course.'

'Now, silence. We are approaching the Emperor.'

The Emperor wore no metal panelling: his body was
plated with sheets of nephrite jade, carved in exquisite
shells that encased him in a creamy green that contrasted
with the emerald of the sunlight glade in which he stood.
Four members of the Imperial Guard stood to the north,
south, east and west of him, their bodies thin and curved,
built of katana metal. They looked like living blades,
curved under tension, ready to spring out in one slicing
movement.

None of them wore ears or eyes. At need, they would
pull them from their bodies and push them into place.

'Emperor, this is Wa-Ka-Mo-Do.'

Wa-Ka-Mo-Do was standing in the middle of the
sunny glade just inches from his Emperor. He lowered
his eyes and found himself gazing at the carvings on his
jade feet, pale and exquisite.

The Emperor spoke.

'Wa-Ka-Mo-Do, warrior of Ekrano. It pleases us to
speak to you.'

'Thank you, oh my Emperor.'

'The High Spires are a long way from the Silent City,
Wa-Ka-Mo-Do.'

'Indeed,' he replied, thinking on how O had told him
not mention the world beyond the garden.

'The land of the Sirens. Did you ever see those fortunate robots, Wa-Ka-Mo-Do?'

'No man may see the Sirens and live, my Emperor.'

There was a long silence.

'Do you mean to correct your Emperor? Are you suggesting that we were unaware of the nature of the Sirens?'

Wa-Ka-Mo-Do looked at the Emperor, and, in a sudden moment of clarity, saw how ridiculous his armless body was. The thought was treachery. Unconsciously he shifted to a fighting position. Surely the guards would know what he was thinking? Surely even now they would be attacking?

But nothing happened. The Emperor was waiting for an answer.

'My Emperor, not for a moment would I think such a thing. The wisdom of the Emperor is recognized by all his subjects.'

'Our wisdom is respected, you would say? Yet you come before me still standing?'

Wa-Ka-Mo-Do fell to his knees at this point. Nobody had mentioned this to him. He was under the impression that subjects remained standing in the presence of the Emperor, ready to serve him.

'You *kneel* before us?'

Now Wa-Ka-Mo-Do fell forward, the grass all around his metal face.

He heard a thin keening above him. Gradually it occurred to him that the Emperor was laughing.

'It would appear that ignorance is still the norm in Ekrano! No one kneels before the Emperor, Wa-Ka-Mo-Do. We are not barbarians in Yukawa!'

He climbed to his feet.

'Wa-Ka-Mo-Do,' said the Emperor. 'You will have heard of the Book of Robots?'

Again Wa-Ka-Mo-Do remembered the words of the aide who had led him here. 'No, my master.'

'We think you are lying. It is well known that the heresy of the Book of Robots is woven deep into the metal of those of the High Spires. We would expect that you, too, have this heresy woven into your mind.'

Wa-Ka-Mo-Do's gaze was still, his current was calm, and yet the Emperor's words were accurate. Wa-Ka-Mo-Do believed in the book. Of course he did.

The Emperor spoke.

'Even so, it must be understood that there are conventions for the lesser subjects, and there are conventions for those who follow a higher calling. We know of the Book of Robots.'

'Have you read the book, my Emperor?'

That same thin keening laughter.

'Our subject is as lacking in guile as he is in intelligence, for not only does he forget that he has claimed not to have heard of the book, but he has also forgotten that no robot is known to have read it, if indeed the book ever existed.'

'My Emperor is indeed wise to point this out to me,' answered Wa-Ka-Mo-Do, and again the treacherous thoughts arose inside him. Did the Emperor, wise above all, think himself clever by employing tricks effective only against those that could not answer back?

'Your Emperor is wise indeed. Wa-Ka-Mo-Do, in Sangrel you will meet the animals that have travelled to our world. And you will look at them and you will wonder how any robot could believe that creatures such as they could claim to have had us built. And yet some do. We trust that our subject will remember his duty, should he encounter such robots.'

'You may be sure that he will, my Emperor.'

'Good, good.'

The Emperor smiled. 'We are pleased with our subject. Now, Wa-Ka-Mo-Do, we do not need to mention that our people place great faith in the Empire. It has stood unchanging for centuries, built on the rule of the Emperor and its queens. It has met new ideas in the past, and woven them into the rich tapestry that is the Empire. Is my garden not eloquent testament to this?'

A golden butterfly fluttered by, as if to confirm this.

'Indeed, my master,' said Wa-Ka-Mo-Do.

'And yet some ideas are not to be contemplated. They throw the weave out of balance, and so they shall not be tolerated. Does our subject understand this?'

'I do, my Emperor.'

'So our subject will be thankful that Vestal Virgins are already in Sangrel. They will watch our subject, and ensure that his mind is on his task. Do you understand, Wa-Ka-Mo-Do?'

Wa-Ka-Mo-Do felt his gyros spinning just a little faster. He forced them to slow.

'I understand, my master.'

Something caught his attention: the butterfly. It fluttered past Wa-Ka-Mo-Do's face, turned to the right, and then changed direction again, heading to settle on the Emperor himself.

There was a flicker of silver, and the butterfly fell to the ground in two parts. An Imperial Guard slowly replaced her sword in her sheath. Wa-Ka-Mo-Do was impressed to note she had not inserted her eyes.

The Emperor did not seem to notice.

'Very well,' he said. 'The audience is at an end. We wish you every luck in your endeavour. You may leave by the Road of Reflection.' He turned to indicate the path that Wa-Ka-Mo-Do had entered by.

For the first time, Wa-Ka-Mo-Do noticed the remains of two robots lying at the edge of the clearing, the metal of their minds twisted around their bodies in blue filigree. He saw the lifeforce flickering around them, and realized the warped creatures were still alive, frozen there in agony. The Vestal Virgins, he thought, as he walked by. The Vestal Virgins did that.

He wondered if some day his body would lie there too.

Kavan

Kavan walked south.

A Scout was standing in the middle of the path ahead, the blades at her hands and feet retracted.

He couldn't go to the right of her: melting ice fuelled the tumbling stream that lay to that side, water dashed white foam off the sharp rocks littering its bed.

He couldn't go to the left of her: even the grass struggled to grow on the rocky slope that sliced into the pale blue sky.

And he couldn't go back. There was nothing behind him but the northern coast of Shull and, beyond it, the iron-grey waters of the Moonshadow sea.

He would have to go past her. Not that Kavan would ever deviate from the path he perceived to be the right one.

He raised his hand in greeting.

'Hello Kavan,' said the Scout. 'I bring the compliments and the congratulations of Artemis City.'

Kavan's gaze travelled the length of the Scout's silver body, the metal unscratched and polished to a shine.

'Have you come directly from there?' he asked.

'I have. Three brigades have been sent to aid in the securing of the North Kingdom, following its conquest by you.'

'Three brigades? That was more than I was given to take the whole of Northern Shull!'

Now Kavan commanded no one. He had expended nearly all his troops in the taking of the North Kingdom. The few survivors would be picking through the melted remains of that ruined land, either that or chasing down the last of the robots who had escaped from the battleground, supposedly carrying the remnants of the Book of Robots in their head. Kavan had travelled to the very top of the kingdom; seeking conquest, not answers, it was true; but even so, along the way he had found nothing but confirmation of his own beliefs.

But that was past. For the moment, he was a leader without troops.

The Scout inclined her head.

'The story of your conquest is told across the

continent, Kavan,' she said. 'Your name has been engraved in the Great Hall of the Basilica.'

'And yet we meet here, in an empty valley at the uttermost north of Shull. No soldiers, no weapons, just you, a Scout in a brand new body and me, a broken-down infantryrobot.' The fresh wind sang in his badly adjusted joints, as if by way of illustration. 'So, what are your orders?'

'To locate Kavan, the hero of Artemis, and to escort him to Spoole, leader of Artemis. You are to be honoured, Kavan. Spoole himself travels north to greet you.'

'Does he, indeed?'

His tone made the Scout shift slightly, the blades at her hands protruding for just a moment.

'Kavan, where have you been? Soldiers and Scouts have scoured these hills searching for you. Rumour has been rife. That you were killed, that you had found the Book of Robots, that you had quit these shores and were travelling the sea roads to the Top of the World itself. Tell me, where have you been?'

Kavan gazed at the Scout, her body so smooth and sleek compared to the scratched utility of his grey infantry panelling.

'I've been thinking,' said Kavan. 'Thinking about new lands to conquer. And I have come to a decision. Tell me, Scout, what's your name?'

'Calor.'

'Your body is polished and unscratched. But that means nothing, perhaps you are freshly repaired. Tell me, Calor, have you ever fought in battle?'

'Yes, Kavan. In the northern states. Two weeks ago. I was caught by three of the mountain robots.'

'That wasn't a true war. The conquest of the northern states was completed three months ago. The few robots who still fight are under-resourced and tired.'

'Even so, they rose from beneath the ground as I ran by; they caught me by the legs, tearing the electromuscles there. I was dragged down beneath the soil. I fought with my arms as they pulled me deeper and deeper into the earth. I cut my own body free beneath the waist, that I may fight better, and then I dispatched them, one by one in the dark. I emerged from the earth, my body scratched and filled with soil, and I dragged myself home with my own hands. I have fought, Kavan.'

'Very well, Calor,' said Kavan. 'You have fought. So, I will tell you this. I have been thinking, here at the top of Shull, wondering at my next move. And finally I have seen what it must be.'

The stream splashed by in that empty land, not heeding the words being spoken on its bank.

'I march south, Calor. My next conquest will be Artemis City itself.'

Now Calor's blades slid properly free of her hands and feet, sharp and deadly in the pale morning sun.

'Treason!' she called.

'Treason? No, I don't think so. Ask yourself this, Calor: which more truly embodies the spirit of Artemis? Spoole and his Generals, living cosseted in Artemis City, cladding themselves in expensive metal? Or me, who has led armies across this continent and conquered all in his path?'

The Scout didn't answer, but her blades retracted, just a fraction of an inch.

'You see? You know I am right. So follow me. We march.'

And at that he strode forward, pushing past the Scout, resuming his march by the side of the stream, heading south, back through the lands he had conquered, heading towards Artemis City. After a moment's hesitation the Scout began to follow him.

'Wait!' she called, running lightly across the sodden turf between the path and the stream. 'Where are we going?'

'I told you, south.'

'But you are heading towards a squad of Storm Troopers.'

'If they are loyal to Artemis they will follow me.'

'If they are loyal to Spoole they will shoot you!'

'Then I will fight them.'

At that Calor looked up along the top of the rocky slope, looked back behind them. She laughed.

'Ah. I begin to understand. Kavan, the master tactician. You have more troops, more weapons. Hidden just out of sight.'

Kavan halted so suddenly that Calor almost tripped over him. She watched, puzzled, as he squatted down by the stream that ran alongside the path. He dipped his hand into the water, it looked blue as he felt for the rounded pebbles on the bed. The plastic grips at the end of his fingers were worn, he had to scrabble in the churning water for a handful, but finally he seized them and held them out for Calor to see, water draining from the dents in his panelling.

'Your claws and a handful of pebbles. These are the only weapons I command now. You are my army.'

Calor nervously extended the blades at her hands and feet once more.

'But there are only two of us!' she said. 'There are hundreds, thousands of soldiers, combing these hills, looking for you. They will kill you if you resist them. Why should I get myself killed too?'

Kavan leaned closer, and she saw the golden glow in his eyes.

'Why?' he said softly. 'Because you know that I am right. Artemis is not a place, Artemis just is. How did your mother weave your mind, Calor? Was she an Artemisian?'

'Yes!'

'Then this is where you learn the truth about yourself.'

'I could kill you now,' said Calor, a hiss of static in her words. She was moving her bladed hands through the killing pattern. 'You wear the body of an infantry-robot. I could slice through you before you have a chance to move. I could disable you and carry your mind back to Spoole.'

'Then why haven't you done so already?' asked Kavan. 'There are many robots who claim to be Artemisians, but their mothers wove their minds to think more of themselves than of the state itself. Are you one of those robots? Some live a long time before they find this out about themselves. You will find out today.'

Calor stilled her killing dance, wondering about what Kavan had said. He stared at her with those golden eyes. Then, slowly, the blades at her hands and feet withdrew.

'It will be my death, but I will follow you, Kavan.'

'Arm yourself, then,' he said, and he handed her a pebble.

Wa-Ka-Mo-Do

How sweetly bloomed the railway station outside the Silent City.

Cherry blossom fluttered down from the branches woven amongst the metal arches of the roof, or was it the metal that was woven around the branches? Wood and metal sprouted from the ground, twisting around each other to form the living canopy of the station. The metal feet of the robots stirred pink petals on the platforms.

Everything looked so normal, so unchanged. It was odd to think that outsiders now walked upon Yukawan soil. And not just outsiders, but animals. Animals that walked upright, like robots. Animals that, if stories were to be believed, had hands and faces. Animals that could think and bend metal to make tools and machines. It was said they had been here for nearly a year, and yet it was odd that so few people had actually seen them. Perhaps they were shy, reflected Wa-Ka-Mo-Do. Perhaps they were embarrassed by the richness and culture of the Empire.

A Shinkansen entered the station in a silent wave of blossom, a white needle threading the living cloth. Petals stuck to the metal shells of the waiting passengers;

they slowly fluttered to the ground as the train drew to a halt.

Wa-Ka-Mo-Do opened the door of a carriage for the pretty young female who stood by him on the platform. There was something about the line of her body, the way she had forged simple metals into a harmonious whole.

'Thank you, warrior,' she said, eyes lowered. 'My name is Jai-Lyn.'

'I am Wa-Ka-Mo-Do.' He followed her into the corridor. 'Where do you travel to?' he asked.

'Ka. They have need of young women there who can twist children.'

Ka was on the west coast, two hundred miles or so from the High Spires of Wa-Ka-Mo-Do's home. A whaling city inhabited mainly by the men who followed the steps down from the city to the sea bottom, there to walk the sea bed, hunting the whales, firing their harpoons up at the great creatures as they passed by overhead. They would wrestle with them for hours, tiring them out before dragging the spent bodies down to their waiting awls and cutters. It was tough, dangerous work for strong robots with plenty of lifeforce. Women who could spin new minds were in short supply.

Wa-Ka-Mo-Do found himself and Jai-Lyn an empty compartment. The seats were of carved and varnished wood set with a chevron pattern of rubber grips to stop metal bodies slipping when the train slowed to a halt. Wa-Ka-Mo-Do waited for the young woman to sit down first, admiring her movement as she did so.

'That's a well-built body,' observed Wa-Ka-Mo-Do. 'You have some ability.'

'Thank you, warrior.'

'You will do well in the city.'

She looked pleased at that, smiled such a pretty smile. 'Do you really think so? I've never left the Silent City before. Still, I follow the Emperor's will.'

A shadow fell across the doorway, and a clear voice sounded out.

'Clear this compartment for the Emperor's Warriors, Dar-Ell-Ji-Larriah and Har-Ka-Bee-Parolyn and their wives.'

Jai-Lyn was already rising to her feet, her head lowered so she did not meet the eyes of the great warrior who stood by the door. Wa-Ka-Mo-Do remained seated.

'This compartment is already occupied by Wa-Ka-Mo-Do of Ko, and his travelling companion Jai-Lyn,' he said smoothly. He waved a hand to the spare seats. 'Though you are welcome to join us.'

One warrior gazed at Wa-Ka-Mo-Do in amusement.

'Wa-Ka-Mo-Do?' he said. 'What sort of a name is that?'

'A warrior's name,' replied Wa-Ka-Mo-Do, without heat. 'Know that I am one of the Eleven sent to the Emperor by the state of Ekrano, newly appointed Commander of the Emperor's Army of Sangrel, travelling there to take up that position.' He looked up politely at the tall robot who stood in the doorway. 'And you are?'

'Dar-Ell-Ji-Larriah, Warrior of the Silent City.'

With that Dar-Ell-Ji-Larriah stepped into the compartment, and allowed Wa-Ka-Mo-Do and Jai-Lyn to look upon his wonderful body, forged of the finest metal by the craftsrobots of the Silent City. There wasn't a straight line on him, every curve that made up his perfectly balanced frame would have been patiently formed by the heating and folding and cooling of metal until his body was strong but sprung. His electromuscles would have been knit from the finest wire, his eyes ground by the most skilled lensmen. It was said that the Vestal Virgins modified the minds of the Warriors of the Silent City, tuning them to make faster and better fighters, but Wa-Ka-Mo-Do suspected that to be nothing more than rumour.

'Did you make that body yourself?' asked Dar-Ell-Ji-Larriah, insulting Wa-Ka-Mo-Do in the politest of tones.

'I did,' replied Wa-Ka-Mo-Do, equally politely. He waved a hand again to the free seats. 'Now, will you join us? For we are both of equal rank and protocol suggests that it would be unbecoming for warriors to fight so close to the Silent City, particularly on a day such as this when the cherry blossom is so beautiful.'

Dar-Ell-Ji-Larriah laughed as he turned to his companion in the corridor.

'The cherry blossom is indeed beautiful! And it is also said that the Eleven Warriors place greater value on poetry than they do on fighting!'

'No,' said Wa-Ka-Mo-Do. 'Equal value.'

A look of anger flickered across Dar-Ell-Ji-Larriah's face.

'I wonder if it is appropriate for you to contradict me before an inferior?'

'Jai-Lyn is my travelling companion, and therefore our equal, at least for the length of the journey.'

Jai-Lyn looked frightened.

'Oh warriors, please do not speak of me in such terms . . .'

She hesitated at the noise from outside. Wa-Ka-Mo-Do and the other warriors heard it too. A shout, a clamour and a clatter of metal. The sound of robots moving, disembarking, the sharp crackle of hurriedly shouted orders. Wa-Ka-Mo-Do leaned out of the door to see that a group of robots had entered the station and were ordering everyone off the train.

'The Silent Wind,' said Dar-Ell-Ji-Larriah in wonder. 'What are they doing here?'

Where the Emperor's Warriors advertised their strength and power in the polish and decoration of their strong bodies, the Silent Wind were panelled in dull grey and green. They wrapped oiled silk around their joints and rubbed carbon black on their hands and feet where metal showed. They moved through the station unchallenged, the polished crowd parting like tree branches blown by the wind.

One of them approached Wa-Ka-Mo-Do's compartment.

'Disembark. This train has been commandeered for the Emperor's business.'

The words were spoken with quiet authority.

Jai-Lyn was already moving to leave the train. Wa-Ka-Mo-Do put an arm at her elbow to halt her.

'Wait,' he said, holding out the metal foil scroll that

declared his status and right to passage. 'I too am on the Emperor's business.'

The Silent Warrior pushed it back.

'That is none of my concern, this train is required immediately.'

Wa-Ka-Mo-Do looked down at the matt-grey hand, looked up into the eyes of the warrior.

'Come along, Jai-Lyn,' he announced. 'We shall leave now.'

Dar-Ell-Ji-Larriah and his companion were already making their way onto the platform. Wa-Ka-Mo-Do and Jai-Lyn followed them out into the blossom-filled daylight.

All around, the station was filled with angry, confused and bewildered passengers. It was rapidly emptying of the Silent Warriors, who slipped on board the waiting train. At the end of the platform, Wa-Ka-Mo-Do could see two more of the Silent Wind climbing into the control cabin. The regular driver stood on the platform, looking confused.

The doors of the train closed, and it accelerated rapidly from the station in a swirl of cherry blossom.

'What's happening?' wondered Jai-Lyn.

Wa-Ka-Mo-Do jumped at the amplified sound of her voice, then turned his ears back down to normal level. He had been listening to the conversations around him. For the moment he said nothing, thinking on what he had heard. One of the Silent Wind had mentioned the word softly as he climbed on board the train. He had heard the name echoed from around the station.

Ell.

Wa-Ka-Mo-Do wondered what it meant. Ell was a city somewhere to the south, only a hundred miles from Sangrel, the place where he himself was headed.

Ell. Something had happened in Ell.

Kavan

Kavan and Calor walked south.

The landscape here twisted around itself, the valleys curling around the rolling green hills, their rocky interiors exposed in cross section by ancient quarries dug by long-forgotten robots. There were paths and roads made by robots that had roamed the countryside hundreds of years ago in search of metal with which to make their children. Occasionally Kavan and Calor passed by an old stone shelter or pile of stones or some other marker.

'We are being watched,' said Calor. 'Two Scouts on the hilltops. Not that experienced, you can see the sunlight reflect from their bodies.'

'I've seen them,' replied Kavan. 'I wonder if they're watching the Storm Trooper ahead.'

The stone path they followed was rising up to the head of a valley.

A black figure stood in the middle of the path, six grey infantryrobots behind him. He held up a hand as Kavan approached.

'Greetings, Kavan.'

'Hello Tams. My army marches south. Join us.'

Tams searched back along the path.

'No, Tams. Here she is.' He pointed to Calor.

Tams seemed disappointed.

'A bluff, Kavan. A pity, seeing how times have changed. Spoole himself is coming north. We are to escort you to meet him. You're a hero now, Kavan.'

'Artemis has no heroes, Tams. That I am declared one goes to show just how hollow a shell Artemis has become. You must realize that?' He looked at the other robot, seeking acknowledgement. When none came, he continued, 'I'm raising my last army to march on Artemis City itself.'

'No, Kavan.'

The voice came from behind him. He turned to see five more Storm Troopers standing there, rifles pointed at the ground.

'Sorry, Kavan,' said Calor. 'I didn't see them. Maybe I'm not so experienced either.'

'Everyone underestimates how quietly Storm Troopers can move when they want to,' said Kavan loudly. 'Don't they, Forban? We fought together in Stark, I think. You served with me in the last battle in the North Kingdom.'

'I did, Kavan.'

Forban's rifle remained pointed at the ground, but it could easily be swung in Kavan's direction. Kavan pretended not to notice.

'You are a true Artemisian, Forban. I wouldn't expect you to follow Spoole and the rest. Join my army.'

'You no longer have an army, Kavan. The battle with the North Kingdom was a battle too far. Barely fifty robots survived the final onslaught. Too many Artemisians were melted in the petrol pits . . .'

'Their metal will be recovered,' interrupted Kavan. 'The battle ended in victory.'

'Too many minds were lost,' said Forban. 'It's over, Kavan. Now that Artemis controls all of Shull, it's a time for consolidation, not conquest. You were a great leader when we were expanding, but your job is done. We need robots like Spoole to lead us now. Fall in, Kavan, we march to meet him.'

Forban waved a hand. The grey infantryrobots shouldered their rifles and fell into position.

'What if I refuse to follow?' asked Kavan.

'We pick you up and carry you.' Behind Forban, the other four Storm Troopers had shouldered their rifles and were marching up the stone path to join their companions. 'If you continue to fight, I will have your mind removed from your body.'

'Very well, I will follow.'

'And what about you?' Forban asked Calor. 'Who do you follow now?'

The Scout looked at Kavan uncertainly. Ahead, she saw the grey infantryrobots looking at each other as they stood, arms sloped, awaiting the order to march. The infantry had always had an affinity with Kavan. After all, didn't he wear the body of an infantryrobot himself? The Storm Troopers, however, had never been quite so loyal. Six infantryrobots and six Storm Troopers. And one Scout. The odds were on Forban's side.

'Well,' prompted Forban. 'Which will it be? Artemis, or Kavan?'

'Aren't they the same thing?' asked Calor. Kavan smiled at that.

Forban pointed his rifle at Calor's head.

'I wouldn't do that,' said Kavan.

'Why not?'

'There are Scouts up there in the hills. If they see you shoot one of their own they will be very unhappy. And they will talk to each other. How far do we have to walk through these hills?'

'I do what is best for Artemis.'

'Forban,' said Kavan. 'I led an army across Shull. Listen to my advice. Let her be.'

Forban looked from Calor to Kavan and back again. Slowly he lowered his rifle.

'Very well. We march. Watch the Scout.'

The Storm Troopers took a step forward. The grey infantry remained still. They were looking unhappily at each other. Forban rounded on them.

'What's the matter?' he shouted. 'Didn't you hear the order? We are to escort Kavan to Spoole! He is a hero!'

Still the grey infantryrobots exchanged looks. Eventually one of them stepped forward.

'What does Kavan say?'

Kavan pointedly looked from the heavily armed and armoured Storm Troopers, to the thin shells of the infantry. When he was sure that everyone there had got the point, he gave his answer.

'For the moment, Forban and I are in agreement. We march south.'

Kavan and Calor, Forban and his troops marched south.

The signs of long-abandoned robot inhabitation

39

seemed to rise and fall across the landscape like tides on a beach. Long ago, robots had followed the Northern Road through this land, bringing news and devices from the Top of the World, carrying the metal they quarried from these hills back up there by way of trade. Kavan had heard something about the history of this land as he had fought his way north, but he had seen little, if anything, of its former glory. The robots who had built these roads and the half-collapsed buildings that stood by them were long gone.

The hills rose and fell as they marched, the Storm Troopers beat a path through the wet turf, shouldering aside boulders, slashing at the twisted and weatherblown plants that clung to life in the thin soil. The infantry-robots marched on, eyes fixed upon Kavan, who walked silently in the centre of the group, his thoughts elsewhere.

Calor's gaze constantly searched along the top of the surrounding hills when they walked through valleys, it flicked from boulder to tree when they walked the high moors, watching the movement all around them.

Because word of Kavan's reappearance was spreading. Calor saw the flickers of sunlight at the top of the hills. Scouts, looking down at the grey and black bodies that marched south, relaying messages back and forth to others who marched nearby.

Forban noticed them, and he spoke into a radio just out of Kavan's earshot. Half an hour later, a squad of twenty Storm Troopers marched in from a side path and joined them.

Kavan and the infantryrobots now found themselves

surrounded by the black marching bodies. The air was filled with the percussion of metal on rock, the hum of electromuscle working and the prickling of electricity. Feet were covered in grey dust, mud and moisture.

And then Calor raised herself up on tiptoes in a dancing, skipping movement, looking over the tall heads that surrounded them. She jumped and spun, dodging through the dark press of bodies, her hand blades slightly extended as she did so.

Four Scouts were running up to join them. Calor dropped back to speak to them, and now Kavan found himself walking alongside an infantryrobot. Coal, his name was.

'You're outnumbered, Kavan,' said Coal. 'Forban has been on the radio, calling up yet more Storm Troopers to join in the escort duty. They have always been more loyal to Spoole. You need to find more infantry! They will support you!'

'Move away there! Get back to your place!'

Forban appeared at Kavan's side. The infantryrobot stared at Kavan significantly and then fell back to his place in line.

'We are bearing a little too far to the west,' said Kavan.

'There is an old road over this way,' answered Forban. 'It runs south across the whole of Northern Shull. Didn't you notice when you marched these lands?'

'It runs north, not south,' said Kavan. 'All the way north to the Top of the World. The robots of these lands believed that Alpha and Gamma, the first two robots, were made up there. Their descendants travelled down the Northern Road to populate Shull.'

'Do you believe that, Kavan?'

'I *know* it's not true. I have seen the proof, up on the northern coast. There is a building there, I have been inside. I know that robots evolved here on Penrose.'

'I think . . . hey, who are you?'

Calor had rejoined the middle of the party, but there was another Scout with her now. They were both speaking to one of the infantryrobots that trudged along. The new Scout looked at Forban for a moment and then turned and quickly ran off, body flashing in the sunlight as she dodged between the black bodies of the Storm Troopers.

A quarter of an hour later they joined the Northern Road, a grass-grown expanse of broken stone, long stamped down by the tread of many robots.

A squad of forty infantryrobots was waiting for them there. Kavan recognized their leader as Gentian, a woman who had served under him in the past. Forban gave no sign of being either pleased or disappointed at their presence.

At the approach of the escort party, the infantry-robots picked up their rifles and joined the procession, heading south.

Spoole

Spoole leaned on the stone balustrade, looking out across the vast landscape of Northern Shull spread out below him, and he felt, for just a moment, his power.

All that he could see, he commanded.

Except, of course, he didn't. Spoole was too much of a realist to think otherwise. It was part of the pattern twisted into his mind, a realization that there was a time to lead and a time to step aside.

The difficulty, of course, was knowing when that time was.

The robots who had built this citadel had not been able to tell. Whoever had built this place must have been way in advance of the other civilizations that inhabited these mountains. Why, they must have been well into the Stone Age whilst the surrounding tribes were still struggling through the Iron Age, and yet, despite that, they were long vanished.

The citadel was an island of rock at the edge of the Northern Mountain range. The builders had taken a mountain just like any of the others around it, and had chipped and hammered and dug and blasted away the surrounding stone, isolating their peak from all the others save for three stone arches leading east, west and south that they left to serve as bridges. But this had only been a prelude to their greatest feat of engineering.

Spoole had heard Kavan's reports of the reservoirs that lined the mountains of Central Range. He had seen them himself as he had travelled north but he hadn't appreciated their use until he had visited the citadel. The robots who made this place had used water to carve their home. The water that had been hoarded behind dams was directed down sluices and aqueducts towards this place, carrying rain and snowmelt and channelling it to just the right point, then they had let the water run over hundreds of years, smoothing the pillar that supported the great city until it shone dully in the sunlight, the bands of rock clearly visible, climbing in tilted shelves almost a mile into the sky.

All the while the water was carrying out its work, the robots were busy on the peak of their mountain, carving it flat to give a circle half a mile across. On this they had used dressed and jointed stone to build walls and forges, keeps and houses. The north side they had left for their final glory: a huge window, five stories high, formed of three arches, empty of glass but looking north across the lands of Shull to the Top of the World.

Now the citadel stood as a gateway to the north, and Spoole and his Generals had commandeered it to await the arrival of Kavan. The Supreme Commander of Artemis stood on the roof of Shull, waiting for its most favoured soldier.

Except, of course, that wasn't quite true either. In any respect.

He heard movement behind him and turned to see General Sandale approaching. For a ridiculous moment, Spoole imagined the General rushing forward and pushing him backwards, sending him tumbling back out of the open window to be smashed on the rocks far below. But, no, General Sandale merely raised a hand in greeting.

'Forban has Kavan,' he said.

'Good,' replied Spoole. 'Good.'

General Sandale remained where he was, gazing at Spoole. His body was polished to a shine, a contrast to Spoole's matt-iron body. It wasn't that Spoole wasn't made of the very best materials; it was just that he didn't advertise it. The leaders of Artemis never had done in the past. When did that thinking change?

Still the General waited.

'Yes, General Sandale?'

'Nothing, Spoole.'

The General joined Spoole by the open window. Again, Spoole had the ridiculous idea that the General would push him out. As if the General would stand a chance. Spoole had fought battles in the past. The General was one of the newer leaders, rarely having left the command post, seldom having felt the surge of current as he rushed into battle, suffered the blistering feedback as an awl pierced electromuscle. But then, at least he had fought, unlike some of the other leaders.

'So, Spoole. We were wondering. What is it you will do with Kavan?'

'Recognize his achievements, of course.'

'And stop him attacking you. He would have marched upon Artemis City if you had let him. He would have replaced you as leader.'

'He would have replaced us all, Sandale.'

'Perhaps—'

'Don't question me, Sandale,' said Spoole mildly, but there was current there. Enough to make Sandale pause. Suddenly, his shiny, unscratched body seemed so ineffectual compared to the workaday iron of Spoole's.

'Perhaps you have work to attend to?' suggested Spoole, and after a moment, Sandale turned and left to join the other Generals, leaving Spoole alone on the wide balcony. He leaned on the stone balustrade, looking out once more across the vast landscape of Northern Shull.

The central mountain range ran east–west across the continent of Shull, effectively cutting it in two, separating north from south. That was until Kavan had blasted a path through the mountains with atomic bombs. The northern end of that path could be seen to Spoole's left, a wide cleft in the mountains through which silver railway lines ran, branching across the green plains of Northern Shull before burying themselves in the low rounded hills that rose up to the north. Kavan was out there some-where, hidden in the twists and turns of those hills, being escorted back here by Forban and his troops.

Standing in this place, it was easy for Spoole to feel invincible, but only a fool felt so. The robots who had built this citadel must have felt the same once, but they were long gone, vanished from this place before even Kavan and his troops had come here.

Spoole didn't care. He was waiting for Kavan.

Kavan

Kavan and Calor, Forban and his Storm Troopers, Gen-tian and her infantryrobots, plus all the various Scouts and other soldiers who had joined their growing band, marched south.

The Northern Road was old and unmaintained, but it had been well built and the troops made good progress over its still mainly smooth surface. The road wove its way through the hills like an animal; only occasionally did it slip and fall. Kavan and the rest of the robots walked through yet another river, the bubbling water cold on their electromuscle, the broken body of the road strung out above them on the hillside. The earth must have shifted over the years, exposing the road's interior, the paved surface, the gravel beneath it, then the larger stones, then the rocks. All the strata reminded Kavan of the body of a whale he had once seen taken apart, back in Wien.

Still the robots marched on, and the band grew larger as robots drained from the surrounding hills to join the procession.

The countryside was changing. Ahead of them, when they rose to the level of the surrounding moors, the robots could make out the snowy peaks of the central mountain range. The character of the Northern Road changed too, the shape of the stones that paved the surface altering, becoming a little smaller and more rounded. The hills were lower, the valleys wider.

Calor ran up from behind Kavan. Her body was developing a slight squeak, she needed oil and grease. They all did. Still, she wasn't complaining. Kavan appreciated that.

'Someone is waiting for us up ahead,' she said. 'Someone important.'

'What is the land like there?' asked Kavan.

'Quarries. The valley has been widened as robots have dug into the hills. There are sheer walls standing to the east and west.'

'A good place for an ambush.'

'Possibly.'

The road wove between the hills before disgorging the growing band into a wide valley. The walls that surrounded them were old and weathered, the quarry works long since abandoned. A few old tumbledown houses stood by the river on the valley floor next to a broken-down forge. Grass and moss had poured down from the hills, leaping from the sheer planes of the quarry walls, like streams in a waterfall to cover the grey stone of the buildings. Some of the robots escorting Kavan broke off from the main party and went sifting through the piles of discarded stones by the buildings, in a hopeful search for metal to repair themselves with.

Gravel roads ran down the hillsides in all directions, leading from the exhausted quarries that surrounded them.

A company of Storm Troopers were waiting for them up ahead, their black bodies sleek and well built, a contrast to the derelict background. At its head was a robot dressed in iron and bronze, silver and platinum and gold.

'General Mickael,' said Forban, and the relief in his voice was obvious. Kavan was no longer his problem.

General Mickael walked forward to meet them, the surrounding troops opening up, leaving Kavan and Forban and the General alone in the centre of a circle of metal.

'General,' said Forban. 'I present to you Kavan. I have escorted him this far. What would you have me do now?'

'General,' said Kavan. 'Have your men fall in and join my army. We march south, on Artemis City.'

General Mickael looked from one robot to the other, his blue eyes glowing. Then he laughed coldly.

'Your army, Kavan?' he said. 'You dare to give me orders? Damn your cheek!'

'You're discredited, General,' said Kavan. 'I marched across this continent with you and the rest of your kind nowhere to be seen.' He raised his voice. 'Now that Shull is conquered you emerge from your city to claim the spoils, walking across the backs and broken metal of the soldiers who fell during the fighting. Soldiers who believed in the cause of Artemis. What did you believe in, hiding back there in the city? Nothing more than cladding yourself in the best metal.'

And he reached out with one hand and scraped a finger across the General's chest, tearing and smudging the gold filigree. The General recoiled.

'Silence him!' he shouted, rubbing at the damage on his own chest. 'You, remove his voicebox.'

'His name is Forban,' said Kavan. 'I always know the names of the soldiers that I fight alongside. How about you? How many of the soldiers here could you name?'

'Be quiet, Kavan,' said Forban urgently. 'I'm still loyal to Artemis. I don't want to have to remove your voice.'

'I don't think that these soldiers would let you.'

Forban looked around the wall of metal that surrounded them. Red and yellow and green eyes glowed. Silver and grey and black bodies were still for the moment, but the hum of charging electromuscle was rising. Forban shifted slightly.

'You are still outnumbered, Kavan,' he said. 'There are still more Storm Troopers than anyone else. General Mickael's troops are clean and tuned, not like the rest of us. Listen, Kavan. I bear you no ill will, but times have changed. They mean to make you a hero. Let us take you to Spoole. You will come to no harm.'

He looked at Mickael for confirmation, but the General pretended not to hear any of this.

Kavan spoke quietly. 'That's what you don't understand, Forban. Whether I come to harm or not is of no concern to me. It does not concern a true Artemisian.'

Kavan and Calor, Forban and his Storm Troopers, Gentian and her infantryrobots, General Mickael and his Storm Troopers, all of the Army of Uncertain Allegiance, marched south.

Kavan's army – or maybe it was General Mickael's army – was growing as the hills sunk down beneath the land and the peaks of the central mountain range rose up before them.

There were now two thousand soldiers marching south down the Northern Road. They spilled over the verges, black Storm Troopers tramping down the borders, smashing trees, crushing stone. Silver Scouts ran in flashing patterns around them, grey infantryrobots plodded across the land, tearing holes and ruts in the mud and grass, all making their way back towards Spoole and his Generals, come to meet the conquering hero.

They had left the uncharted lands of the far north and were back amongst the signs of Artemisian expansion. Railway lines threaded north, trains could be seen in the distance carrying metal and plate and wire and coal.

Still they marched, and around them new forges were springing up, new buildings and barracks and warehouses, dropped amongst the stone castles and buildings that had been constructed by the former rulers of this land. The robots who worked in the new buildings came out to watch the passing band. Some of them waving and cheering, some merely standing in silence, eyes glowing as the procession marched by.

Kavan found himself marching in the centre of growing space. No one seemed to want to come too close to him. No one but Forban and Calor.

'No one knows which way this will go,' said Forban. 'They want to be on the winning side.'

'What about you, Forban?' asked Kavan. 'What do you want?'

'I want what's best for Artemis,' said the Black Storm Trooper, miserably.

Calor joined them.

'The land seems to be drained of soldiers,' she said. 'All the troops that should be out here have vanished.'

'Spoole will have ordered them to withdraw,' said Kavan. 'He will have them grouped safely around himself.'

He looked up at the mountains ahead. They seemed to fill the sky.

'Not long now,' he said.

And so the Army of Uncertain Allegiance left the hills of the north and approached the mountains of the central range, where they saw arrayed against them the armies of Spoole and Artemis City.

Row upon row of black Storm Troopers, thousands

upon thousands of grey infantryrobots. The high peaks shone with the glimmering array of Scouts. All new and unscratched, freshly minted by the Artemisian forges, and untouched by the glamour of Kavan. These soldiers had not marched with him. They had not fought alongside him, and they bore him no loyalty.

The troops of the Uncertain Army gradually halted, stopping in ones and twos, looking to their companions for a lead. Only Kavan and Calor and Forban continued forward.

'It's over, Kavan,' said Forban.

Kavan continued to walk. Calor and Forban followed hesitantly.

Spoole had chosen a good place to meet the Uncertain Army. They stood on a rocky plain between the hills and the mountains. The only way south was between the arms of the mountains, into the valley that Kavan himself had blasted all those months ago.

'Enough of this!'

The voice came from behind. General Mickael, who had kept well clear of Kavan since they had met, was coming forward.

'Why are we hesitating?' he called, blue eyes flashing. 'Move out, now.'

Forban and Calor looked at Kavan. All eyes were on Kavan.

'I said move out!'

Kavan ignored him. He waited a moment, thinking, and then turned to face Spoole's troops.

'Soldiers of Artemis,' he called. He waited, waited for their attention. Then he raised his hand, pointed forward.

'There is your enemy,' he said. 'There, arrayed before you in polished metal.'

He waited for his words to sink in.

'And so it is time. Take up your weapons, and charge.'

He barely raised his voice, but the words rippled out-wards from where he stood. Infantryrobots lifted their rifles. Storm Troopers turned in warning, told them to lower their arms. But not all of them. Scouts began to dance at the perimeter. A wave was set up. Robots pushing this way and that, but with no overall direction.

'Put down those weapons!' called General Mickael. 'Put them down at once.'

Nobody listened. More and more soldiers were raising their arms, pulling out awls, moving this way and that. Storm Troopers' voices could be heard, ordering infantryrobots to stand down.

Somewhere there was an electronic cry, and then silence. It took a moment for the ranks to figure out what had happened. An infantryrobot had been cut down by a Storm Trooper. All eyes turned to see the black robot, blue wire twisted around its hand. An electronic growl sounded. A shot rang out. Then another.

'Put down your weapons! Forban, order them to stop!' General Mickael was growing angry.

Kavan held out a hand to Forban.

'Your awl,' he said.

And just like that, the motion in the Uncertain Army ceased. Kavan could feel them all, looking in his direc-tion. 'Your awl,' he repeated.

Forban looked from Kavan to the General.

'No, Kavan . . . I can't . . .'

'What's going on?' demanded the General. 'Forban. What are you doing?'

'For the last time, Forban, give me your awl.'

No one spoke. In the distance, Spoole's troops were motionless.

'Kavan, this is not the way. You can't—'

'Who would you rather serve, Forban? Him,' Kavan pointed at General Mickael, slowly backing off, eyes glowing, 'or Artemis?' A group of infantryrobots moved forwards to surround him. Storm Troopers looked on, uncertain what to do.

'Forban, I order you . . .'

Forban looked from Kavan to the General. Finally, he decided. Quickly, he passed the awl across to Kavan. Kavan looked at the awl for a moment, and even the wind stilled. Then suddenly, so quickly, Kavan dived forward. The General jerked back, held up a hand, but he was no fighter. Kavan feinted, dodged around behind him, got hold of him around the neck and pulled him backwards, off balance. He reached around with the awl and stabbed up beneath the General's chin, up into the brain. Again and again.

'Take this, Kavan.' An infantryrobot was suddenly at his side, handing him a blade with a nick in the end. The General was struggling now. Kavan took the blade and stabbed upwards, catching the twisted metal of the General's mind in the nick of the blade. He pulled it out, unwinding the blue wire that held the General's thoughts. The General struggled harder and harder, and then, all of a sudden, he went limp.

Kavan let the body slip to the ground. It fell in a clatter

of metal. So much expensive plating was now nothing more than spare parts.

Forban looked on in horror.

'Okay,' said Kavan. 'Now, Forban, sound the attack.'

The standing wave that wobbled up and down the Uncertain Army was resolving itself.

'The attack,' said Kavan.

Forban turned towards the troops arranged before them. He raised a hand, pointed forward.

'Artemisians,' he said. He collected himself. 'Artemisians! Attack!'

First one or two soldiers, then a handful, then a trickle, and then a great wave of metal began to pour south, towards Spoole's waiting troops.

Metal pounded forward, clanking thundering metal.

Kavan's army charged!

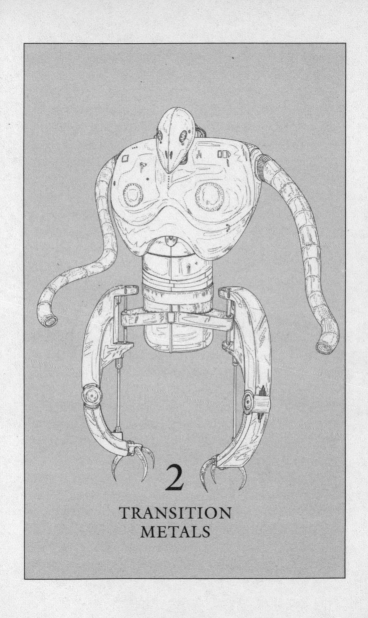

2

TRANSITION
METALS

Susan

'The city seems so empty at the moment,' said Susan. 'Listen. When was the last time you heard the wind?'

The two women tilted their heads, listening to the breeze as it hissed through the gratings. It blew notes on the drainpipes as it sent thin streamers of ash dancing through the gutters of the street.

'Isn't it lovely? To think that this is always here, only drowned out by the hammering and the pounding of feet. To think, there is beauty even here in Artemis City . . . '

'The Generals have all gone north with Spoole,' said Nettie. 'They've taken their troops with them.'

'I suppose they all want to be there at the capture of Kavan.'

'Not at all. Spoole ordered them to go. He didn't want them left here in the city, plotting against him.'

'I suppose.'

'Oh, help me with this, Susan. It's stuck again.' There were railings in this part of the city, screwed to the red brick walls that lined the tarmac road, intended to help steady newly made robots, unused to their bodies. Nettie held onto a rail with one hand and bent down to fiddle with her foot. The segmented plates were new and badly fitted, they kept catching on each other. Susan knelt down, and, taking hold of the foot in one hand, she prised at the plate with the other.

'It's no use, it's stuck. Do you have an awl or something?'

'Why would I have an awl?' asked Nettie.

Susan cast about for something to use. The trouble with Artemis City was it was just too clean and well kept. Every bit of metal was accounted for, neatly assigned to make walls or electrical wire, girders or fingers, railway lines or minds. Not a twist of swarf, not a lost link of chain was left lying on the floor or brushed up as scrap. In the end she pulled the grey plate from the back of her hand and used it to tap at Nettie's foot.

'Will that work?' said Nettie.

'It does sometimes,' said Susan. And with a click, the foot could suddenly move again.

'Thank you Susan,' said Nettie, and she looked so sad. 'I'm really no good at this am I? I'm no good at making things.'

'You do fine,' lied Susan, sliding the plate back onto her hand. 'I was lucky. I was raised where there was plenty of fine metal.'

The answer seemed to cheer her friend up a little.

'Now come on, where should we go?'

'Let's go to the radio masts,' said Nettie. 'I like to feel the patterns they make.'

The radio masts lay to the south-west of the city, and the two women cut through the half empty streets of the Centre City. They were both dressed in similar grey bodies, but there was a workmanship to Susan's that drew admiring looks from the few men that passed down the neat streets. Many approving looks, but no comments, for it was obvious what Susan and Nettie were.

They were mothers of Artemis, they were women who worked in the making rooms of Artemis.

Once, Susan had been a free citizen of Turing City, but then Kavan and his troops had marched south in conquest. Now her son was dead, killed by an infantry-robot's bullet. And her husband was gone, captured on the night of the invasion.

As for Susan, she had been brought here and indoctrinated in Artemisian philosophy. Now, every night, she knelt at the feet of yet another Artemisian soldier and drew forth his wire, twisting it into a mind that embodied Artemisian principles. Another mind bent to see metal as nothing more than metal, nothing more than something bent to the continued expansion of the Artemisian State.

And the Artemisian State kept expanding. The Centre City grew from metal stripped from across the continent. Where the rest of Artemis City was built of brick and prefabricated steel, the Centre City was where the copper ended up. It was where the chromium and nickel was plated on the arches and columns. Not that it remained there for long. It was constantly stripped back and put to more prosaic uses elsewhere. There was no sentiment in Artemis City.

Unlike Turing City. But Turing City was no more. So what did that make Susan? An Artemisian? Certainly she was now held in some respect by the members of that state. She was a mother, a woman who twisted the minds of the future generations. After weeks of imprisonment in the making rooms beneath the city, she had proven her loyalty by her actions every night. Now she was allowed out by day to walk the streets of Artemis City. This she did, and she was welcomed and acknowledged wherever she went.

She felt a traitor to herself. The memory of a conversation she had had back in Turing City was constantly at the edge of her memory. She repressed it.

'I wonder what the radio masts are saying?' she asked.

They had come to the far side of the Centre City, and Nettie was looking down a long straight road, lined with the prefabricated steel buildings of the cable walks. One of the masts stood clearly framed at the end of the road, a lattice tower six hundred feet high, guyed by steel cables. Susan could only see the ripples of the electromagnetic spectrum that ran up and down the structure. Nettie, however, could read them. Sometimes.

'They're talking about Kavan,' she said. 'Kavan, Kavan, Kavan. They've found him. And yet, that can't be right, they also say that he is attacking.'

'I don't want to hear about him.'

Nettie was immediately chastened and Susan felt ashamed of her words. She reached out and took hold of her friend's hand, the only friend she had here in Artemis City.

Possibly the only friend she had in the world. After all, the other mothers of Artemis distrusted her. They had been Turing Citizens too. They remembered Karel, her husband. Many robots back in Turing City had thought him a traitor. Karel had been an immigration officer, he believed in new ideas, welcoming in those whose minds were woven in a different fashion. Many robots were convinced that this had hastened Turing

City's downfall, that their philosophy had been diluted by these strangers.

Karel had been taken from her on the night of the invasion. She had thought he was dead, but just a few weeks earlier, the robot she had been kneeling before in the making rooms had assured her he still lived. The robot would not reveal how he knew, nor why he was telling her. Still, she hoped it was true. Karel and Nettie were all she had left. Nettie, who had never woven a mind in her life, but who was responsible for directing the other women in patterns they should weave. The other women scorned Nettie: in their eyes Susan's friendship with her was proof that she was a traitor.

And, truth be told, she was. They all were. What had she been asked, when she had first learned of the Book of Robots? When it came down to it, would she be strong enough to twist a mind in the way she knew was right?

The answer, it had turned out, was no. When it had come down to it, when Turing City had been destroyed and she had been brought here, she had bowed down before her captors and subdued her will to theirs. The minds Susan twisted each night were Artemisian minds.

She was a traitor; there was nothing else to say.

The radio masts were set in an expanse of flat ground to the west of the city. Three tall lattice towers cradled by iron cable. A fourth, smaller tower stood some distance from them. Susan and Nettie stood at the perimeter of the radio ground and watched the rippling patterns as they climbed the masts.

'You know they're thinking of stepping up production,' said Nettie, suddenly.

Susan felt her gyros spin a little faster. 'How?' she asked.

'A mind every day as well as every night.'

The news didn't fill Susan with the horror that she would have imagined. Rather, she felt annoyed at the stupidity of it all.

'It can't be done,' she said simply. 'We need a rest. A woman needs time to get her thoughts in order after making a mind. If not then she runs the risk of weaving the second mind imperfectly.'

Nettie looked away from her, ashamed.

'I know that,' she said. Of course, she didn't. Nettie had never woven a mind in her life, nor would Artemis ever allow her to. She was too clumsy a craftsrobot.

'Artemis doesn't care about imperfect minds,' Nettie retorted. 'They have worked out that if two minds are woven every day, around one point six of them will be usable on average. That's a net gain on the current rate.'

'So what about the minds that don't work?' asked Susan. Nettie didn't answer. She just stared at the ground. Susan figured it out straight away.

'Oh no,' she said. 'No. They'll just recycle the metal, won't they? Start all over again . . .'

Radio waves rippled against the empty grey sky. Susan felt as if the little comfort she had gained was radiating away too.

'Oh Nettie, I hate this place,' she said. 'It becomes so comfortable, you almost convince yourself you're part of it, and then something like this happens and reminds you just how awful it really is.'

'I know.'

'I don't know what I'd do without you here, Nettie. You're the only friend I have left.'

For a moment, just a moment, a picture of Karel, her husband, appeared in her mind. She suppressed it, it was just too painful.

'How long?' she asked. 'How long can this go on for?'

'I don't know,' said Nettie. Shyly, she reached out a hand and sent a soothing wave of current into Susan's own.

'Why are they doing it? They've conquered the entire continent. What else could they want?'

Nettie looked around. They were two tiny figures dwarfed by the sky and the city behind them, the silver shapes of trains moving across the horizon. Even so, Nettie lowered her voice.

'Susan, there are rumours. Rumours about the Book of Robots. Have you heard them?'

Susan looked at Nettie.

'Nettie, I've heard nothing. The other women don't speak to me, the only friend I have in here is you.'

Nettie looked around again.

'I speak to the other supervisors. There is another who knows of the book. She speaks to me sometimes.'

Nettie leaned closer.

'They have come, Susan. The writers of the book! The creators of the first robots!'

Susan didn't know what to feel. She didn't have belief of the book woven into her mind like some other robots did. Her mother had believed, she had woven Susan to be nothing more than a companion for Karel, her husband. Karel was important in some way, she understood that. His mind was different. Beyond that, she really did not care about the book. If only the others who had spoken to her about it understood that. Nettie was gazing at her, excited.

'Well?' she said. 'Don't you see what that means? They have come to free us! Surely they won't allow Artemis to continue as it is?'

'Why not?' asked Susan. 'Maybe Artemis is what they want. How do we know what the creators want?' *If they really exist*, she added to herself.

Nettie looked troubled for a moment. Susan pressed home her point.

'And how do we know they *are* the creators, Nettie? What are they like?'

At that Nettie looked even more troubled.

'Oh Susan. I don't know. There are so many rumours. Messages become garbled and twisted—'

'What have you heard, Nettie?'

Nettie looked around once more.

'Animals, Susan. They are animals! They walk like robots, they have two arms and legs and a head, but they are animals! It surely can't be true!'

'Animals?' said Susan, disbelievingly.

'Yes, they say they . . .'

Her voice trailed off. Three people were approaching, walking towards them across the bare field of the radio masts. A computer, a young man in a body painted green. He was flanked by two Storm Troopers.

'Good afternoon ladies,' he said. 'What are you doing here?'

There was something unsettling about the two Storm

Troopers. Susan knew she shouldn't feel intimidated by them, but she felt as if she were back in Turing City, coming face to face with the invading forces. Yet what could they do to her? The worst had already happened.

Nettie spoke up.

'We're mothers of Artemis,' she said, primly. 'We need to walk the city in order that we do our job properly at night.'

One of the Storm Troopers laughed.

'You keep walking,' he said, staring at Susan. 'You could twist my wire any day.'

'Shut up,' said the other Storm Trooper to his companion. He turned to Nettie. 'Why do you need to be here?'

'I like to watch the patterns of the signals,' replied Nettie, truthfully.

'Not any more. This area is off limits. General Sandale's orders.'

'But why?' said Nettie. 'We're doing no harm.'

'That's irrelevant. Come back here and I will have you both recycled, mothers or not. Do you understand?'

'Yes,' said Susan.

'I'll escort them back,' said the young man in the pale green body. 'I need to report to the Centre City.'

'You do that.'

Susan could feel the two Storm Troopers' eyes on her as she and Nettie followed the green robot back into the city.

'Rusting Storm Troopers,' said Nettie. 'I hate them. Those big bodies, and yet their wire is so thin and insipid.'

Susan said nothing in reply. What would Nettie know about twisting wire? And yet she was right. They may have big bodies, but there was something about those Storm Troopers that was strangely weak and ineffectual compared to her husband's thoughts . . .

Too late. The image was there now. Karel. Karel in his finely built body, painted by Susan herself. Karel with Axel, both of them telling stories together. Both of them now gone . . . A soft electronic whine erupted from her voicebox.

She stilled it.

Karel

Karel's anger was like a diesel engine, constantly churning, belching dirty black smoke that left a trail behind him. Most of the time it was there, running in the background, but then something would rev it up and the air was filled with that rattling purr and his vision was obscured by a black cloud of unreason . . .

For the moment, though, it was under control. Karel worked his way up the valleys and river beds that wound their way back down to the sea. He stuck to cover as he picked his way southwards towards Artemis City. That was where Kavan would be heading, and Kavan was responsible for the death of his child and, in all likelihood, his wife.

This green, windblown land was nearly deserted. Occasionally he would see a soldier in the distance, catch the flash of a Scout as she ran along the hillside, hear a distant shout carried by the wind. At first he had dropped to the ground for cover at any sign of life, more recently he had just continued walking. He was wearing the body of an Artemisian infantryrobot, after all.

But for the most part he was alone. Kavan's army seemed to be draining from the northern hills, leaving nothing but broken and twisted metal to show for his conquest. The north had been tamed, but at tremendous cost to Kavan himself.

Good, thought Karel. *Good!*

The stream he was following led to a busy river, flushed with the snowmelt that ran from the surrounding hills. Karel looked at the churning waters and tensed the electromuscles in his weak body, gauging whether or not he should cross. The slope on this side was uneven, giving way to rocky walls that sliced down into the water. The far side was flatter, paved in the rough grass that clung wherever it could in these wild lands.

He decided to try it, and managed to wade halfway across before the current caught him and swept him off his feet. He was sucked below the surface and swept back northwards, his body crashing and scraping on the rocks of the river bed. He snatched for handhold after handhold, eventually managing to find a purchase, hands and feet wedged in the rocky bed. He rested for a moment, looking up through the white swirling patterns of water that streamed around him, seeing the pale glow of daylight above. Then, moving carefully on all fours, he picked his way to the opposite bank and began to climb free of the water.

As he did so, someone grabbed hold of his arm and pulled him clear.

Karel sat for a while on the bank, letting the water drain from his battered body. His electromuscles were shorting with the moisture, he felt weak and uncoordinated. Everything about this land seemed unnatural, the grass that covered the soil, the twisted organic trees that thrust roots into the cracks in the grey rocks, tearing out stones that tumbled into the cold water. And so much water! More than a robot needed.

Still, he had a more pressing concern.

'Who are you?' he asked the tall robot who stood silently looking down at him.

'Banjo Macrodocious.'

'I should have known.'

Karel had met the robot, or more likely, one of his brothers, before. Banjo Macrodocious. They all had the same name, they were all unnaturally strong. And, despite the fact they were obviously intelligent, they had no sense of self.

'You shouldn't stay here,' Karel warned. 'Kavan has his troops out hunting for you. He knows that you escaped from the Northern Kingdom before it fell and he wants you all destroyed. Kavan doesn't believe in the Book of Robots, he thinks it's nothing more than sedition.'

'It's no matter,' replied Banjo Macrodocious.

'Why not? I thought the book was important to you! Don't you carry it in your mind? I thought you all did!'

Banjo Macrodocious was unconcerned.

'We do. But Kavan and his troops are currently no threat to us, if it can be said that Kavan still commands any troops. The soldiers that once filled our land are marching south. Artemis is undergoing a time of change. Spoole and Kavan and the rest will fight to determine who leads Artemis and what its future direction will be.'

There was an iron-grey lid on this strange land. Karel stared at the dull sky, trying to remember another world, one filled with metal and stone and singing with the current of life.

'Who leads Artemis has nothing to do with me,' said Karel.

'It does. Your wife is in Artemis City.'

Karel felt as if he had been struck by a hammer. For a moment, his head seemed to ring like a bell. Susan was still alive. Happiness and fear mingled within him.

'Is she okay?' he asked, his voice almost crackling with joy. Banjo Macrodocious didn't seem to notice.

'She is healthy. She works in the making rooms, twisting new minds.'

Now Karel felt his gyros lurch.

'They're . . . raping her,' he said.

'Every night.'

He struggled unsteadily to his feet, water still dripping down the grey metal panelling of his body. Mud covered his fingertips.

'I've got to go,' he said, wiping his hands on the grass. 'I need to save her.'

'Not now. Not like that.'

Weak as he was, Karel bunched his fists, squeezing more water from them as he did so. 'Who are you to tell me what to do?' he asked, anger surging within him.

Banjo Macrodocious moved forward, blocking his way. He was a big robot, humming with power. Karel was well aware that, even were he not in his current, weakened state, the other robot would have no trouble subduing him. Karel lowered his hands, dampened the anger that was telling him to push the big robot out of the way.

'Why won't you let me go?' he asked.

'I've come to take you to someone who may help you. His name is Morphobia Alligator.'

'Morphobia Alligator? Who is he?'

'He's a pilgrim. He has been looking for you.'

Wa-Ka-Mo-Do

Jai-Lyn was young and sheltered, she had never been outside the Silent City before. Now she was torn between the view from the window of the train and the company of Wa-Ka-Mo-Do.

'Is it really true that you have travelled all the way from the High Spires to the Silent City, Warrior?' she asked in awe.

'Much of the journey takes place on metalled roads, Jai-Lyn, and through the lands of the Emperor. There are few of the robbers and the other dangers of the old tales.'

'You say few of the robbers! Did you meet any?'

'Some. When they realized who I was they did not attack.'

'I suppose you made them hand their ill-gotten gains back to the peasants. Am I not right, oh my master?'

'It is true that the peasants benefitted from my passage.'

The robbers he had met were poorer than the peasants upon which they preyed, reflected Wa-Ka-Mo-Do. He had dispatched the unfortunates with a blow of his sword, cutting cleanly through the metal of their minds, then he had dragged the metal of their bodies to the closest forge, where it was recycled to the benefit of the people, and through them, their Emperor.

'And what about monsters? Did you meet the Nightwalker?'

'There are few monsters in the Empire, Jai-Lyn,' he laughed. 'But I saw many marvels. The metal forests of La Wen, where acid is poured into the ground and left to evaporate, and the metal that is washed from the salts blooms as trees under the soil, to be excavated by farmers over the centuries. I saw the great animal farms of Mel-Ka, where the organic cattle roam over grassland and come to slaughter when called. I crossed the four rivers of Fla. I fought there, it's true, cutting myself free of the squid that reach for metal from the water—'

'Surely you are the best of all warriors!'

Wa-Ka-Mo-Do smiled at the way Jai-Lyn's eyes glowed as he spoke.

'The Imperial Guard would think otherwise.'

Jai-Lyn reminded Wa-Ka-Mo-Do of his younger sister, La-Cor. Bright and skilled in the working of metal.

His sister had built a body that caused Wa-Ka-Mo-Do to walk with one hand near his sword when the young men came calling; her conversation had the same eager questioning, always seeking out new knowledge and experience. So similar. At one point Wa-Ka-Mo-Do had traced the symbol of the Book of Robots: a small circle on the circumference of a larger one, but Jai-Lyn did not seem to notice.

Wa-Ka-Mo-Do realized he had been careless in almost revealing himself like that, but she was so like La-Cor . . .

Sweetest of all was the way that both of them seemed to regard Wa-Ka-Mo-Do as the most skilled of warriors. Jai-Lyn would not be dissuaded from this point of view, and she spoke most prettily in his favour.

'But, oh my master, it is true that the Imperial Guard have the best metal, the best training. Who can deny that? Surely it would be treason to suggest that the Emperor would do otherwise than ensure the best of all is made available for his own soldiers. Without doubt, their bodies are shaped from the purest iron and aluminium by the most expert craftsrobots!'

She lowered her face most delightfully.

'But what of their minds?' she asked. 'I am sure they have not your experience, warrior! They would not have stood in the snow of the High Spires and looked north across the Empire! They would not have learned to fight in those cold and sparse lands. Robots who spend their life in the Silent City would not have been tempered by their journey from the south!'

Wa-Ka-Mo-Do laughed delightedly.

'I am sure, Jai-Lyn, that you will be a huge success in the city of Ka! If you twist a man's wire as surely as you build his ego, you will produce minds at which robots may wonder!'

Her eyes glowed brightly.

'I only speak the truth, my master. The robots of the Imperial Guard are not like you! Nor have they been granted such a high command. The city and province of Sangrel!'

Wa-Ka-Mo-Do smiled back at her, but he felt uneasy. Commander of the forces of Sangrel was indeed a high honour. It was almost unknown for the Emperor to place one of the Eleven in charge, and not for the first time he wondered whether some deeper scheme was at work here. His thoughts wandered to the sudden evacuation of the train back at the station. It was unheard of for the Emperor's railway to be so disrupted, for such an event implied a lack of planning on behalf of the Emperor: it implied an unseen event, and this was impossible in Yukawa, for did not the Emperor see all?

It had taken Wa-Ka-Mo-Do a good day to find another train to take him on his way, a task made doubly difficult by his insistence that Jai-Lyn be allowed to accompany him. In all this time he had found no one who could tell him what had happened in Ell. He suspected that this was not due to robots withholding information: genuinely, no one knew. And yet Ell was not so far from Sangrel. Barely a hundred miles . . .

'Look, warrior!'

Jai-Lyn interrupted his thoughts. She was pointing out of the window.

'Jai-Lyn, perhaps if . . .' but his words trailed away.

For most of the morning the train had travelled through the green forests of An-Dara Province, and Jai-Lyn had gazed at long lines of trees, carefully farmed to feed the forges of nearby Ban City. But now they had left the trees behind. They were gliding through the grass plains of northern Sangrel Province.

A robot could see for miles here, look across plains that fed the thin cattle and sheep, bred by Yukawan robots throughout the centuries to remove as much of the muscle as possible to leave the skin and bone that were so useful to industry. Oily crops flowered in the distance, bright yellow marks against the horizon, punctuated by the glint of sunlight on the metal skins of robots tending the fields.

But something disturbed the harmony. The earth had been churned up to leave great brown scars in the ground.

'What is it?' asked Jai-Lyn. 'What's happened there?'

'I don't know,' said Wa-Ka-Mo-Do.

They gazed from the compartment in silence, two robots in a little place of metal and wood looking out on a world seemingly destroyed. The carefully harmony of fields and cattle and trees, cultivated over hundreds of years of Empire, had been ruined. It was like a robot had wiped his hand across a picture on a sheet of metal, erasing it. The brown churned earth seemingly stretched for miles.

'It's like when a farmer plants crops,' said Wa-Ka-Mo-Do slowly. 'Only much, much bigger.'

'I have never seen a farmer plant crops,' said Jai-Lyn.

'I grew bonsai trees, back in Ekrano,' answered Wa-Ka-Mo-Do, engrossed by the scene before him. The excavation was so large. What possible use could it be? And then he saw something else.

'Do you see it too?' asked Jai-Lyn.

'Yes,' replied Wa-Ka-Mo-Do, staring at the yellow machine that worked its way across the grassy plain in the distance. The machine was so big, and so smooth. So much metal, it seemed to have been poured in one piece. Behind the machine stretched a brown ribbon of churned earth.

'That's what's causing those marks,' said Jai-Lyn. 'But I have never seen a machine like it. What robot could have built that?'

'I don't think it's robot-built,' answered Wa-Ka-Mo-Do. He caught a movement high up in the sky. He and Jai-Lyn looked up at the silver shape that drew a line of condensation through the heavens.

'I think the animals have done this.'

Karel

Karel followed Banjo Macrodocious through the hills. His metal squeaked as he strode after the other robot: it had been too long since he had had time to tend to it, but of his mental turmoil, there was no sign.

'What's a pilgrim?' he asked carefully.

'The opposite of my kind. Morphobia Alligator will explain everything to you.'

Karel didn't press the point. If Banjo Macrodocious

had been told to say nothing, then he would say nothing. Still, he was distracted by other thoughts. Susan was alive! Somewhere to the south, his wife knelt in Artemis City to twist the wire of other men. He should be heading there right now, yet Banjo Macrodocious was leading him west. He caught glimpses of the Northern Sea to his right as they traversed the rough green hills, cutting across this foreign land of grass and stone. A grey beetle watched him as he walked by, metal shell warming in the sun, then he felt a boiling of electricity at his feet and looked down to see he had kicked an ants' nest, the little creatures swarmed around his feet, scraping nicks of metal from his soles. He leaped forward, stamping his feet hard.

Banjo Macrodocious watched him.

'Insects everywhere,' said Karel. 'We must be getting near to ore.' He paused, tasting his surroundings. 'I can feel it in the ground. Very faint.'

'We are heading towards Presper Boole,' Banjo Macrodocious volunteered. 'Its prosperity was built on metal ore and trade.'

'I've never heard of it,' replied Karel.

'That was a long time ago, when many robots still travelled the Northern Road to the paths beneath the sea. There was much trade between Shull and the robots at the Top of the World.'

'You believe in the robots at the Top of the World?' asked Karel. He smiled. 'I suppose you do. You believe in the Book of Robots after all.'

'I don't believe,' said Banjo Macrodocious. 'I *know* it to be true.'

Of course he did, thought Karel, it was woven into

his mind. Banjo Macrodocious really would think that he had part of the plan for the original robots there in his head, he really would believe that he knew a little about how robots should behave.

And yet, who was he to feel anything but envy? At the moment, Karel was certain of nothing more than the fact he wanted his wife back.

'How much further?' he asked, as they crested the top of another low hill.

'Nearly there,' answered Banjo Macrodocious, and they both looked down.

The land fell into a wide sea inlet fed by a river that flowed from the south, the waters churning against the incoming tide. Across the way Karel saw more land, rocky cliffs and edges dressed in green grass. He felt caught between the elements, exposed to the choices of the world. Which way now? North beneath the vast expanse of the Moonshadow sea, down the river to the south, or follow the coast to where it took him? Then, further down the hillside, he saw the ancient remains of a town. Grey stone buildings, long broken by the elements. All the metal stripped away.

'That was Presper Boole,' said Banjo Macrodocious. 'Across the way you can see Blaize.'

Karel looked across the water and saw the other town. It looked much bigger than Presper Boole, and better constructed. The buildings rose higher, they were squarer and topped by spires and towers that gleamed white even under the dull skies.

'Blaize must have been quite impressive in its day,' he ventured.

'Both cities were,' said Banjo Macrodocious. 'I have the memory of them woven into my mind. They were built of the riches that flowed down from the Top of the World.'

Seeing the spectacular remains of the two cities there, Karel almost believed it was true. That there really were robots at the Top of the World.

'Greetings, Karel.'

The voice came from somewhere to his side. Karel turned to gaze at the strangest robot he had ever seen. Everything about it was different. The proportions of its body were all wrong: its arms far too long and jointless, they waved and rippled like snakes. Its head was the shape of a droplet of water turned upside down, rounded at the top and then curving inwards and downwards to meet at a sharp point well below its neck. It had two large black hemispheres for eyes, set wide apart, so that Karel gained the impression it could see behind as well as in front. It had a fat body, like a light bulb, bulging at the top and pinched in where the short legs joined on. It didn't have feet as such, instead four rods curved out from its ankles like blunt claws. They pierced the grass as it walked towards Karel, making him feel deeply uneasy. He quelled the feeling.

'Greetings,' replied Karel. 'You must be Morphobia Alligator.'

Morphobia Alligator bowed in a complicated movement that made Karel's gyros wobble. The other robot seemed to have joints in all the wrong places.

'You are Karel, yes, yes? Formerly of Turing City, now stateless since the fall of the Northern Kingdom.'

'Were you there?' asked Karel.

'No, no. But Banjo Macrodocious was. All of them were. When that place was on the brink of collapse, they were sent out to find safer lands so that the knowledge they held in their minds would be preserved. Some of them found me. Strange how old enemies work together in these times.'

'Banjo Macrodocious is your enemy? You don't believe in the Book of Robots?'

'Oh, we believe what it says is the truth. Oh yes, yes! But that misses the point.' His eyes brightened, and Karel sensed he was amused. 'Anyway, I was told that you were nearby. I asked them to bring you to see me.'

Karel was confused. The robot's words made little sense. Even its voice sounded wrong, like it was being modulated in a different way. And then Karel noticed the strangest thing about the robot.

'Your body. That metal, what is it?'

'Aluminium,' said Morphobia Alligator.

'The mythical element?'

'Obviously not a myth.'

'Where are you from?' Karel looked aghast as realization dawned. 'You're from the Top of the World!'

Wa-Ka-Mo-Do

They glided on in silence, gazing from the windows. The vast patches of churned brown earth had given way to something even more disturbing.

'Warrior, I have never left the Silent City before. Surely these plants are not natural?'

'They are not,' replied Wa-Ka-Mo-Do. 'Not natural to Penrose, anyway.'

The plants were tall as robots, straight green stalks swelling to a cylindrical bulge at the top. They were planted in staggered rows that allowed long views along the green lines as the train rolled past. Wa-Ka-Mo-Do had never seen anything so alien.

'Do you think that the Emperor is aware of what the animals are doing in his kingdom?' murmured Jai-Lyn in a voice that hummed with static.

'Be quiet, Jai-Lyn,' warned Wa-Ka-Mo-Do, glancing around the otherwise empty compartment. 'I am sure the Emperor is aware of all that happens in Yukawa.'

'Then how could he permit this? Those plants should not be here! They look so wrong!'

Wa-Ka-Mo-Do gazed again at the long rows of green stalks. Some of the bulging tops had peeled back to reveal the yellow segmented fruit that lay inside.

'The rumours are true . . .' said Jai-Lyn, softly.

'What rumours?' asked Wa-Ka-Mo-Do.

Jai-Lyn lowered her eyes, well aware she had said too much.

'Jai-Lyn. What are the rumours?'

'Oh my master! I should not have spoken.'

'But you have. Tell me, Jai-Lyn, what have you heard?'

Green speckled with yellow flickered by the window. Jai-Lyn stared at his feet as she spoke.

'Oh my master, back in the Silent City, some of the women would service the Emperor's messengers. Robots who had been the length and breadth of the Empire. They would remove their plating for polishing, they would dip their electromuscle in fine oil and reweave it, they would listen for the singing of the current in the wire, all to ensure the smooth running of the messengers. And sometimes, as they did this, the messengers would speak of what they had seen on their travels.'

'What did they say?'

'What we have seen, warrior. The messengers who had been to the south spoke of whole swathes of land given over to the animals that they might grow crops for themselves.'

'Well, it is true. We can see that for ourselves!'

Jai-Lyn wore only cheap metal, and yet she moved with an elegant grace. Even looking at the floor, her hands pressed together so nervously, she looked so pretty.

'There was worse, my master,' continued Jai-Lyn, miserably. 'For what is land to a robot but a luxury? Crops and cattle help one to live a more comfortable life, but they are not essential.' She looked around again, to see if anyone was listening. 'I . . .'

'Go on, Jai-Lyn,' urged Wa-Ka-Mo-Do.

'I . . . Oh, my master, it cannot be true, but I also heard it rumoured that the animals were to be given mining rights. That the Emperor had granted them leave to take coal and ore from his mines. Oh, I am sorry.'

She lowered her head now so that it touched her chest. Silence descended, underscored by the sound of the wheels on the track.

'Be very careful that you do not speak these words outside this carriage, Jai-Lyn,' warned Wa-Ka-Mo-Do.

'They are highest treason. The Emperor would never allow what you say to be.'

'I know it is true, but that is what I heard, warrior. And it troubled me, for I also heard that the animals had no use for the robots who worked in the mines.'

'No use for them?' said Wa-Ka-Mo-Do. But he knew what she meant. He had seen the silver machines in the fields. If the animals could make a machine that would plant and tend crops, then surely they could make one that would mine for ore.

'No use, my master. The robots of the mines were cast out to walk the land, with access to neither fire nor forge until their bodies fell apart and they were left broken and unmoving.'

'Be silent, Jai-Lyn!' He hadn't meant to shout, but he was rattled by her words. He already nursed doubts about this command; this news only unsettled him further.

Jai-Lyn had fallen to her hands and knees, her face close to the floor.

Wa-Ka-Mo-Do centred himself. 'Be silent,' he repeated, though more softly. 'Such things cannot be true. The Emperor is just and wise. He would never countenance such actions.'

Wa-Ka-Mo-Do had met the Emperor, and had seen him to be neither wise nor just. Surely, though, he would not contemplate this? To give metal to animals?

'Warrior?' said Jai-Lyn, face still turned to the ground. 'I'm sorry.'

Look at me, thought Wa-Ka-Mo-Do. *One of the Eleven, taking out his anger on a young unarmed woman. What*

*would those robots of the Imperial Guard think if they were
to see me now? They were right. I am uncultured.*

'Jai-Lyn. Please get up. I'm sorry I shouted. Here.'

He bent down and held out his hand, helped her to
her feet. He smiled in apology.

'Jai-Lyn, will you forgive me?'

'I have nothing to forgive you for, warrior. I shouldn't
have spoken as I did.'

'No. The fault is mine. I commanded you to speak.
Please, forgive me.'

She looked at him hesitantly; more than ever she
reminded him of La-Cor, his sister.

'I forgive you,' she said. 'Warrior, may I ask you a
question?'

'Of course you may.'

'Warrior. You are to command the warriors of Sangrel, are you not?'

'I am.'

And that feeling of unease returned to Wa-Ka-Mo-
Do. Just why was he being sent to command the city?

'Warrior, if you saw injustice in Sangrel, you would
address it, would you not?'

'Of course I would,' answered Wa-Ka-Mo-Do. He felt
more confident now. This he was sure of.

'Then I am pleased,' replied Jai-Lyn. 'For I know that
I can trust you. Look, we are approaching Sangrel . . .'

She pointed out of the window. Over the high heads
of the crops, Wa-Ka-Mo-Do saw the hilltop town of
Sangrel. Old stone and iron buildings clustered within
walls that gathered the town to safety at the top of
the steep slopes and cliffs of Sangrel Mound. The town

commanded a view for miles around, and in turn it commanded respect of those who looked up at it.

'It has been a pleasure to travel with you, warrior.'

Wa-Ka-Mo-Do looked down at the young robot, at her cheap but beautiful body, and worried at how she would fare in the city of Ka with its predominantly male population. All those whalers with their thick metal bodies, all that current surging within them, looking for release . . .

'It has been a pleasure to travel with you too, Jai-Lyn,' he said, and he took her hand. 'Remember, you have a friend in Sangrel. If you ever find yourself in need whilst in Ka, just mention that you know the commander of Sangrel.' He gripped her hand all the tighter as he spoke.

'No one would ever believe me,' laughed Jai-Lyn, gently disengaging her hand. 'And besides, your duty will lie elsewhere.'

'Perhaps,' said Wa-Ka-Mo-Do. 'But, for friendship's sake, if nothing else, if there is ever a need, you will promise to send me a message?'

He felt the surge of electricity in her hand.

'Friendship? Oh my master, thank you!'

'Then you promise?'

'I promise.'

Wa-Ka-Mo-Do felt a little happier.

'Then I vow that I will do what I can to aid you.'

'Don't make such a vow, warrior!'

'It is done.'

She gazed at him, golden eyes shining.

'Thank you,' said Jai-Lyn. 'Thank you, my master.'

The note of the engine changed. The train was decelerating, magnetic motors slowing it rapidly to a halt.

Wa-Ka-Mo-Do was approaching his command.

Karel

Morphobia Alligator might have been smiling at Karel, but Karel couldn't tell. If Morphobia Alligator did have a mouth, it was hidden behind the long tapering point that extended down from his head like an elongated chin.

'You think I'm from the Top of the World?' he was saying, and there was something about the timbre of his voice that wasn't quite normal. 'Yes, yes, that is right. You would think that, of course. You see the aluminium in my body and so you naturally assume that's where I would come from.' He held his arms wide as he spoke, each of them twice as long as he was tall. He shook them, sending a sine wave sinuating to each hand and back again to his body. 'No, No. I'm not from the Top of the World.'

'Then where did you find aluminium?' asked Karel. 'There is no such metal anywhere else in the whole of Shull!'

'Karel, Karel! Shull is riddled with it! Yes, Yes! I noted limestone hills to the south of here that are doubtless full of aluminium, but the quantities therein will be too diffuse to be mined! The same is true of the lands around your former home. What they lack, though, is this hot, wet climate that will lead to the chemical weathering, which concentrates the metal as stone erodes. The central coast of Yukawa is rich in aluminium! It has such a climate! Yes, Yes!'

'Yukawa? I've never heard of it.'

'Yukawa is probably the most advanced state on Penrose,' said Morphobia Alligator. 'They have certainly heard of Shull, yes, yes!'

'Are you from Yukawa then? Do all the robots in Yukawa look like you?'

'No, No! I'm not from Yukawa, Karel. No land can lay claim to a pilgrim.'

Karel felt the familiar anger rising within him.

'Don't play games with me, pilgrim. I have just learned that my wife is a prisoner, way south of here in Artemis City. Why am I wasting my time with you?'

Morphobia Alligator shook his arms again in that sine wave pattern. Karel wondered if he was being laughed at.

'Why are you here, Karel? Why are you here? Because if you're left to your own devices you will rush towards Artemis City in such a great temper and you will probably get yourself killed or captured in the process. Yes, yes! It's true, isn't it, yes, yes? I'm right!'

Karel calmed himself. Morphobia Alligator was speaking the truth, and they both knew it. A long arm snaked around his shoulder and gently turned him.

'Come, look out over this seascape with me, Karel. Though you do not have the mental capacity, the senses, the learning to enjoy it as I do, you may still gain some small measure of peace as we speak.'

'I don't want to gaze at the scenery, I want to see my wife.'

'But which way would you go, Karel? South, straight into Kavan's arms, or west to Presper Boole and the Northern Road? Or maybe north, to where the past lies?'

Karel pushed the arm from his shoulder. He looked out across the grey waters.

'I don't know, Morphobia Alligator. You tell me, which way should I go?'

'Ah! A pilgrim would not presume to *tell* you what to do, Karel. No, no! Your mind is a special thing; it is free to make its own decisions. Not many robots on this planet could say the same.'

'So I've heard. I have free will, and what difference has that made to me? My child is dead and my wife a prisoner. I was captured by Artemis and forced up here to the top of Shull, where I watched as two armies destroyed each other, and then I was abandoned to my own devices. Believe me, my life these past few months has not been of my choosing. Free will has made precious little difference to my circumstances, Morphobia Alligator. Dare you say any different?'

He gazed at the other robot in challenge, noted the odd glow to his eyes. Was there any part of Morphobia Alligator that was normal? The other robot answered in that strange voice.

'Dare I say any different? Long ago we won a battle and lost a war over robots like you. But Penrose is changing. For centuries the robots on this planet have woven the minds of their children to believe definite things and to possess definite skills. Some patterns of mind were more appropriate to the world than others, and those robots and their descendants prospered, so that now this world is a suitable place for robots with certain mindsets to live.'

What Morphobia Alligator said was true. Karel thought of Artemis, and how their state of mind had enabled the conquest of Shull.

'But all of that is changing,' continued the other robot. 'A new species has arrived on Penrose. Animals! They stand like robots, they walk and think and talk like robots, but they are animals!'

'Animals?' said Karel, disbelievingly.

'Yes, yes! Animals! I speak the truth, Karel. Animals! They have not yet visited Shull, but they will. They are clever, these creatures. They build ships to bring them here, ships that carry them across the stars from their own planet, many, many miles away. They use materials that we have never seen, plastics and alloys manufactured by processes we cannot begin to guess at! These animals are rich in knowledge and learning and metal. They have strong machinery that rips apart the land and rocks without effort, they have delicate devices that can change the passage of a breeze, machines so large you could build a city inside them, and devices so small you could hold one in your hand, balance it on a finger tip; devices so fast they fly across this land in minutes—'

'What are they doing here?' interrupted Karel. A sudden suspicion seized him. 'If they exist at all, of course.'

'Oh, they exist, Karel. Yes, yes they exist! You will see them soon. As to why they are here, well, they have come to trade, or so they say. The Emperor of Yukawa has granted them land to grow their crops, given them mines so that they may own metal—'

'Crops?' asked Karel.

Morphobia Alligator tilted his head, and then his eyes glowed with understanding.

'Of course, you're from Turing City! You don't know that the robots of Yukawa have not sterilized their land like the robots of southern Shull. You don't realize that in Yukawa they still plant crops and farm animals, harvesting the oil and skin and bone that they produce! Yes, yes? And so the animals, presumably seeing these crops and farms as they approached Penrose from space, have landed in Yukawa and have begun trade with the robots there. They take metal and work it to make wondrous devices that they give as presents to the Emperor in order to flatter him. The animals are skilled in *agriculture* – a *Tokvah* word relating to the growing of crops, Karel, and they are teaching the Emperor this lore.'

Karel looked around at the shiny grass, blown in patterns of light green and dark green by the fresh sea breeze. He found the sight vaguely unpleasant. Now he imagined the whole of the continent covered in the same vegetation, farmed by the animals. The thought made his gyros spin. It was obscene!

'But what has all this to do with me?' he asked.

Morphobia Alligator turned his head towards the silver sea, a strange movement given his odd body.

'What has this to do with you, Karel? Everything or nothing! Who knows which it will be? You are unusual, Karel, in these times. Not unique, understand, there are other robots with minds such as yours. But not many. You are unusual. Yes, Yes!'

'So I'm unusual. So what?'

'Think of this. Suppose the animals had come to Shull forty years ago, how would the robots have responded?'

Karel gazed at the robot, hurt to be asked such questions. They reminded him of his past.

'I'll tell you,' said Morphobia Alligator, not seeming to notice his silence. 'The robots of Stark would have studied their technology so that they could become stronger, the robots of Wien would have traded coal and their own serfs and slaves with the animals in order to gain more power, and the robots of Bethe would have observed them and waited to see what they did next. And as for the robots of Turing City—'

'We would have spoken to them. We would have tried to understand who they were and what they were.' Karel spoke softly. That had been his job. He used to negotiate with outsiders. To think that he might have been summoned to speak with the animals, back when Turing City was at its height. What an opportunity that would have been!

'But that was then,' said Morphobia Alligator. 'What about now? What will happen now, when the animals come to Shull?'

'Artemis will attack them, they will try and defeat them.'

'Is that the right course to take, Karel?'

'Of course not! There is a time for fighting, but one should always speak first!'

'Yes, yes, but of course you would say that, Karel! That is what Turing City robots do! That is the way you were made. But you will be made that way no longer, because all the minds that will be twisted on Shull from now are to be twisted in the fashion of Artemis.'

Karel nodded. He understood what Morphobia Alligator was saying now.

'So Artemis will fight the animals. Well, that may not be a bad thing.'

'It may not be. But the animals are very clever. They are very powerful. What if they defeat us all? What if they melt down all the metal life on this planet and place organic life in its place?'

'Zuse, yes,' said Karel. His gyros were churning. 'But what difference does it make now? Artemis is strong. If the animals had come forty years ago.'

'Yes, yes. If they had come forty years ago. What then, though? How do we know that Stark or Bethe or Turing City or any of the other states would have had the right mindset to deal with the animals?'

'How am I supposed to know that?'

'How indeed, Karel? How could a robot with a mind such as yours possibly be expected to understand that? Now, I on the other hand . . .'

Morphobia Alligator let the sentence trail away.

'Who are you?' asked Karel.

'I am a pilgrim. I am a mule. I am only one hundred years old, yet I was one of the first robots to walk on Penrose. I was there when the truth of the Book of Robots was first understood and yet my mind was not yet twisted.'

'Spare me the riddles, Morphobia Alligator. You know I have a temper.'

'I know you're not a fool, either, Karel. You've been

to the reliquary on the northern coast of Shull. You've seen what is in there; you've seen the mind patterns engraved around the outside of the building. You should realize that there are more types of robot that walk on Penrose than those like yourself. You have met some of the others. Robots like Banjo Macrodocious, who once fought the pilgrims. Robots like myself. Maybe we are not so plentiful as your own species who have spread their offspring across this planet, but we all have our place on this world.'

Karel looked again across the waters to the town of Blaize. He had spent nearly all of his life in Turing City. He had thought of himself as educated and urbane, he was increasingly aware of how wrong that impression was. He felt as out of touch and provincial in the eyes of this robot as the robots of Artemis had once seemed to himself.

'So I ask you again, Morphobia Alligator. What do you want with me?'

'I want nothing with you personally, Karel. But at times like this, pilgrims have always paid special attention to robots such as you. Robots whose minds weren't made up for them by their parents.'

'Why? Am I so special?'

'I don't know, Karel. Most of you die young, you know. But, just occasionally, one of you has a thought so original it can change the path of life of Penrose. Nicolas the Coward was one such robot.'

'Are you saying I am a coward?'

'You know that I'm not. Nicolas the Coward realized that the mind was more important than metal.'

'That's not how the story goes.'

'Stories have a way of changing as they are twisted into new minds. Stories change with each telling, slowly evolving into new stories. Perhaps some day there will be a story about Karel and Kavan?'

Karel gazed at the pilgrim, suspiciously.

'So you *are* saying that I'm special?'

'Who knows, Karel? No one ever knows until afterwards. In all probability, the chances are that you are not such a robot. There are around two hundred of you that we know of on Penrose at the moment, and most, if not all of you will die young and unfulfilled.'

'I had a sister,' said Karel. 'She was just like me.'

'I know. Eleanor.'

'Kavan killed her.'

'Robots such as yourself usually die young, Karel. I told you that.'

'All I want to do is free my wife.'

'Just maybe, I can help you do that.'

'Then why are we wasting time here? Let's go!'

'No, no. You don't understand, Karel. I am not going anywhere. I have seen you and spoken to you, and I have played my part. All that remains for me to do is to give you some advice, give you a direction in which to travel. Not south, Karel. At least, not at first. Climb down this hillside to the water's edge, and there find the heaviest rock that you can carry. Pick up that rock and then follow the road beneath the water to Blaize.'

'Why take a rock?'

'The currents in the inlet are strong. They can sweep a fully grown robot out to sea.'

Karel looked across the grey water to the distant town.

'What do I do when I reach Blaize?'

'There is another robot waiting there. He is a soldier, or at least he was once. He might be able to help you. And you him. He needs to redeem himself.'

'Redeem himself? From what?'

'Perhaps he will tell you himself.'

'And what about you?'

'I will continue on my way . . .'

At that Morphobia Alligator was silent.

Karel looked once more across the grey choppy waters. The clouds were dispersing a little, allowing sunlight through in red bands. It cast a red glow over the far-away town, giving it an alien air.

'Will I see you again?'

'Perhaps.'

There was nothing else to say. Karel had already made up his mind; he wanted to be on his way, off to rescue his wife. He quickly descended the slippery green hillside, skirting the grey ruins of Presper Boole. The town had an eerie, dead aspect, empty of all iron. Childhood stories of northern ghosts arose in Karel's mind.

Down at the water's edge he found a wide, paved road that led down beneath the waves, and he wondered once more at the robots that had once inhabited this land, wondered at the journeys they had formerly made between the two towns. He found a large stone by the road, remnants of a collapsed column. He picked it up and made his way into the water, his electromuscles aching with the cold once more.

Just before he vanished beneath the waves, he turned and looked back up at Morphobia Alligator, still standing there on the hillside, arms waving in sine waves.

Karel hoisted the stone and followed the road under the water.

The road to Blaize was old and mostly overgrown with slippery weed, yet the path down the centre was a little clearer, suggesting that a few robots still travelled this way. Karel turned his eyes right up, and strode determinedly on, his field of vision extending only a few feet before being lost in the gloom of the surrounding water. Faint streamers of light rippled in the ceiling somewhere above his head. The currents in the water swirled around him, tugging him this way and that; his feet skidded on the writhing weed.

Still, he walked on, feeling the path descend as he approached the centre of the wide inlet, wondering all the time at Morphobia Alligator. Was he wasting his time coming this way? He didn't know. Morphobia Alligator was right, if he had been left to his own devices, he would have blindly walked south until he had been killed or captured by the Artemisians. On and on he walked, the ache in his electromuscle increasing all the time.

Eventually the road ceased its descent and began to climb upwards. Karel had passed the halfway point, he guessed. Just as he began his struggle up the far side of the inlet, the road split in two. One fork bent to the right, heading north, and for a moment Karel hesitated.

Did that path lead to the Top of the World? For just a moment, he was tempted to follow it but the image of Susan appeared in his mind and he resumed his climb.

He reached the far side as the sun was setting. Across the inlet, Presper Boole was lost in shadow. Behind the hills upon which it stood, the low sun had set the sky seemingly on fire. Karel realized he was still holding onto the rock, and he let it fall into the sea, water splashing up over his knees, water draining once again from his grey infantryrobot's body. Not for the first time, he noted that though the Artemisian robotics might not be as sophisticated as those of Turing City, they could take a lot more punishment.

Now that he had reached Blaize he had his first inkling of how enormous the place was. The city was comparable in magnitude maybe even to his former home of Turing City. Morphobia Alligator had said he was to meet someone here: a soldier. That could take some doing in a place of this size.

Just as he was thinking this he saw, lit up in scarlet sunlight, the metal shell of another robot. It was sitting near the top of the road, just where it ran up through the remains of a wide arch into the city proper.

Karel raised a hand, and slowly, the other robot returned his gesture. As Karel made his way towards it, he realized that there was something odd about the other person. His body seemed half melted. The joints and seams of his panelling looked as if they were soldered together. Karel felt the current drain from his electromuscles. The thought of having his mind placed in that body made him feel fuzzy with static. It would be like being trapped in a prison.

The other robot got up with some difficulty. Stiffly, it made its way towards Karel.

'Hello,' said Karel. 'My name is Karel. I have been told that you could help me.'

'*I* help *you?*' said the other robot. 'I don't think so. I can't even help myself. Tell me, do you know who I am?'

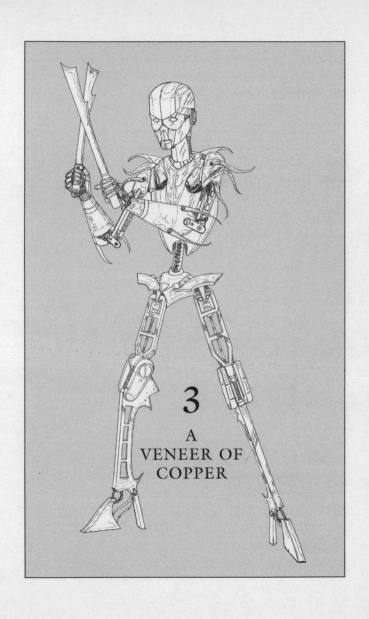

3

A
VENEER OF
COPPER

Kavan

The Uncertain Army charged, and a storm of metal arose upon the face of Shull. Metal pumping and flexing, pistoning and scraping, stretching and bending across the earth, metal tearing into the ground, thudding deep into the soil, metal rising up into the air in a swarm . . . The swipe of blades, the crash of cannonballs, the spung and ricochet of bullets, the whirling of saw-edged discs, flares of wire, rains of chaff, explosions of shrapnel, swarf springing up all around . . .

Through it all danced the energy of electricity, jumping in blue sparks, crackling down arms and legs, earthing itself on blades, shorting out between electro-muscles, singing in the mind . . .

The noise of explosions, crackling orange and yellow flames, burning phosphorus, the clash of metal, the squeal of drills slipping across plate, the scrape of knives, the thud of lead on iron . . . The atmosphere was squeezed and sucked this way and that by explosions, smoke and iron filings pushed through panelling in great gasps that sent the gyros shuddering, eyesight and hearing baffled by the flash and crash and roar . . .

And amongst it all, the Uncertain Army stumbled forward, retreated back, reeled sideways, was pushed and knocked and tumbled over itself, the whole force swaying this way and that, but all the time slowly advancing on the Artemisian army.

Spoole had positioned his troops well; he had given his cannon clear lines of sight at Kavan's approaching army. They fired round shot and chain shot, canister and shrapnel, shell and carcass and magnetic bolas: pairs of magnetized balls that orbited each other as they flew, whipping and crashing their way through the approaching ranks. File after file of robots were smashed down, bodies crushed, electromuscle torn, blue wire tangling across their comrades, and still the Uncertain Army came on.

Seen from above, the fighting didn't just occur at the boundary between the forces: it boiled all the way through the troops. The robots of the Uncertain Army fought amongst themselves, they fought to get away from the charge, they fought to be at the front of it, they fought just to keep their feet. Kavan moved in the eye of the hurricane, surrounded by grey-bodied infantry-robots who marched with cold determination, but also with an air of homecoming: they had marched for Kavan before, they were marching for him again. Iron-tipped bullets rained down from above, they rattled off their grey shells. They were fired by the robots that lined the distant mountain peaks, their killing energy spent by the time it reached them.

'Onwards,' called Kavan. 'Onwards! Aim for the centre!'

The Uncertain Army was getting less spread out: they were being funnelled between the low hills that led to the pass Kavan had once blasted through the centre of the mountain range. Now that passage was being choked with railway lines. He guessed that somewhere safely beyond Spoole's troops would be marshalled the trains that had brought his army north. They would be waiting to carry the broken metal from this battle back south to Artemis City to be remade anew once the war was over.

A volley of shots sounded to Kavan's right, and a huge explosion fountained brown soil into the air, smeared clinging dust across eyes and bodies. Black and grey and silver robots lost their nerve and began running for the surrounding hills, barely seen through the smoke and flame: they were cut down by shots fired by the grey robots that Spoole had stationed up there. A gust of wind blew clear the smoke for a moment, revealing silver Scouts running down the hills towards them. Some of his own Storm Troopers stepped forward to meet them, then the smoke drew back in, blotting out the scene. Were the Storm Troopers defecting to Spoole's side, or were they fighting the Scouts?

Still the Uncertain Army moved on, a creeping determination spreading through the ranks as they realized they were now committed: there was no way to go but forward. The army moved like a robot carrying a large rock, unsteadily but with an unstoppable intent.

Grey infantryrobots spilled down from the hillside in front of them. Kavan thought that this was an attack, then saw the soldiers on his side that charged to intercept them pause and open their lines, welcome the infantryrobots back into their ranks. Kavan realized that the message was spreading.

Kavan was returning, and he was raising an army.

Silver Scouts came rushing up to join the battle on the hillside; they fought the Stormtroopers and the infantry alike, and Kavan saw the careful arrangement of Spoole's troops unravelling, a tearing in the ranks that spread back along the hills further and further to the distant mountain peaks. Robots were changing sides as the fight reached them. Spoole's and Kavan's armies were flowing together and splitting apart and changing allegiances too fast to follow.

The grey band of infantryrobots that surrounded Kavan was growing thicker and thicker as more soldiers defected to his side. The infantry had always been loyal to him, he was one of them after all. The ground was shaking with the stamp and crash of so many feet. And then there was another noise, a high-pitched whistling.

The battle seemed to freeze for just a moment. So many robots halted, looking into the dark smoke, listening . . .

The area ahead of Kavan erupted in incandescent white fire. Metal and shrapnel exploded into the air, molten lead droplets rained down upon Kavan, melting into his panelling, searing the electromuscle beneath. The Uncertain Army moved forward once more, the fighting reforming itself around the smoking pit ahead.

'What was it?' Kavan realized he was asking the question of himself. Then he heard the answer. 'Magnesium. They're burning magnesium.'

The sense of outraged indignation spread through the robots battling in the flare and the noise. They were wasting metal! Those people who called themselves Artemisians were destroying metal!

Again, that same high-pitched whistling, and Kavan looked up to see something falling overhead. A dark metal sphere, it burst in the ranks behind him in another bright white flare. Hot air rushed forward, coating him with soot.

His ears were singing, some of the circuitry had been damaged by the blast, but he still heard the faint crump ahead of him, he saw the flames there on the slopes of the distant mountain. He stood taller when he knew what was happening.

The robots who fired the missiles had realized what they had done. It was the tipping point, even for them. Now those same weapons were being turned back on Spoole's own troops. The mutiny had reached the artillery even as the Uncertain Army came within its range.

'We are winning,' shouted Kavan, 'We are winning!'

He stamped his feet, once, twice, three times. Stamp, *stamp*, stamp; stamp, *stamp*, stamp. It was an old beat, one that the Storm Troopers had used in the past. Now Kavan adopted it for his own. His growing army marched on, with the sound of stamping rolling before it, shaking the very mountains themselves. It echoed from the mountains, it was taken up and copied by the soldiers that Spoole had brought to capture Kavan.

'We are winning!' shouted Kavan.

We are winning! We are winning!

The shout was echoed by the infantryrobots around him. It echoed down the ranks, spreading out in a circle, losing itself in the crash of the battle.

Kavan raised his arm and shouted into the noise.

'And now, everyone who is with me, the time is at hand! This is the time of the final charge! Pour all your shot forward, slice every body that stands against you, claw with your hands, discharge every last watt of power from your electromuscle! Break yourself on the enemy, and watch as their ranks crumble and retreat! For this is the day when Nyro's dream is finally realized!'

They couldn't hear him, but it didn't matter, it was already happening, Kavan could see it. Lines of metal peeling away from Spoole's ranks: walking, pushing, running, heading for the trains and the route back to Artemis City. Spoole's army was retreating.

Kavan sent all the power he had into his voicebox, almost rupturing it in the process.

'Charge!' he called.

It wasn't a rout. It wasn't a glorious victory. It wasn't even a battle in the end. It was what happened when soldiers no longer believed in what they were doing, that point when they turned and ran, thinking of nothing but the twisted metal of their own minds. All the noise, all the violence seemed to pass away, rising into the sky as gently as the black smoke smouldering from the battle-field.

Peace settled on the broken scene. Robots lay crushed and broken across the valley floor. Smashed by bullets and shot, trampled by other robots rushing to the charge or to the retreat.

Voiceboxes whined and whistled and screeched. Blue twisted metal lay tangled around arms and legs and hands and feet. It had tripped up robots; it had bound and sliced friend and foe alike. It was the same as on any

battlefield, but this was only the visible sign of destruction. There was also the unguessable number of minds
that lay trapped in bodies, on the valley floor, in the hills,
on the mountains, fallen between cracks and down cliff
faces and gorges. Minds whose coils had been broken,
leaving the thoughts trapped in darkness for the rest of
the robot's life, or worse, minds where the coil had suffered a few breaks, leaving current surging agonizingly
through the twisted metal. How many robots lay in silent
agony, hoping, waiting for the salvage teams to discover
them, to reclaim their metal and to crush the metal of
their minds, ending their life and their pain?

Kavan didn't care. As far as Artemis was concerned,
there was no mind, there was only metal.

Kavan walked to the head of the pass, saw the broken
podium where Spoole must have stood, waiting for
Kavan to be brought to him. It was deserted. Spoole and
the rest of the Generals were long gone, the first on the
trains that had loaded up and headed south as the tide
of battle turned. The railway lines were littered with the
metal of those robots that had not made it on board the
trains; mostly raw, untempered recruits, chased down by
the silver Scouts, their coils broken by one swift swipe.

Later, some of Kavan's troops would walk the broken
railway lines, the metal twisted, the sleepers and ballast
wrecked by Spoole's retreating army, and they would
follow a line of dead bodies that led through the mountains to the very edge of the Artemis plain itself.

But for now, they looked around at the carnage,
incongruously roofed by the fresh blue sky, sharply illuminated by the clear spring sun.

His army was taking shape, all by itself. Robots were forming ranks around him. Infantryrobots, Storm Troopers and Scouts. Even some Generals and engineers, recently defected from Spoole's army. Did they really believe, or were they just taking the most likely route to survival?

He would find out soon enough.

He counted his troops. Nearly three thousand, he guessed, arranging themselves in squares on the floor of the pass, in tiers up the sides of the low hills to the north. Not bad. But not enough to launch an attack on Artemis City.

At least, not yet.

He raised his voice.

'Robots of Artemis,' he called. He paused. He heard his words being relayed back through the crowd, and he felt an electric glow of satisfaction. This was how it had been in the old days, standing in the trenches, passing on commands. This speech would take some time for the message to get through. But for all the old soldiers out there, it would be more poignant for the method in which it was delivered.

'Robots of Artemis,' he repeated. 'This was our easiest fight, out here, on *our* territory, on the battle-field, the place we are familiar with, the place that Spoole and his City Generals have forgotten or have never visited. This battle was *always* going to go our way.'

He paused, hearing his words relayed out, a diminishing electronic whisper.

'Of course it would go our way! We had the will! Our former leaders are no longer true to Nyro, they dwell too much on their own lives and comforts, to the exclusion of Nyro's way. It is obvious that their day is past!

'But now we face a harder struggle, for we cannot remain here long. What would you have us do? Lurk here in the mountains, preying on the folk who live here, building our strength, for the day we feel comfortable attacking Artemis City? That would be the easiest way, but it is not the Artemisian way!'

The cheer was ragged. This was where the true followers of Nyro would show themselves, thought Kavan. Those who had followed him all this time would understand the necessity to move now. It would be those who had joined his army out of convenience who would be having second thoughts.

'And so,' continued Kavan, 'we march on Artemis City itself! Not in a month's time, or even a day's time, but now! Because that is what we must do, even if that is the dangerous choice, because *we* are the true Artemisians! Because we are true to Artemis, we must march to where the Generals are on their home territory. To where the soldiers will huddle safe within walls and behind trenches. We must march to where we are outnumbered.'

More cheers. Were they more or less enthusiastic? It didn't matter.

'But do not be too disheartened. Our numbers will grow as we march south. Some of you will slip away into the night. We will reclaim you in the end, for those robots who see the truth in what we do will be marching to join us even now, and, cowards that you are, you will see that your path returns you to us. But most of you will follow because you know what we do is *right*! Even though the journey will be hard, for you know that Spoole and the rest will fight us every step of the way . . .' He paused, turned in a circle to see all of his troops. 'But from a distance,' he continued, 'and half-heartedly. Because that is all that Spoole and his Generals will know and will dare. That is why we *know* we will triumph, because we have the will. And because we are right!'

Somewhere behind him, back where the infantry-robots assembled, someone began to stamp their feet. Stamp, *stamp*, stamp; stamp, *stamp*, stamp. The beat spread out to fill the whole of the pass, and Kavan did something he very rarely did.

He smiled.

Spoole

'What you should have done . . .' began General Sandale.

'Later,' said Spoole, evenly.

'I only meant to say—'

'General,' Spoole was aware that all the Generals in the railway coach were attending. This coach was made of the best metal and insulated with plastic. The noise of the wheels on the track outside could barely be heard, and the Generals were listening closely to what was being said. He knew what they were thinking: they were wondering *is today the day we get a new leader?*

'General,' repeated Spoole, and he lowered his voice a little further so that all present strained to hear, 'I don't want to hear what you *only meant to say* or what you were *only asking*. I don't want any suggestions about what *we* could have done after the event.'

He stressed the word *we*. General Sandale's voice was smooth.

'I do think a thorough examination of what went wrong would be appropriate.'

'And this shall be done, when we return to Artemis City. Although I think it obvious already what happened back there, General. Kavan is right. Artemis has lost its way. Its own soldiers obviously believe that.'

'You're the leader, Spoole. The state is what you made it.'

'It's what *we* made it, Sandale,' answered Spoole. 'Look at us all, look at this coach. Gold and copper and plastic. This isn't the way that Kavan will travel, I bet.'

'A leader does not need distractions—'

'Leaders?' interrupted Spoole. 'Leaders stand at the front of their troops. What's the last battle you fought, Sandale? How long ago was it?'

Before Sandale could answer, Spoole was looking around the rest of the Generals.

'And you Spine, and you Pont? Ossel? Wines? Chekov? At least Sandale has seen action. You younger ones have never been out in the field, have you?'

The silence in the carriage deepened.

'I think—' began Sandale.

'No,' said Spoole. 'I don't want to know what you think. Not now. Perhaps when we get back to Artemis City.'

'I really think that we should talk now, Spoole.'

'No, Sandale. As you said, I'm the leader. Unless you think otherwise? Perhaps you want to fight me?'

General Sandale gave a faint smile as he turned away from Spoole.

'I don't think fighting is appropriate for Generals, Spoole,' he said.

'I know,' said Spoole. 'And I can't help thinking that's just another example of where Artemis has lost its way.'

Karel

Karel felt as if he was in a tale from his childhood. He racked his memory: had there ever been a story of someone who travelled to a land of fire at the northern edge of Shull in order to meet a melted man?

If not, then there should have been.

The towers of the ancient city beyond were lit up by the crimson light of the setting sun. The sea was dark with pink highlights. The strange robot seemed almost black, as if made of lead.

'My name is Karel,' repeated Karel.

'I thought it might be. He said you would come.'

'Who did?'

'Morphobia Alligator. Before he left me last night, he said he had left oil and metal and a fire for us to repair our bodies. It is waiting in a forge, just beyond the gates to the city.'

Karel turned towards the gates.

'Then take my arm,' he said.

He supported the other robot as they made their way up the slope of the beach.

'How do you know Morphobia Alligator?' asked Karel.

'I don't know. I was coughed up on this beach by a whale. Morphobia Alligator was waiting for me. He said I might be able to help you find your wife.'

'Coughed up by a whale? What were you doing in a whale?'

'I don't know. Look at my body, how melted it is. My mind must have melted a little, too. All the memories have run together. I can see mountains and cities and the sea. I can see different lands through which I must have travelled, but I don't know the order in which I visited them.'

'You don't know who you are?'

'I can see faces of robots, but none of them can be my own, can they?'

'Can you see a robot's face in a mirror?'

The other robot paused, remembering.

'Clever. But no, the memories are all jumbled; I can't tell where one person ends and another begins. How can I tell who I am?'

'You must know some names?'

'Part of me is missing, Karel. Part of my mind has melted too far.'

Karel wondered if the other robot was telling the full truth. He had met robots in the past who had claimed to have lost their memories, back when he worked as an immigration officer in Turing City. Those robots had a reason to not admit the full truth of their past. What reason could this robot have for wanting to do so? It occurred to Karel that maybe he was ashamed of his past.

'But still, I have to call you something,' he said.

The other robot's face didn't move. It was melted into an expression of permanent surprise.

'A name,' said the robot. 'Then how about Melt? It describes me, at least.'

'Melt,' said Karel. 'And you are going to help me? Morphobia Alligator says you used to be a soldier.'

'Yes, that feels right.'

'Who did you fight for?'

Melt paused. This time Karel had the definite impression that the other robot knew the answer to this question.

'I don't know,' said Melt, slowly.

The two robots passed under the broken arch of the city entrance, and they paused a moment, looking at the strange architecture of the ancient buildings around them.

'Does this feel right to you?' asked Karel, 'that we should do what Morphobia Alligator tells us?'

'I don't know what feels right any more,' said Melt, and there was a sincerity to his tone that had been lacking in his previous speech.

Karel pointed straight ahead. 'There is a glow coming from that building. Do you think it's the forge Morphobia Alligator mentioned?'

'What else could it be?'

They walked towards it, and Karel felt a sudden sense of homecoming. Despite the strangeness of his surroundings, despite the distance he had travelled from his

broken city, there was something about the glow of a
forge that always reminded him of home. The memory
of his dead son glowed for a moment, but it quickly
faded, and a picture of Susan arose instead. He felt a faint
satisfaction.

He was coming for her.

Well, he was beginning the journey.

The inside of the building was at once familiar and alien.
The doorways were a little smaller than was comfortable,
some of them so small he wondered if the robots who
had once used them crawled through on all fours. A
frieze was carved into the stone near the ceiling, pictures
of creatures with the head, arms and chests of robots,
but with the bodies of horses. Karel stared at them for
a moment, wondering if the animals they depicted had
once existed. His gaze was drawn back to the red glowing
fire in the corner of the room. A bucket of good, hard
coal stood at the side, there was a trough filled with sea
water nearby. Plates of iron and copper and tin lay stacked
on the floor and, on closer inspection, joy of joys, Karel
found two cans of thin, clear oil.

'Oh, to clean out my feet,' said Karel. He sat down
on a metal stool and began to strip the panelling away
from his legs. 'Or maybe we should start with each
other's hands?'

Melt said nothing, he just remained standing by the
door, watching Karel.

'Come on, Melt, what's the matter?'

'Nothing. You go on.'

Karel rose to his feet and, electromuscles bare from the knee down, walked to Melt.

'Come on, I'll help you get this panelling off,' he offered.

'You can't,' said Melt. 'It's welded to the electro-muscle.'

Karel felt a wobble in his gyros. He peered closer at Melt's dark metal body, looking at the faint lines where the seams of the panelling had melted together.

'What happened to you?' he murmured.

'I don't remember,' said Melt, and once again Karel had the impression that this wasn't quite true.

'You know,' said Karel, 'I used to work as an immigration officer, back in Turing City.'

'What is that?'

'I used to speak to people, communicate with them. See if they were suitable to join our state. I got to know when people weren't telling the full truth.'

'Really?' said Melt. Karel wondered for a moment, but didn't press the point. He ran a hand down the seam in Melt's arm, feeling the mix of metals there.

'What are you made of?' he asked. 'I can feel cast iron in there, and lead, and steel. How can you walk around in that body? It must weigh so much! We should just remove your mind and start again.' Karel glanced back towards the fire. 'There isn't enough metal here, but I'm sure if we head back to the battlefields we'll find a body there we can use. Or maybe we can put it together from parts. These Artemisian bodies are pretty standard,' and he rapped his knuckles on his chest for effect as he spoke.

'There's no point,' said Melt. 'My coil is fused to this body. I'm trapped in here.'

Karel felt as if his gyros had been dropped in the fire, as if they were melting, spinning out of true, jamming. He had seen death and destruction on the battlefields of Artemis. Nothing had been quite as nasty as this.

'So as you can see,' said Melt, 'there is no point waiting for me. Tend to yourself. That body needs cleaning and adjustment. We will travel easier once you are repaired.'

'No way,' said Karel. 'Not with you fighting against that body to make every step. Come over here to the fire. I'm good with metal, all Turing Citizens are. My wife was . . . *is* . . . much better than I. When we find her she will fix you up properly. In the meantime, if we are ever going to get to her, I need you working as best you can. You're a soldier, aren't you?'

'I think so.'

'Well, there you are. We'll need to fight, I'm sure. Now sit down here on this stool while I see what I can do.'

'I can't sit down. I can't bend my legs enough.'

Karel thought about that. Melt couldn't even sit down to rest from the weight of his body. What other hardships did he suffer?

'Okay,' said Karel. 'We'll start on the legs.'

He selected a piece of metal from the pile by the fire, and started to shape it with his hands, folding and pulling it, making it into a crude knife. 'I'll see if I can open up these seams a little. Maybe plane away some of the metal from your body, reduce the weight a little. The least we can do is loosen you up, restore some movement to your body.'

He thrust the proto-knife into the fire. Oddly enough, he felt quite positive. For the first time in months, he was doing something useful. He was helping someone. It felt good.

Wa-Ka-Mo-Do

Sangrel was built on a rocky plug of stone thrust clear of the rolling grassy countryside that surrounded it. Centuries ago, robots had chipped away at the natural outcrop, making its walls more sheer, carving steps and passageways into the slopes leading to the summit. They had dressed stone to make bricks and flags and used it in building gates and archways and walls, making a maze of passageways and courtyards overlooked by firing steps and loupes, the better to defend the city they planned to grow on the flattened top of the hill. Sangrel was a fortress at its foundations, but something more beautiful had risen from them.

Wa-Ka-Mo-Do had watched the multicoloured roofs and domes of the city rising above the city ramparts as he approached, gradually losing sight of them as the railway line tucked itself into the shadow of the hill upon which Sangrel stood. As the train slowed, squeezing between the cliffs and the clear blue waters of Lake Ochoa, Wa-Ka-Mo-Do looked across the lake to the dark wooded hill that stood on the far bank. The surrounding hills seemed to have drawn back to leave it standing on its own, as if even they knew of the stone temples that hid amongst the dark green foliage of the Mound of Eternity, those temples that had made the place infamous throughout the whole of Yukawa.

Wa-Ka-Mo-Do stepped from the train into the shade cast by the Mound of Sangrel. He wanted to turn, to wave goodbye to Jai-Lyn, who he was sure would be watching him from the carriage, but protocol forbade that. Further down the platform, a captain stood waiting, four soldiers standing to attention behind him.

Only four, noted Wa-Ka-Mo-Do. He wondered if this was a deliberate slight, given his low parentage. Before he had time to ponder on this, the captain stepped forward and saluted.

'Wa-Ka-Mo-Do. Welcome to Sangrel. My name is Ka-Lo-Re-Harballah. I must apologize for the paucity of your welcome, but there are precious few troops to spare here in Sangrel.'

Wa-Ka-Mo-Do took an immediate liking to Ka-Lo-Re-Harballah. He was young, his body work suggested nobility, but there was an honesty about him that Wa-Ka-Mo-Do recognized straightaway.

'And so you decided that my reception was less than essential, given the circumstances.'

'No, Honoured Commander, but—'

'And that was an excellent decision. I can see that you are a robot who understands the exigencies of command. Now, I would be obliged if you would escort me to the command rooms.'

'Certainly, Honoured Commander.' Ka-Lo-Re-

Harballah stood to attention and about-turned. Wa-Ka-Mo-Do was impressed to see the four soldiers do the same in perfect synchronization. At the same moment, there was a roar of a diesel engine, and the train began to roll from the station. Wa-Ka-Mo-Do watched it go, rounding the far corner of Sangrel Mound as it began the journey from Sangrel province, heading for the marshland that surrounded distant Ka.

'We will enter the city through the Emperor's Gate,' said Ka-Lo-Re-Harballah, indicating the tall arch behind the railway station, the underside carved with shapes of hanging icicles. Centuries ago, the commander of Sangrel displayed his power by having ice brought from many miles away and hung from the gates, glistening in even in the hottest summers, for no other reason than to show that he could.

'You occupy the Copper Master's house, facing onto Smithy Square.'

'The Copper Master's house? An exalted position indeed. With views over the western terrace and the lake, I believe.'

'You are certainly well informed, Honoured Commander.'

Wa-Ka-Mo-Do had read up on his command before leaving the Silent City. However, a question remained.

'But what of the Emperor's Palace? Surely that is the traditional residence for the commander of Sangrel?'

Ka-Lo-Re-Harballah gave Wa-Ka-Mo-Do a sideways look.

'That building has been given as embassy to the animals, as you are of course aware, Honoured Commander.'

The young robot seemed almost ashamed by his answer.

'Of course,' answered Wa-Ka-Mo-Do. It was unheard of, by any protocol, for the Emperor to give up any of his residences, for was not the Emperor supreme? What signal did this send to the robots of Sangrel, seeing that the animals had, quite visibly, been placed above the Emperor himself?

At that moment something appeared from the gates of the city that drove all other thoughts from Wa-Ka-Mo-Do's mind. He found himself slowing to a halt, turning to watch.

Three of them, walking upright like robots, walking through the Emperor's Gate. They strode beneath the stone icicles without so much as a second glance, as if they were peasants heading from the mine after their shift, not as if they were honoured guests to take this most glorious of paths.

Wa-Ka-Mo-Do didn't mean to stare, but he couldn't help himself. They moved like robots. Almost like robots, but with less ... formality? Was that the word? They strode through the sunlight as if they weren't really part of their surroundings. Perhaps they weren't, they were strangers to this world, after all. There was something so odd about them though, something almost ethereal. Was it simply because they weren't made of metal? Look at them, clad in green-cloth panelling, hands and faces emerging from the strange material that they wore, their flesh an odd colour, and so different, even to each other. Two of them were pale pink, the other a brown colour. An unnatural hue, no metal was of that shade.

'Honoured Commander?'

Wa-Ka-Mo-Do was embarrassed by his rudeness.

'Thank you, Ka-Lo-Re-Harballah,' he said, lowering his face in shame. 'I did not mean to stare. Only, I have never seen the animals.'

'One never quite gets used to them, Honoured Commander. There is an emptiness about them. You can see them with your eyes, and hear them with your ears, but you cannot sense their metal. They seem so insubstantial . . .'

Wa-Ka-Mo-Do turned to watch the animals as they walked down past the railway station.

'Where are they going?' he asked.

'To the lake, probably. They float upon the water there, or lie upon its shores.'

'Why?'

'Recreation, I think.'

Wa-Ka-Mo-Do passed through the Emperor's Archway and followed Ka-Lo-Re-Harballah up the Emperor's Road into the city. Sheer stone walls rose up to their left, studded with balconies and loupe holes from where defenders had once dropped magnetized iron snow and forced water at high pressure over invading troops. Channels were cut in the road down which heavy iron balls were rolled. Some of them were fused to explode, others simply rolled over the attackers, plating their bodies onto their huge mass, their size growing with each attack.

Wa-Ka-Mo-Do was still wondering at what he had seen.

'They look so weak . . .' he began.

'No, Honoured Commander,' interrupted Ka-Lo-Re-Harballah. 'No, they are not weak. The animals are so strong. They speak softly, but they have terrible power.'

'You speak with them?'

'Yes. They have machines that help them to do this.'

'Machines?'

'The humans build machines to do everything for them.'

'Humans?'

'This is the name they give themselves. Or at least, the word that the machines speak.'

They reached the end of the Emperor's Road. The Silver Ice gates stood open at this end.

'Why are the gates left open for me?' asked Wa-Ka-Mo-Do.

'Not for you, Honoured Commander,' said Ka-Lo-Re-Harballah, and you could hear the shame in his voice. 'The animals requested it. This road is the most convenient for the lake. The Emperor himself approved the request.'

Wa-Ka-Mo-Do felt sorry for poor Ka-Lo-Re-Harballah. He was one of the nobility. The shame he felt would be like a physical pain to him. It would be woven into his mind to be so. What did Wa-Ka-Mo-Do himself feel, he wondered? A little shame, it was true, but something else too: the awakening urge to fight. After all, wasn't this what he had been woven for? It was a dangerous thought. He wasn't here to fight the animals.

They passed through the Silver Ice gates into the lower city. Tall buildings made of stone and brick, their small windows set high up. Shiny green and red tiles decorated their roofs.

'The animals are powerful, Honoured Commander.' Ka-Lo-Re-Harballah lowered his voice, 'More powerful than we are. The Emperor maintains that he is pleased to trade with them, but I suspect the reverse is the truth. The humans have the advantage in all negotiations.'

Wa-Ka-Mo-Do looked carefully at Ka-Lo-Re-Harballah, wondering if this were some sort of test.

'This is treasonous talk, Ka-Lo-Re-Harballah.'

'I know that, Honoured Commander, and it shames me to speak in this fashion, but is it not more shameful to deny the truth?'

'This is a wise thought.'

'You will see, Honoured Commander, the humans roam far and wide across this land, much wider than they are permitted under the terms of the trade agreement. They move so quickly in their flying craft. They are taking up good land to grow their strange crops. The chemicals they use stunt the growth of our own farmers' crops.'

'What do our farmers say to this?'

'I don't know. La-Ver-Di-Arussah says that is not important.'

'La-Ver-Di-Arussah?'

'The acting commander. She is waiting upon your arrival. She says that the Emperor does not listen to the opinion of peasants. Rather, the peasants listen to the Emperor.'

'This is indeed true, but sometimes a little conversation can prevent conflict . . .'

Now Wa-Ka-Mo-Do could feel the current humming

through Ka-Lo-Re-Harballah. The young robot was obviously upset at what was going on here.

'The farmers are merely part of the problem, Honoured Commander. The humans are turning robots out of the mines and filling them instead with their own machines.'

'They are turning robots out of the mines? Surely the Emperor would not allow this?'

The hum of current through Ka-Lo-Re-Harballah's body increased. His voice modulated up a couple of tones. 'The Emperor insists that this is his will, that he seeks further trade advantage, but all the while more and more robots are being displaced from this land.'

'Then where are they going?'

'Everywhere and nowhere. This is your problem, Honoured Commander. There are displaced robots everywhere throughout Sangrel province, all the way to the borders of Ka province.'

Ka? Wa-Ka-Mo-Do felt a lurch as he thought of Jai-Lyn, travelling there on her own. 'And there is growing anger at the humans' actions,' continued Ka-Lo-Re-Harballah. 'They are asking why we of the Imperial Army are not protecting them.'

'They never asked such questions in the past.'

'They have never lost so much in the past.'

They walked through the third gate into the middle city. Now the houses were well built, of stone and freshly painted wood and metal.

'Well, the first thing to do is straightforward,' said Wa-Ka-Mo-Do decisively. 'We will form an army of the dispossessed. Make good use of their skills and talents.

All those robots that have lost their mines and fields can be put to work building roads and bridges. They can delve deeper into the earth for metal.'

He looked at the young robot by his side.

'I sense a lack of enthusiasm for my order, Ka-Lo-Re-Harballah.'

'Your predecessor tried that, Honoured Commander. I fear events have moved beyond that. There is growing resentment amongst the dispossessed. There has been minor damage and vandalism against the Emperor's property, insolence towards the Imperial Army.'

'This will not be allowed to continue,' said Wa-Ka-Mo-Do mildly.

'Your predecessor said the same, and he is no longer with us. La-Ver-Di-Arussah, your second in command, is of a good family. Her voice is heard in the Imperial Court. She does not believe in capitulation to the peasants, under any circumstances. Yet I fear that if we continue to ignore them, their anger may drive them to do something worse.'

'Worse than to refuse to follow orders? Such a thing is almost unheard of within the Empire! What could be worse than a disobedient robot?'

Ka-Lo-Re-Harballah's voice was so low that Wa-Ka-Mo-Do had to strain to hear it.

'One who attacks the humans themselves?'

'Attack our honoured guests? That would bring shame upon us indeed.'

'Shame upon us?' There was a squeak in Ka-Lo-Re-Harballah's voice. He was close to breaking point, Wa-Ka-Mo-Do realized. What was going on here was deeply affecting the young soldier. 'Honoured Commander, it would bring our utter destruction! You do not realize just how powerful the humans are.'

Wa-Ka-Mo-Do was a warrior of Ko. One of the first lessons he had learned was how to avoid conflict. He spoke calmly.

'Ka-Lo-Re-Harballah, you are an honourable soldier who works hard in the service of his Emperor. Together, I am sure that we can . . .'

His voice trailed away as he saw what Ka-Lo-Re-Harballah was looking at. There was a message painted on the wall of a nearby house. The robot's whole body sagged.

'You must understand, Honoured Commander,' he said, 'this street is busy with robots at all hours of the day. Many people would have seen this message being painted here, and yet no one thought to stop it, or to report the perpetrators to us.'

Wa-Ka-Mo-Do read the message.

What happened in Ell?

Wa-Ka-Mo-Do felt as if the current was draining from his electromuscle. He remembered the scene in the railway station just before he left the Silent City. All those soldiers, commandeering the train. They were heading to Ell.

'Just how far from here is Ell, Ka-Lo-Re-Harballah?'

'One hundred and nine miles.'

'What *has* happened there?'

'I don't know, Honoured Commander.' And again, there was a squeak in his voice, 'we are too busy with the problems here in Sangrel.'

He turned to one of the escorting soldiers, and pointed to the wall.

'Clean this,' he said.

The soldier was already moving to do so. Two of the other soldiers, meanwhile, had drawn their swords and had seized two people from the crowd.

'What are they doing?' asked Wa-Ka-Mo-Do.

'La-Ver-Di-Arussah's orders, Honoured Commander. For every act such as this, four peasants are to be executed, as an example.'

'Hold,' said Wa-Ka-Mo-Do. It wouldn't do to undermine his second-in-command, he knew that. But at the same time, these were bad orders. They would heighten rebellion, not quell it. He came to a decision.

'Bring them with us,' he said. 'I wish to meet La-Ver-Di-Arussah directly.'

Karel

The last of the evening sun died in the doorway, as Karel set to work on Melt by the light of the fire. The knife he had made was not as hard or as sharp as he would like, but it would do for now. He scored a line down the side of Melt's left thigh, cutting his way into the dissolved seam there.

'As we travel south we may find better-equipped workshops,' he said. 'We should be able to keep on improving you.'

'Thank you.'

'How long were you waiting here for me?'

'I don't know.'

'How many days? How many sunsets?'

'Four sunsets. I sat with Morphobia Alligator. We talked.'

'What about?'

'This planet. Shull.'

'Morphobia Alligator is a strange robot. Have you met any like him before?'

'No. I'm sure of that at least. None that look like him, nor any that think like him. He asked me a question: how do beetles and whales and all the other robot animals reproduce when they don't have hands?'

'I don't know!'

'It's a good point, though, isn't it? When robots reproduce, the female twists the metal that comes from a male to make a mind. Then they place that mind in a body they have built themselves, with their own hands. How do animals make bodies, when they have no hands?'

Karel worked away at the seam. The metal there was so hard, he was struggling to scrape it away.

'Does it matter?'

Melt didn't answer. He was thinking of something else. 'Do you know he counts days backwards? Wednesday follows Thursday by his reckoning.'

'Why?'

'I don't know. I'm not sure that Morphobia Alligator is the same as us. He's not quite a robot.'

Karel thought of the building at the northern coast of Shull, the one Morphobia Alligator had called the reliquary. He thought of the mind patterns drawn on the wall there. Did Morphobia Alligator really have a mind twisted in a different way? Was such a thing possible?

'I think he's waiting for something. Something in the future. Every sunset was one less to him, not one more, eeeeeeeeeeee!'

The last word was lost in an electronic squeak. Karel had felt the surge of electricity through the knife.

'I'm sorry!' he said. 'Did I hit the electromuscle?'

'Not exactly. But the muscle and the metal are joined together.'

'I'll stop then. I'll try the other side.'

'No, go on. I can ignore the pain.'

Karel looked up into Melt's dim grey eyes, then he steeled himself. He resumed his hacking at the seam, hesitating when he felt the surge of current, going on when Melt commanded him to.

The night passed. The doorway to the forge was lit up in pale green.

'I've done all I can,' said Karel, dropping the knife and flexing his fingers.

Melt stretched, this way and that.

'I feel a lot freer, thank you.'

'I'm sorry I hurt you.'

'You did your best. It wasn't easy for you, either.'

Karel looked through the forge door. The broken archway to the sea framed the distant town of Presper Boole, now lit by the dawn. The robots who had built this city were fine architects, he thought. What could have happened to them? He dismissed the thought for the moment. He had more pressing concerns.

'Another clear day coming. We should set off now, get some miles covered.'

'But you haven't attended to your own body yet.'

'No matter,' said Karel, looking wistfully at the containers of thin oil. But he didn't feel as if he had anything to complain about, having seen how Melt was suffering.

'No, it does matter,' said Melt. 'Here, let me see what I can do. I was a soldier once, and that's a soldier's body you are wearing.'

'If I could, I would exchange it for another.'

'Then we shall find one for you.'

'Thank you, Melt, but for the moment I will keep this body. It will be to our advantage to pass as Artemisians.'

Melt came around behind Karel.

'Take off your panelling, and I will straighten it for you and hammer out its dents. I will file it and apply solder and rub in oil.'

Karel didn't need to be told twice. He fumbled a little at first with the joints. The body was built so that an enemy would find it difficult to pierce its seams, and Karel was unused to this design. Finally he stripped away the panels of his upper body and sat there, naked electro-muscle glinting in the firelight. He examined its pattern. There was nothing fancy there, just simple arrangements that any soldier would be able to knit and maintain. The last owner of the body had done a reasonable job of keeping it in order. There wasn't time to knit new muscle, so for the moment Karel did the best he could, straightening out kinks here and there and applying oil or the hot knife as appropriate. He cleaned out his feet and his legs, he did what he could with the cogs and gears of his chest section. All the time behind him came the scrape and tap and bang of Melt working on the panelling.

Eventually they were both done. Karel accepted the panelling and was impressed by the neat job Melt had made of it. Everything fitted smoothly back together. Karel swung his arms and stamped his feet, feeling how easily the metal slid over itself. There were none of the annoying clicks and catches he had grown used to over the past few days.

'A good job,' said Karel. 'Whoever you were, Melt, you were a skilled builder.'

'Thank you,' said Melt, obviously pleased.

They made their way from the forge into the clear morning. A fresh breeze blew off the sea, and Karel was pleased to note it no longer penetrated his body.

They looked around the large square into which the sea road emerged. They were in the middle of a cross-roads. Another road ran southwards, through the remains of the city. Once grand buildings lined either side of the road, their facades broken, their upper stories missing. Rusty trails ran down marble facings, metal-work long dissolved by the rain.

'The Northern Road,' said Melt. 'Morphobia Alligator said that was the way to your wife.'

'Morphobia Alligator,' said Karel. 'I wonder where he is now? Is he watching us, do you think?'

'I don't know.'

Karel gazed southwards, down the lines of buildings to the distant hills.

'Very well,' he said. 'Let's go. Susan, I'm on my way.' They set off.

Wa-Ka-Mo-Do

Sangrel had grown rich on copper. Green copper was a constant theme in the patterned roofs of the city. In the past, on special days, the most honoured robots of the city had dressed in new copper skins, the metal so fresh it shone pink in the sunlight.

No wonder the second most important building in the city was the Copper Master's house.

Smithy Square was the highest plateau that had been levelled on Sangrel Mound. The Copper Master's house stood at the south side: a low white-painted building that gleamed brightly in the midday sun. Its windows and doors were bordered in gold and silver. Four bell towers rose from the top of the house, each containing seventeen bells of varying copper alloys. The peels of music that rang forth on special days could be heard for miles across the province.

'This is a beautiful place, Ka-Lo-Re-Harballah,' observed Wa-Ka-Mo-Do.

Smithy Square was thronged with both robots and animals, and all of them walked and sat and chatted amongst some of the loveliest scenery in Yukawa. The patterned domes of the Emperor's Palace lay to the north, the bell towers of the Copper Master's house to the south, and as for the view from the western edge of the square . . .

A woman was coming towards them. She wore the body of an Imperial Warrior, but the metal and the quality of its construction told of her true rank. She moved with a grace that only the best engineering skill could achieve. This was a woman who had had access to the finest materials since the day of her making, a woman who had been trained well in the arts of metalwork. Her panelling was of brushed aluminium, her arms and legs were curved and sprung, there was a pattern of gold filigree around her head, tracing loops around her eyes and ears.

Ka-Lo-Re-Harballah stepped forward.

'Honoured Commander, may I present La-Ver-Di-Arussah, Commander of the Copper Guard. La-Ver-Di-Arussah, this is Wa-Ka-Mo-Do, Commander of the Emperor's Army of Sangrel.'

They touched each other's upper arms, felt the current there. Wa-Ka-Mo-Do noted the knot patterns engraved just above her shoulders, emblems of one of the imperial families.

'Honoured Commander, and how is life in the High Spires?'

For a moment Wa-Ka-Mo-Do thought this was a gentle insult, and then he felt La-Ver-Di-Arussah's finger slip into his palm and trace a shape. A circle on a circle. Current sang into life as he realized what she was doing. The Book of Robots. Did she know? Was the truth woven into her mind too?

'You pause, Honoured Commander,' said La-Ver-Di-Arussah, and there was something in her gaze that caused Wa-Ka-Mo-Do to remain still for the moment. 'Do you recognize the sign?'

'I do, La-Ver-Di-Arussah. It is the symbol of those who believe in the Book of Robots. Those who believe that there is a shape and a philosophy that all robots should adopt, a shape given to them by the makers of the first robots.'

'And do you believe that, Wa-Ka-Mo-Do?'

'Such beliefs are treason, La-Ver-Di-Arussah, as I'm sure you know.' He changed the subject. 'There are more important things to discuss. Someone has been defacing the walls of this city with graffiti. Are you aware of this?'

'Indeed, Honoured Commander. You will be pleased to know that such incidents are dealt with immediately. Punishment is swift and severe.' She looked at the robots who had accompanied Wa-Ka-Mo-Do to the square.

'These robots were found in the presence of graffiti not five minutes ago,' said Wa-Ka-Mo-Do. 'They were to be executed by the Copper Guard.'

'As is right and proper.'

Wa-Ka-Mo-Do gazed into her eyes. They shone a blue-silver colour he had never seen before.

'I have spared them.'

'Is that wise?'

'Only the guilty are to be punished, La-Ver-Di-Arussah. I believe that making an example of the innocent will only inflame the situation.'

There was the merest flicker in La-Ver-Di-Arussah's eyes, but she controlled her anger quickly.

'As the commander wishes,' she said, and then she smiled. 'Sparing peasants? Doesn't it say something in the Book of Robots about all robots looking after each other?'

'You seem to know a lot about the book, La-Ver-Di-Arussah.'

'A little, a little. I must say, Honoured Commander, I am surprised that you do not. The belief is rife in the High Spires, is it not?'

'I am a warrior, La-Ver-Di-Arussah.'

'I notice that you do not deny your belief, Honoured Commander.'

'I am also your commander, La-Ver-Di-Arussah. You will be silent now.'

'Honoured Commander, surely we have much to discuss?'

'No. This is a time for you to listen. I have new orders. Innocents are not to be executed by way of example. You will ensure this message goes out to the Copper Guard immediately.'

'Ka-Lo-Re-Harballah can do that.'

Wa-Ka-Mo-Do's voice remained level.

'You question my orders? Do you wish to fight me now? Challenge me to a duel, if you believe you would make the better commander?'

He held her gaze. This was the true warrior's duel, Wa-Ka-Mo-Do knew. Before the swords were drawn, before the bullets were fired: when two robots gazed into each other's eyes to see who would falter first.

That robot was La-Ver-Di-Arussah.

'Fight a duel, Honoured Commander?' she smiled. 'That may be the way in the High Spires, but certainly not in the Silent City. And not even here in Sangrel. Of course I will carry out your orders immediately.'

At that she turned and walked away.

Wa-Ka-Mo-Do looked at Ka-Lo-Re-Harballah, hot current humming within him.

'Well, Ka-Lo-Re-Harballah?' he said.

'Honoured Commander?'

'Release the prisoners.'

They turned to the four robots.

'But Honoured Commander, they will have seen and heard everything!'

'Good! Then the word will spread, that the new commander will not tolerate anything that will bring the name of Sangrel and the Emperor into dispute.'

'As you wish, Honoured Commander.'

Whilst Ka-Lo-Re-Harballah gave the orders, Wa-Ka-Mo-Do turned and gazed around the square. There were so many people here, robot and animal. But it was the humans who drew his attention still, so alien, so unnatural in their strange panelling, their insubstantial bodies. They seemed so ineffectual, and yet look at the trouble they had already brought to Sangrel.

'Tell me, Ka-Lo-Re-Harballah. Do you think that the animals have souls, as we do?'

'Souls, Honoured Commander?'

'I mean, they are obviously intelligent, I have seen evidence of their machinery as I travelled here. But do they have that capacity twisted into their wire that means they can appreciate beauty, as we can?'

'I think so, Honoured Commander. Look over there.'

Wa-Ka-Mo-Do had already noticed the animals that leaned on the stone balustrade at the western edge of Smithy Square. Now he saw how they were looking out over the western lands of Sangrel province, over the rolling green hills, over the neat orange squares of the open cast mines and quarries, over the tall mine towers. They were gazing at the still blue waters of Lake Ochoa and the Mound of Eternity beyond. They were obviously enjoying the view.

'I would fear a robot with a soul far more than a merely intelligent animal,' quoted Wa-Ka-Mo-Do. 'For only a robot with a soul would understand cruelty.'

He gazed again at the animals standing by the balustrade. They all wore grey and green panelling, and something about the way they moved put him in mind of soldiers. The other animals in the square wore different colours, striking colours, many of which Wa-Ka-Mo-Do had never seen before. Pale greens that seemed to fluoresce in the sunlight, strong reds like iron in the fire. Their panelling reminded him of the flowers of the forest.

'Look around and one may believe that all is harmony,' said Wa-Ka-Mo-Do.

'Indeed,' answered Ka-Lo-Re-Harballah.

'I wonder just how aware the Emperor is of what is happening in Sangrel?'

Ka-Lo-Re-Harballah waited for two young women to walk past. Their panelling was of the thinnest aluminium, their golden electromuscle lovely to behold. They were carrying bundles of red cloth in their arms. Now Ka-Lo-Re-Harballah spoke in low tones.

'I have heard that the Vestal Virgins walk abroad. There is talk that they once more inhabit the Eternal Mound.'

'The Vestal Virgins?' Wa-Ka-Mo-Do feigned innocence,

but he remembered the Emperor's words back in the Silent City. He knew the Vestal Virgins had been sent here to watch him. 'But why would the Emperor send them here?' he asked.

'To ensure that Emperor's wishes are followed.'

'Am I to command them too?'

'Honoured Commander, you joke. For you know, of course, that the Vestal Virgins answer to none save the Emperor.'

And perhaps not even him, Wa-Ka-Mo-Do added to himself.

'There may be another reason for the Vestal Virgins' presence, Honoured Commander. For it is known that where the Emperor wishes to forge peace and harmony and accord, there he sends his Imperial Army.'

'Indeed.'

'And where the seeds of discord are to be sown, then the Vestal Virgins can be found, tending and watering and pruning.' Ka-Lo-Re-Harballah lowered his voice further, and Wa-Ka-Mo-Do could feel the burning shame he felt as he gave his warning. 'Watch the humans, Honoured Commander. Listen to their words. For I do not think they are telling all.'

Wa-Ka-Mo-Do looked around the square, felt the peace and the tranquillity of hundreds of years of history.

'It is difficult to think that such things can come to an end, Ka-Lo-Re-Harballah.'

'I fear they have ended already,' said Ka-Lo-Re-Harballah, gazing at the green-panelled humans by the balustrade. They had finished their contemplation of the view and were walking back to the Emperor's Palace. They seemed to march almost in step.

'Come, let us enter the Copper Master's house, Ka-Lo-Re-Harballah. I'm sure that things will not be as bad as you describe.'

'Perhaps not.'

Wa-Ka-Mo-Do placed his foot on the steps leading up to the white house, but Ka-Lo-Re-Harballah touched a hand to his elbow.

'Before we do . . .' Ka-Lo-Re-Harballah seemed to be struggling with his conscience. 'I do not like to say this, Honoured Commander, but I would speak the truth. You are an outsider, one of the Eleven from the High Spires. Robots famed for their skill on the battlefield, robots who proved themselves in the past when Yukawa had enemies on its borders, but who are rarely required in these more, shall we say, *settled* times.'

'That may be so, Ka-Lo-Re-Harballah.'

'Indeed. I am sorry to say this, Honoured Commander, but do you not feel that you are a strange choice for such an important command as this?'

'Explain yourself, Ka-Lo-Re-Harballah,' said Wa-Ka-Mo-Do sternly, though the same suspicions walked his own mind.

'I am sorry, Honoured Commander, but animals walk abroad in Sangrel, dissent is rife among the population. Surely this is a job for a commander of the Imperial Army, one versed in politics, one who knows the area? A robot such as La-Ver-Di-Arussah? Yet when the call came, no such robot was found to be suitable.'

Wa-Ka-Mo-Do said nothing. Emboldened, Ka-Lo-Re-Harballah spoke on.

'I wonder why the Emperor has had you sent here, and I feel it is because it will not matter so much if you fail.'

The young robot gazed directly into Wa-Ka-Mo-Do's eyes.

'I fear that you are to be made a scapegoat, Honoured Commander.'

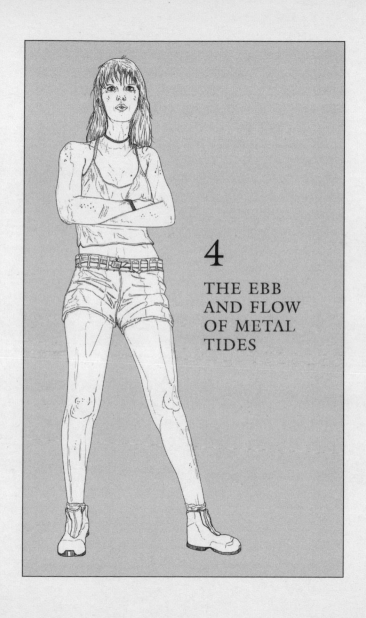

4

THE EBB AND FLOW OF METAL TIDES

Susan

Susan knelt in the making room, twisting the metal of the Storm Trooper who sat before her.

She hated the Storm Troopers, hated the thick feel of their wire in her hands, hated the sharp feel of the potential current in there.

'There we are, ladies, you may put down the minds.'

Susan remembered the first time she had put down a half-completed mind, the horror she had felt at seeing the wire untwist and the potential life die. Now it was such a common occurrence she felt nothing except an emptiness inside, like someone had scooped out all the living parts of her body, leaving behind nothing but the metal shell. She felt like a ghost.

There were nineteen other mothers in Susan's making room, all of them women who had been captured from Turing City, all of them united by their hatred of her. They hated her for her friendship with Nettie, hated her for what she had been back in Turing City: the wife of Karel. They thought Karel was a traitor, because of who his father was. Yet was it Karel's fault that his mother had been raped by an Artemisian soldier? After all, it was no more than what was happening to them all now.

The twenty Storm Troopers in the room filed out, their wire cooling on the floor where the women had dropped it. Susan could feel the current surging in their strong bodies, and she hated it. She hated their arrogant swagger, hated the way they looked at the women, at everyone, like they were inferior beings. Didn't they realize that such thoughts weren't the Artemisian way? She wanted to scream that truth out to them, even though she wasn't an Artemisian herself.

Nettie waited until the last of the Storm Troopers had left the room; she listened to their heavy tread ringing down the metal corridor. When she was sure they were out of earshot, she spoke up brightly.

'Now ladies, what have we learned?'

The women looked at Nettie with contempt, all of them except Susan. Nettie had never woven a mind herself, yet she was responsible for training them all how to weave minds for Artemis. But there was something else, Susan recognized. Nettie was always at her brightest when she was unhappiest.

'I don't get it,' said Diehl, more in frustration than anything else. 'The minds will be strong, but they won't be able to think properly.'

Some of the other women murmured agreement.

'Don't worry about that, ladies, it doesn't matter,' said Nettie. 'Is the basic pattern sound?'

She looked at Susan for help.

'It's sound,' said Susan, ignoring the looks of the other women. 'It just doesn't make any sense. Seriously, Nettie, I really don't understand. Why are we doing this?'

'Nyro's will,' said Nettie, and she smiled at them all.

The women said nothing. They had learned long ago that Nyro's will was a euphemism for orders from Artemis command.

Nettie looked back to the doorway of the making room, and there was a flicker of uncertainty in her eyes.

'Listen,' said Nettie, 'Please! Don't make a fuss. It could be so much worse. Really! The other women are making two minds a night now, you know that, don't you? I had to push to get this assignment for you, ladies. Really, I did!'

'We know,' said Susan. The other women made grudging noises of agreement. 'We believe you, we're grateful, honestly. But what is going on?'

'No one will tell me,' said Nettie, and she sagged suddenly as a wave of misery overwhelmed her. 'I don't know what's happening! Everything is confusion within the city. Something happened up in the north. Something bad. Spoole and the Generals returned to the city much earlier than expected and suddenly everything has been put on a war footing. We have stepped up production of everything: minds, robots, metal.'

'It will be Kavan,' said Diehl. She looked around the assembled women. 'Come on,' she said. 'You've all heard the soldiers talk as we kneel before them. They think that Kavan is some sort of hero. Another Nyro, almost, and you know how much they think of her.'

'Not all the soldiers,' said another woman. 'The Storm Troopers aren't so keen on Kavan.'

Kavan, thought Susan. He was the robot who had destroyed Turing City. He had killed her child and had taken her husband away from her. Now, maybe, he was returning to Artemis City.

She wondered what she would do if she ever met him.

Kavan

The Uncertain Army moved south like a silver tide flowing through the valleys of the central mountain range.

Just like a tide, reflected Kavan, for he had as much command over the army as he had over the waters. The robots sloshed forwards and backwards, rushed up into the surrounding hills and mountains, spilling over the edges, sometimes never to be seen again, sometimes to come trickling back in metal streams.

The trouble was, there was no certainty up here amongst the high peaks. No one really knew who was on whose side, and just where all of this was going to end up. Not even Kavan. There were too many variables.

When Spoole had retreated, he had taken as many of the Artemisian troops back with him as would follow: he didn't want them deserting to join Kavan's army as it advanced. All those little mountain kingdoms that Kavan himself had so recently conquered suddenly found themselves drained of their new rulers, found themselves free once more. Free to take back their own land and lives, to refortify themselves, to run away, higher into the mountains and safety. Free to launch attacks on the Uncertain Army.

Or even, in some cases, to join it. After all, wasn't Kavan intending to attack Artemis itself? For some, it didn't matter that the Army was led by their former conqueror, it was enough to follow it to where it was going. For safety, for revenge, for profit.

Then there were those troops who had found themselves unwilling conscripts in the Uncertain Army, who took the chance to slip away, in ones or twos, in squads and even platoons, to seek freedom, or perhaps to set themselves up in one of the abandoned kingdoms, maybe to rule over those who still remained, or merely to find somewhere to hide whilst the events unfolded without them to the south, waiting to join the victors later on.

Whichever side that was.

Finally, there were those who still saw Kavan and his army as the enemy. Whether Artemisian soldiers loyal to Spoole and the Generals, or the remnants of the armies of the Northern Kingdoms who still held out in the high caves and passes, swooping down occasionally to fight their guerrilla war, there were still enough robots to ambush and bomb and trap and attack Kavan and his troops. Sailing down from the skies beneath silver parafoils, rolling rocks in avalanche down the mountainsides, pouring petrol to fill the streams, filling the air with iron filings and chaff, ricocheting cannonballs from the rocky walls, igniting magnesium flares that filled the night with harsh light that burned out the eye cells, or simply attacking in a chatter of rifle shot and a clatter of knives and awls, Kavan found his progress constantly slowed and frustrated.

As if he was wading against a tide of his own design.

And yet, it didn't seem to make any difference to the size of his army. If anything, it continued to grow. A constant stream of robots found their way to him, offering advice and allegiance.

Robots like the one that stood before Kavan at the moment.

Calor had brought her to meet him. She wore an engineer's body: blue panelling, the machinery beneath it adapted, tuned, altered from the standard pattern that Artemis imposed on its robots. Oddly enough, this didn't upset Kavan. He recognized the Artemisian State's need for engineers. So long as they helped to advance its cause he never felt a need to understand them.

'Her name is Ada. She says her mother was a Raman, her father an Artemisian.'

'And do you follow Nyro's way?' asked Kavan, looking at the robot's elongated body.

'I do,' answered Ada. 'Should my parentage cast doubt on my loyalties? Your mind wasn't twisted in Artemis, either, Kavan. It's not about where you were made, it's what you believe in.'

Kavan noticed the way Calor was looking at him, as if surprised at what she had just heard. She covered up her confusion. 'I found her up there,' she said, pointing to the rocky peaks to the west. 'She was making her way towards you.'

'I was,' Ada said, 'I've been looking for you. You're making a mistake, Kavan.'

Kavan took a closer look at Calor. He could hear the hum of the current running through her body. Scouts always pushed themselves too hard. In Kavan's opinion they were already half mad when they were made: you never knew which way they would jump. Calor now belonged to an army whose direction changed by the hour. No wonder she was tense. 'Perhaps you should walk with me a while, Calor,' he suggested.

Calor shook her head.

'Got to get back to the mountains, Kavan. Keep watching your path.'

'As you wish,' said Kavan. He watched her silver body as she sprang up the side of a cliff, jumping from ledge to ledge, scrabbling with her claws for purchase in the smallest cracks. Showers of stones rattled to the ground behind her, marking her passage.

Kavan turned back to Ada.

'You said I was making a mistake? Do you think that Spoole and the rest are the true leaders of Artemis?'

Ada's blue eyes flashed. Whether in humour or anger, Kavan couldn't tell.

'Of course I don't,' she said. 'You're the right robot for the job. It's just that you're going about it the wrong way.'

'Go on.'

'You're thinking like you've always done, Kavan. It's not your fault; it's the way your mind was twisted, to think of leading soldiers to the expansion of Artemis. Well, the conditions no longer apply. The continent is conquered and you're not in full control of this army. Although there are many who believe in you, there are just as many who don't. You don't have the backing of Spoole and the Generals any more, even the backing that they gave you under duress of circumstances. You're the right robot for the job of overthrowing the Generals, but not for the job of getting this army down to where it's needed.'

Ada's blue eyes flashed again, and this time Kavan saw the humour there. He was reminded of Eleanor, his old second in command. But whereas she was twisted a warrior and had always subtly challenged him for leadership, Ada was an engineer. She would be more interested in getting the job done.

'So who is the right person? You?'

'I know these mountains well, Kavan. I know what Spoole's engineers will have done to the road before you. Blowing bridges, mining the roads, setting avalanches. All the traps that I would have set if I were in their position.'

'And do you know of another way south?'

'Yes. Head west and follow the Northern Road.'

Kavan gazed at her blue eyes.

'The Northern Road? I didn't realize it extended into the mountains.'

'There's a lot you don't know, Kavan,' said Ada. 'What does Artemis care for but Artemis?'

'Nothing, and that is how it should be. Why is there a road through the mountains?'

'The Borners, or those who became the Borners, followed the road here from the Top of the World. They came to these mountains for iron, and they carried it back to their home.'

'What happened to them?'

'War,' said Ada. 'The people who settled in the mountains wanted to keep the iron to themselves.'

Kavan nodded. That made sense to him.

'How far is this road from here?'

'Barely a mile,' said Ada, and she laughed. Kavan

understood why. This was a land of sheer peaks and deep valleys. A robot could travel a hundred miles to get to a point a mile distant.

'There is a path to that road not far from here. Send your Scouts ahead, they will confirm what I say is true.'

'Is it safe?'

'Safe? Of course not. But under the circumstances it's the right path. Your mind is set on marching a path of conquest. What you need is a path of stealth and convenience. This path will deliver you through the mountains and onto the Artemisian plain. It is the right path to take. I can see that.'

Kavan thought of the road he had travelled so far and then he gestured to a nearby Scout.

'Listen to this robot,' he said. 'Search the path that she suggests. See if it is suitable for us to traverse.'

Of course, thought Kavan, it could be a trap, but no more so than the path they currently followed.

And Ada was right about one thing at least. Kavan was not the right robot to make decisions at this point. He wasn't commanding an army as such, he was more caught in the middle of the events that were unfolding on the continent. Robots moved this way and that, and for the moment Kavan was following the ebb and flow of the metal tide.

He had no ego in these matters. What he followed was Nyro's will. If the moment came, he would resume command of the army.

Wa-Ka-Mo-Do

Wa-Ka-Mo-Do met Rachael as he descended the Street of Becoming. At the time she looked like any other animal; he was not yet at the point where he could identify a young human female of around fourteen or fifteen. She walked with her arms folded around her middle, a look on her face of withering contempt for the world. She was coming up the hill, heading directly for him, and Wa-Ka-Mo-Do realized that she wasn't going to give way as protocol directed. He signalled to the Copper Guard who flanked him not to intercede.

Her long straight hair was the colour of copper, her eyes like copper sulphate, her skin the colour of titanium dioxide. Her body was not as curved as an adult human female, it more resembled that of a female robot, the same hint of an indentation to the waist that many women built, the same long arms and fingers.

Wa-Ka-Mo-Do stood still, smiling slightly as the girl halted before him. She raised her gaze almost to his, made a loud tutting noise.

'Excuse me,' said Wa-Ka-Mo-Do politely, 'but this is my right of way.'

The girl rolled her eyes and made to walk around him.

'I know that you can understand me,' said Wa-Ka-Mo-Do. 'I see the light flicker on the little device you wear by your ear when I speak.'

The girl rolled her eyes. Wa-Ka-Mo-Do had never seen that before, he struggled not to laugh.

'I was walking this way first,' she said.

'Ah yes, but I'm the commander of this city. Strictly speaking I could have your coil broken for failing to show me respect.'

The girl just rolled her eyes once more and turned her back on him. The Copper Guard saw the slight and began to move forward. Swiftly, Wa-Ka-Mo-Do reached out and seized her arm. It felt softer than he expected, but stronger too. There was a hardness at the centre. The bone, he later discovered.

'Aaaoow!' yelped the girl, pulling her arm free. She rounded on him, face flushed with fury. 'That hurt! What are you playing at?'

'Saving your life.' *And preventing a diplomatic disaster*, he added to himself. 'Yukawa is a land steeped in tradition, young lady. You should never turn your back on a superior.'

'Your hand is burning!' She rubbed her arm. 'You robots stand in the sun all day and you don't realize how hot your metal gets.'

'I didn't realize,' said Wa-Ka-Mo-Do. 'I've never touched a human before. I didn't expect you to be so sensitive.'

'Sensitive? Look! You made a mark! And I turn my back on who I want. What gives you the right to tell me otherwise?'

'Four hundred fully armed troops garrisoned within the city,' replied Wa-Ka-Mo-Do. 'Plus another two thousand spread across the surrounding land. Plus the fact that I am trained in the seven arts of combat, and the nine arts of weaponry. Oh yes, and the fact that I am the commander of this city, and what I say goes.'

That brought a faint smile to the human's lips, and Wa-Ka-Mo-Do felt a kindling empathy with this strange creature. She reminded him of his sister, and of Jai-Lyn.

The thought brought a certain symmetry to his life. Three young females.

'What's your name, human?' he asked.

'Rachael. What's yours, robot?'

'Wa-Ka-Mo-Do.'

'Wa-Ka-Mo-Do. That's a stupid name.'

'I think Rachael sounds rather pretty.'

'Really?' She gave a smile that vanished as soon as it appeared. Now she just looked bored. 'Can I go now, or are you going to get your men to cut off my head for showing your name disrespect?'

'They're women, actually,' said Wa-Ka-Mo-Do, gazing at the Copper Guard. 'You can go in a moment. But first, Rachael, I want to ask you something. You're the first human I've ever spoken to. I want to know, what do you think of Sangrel?'

Rachael stared at him with those copper-sulphate eyes. Two lines of hair like copper wire were stitched above them. From that moment on, Wa-Ka-Mo-Do thought of Rachael as his copper girl.

'What do I think of Sangrel?' she said. 'Do you really want my opinion, or are you just trying to win me over?'

'Oh, both,' replied Wa-Ka-Mo-Do. 'Congratulations, though, for seeing through my strategy.'

'Now you're patronizing me.'

'I wouldn't dare. Go on, tell me what you think of Sangrel.'

'I think it's a lovely place,' said Rachael, and Wa-Ka-

Mo-Do wondered if she was being sarcastic. 'But I don't like how you run it. Yukawa is a cruel Empire. Cruel and stupid. You're selling yourself far too cheaply, you know that?'

'Selling ourselves too cheaply? What do you mean?'

'You've given away your mines and your land for a song. *Now* can I go?'

'For a song? I'm sure the Emperor is being generous to his guests—'

'Oh, the Emperor! But we have to be nice to him. Look, I'm late. May I go?'

'You may,' said Wa-Ka-Mo-Do, thinking about what she had just said. Just in time he remembered the Copper Guard, standing to attention either side of him. 'But make sure you don't turn your back to me. I don't want my Guard to have to kill you.'

Rachael rolled her eyes once more and walked on her way. But she kept her back away from him as she did so.

Kavan

Ada was a true Artemisian, and a true engineer. Kavan could see it in the way she organized the movement of the Uncertain Army through the mountains. She approached the problem of moving metal from one location to another just as she would any other project, whether it was navigating a railway line or building a bridge.

The robots marched along narrow paths at her guidance, disassembling themselves to be carried by others or even shaping their own bodies into ramps and ladders to enable other robots to climb over them to higher paths, trusting in their fellows to reassemble them afterwards.

She was right, realized Kavan. He had been treating the problem as yet another attack, charging down a path, pushing aside all resistance, but as he climbed from shoulder to shoulder on a pyramid of robots arranged up a rocky slope, he acknowledged that her way of thinking was more appropriate here.

It took them four days to travel the distance to the Northern Road, and often Kavan would look down on a windblown valley, silver and black robots clinging to the sheer sides, body parts being passed hand-to-hand along the edges of ridges. Always there would be blue engineers organizing winches and cranes to collect bodies from the deeper ravines, in order to save the precious metal, and always there was Ada, moving back and forth, organizing and planning and building.

'Good work,' he said to her on the evening of the last day. Ada had ordered the robots to remain still at night. Better to lose ten hours' travel than to waste twenty retrieving broken metal from the foot of a mountain, she had said.

'I'm impressed. How much further?'

'You'll see the Northern Road in the morning,' said Ada. 'After that, you only need point your army south.'

'I want you to remain with me. You've proven your worth.'

'I intend to,' replied Ada. 'You'll need me yet.'

*

The Northern Road had been impressive enough as they had travelled through the hills of northern Shull. Up here in the mountains it inspired awe in the robots that gazed upon it. Even Kavan found himself wondering at the robots who had imagined it, wondered at the state that had the vision, the planning and the technical proficiency to build it. How would Artemis have fared against them, if they had faced them at the height of their strength?

Kavan was in no doubt, Artemis would have prevailed. Still, the Northern Road was a worthy artefact.

'I'd say this road even surpasses the railway system of Artemis,' said Ada, at his shoulder.

The road was built of stone, not metal. Sometimes made of bricks, sometimes of huge boulders, sometimes even carved from the side of the mountains themselves. Seven yards wide and surfaced in cobbles, a low wall on each side, it ran in the shadows of the mountain peaks. Kavan marched amongst the Uncertain Army, part of the metal river that flowed up steep inclines where steps were cut into the road's surface, a river that ran by the sheets of snow that still lingered up here despite the approach of summer, a river that plunged into the shadows of hanging valleys.

The robots of the plains weren't used to these high passes; the days when the sun reflected so brightly from the snow that their eyes filled with flashing interference, the nights where the temperature dropped so low that metal became brittle and electromuscle would tear if flexed too quickly. They were playful in the cold, scooping handfuls of snow from the banks as they passed by, kicking at the ice formed in the lee of the low walls. And then the temperature dropped further and they tapped at joints that seized up through contraction, they looked at canisters of diesel turned waxy by the cold.

Kavan walked with Ada.

'What if we are attacked here?' asked a Storm Trooper, its body emitting clanking, popping noises as it stamped along beside them. The cold was not kind to its large frame.

'We fight,' replied Kavan, simply.

Only the Scouts seemed happy. Or not so much happy as manic. They jumped and skidded down steep banks of snow, skiing on extended claws towards sheer drops, only flicking a foot at the last moment to veer clear of the edge. Sometimes they went over and Kavan and the rest listened for the distant clatter of metal hitting rock.

There was no sign of any other robots this high up.

'Oh, they're here,' said Ada. 'They'll be watching you.'

'Who will be?'

'The Borners. This is their territory.'

'Artemis territory.'

'No. This isn't the part we conquered. I'm talking about the real Borners. The robots of the mountains.'

'You like to draw questions from me, don't you Ada? Very well, there is time whilst we walk. Tell me about the robots of the mountains.

The Story of the Robots of the Mountains

'Long ago, robots found the land of Born, a thin stretch of land squeezed between the sea and the mountains. Now, some say that the first inhabitants of that land descended to it from the peaks, and others say that the first inhabitants climbed from the sea, but all are agreed that the land of Born was a paradise for robots. The ground was rich in coal, buried so shallow that a robot did not have to mine, but could pull it straight from the earth. All they had to do was hold out their hands for iron ore to tumble onto them from a nearby mountain. Some days, it was said, even molten lead would rise from the earth around their feet, ready to be scooped up and used. A robot could stand in one place and wait for the materials of the forge to come to it.

'And so robots flourished in the land of Born. It is said that the whales would come to the shore to speak, secure in the knowledge they would not be harmed, such was the abundance of metal in the land, and so a friendship grew up here between the two species.

'Some even say that robots travelled from the Top of the World, riding in the bodies of the whales.

'So the robots lived a life of ease. But such ease does not suit robotkind. For sloth and indolence took hold of those robots, until there came the day that the best women of Born looked at the men, and they found them wanting.

'There was much iron to be found in the mountains, so much so that the men took it for granted, making themselves bodies of iron, and never bothering to roam further afield in search of copper or chrome or nickel. Therefore the best of the women began to complain of the diminishing quality of the men's wire, for the minds that they wove would be much improved by the presence of silver or a little gold, but the men just laughed and said the women were being too demanding, and wasn't that the way of women?

'Eventually the best women tired of this. So one night, when Zuse and Néel shared the sky and the snow of the mountains seemed to shine palely itself, the women took themselves along the paths into the high peaks. There they built themselves castles and towers out of rock, and they set traps and deadfalls and did all they could to make the passage to themselves as difficult as possible, that only the most worthy men could reach them—'

'I've heard this story before,' interrupted Kavan. 'In the North Kingdom. And in Stark.'

'This is not a story,' said Ada. 'Follow this path and you will see the places in the mountains that the women built. You will see the high balconies upon which they waited.'

'Very well,' said Kavan, 'I believe you.'

Ada resumed her story.

'The women waited. Eventually, the first men came climbing up to meet them. Those women looked down from their high towers that pierced the clear blue sky and saw the robots climbing the icy paths. But these robots were not the men they had left behind in the lowlands of Born. For the weak, iron-bound bodies those robots had worn would not have withstood the journey up into the high peaks. The men who approached the women in their towers had, of need, built themselves better bodies. They had been forced to travel in search of new metal and new ideas, and these they had incorporated into themselves. Furthermore, these robots were the few who had the bravery and the skill to climb the mountains to meet the women. And so the only men who showed the necessary skill and engineering to climb the mountains and make it past the traps and the deadfalls were judged worthy to make new minds with the women.

'Time passed. And it came to be that the robots who dwelled in the highlands thought less and less of their brothers and sisters of the lowlands. For did not those robots who had remained behind still have the same iron bodies that they always had? Had they not remained in place whilst others had been tempered by the fire? And so those highlanders gradually separated themselves from the world below. They lived a harsh life in the mountains, and through this they became stronger and better engineered.'

Kavan listened to the story with interest.

'Well, that would explain why the robots of Born were so easy to conquer,' he said.

'You never met the true Borners,' said Ada. 'You may see them yet.'

'You said your mother was a Raman. You admire the Borners?'

'I appreciate good engineering.'

Kavan nodded thoughtfully. He looked out to his right, down the sheer wall along which the road ran.

'Was it *really* the Borners who built this road?' he asked.

'Possibly,' said Ada. 'That's what they claim.'

Kavan nodded. He understood this much at least. 'I'd do the same. It would help to inspire fear in my enemies.'

Night fell, and the army came to a halt.

Robots sat down, they pooled coal and charcoal, piled it against the low walls at the side of the road and made fires on which they could heat metal and make some repairs to themselves.

Kavan had spent only a short time in the polluted lands of Artemis; most of his adult life had seen him wandering the continent of Shull. Even so, he had never seen a sky as clear as this. The stars seemed to billow in great sheets of light above him, darkening the surrounding peaks still further by comparison. He gazed up into the sky, thinking.

'You can see the planet Bohm over there,' said Ada, still there at his side. 'The bright light, just through the peaks.'

Kavan looked over to where she indicated.

'They say the robots who travelled down the Northern Road liked to look at the stars,' she continued. 'They built an observatory up here in the mountains. The air is thinner, you get a better view.'

'I saw an observatory on the northern coast,' began Kavan, but his voice trailed away. All around him robots were pausing in their repairs and staring up into the night sky. Kavan followed their gaze and saw why.

Zuse, the night moon, was on fire.

Kavan was not a superstitious robot, but as he stared into the sky as rainbow light arced from the moon, he wondered what it signified.

'Is this an atmospheric phenomenon?' he asked Ada, not quite concealing the note of hope in his voice.

'No,' she said softly. 'Look, you can see how it's erupting from the surface of the moon.'

Kavan looked back down the path behind him. Thousands of pairs of eyes were turned to the sky, yellow and green and red lights shining in the darkness.

Then he turned back to the sky. A long flare of light trailed from the moon into the darkness. What was going on?

Wa-Ka-Mo-Do

Wa-Ka-Mo-Do heard the Copper Market well before he entered it. The noise of so many robots speaking and shouting; the ringing of metal being beaten into shape; the cackle and lowing of animals: the sounds echoed through the narrow streets of the mid-city.

He entered beneath the bone arch and found himself amongst the seemingly random collection of close-packed stalls and booths that had been gathering here in Sangrel for hundreds of years. Commanders had come and commanders had gone, but the Copper Market had sailed on through time untouched by higher events. There were stalls here whose position had been handed down from maker to robot for generations; there were traders whose lineage went back to the time that San-grel had been carved from the rock.

Originally, this had been the place where copper was traded, but as the fame of the market spread, so other stalls had been set up, until the Copper Market had become the principal place to buy and exchange goods for all of southern Yukawa.

Wa-Ka-Mo-Do had entered the market by the live-stock gate, and he found himself jostled by two skinny cows pushing their way through the crowd. Their owner, an iron robot carrying a long wooden stick, fell to his knees before Wa-Ka-Mo-Do in horror and supplication.

'Peace,' said Wa-Ka-Mo-Do, signalling to the Copper Guard to remain still. 'They are fine animals,' he said to their owner.

'Thank you, oh my master.'

'This is a breed prized for its leather, is it not?'

'Yes, my master.'

The robot remained kneeling before him, eyes fixed on Wa-Ka-Mo-Do's feet.

'You had better retrieve your animals before they cause some damage,' said Wa-Ka-Mo-Do, and he went on his way into the crowded square.

There was so much to see here. Birds with clipped wings fluttered and squawked in cages, lizards baked in the hot sun. A frantic bellowing sounded, and Wa-Ka-Mo-Do turned to watch a cow being carefully cut apart. Two strong robots held it in a metal grasp whilst a woman drew a knife beneath its throat. Rich red blood squirted over her body, it dripped from her elbows onto the stone ground. Wa-Ka-Mo-Do looked down to see that he had been walking in the sticky fluid: red metal footprints tracked his progress through the market.

There was a sudden commotion, the sound of someone shouting, and laughter spread through the crowd. The noise reminded Wa-Ka-Mo-Do of home, it was so long since he had heard people laughing like this, and he moved to see what had happened, the Copper Guard clearing a path for him as he went. He came upon a woman scolding her child, holding up the bodies of four dead animals by their tails. Rats, he thought. What use a robot would make of their skin and bones he didn't know, but poverty found a use for most things.

'No!' she was shouting. 'They're animals. Animals! You can't swap their heads around!'

The crowd laughed all the louder as the child tried to stick the heads of the dead animals back on their bodies. They laughed at the woman, at her frustration at losing stock, but the laughter died away as they saw Wa-Ka-Mo-Do standing there in their midst.

'Madam, he made an honest mistake,' said Wa-Ka-Mo-Do, but already the crowd was dissipating. The woman fell to her knees before him, and at that moment Ka-Lo-Re-Harballah appeared at his shoulder.

'Honoured Commander, I have found you at last!'

'Greetings, Ka-Lo-Re-Harballah.'

'Honoured Commander, if I may say, it does not do to be too approachable to your subjects. Not ever, but especially not now, when they talk and plot against you.'

'Against me, Ka-Lo-Re-Harballah?' He laughed. 'I have only just arrived here!'

'They plot against the Emperor, and so by default, against his representative here. Honoured Commander, the people here are angry. Rumour sweeps the city and the surrounding lands.'

'The people here seem quite content, Ka-Lo-Re-Harballah.'

'The people here haven't lost their jobs in the mines and the fields. The people here still have goods to trade.' For just a moment, the frustration sounded in Ka-Lo-Re-Harballah's voice. 'My apologies, Honoured Commander, I speak out of turn.'

'No, not at all. It's your duty to keep me informed. Now, lead on. What is it you wish me to see?'

A shadow passed over Ka-Lo-Re-Harballah's face. 'Not out here, Honoured Commander. For the moment, you are merely taking a walk in the market, inspecting the produce. Follow me, and I will show you.'

Puzzled, Wa-Ka-Mo-Do followed Ka-Lo-Re-Harballah out of the livestock market and through the tanner's quarter, where he saw slowly turning drums filled with chromium sulphate and animal hide.

'I knew a robot with a nose who walked through here,' said Ka-Lo-Re-Harballah, in an attempt to appear nonchalant. 'She said the smell was terrible!'

'Really?' said Wa-Ka-Mo-Do, looking at a rack of pale blue skins, drying in the sun.

They passed into the Copper Market proper, and Wa-Ka-Mo-Do halted for a moment, struck by the scene.

The stalls here were older, but more substantial. They were made of iron decorated with a fine filigree of copper. And set out on them, glowing pale pink, looking so pure it made Wa-Ka-Mo-Do ache to touch them, were ingots of copper. Beautiful, clean pink copper.

'What couldn't a robot make with such metal?' he said in awe.

'Oh, indeed,' said Ka-Lo-Re-Harballah, 'but not now. This way.'

They passed on, Wa-Ka-Mo-Do looking about him at the pure ingots of iron and aluminium and gold and feeling the pull of them throughout his electromuscles.

They came to the poorer part of the market, the northern end, built up against the walls and cliffs that rose up to the high city where Smithy Square and the Copper Master's house were built. The light here was dimmer, the stalls crowded closer together. The wares on sale were of poorer quality, the robots that thronged the narrow ways were of poorer construction. Wa-Ka-Mo-Do watched a young woman searching through a selection of scraps of tin and poor alloys, hunting for the best-quality metal. Her body was cheaply made, dented and scratched. In that she resembled the other robots who walked here. Fires glowed pale red, lit by poor coal, and black smoke drifted by. Wa-Ka-Mo-Do was aware of how the robots here gazed at him. There was still fear, yes, but there was envy too. Envy of his strong body, envy of who he was. And underneath it all, resentment.

'We're here,' said Ka-Lo-Re-Harballah, and Wa-Ka-Mo-Do saw he had been led to the very edge of the market. The old stone walls of the city rose high up above him, partly rockface, partly bricks. Caves and rooms had been cut out of these walls, and robots had set up more stalls and forges and storerooms within them. Despite the bustle of the market, the area in front of one of the caves stood empty. There was a leather curtain draped across its entrance, and it was to this one that Ka-Lo-Re-Harballah was leading Wa-Ka-Mo-Do.

'What is it?' asked Wa-Ka-Mo-Do.

'It is best that you see, Honoured Commander.' He pulled aside the curtain, just a little, and Wa-Ka-Mo-Do stepped into the darkness beyond.

A silver robot moved towards him, drawing her blade. She let it fall when she saw who it was.

'My apologies, Wa-Ka-Mo-Do. I did not immediately realize it was you.'

'Peace, La-Ver-Di-Arussah.' Wa-Ka-Mo-Do recognized her insult: she was implying that he dressed himself in the manner of a peasant.

'At the back,' said Ka-Lo-Re-Harballah. The cave was deeper than Wa-Ka-Mo-Do expected. An oil lamp didn't quite illuminate its furthest reaches.

Wa-Ka-Mo-Do moved into the dimness, and he saw the body. He could not quite hide the shock in his voice.

'It's one of the Emperor's army!' he said. 'One of the robots under my command!' He looked closer. There was something strange about the body. The metal panelling didn't look right, it didn't look like steel and aluminium should . . .

'It's leather,' he said softly, reaching out to touch the skin. 'They took off the metal panelling and dressed him in animal skin.'

Wa-Ka-Mo-Do knew that he could not show his concern to his inferiors, yet it was a struggle to remain calm in the face of this obscenity. What minds would do this to a robot?

'There was a note around his neck,' said La-Ver-Di-Arussah.

She held out a thin sheet of foil with words inscribed upon it. *A human next time . . .*

Wa-Ka-Mo-Do felt as if there was a current running through the metal of the note. It seemed to surge through his body, burning him.

'When did they find him?'

'Last night. The brothers who owned this place have vanished. There are rumours that they were involved with the resistance.' Ka-Lo-Re-Harballah's voice was laced with static. 'These were robots who did this. Robots will suffer because of this. Children will lose their parents. Husbands will lose wives.'

Something occurred to him. 'Does the Emperor know of this?' he asked Ka-Lo-Re-Harballah.

'Not yet.'

Wa-Ka-Mo-Do looked at the dead guard again. 'Then he shan't,' he decided.

'That isn't your choice to make,' observed La-Ver-Di-Arussah.

Wa-Ka-Mo-Do spun to face her.

'Would you question my orders?'

'Not at all, Honoured Commander,' she replied, and she rested her hand on her sword. 'But I consider it my duty to advise you.'

'But not in such a manner that I lose face,' replied Wa-Ka-Mo-Do, and he drew his own sword so quickly that even La-Ver-Di-Arussah's eyes flashed in surprise.

'And so for the second time I wonder if you are challenging me to a duel. Or would you rather apologize for insulting me before an inferior?'

'Honoured Commander, I—'

'Silence, Ka-Lo-Re-Harballah. Before you answer, La-Ver-Di-Arussah, I should explain. Whoever did this is expecting an extreme response. They are hoping that arrests will be made, and that examples will be set. They are hoping to see coils being crushed in Smithy Square as they believe that will galvanize the people to more acts of defiance and subversion.'

La-Ver-Di-Arussah remained motionless, her hand still on her sword.

'Would you force the Emperor's hand, La-Ver-Di-Arussah? I suggest that there are some things the Emperor would prefer not to know! Would you have it said that the Emperor knew of this outrage, of one of his soldiers humiliated so, and yet he stayed his hand for fear of inflaming the uprising that would lead to the humans being harmed?'

'The Emperor does not fear the humans!'

'Of course he does not. Yet who would seek a fight where none is necessary? Let us second guess those who perpetrated this atrocity, let us choose the cultured way, let us listen in the silence, let us ask the quiet question, and then, when we find the answer, strike quickly and mercilessly, decapitating this monster, rather than feeding it.'

La-Ver-Di-Arussah held his gaze for some time, and then, slowly, she withdrew her hand from her sword. Wa-Ka-Mo-Do resheathed his own.

'You are right, *Honoured Commander*.' There was the

faintest edge of sarcasm to her words. 'And I thank you for your instruction. May I say, it was never my intention to challenge you to a duel, or to hurt you.' And she drew her own sword, brought it flashing through the air to stop just before Wa-Ka-Mo-Do's head. He looked at the blade, so sharp, poised just between his eyes, watched as it fell to the ground, La-Ver-Di-Arussah's hand still gripping the hilt.

All three robots looked to Wa-Ka-Mo-Do's sword, they marvelled at the way it had been drawn and cut through the wrist, all in one movement.

'And it was not my intention to hurt *you*,' replied Wa-Ka-Mo-Do. 'The hand will be easily reattached.'

'Of course, Honoured Commander.'

Using her other hand, La-Ver-Di-Arussah took the sword from the floor, resheathed it, bowed, and then retrieved her hand. Just as she was leaving, Wa-Ka-Mo-Do called to her.

'One last thing, La-Ver-Di-Arussah. What do you know of the city of Ell?'

'Ell, Honoured Commander? What do you mean?'

She was hiding something, Wa-Ka-Mo-Do knew it.

'It is nothing,' he said.

La-Ver-Di-Arussah left, pushing her way through the leather curtain.

Ka-Lo-Re-Harballah waited until she was out of earshot and then turned to his commander, eyes glowing in awe.

'Honoured Commander. Such speed—'

'Do you know who this is?' interrupted Wa-Ka-Mo-Do, pointing to the dead soldier.

'Zil-Wa-Tem. Originally from Ka.'

Ka. Wa-Ka-Mo-Do had a momentary thought of Jai-Lyn.

'Ka,' he repeated. 'Look at this leather, look how carefully it has been stitched to make this skin. Who can have done this?'

'There is a whole market full of people out there who could have done it,' said Ka-Lo-Re-Harballah.

'Yes. But some of them will know.'

Wa-Ka-Mo-Do stared at the dead robot. Zil-Wa-Tem's coil was cut, his eyes dim. Someone had pushed an awl up into his mind, tangling and shorting the twisted metal there.

'I really don't understand!' said Ka-Lo-Re-Harballah in despair. 'Where is this dissent coming from? The robots of Sangrel province are woven to be loyal. For generations loyal parents have woven loyalty into their children.'

'But loyalty to whom?' asked Wa-Ka-Mo-Do, thoughtfully. 'Loyalty to their Emperor, or to Sangrel, or to themselves?'

He came to a decision.

'Ka-Lo-Re-Harballah, fetch two trusted soldiers. Strip this robot and then disassemble his body, carry it from this place. Then I want you to return here and take the skin. Carry it, carefully concealed, around the market, looking for robots who stitch leather for a trade, and show it to them, and when you show it to them, watch their reaction.'

'Understood, Honoured Commander.'

'I will return to the Copper Master's house to think.'

Wa-Ka-Mo-Do rose to his feet. As he made to leave Ka-Lo-Re-Harballah called out to him.

'Honoured Commander?'

'Yes Ka-Lo-Re-Harballah?'

'Are we right not to tell the Emperor what has happened here?'

'Would you prefer that we take arms against this market place, Ka-Lo-Re-Harballah?'

The young robot didn't say anything.

'Then there is your answer.'

Kavan

The following day dawned tinged in silver. The strange light from the night before hung in the air, turning the rocks to the colour of metal. Kavan stood in a land of frozen mercury, solidified as it poured from the sky. The snow glinted oddly like quartz in neon.

Calor appeared before Kavan, her bright body covered in scratches. Melting snow dripped from her body.

'There's a trap ahead, Kavan,' she said.

'How far?'

'Less than a mile. There's a bridge, the biggest I've ever seen. It crosses between two mountains. Several Scouts have gone across it, none have come back.'

'Can you see anything on the far side?'

'Movement. I can't tell what.' Calor looked around and buzzed. 'What's happened to the moon, Kavan?'

'I don't know.'

He looked around for Ada. She was balancing on one

leg, holding onto the wall of the road with one hand as she fiddled with her foot with the other.

'Ada,' he called. 'What do you know about a bridge ahead?'

'The Evening Bridge,' she said. 'It marks the border of Born.'

Kavan looked back to Calor.

'They will guard their border. Whether they mean to attack us or allow us to pass remains to be seen. Come on, let's go and see.'

Kavan stood near the start of the bridge, looking at the biggest bolt he had ever seen. It was screwed into a wide metal plate riveted into the black rock. Red paint covered the large mushroom rivets that held the construction against the mountainside. Turning around, Kavan saw a huge red pipe looping up into the air, arching out over the sheer drop of the chasm by which they stood, and then dropping down to the pier of stone that rose from the centre of the chasm, a stepping stone between the mountains. Another red pipe did the same in parallel, a hundred feet away. And suspended beneath these two pipes, a road.

It was a bridge, but a bridge like none that Kavan had ever seen before.

'How come we never saw anything like this when we conquered these mountains?'

'We never came this far west,' answered Calor.

'They have to keep it painted,' said Ada, 'or the iron would just flake away.'

'How do they do it?' wondered Kavan.

'Magnetic feet,' said Ada.

He gazed across the bridge, felt the wind whipping through his body.

'It would be the easiest thing to defend the far side.'

'Then what shall we do?' asked Calor.

'I'll cross,' said Kavan. 'Perhaps they will speak to me.'

'And if they don't?'

'The Uncertain Army will find its own way south. Ada can guide it out of the mountains, and after that Nyro's will shall prevail.'

'I'll come with you, Kavan,' said Calor. Kavan looked at the Scout, saw how she twitched and buzzed.

'No, Calor. I need you to stay and organize the Scouts. Don't let any more of them across.'

'Okay, Kavan.'

Kavan stepped onto the bridge. So much metal, it was a wonder it hadn't been taken and twisted into more minds and robots. Whoever guarded it must be strong indeed.

He began to walk, listening to the wind singing through the struts and cables, looking down at the peaks below him, wrapped in clouds and mist. This would be a clear blue morning, were it not for the fading silver light that filled the sky. Now Kavan reached the central pier: an island of stone on which an iron and brick support for the bridge had been built. He looked down. There were buildings there, clustered on this island in the sky, and on the roof of one, the silver body of a Scout lay, unmoving. Someone would retrieve the metal later, one way or another.

Now he moved on to the second span. He saw movement ahead. Figures on the other side of the bridge.
More and more of them, crowding in. Robots, but oddly
built. Too tall, too thin.

Kavan walked on. A robot detached itself from the
group ahead and came forward onto the bridge to meet
him. They met halfway across the second span, standing
in the wind above the swirling mists below, the silver
light fading from the sky above them.

'You are Kavan, and behind you is your army.'

'Sort of,' said Kavan. 'They may become my army.
Will you join us or fight us?'

'I haven't yet decided.'

Kavan looked at the other robot. It was much taller
and thinner than he was. Its limbs seemed to bend like
springs when it moved, and Kavan wondered how it
would look climbing from rock to rock up here in the
mountains, how it would swing its body from ledge to
ledge.

'Who are you?' he asked.

'My name is Goeppert.'

'Are you the leader of these troops?'

'They aren't troops, and I am not their leader. A robot
must follow the path woven into its own mind. Some
paths lead up into the mountains, and some down to the
plains—'

'No,' said Kavan. 'I have marched from the top to the
bottom of this continent, and I have conquered all that
I have seen. I've heard robots issue challenges, I've heard
robots plead for mercy, and I have heard robots spout

philosophy. It all means nothing to me in the end. Tell me who you are, Goeppert.'

'I am a Speaker. Some days ago another army came through these mountains. A small group of Artemisians. They were fleeing a robot named Kavan, they said that he might follow them down this path. They gave us much metal. Gold and silver, platinum, lead. Metals that we do not often see in these mountains. They promised us more if we were to fight him, should he come this way.'

'And what did you say?'

'We promised that we would, and we took the metal.'

Kavan shifted, his left side squeaking.

'I would have promised the same,' he said. 'That way I would have the metal. So you will fight us?'

Goeppert held his gaze.

'We don't know. Promises made to lowlanders mean nothing.'

Silence in the silver light.

'Then will you let us pass?'

'What would you offer us if we were to do so?'

'The chance to follow Nyro. I go to take control of Artemis.'

'And if we allowed you to pass, but we chose to remain here?'

'Then I would take my army to Artemis. If I were successful in my conquest I would someday return here and conquer this land.'

Goeppert smiled.

'I think you might find that more difficult than you would imagine. Even so, I appreciate your honesty. The world is not an honest place at the moment. Even the sky is wrong.'

'Zuse flared last night,' said Kavan. 'I've never seen that before. Is it a feature of these mountains?'

'No.'

Kavan said nothing.

'Do you know the whales are dying?' said Goeppert, suddenly.

Kavan was little unsettled by this change in the conversation. 'The whales?' he said. 'What do you know about whales, living up here in the mountains?'

'We listen to their songs. They are in constant communication with each other. Didn't you know this?'

Kavan didn't care.

'Goeppert, I travel with an Uncertain Army. It will follow me forwards, it will not go backwards, and if it stands still for too long it will simply evaporate to nothing. I cannot afford to stand here all day, so tell me, will you fight me, or let me pass?'

Goeppert didn't say a word, but somewhere behind him, somewhere out in the land of Born, robots were detaching themselves from the mountainside, coming into view, forming themselves into lines on the road beyond the bridge.

'Both,' said Goeppert. 'For the moment we will let you pass. We will even give you troops to accompany you. They will learn how to fight, and maybe return here with more metal from the plains.'

'Good,' said Kavan.

'The robots who return here will be stronger for

having travelled. They will bring us new knowledge that we will put to use.'

Kavan understood. 'You seek to temper yourself further.' He looked back to the far side of the bridge where his troops waited. 'I feel no such need.'

Spoole

Spoole gazed at the map of the city.

'Is this the best they could do?' he asked.

'They did well, given the time they had available,' said General Sandale reprovingly.

Spoole doubted it. Someone had taken a sheet of polished steel and engraved a map upon it. The Basilica was a rectangle in the centre, the forges clustered around it. Beyond it was Half-fused City, the railway stations, the goods yards, the chemical tanks, the construction yards, the making rooms, the barracks, the gasometers and cable walks . . . All the signs of a busy city. Beyond all that, there was a planned outline of the defences.

He looked at the lines of the trenches, represented on the map. They were well laid out, offering clear, overlapping lines of fire. The railway lines picked their way through them, offering an effective way of keeping the front lines stocked with ammunition.

'We thought of running lines out beyond the defences,' said Sandale. 'Fill a load of wagons with guns and send them out to fire a broadside into Kavan's troops.'

'It would only work once, but it could be effective. Still,' he said grudgingly, 'the overall plan looks workable.'

But will it be enough? he wondered. He had seen the way the troops had retreated back in the mountains. Kavan hadn't even had a proper army then. If he reached Artemis City, and he would, then he would do so with troops hardened by the march, and tempered by the fighting they would have been forced into on the way.

Still, Spoole was fighting from his home territory. The land beyond the city was mined, the trenches could be flooded with petrol, trains could be loaded with explosives and sent running on railway lines buried beneath the sand and soil of the plain towards the attacking troops.

That thought gave Spoole pause. Once Artemis City had been connected to the continent by railway lines. Now those joins were severed, the city cut off from the rest of Shull. What were they doing, he wondered. Surely this wasn't Nyro's will?

He wasn't a superstitious robot, none of the Artemisians were; it wasn't woven into their minds. Nonetheless, he remembered the lights in the sky from the night before, the way that Zuse had lit up. The whole city had stopped work, robots had thronged the streets looking to the skies whilst fires burned unattended in forges and robots remained half assembled.

He pushed the thought from his mind and turned his attention back to the job in hand.

'We need to do something about the aerial masts,'

said Spoole, pointing to the map. 'Kavan could take them out easily, and thus cut off our communications.'

He scanned the map.

'Here,' he pointed. 'The northern quarters. Demolish this sector and move the aerials there. They'll be safe behind the forges and the garrisons.'

He looked up, saw Sandale and the other Generals exchanging looks.

'Well?' he said. 'What's the matter with you?'

'Spoole, that's where *we* are quartered. Don't you think our capacity to lead will be severely reduced if we cannot guarantee our bodies are in working order?'

'Surely we will be quartered here, in the Basilica?' said Spoole. 'A little privation during the course of the conflict is normal, surely?'

General Sandale took a long rod of iron and pointed.

'I suggest we relocate the aerials here, just a little closer to the city than their current position. We leave the area where they stood empty. It should give a good line of fire on any robot that tries to attack across the ground there.'

Spoole inspected the map.

'It's not that bad an idea,' he admitted, 'but what's to stop Kavan simply moving his troops onto the land and occupying it?'

The Generals exchanged looks once more.

'Nonetheless,' said Sandale, 'we think this is a better idea.'

'Since when was this a democracy?'

'Since your decisions began to lose their effectiveness.'

Long ago, Spoole had seen the mugger snakes of

Stark, watched them as they slipped out of their bore holes to capture a passing insect. They didn't move that quickly, but they moved with an ease and assurance that meant they could often capture their prey before it was aware of the movement. Spoole moved in the same manner now, he had his hand behind General Sandale's neck before the soldier knew what was happening.

'You've lost your edge, General,' said Spoole. He dragged a finger down Sandale's chest panelling, scratching it.

'And you are losing yours, Spoole,' said Sandale. 'Enough of this charade. Let me go.'

He had pushed a magnetic bomb against Spoole's chest.

'It's not armed,' he said, 'but if it were, it would freeze your body before you could harm my coil.' He smiled to the other robots. 'There's a time for action, and a time for thought.'

'Want to try it?' asked Spoole. 'Put it to the test?'

'There's no need,' said General Sandale. 'Your moment has passed Spoole. Other arrangements have already been made.'

'What arrangements?' asked Spoole.

'Troop deployments,' said General Sandale. 'We have a plan.'

Again the Generals looked at each other.

'I think it's time we told you,' said General Sandale. 'Come with me, Spoole.'

Wondering, Spoole followed General Sandale from the room.

He was heading for the topmost level of the Basilica.

For the staterooms. Spoole's own quarters were located up here, along with the radio centre. Spoole wondered if this was when the coup would finally happen. Still, he walked on.

He was Artemisian to the core. Whether by Kavan, or by Sandale and his cronies, if he was overthrown by other Artemisians, then that would be the will of Artemis.

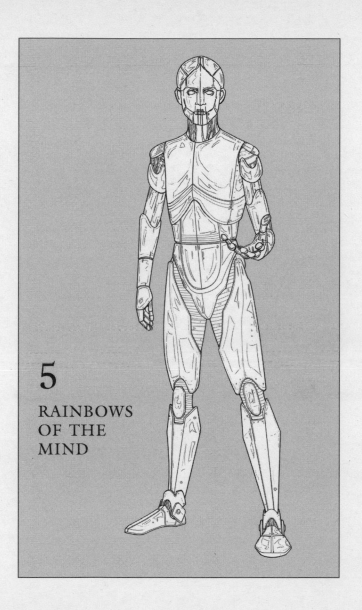

5

RAINBOWS
OF THE
MIND

Susan

The women filed into the lecture room.

'Where's Nettie?' asked Susan.

'I don't know,' said the woman next to her, forgetting her old hatred for Susan. She too was unsettled by the stranger standing in Nettie's place, preparing to give the morning lecture. Susan and her neighbour held each other's gaze for a moment. Life had become almost comfortable in Artemis City. What did this change signify?

The new woman at the front smiled brightly. 'Good afternoon, ladies! My name is Gretel, and I'm here to show you a new pattern.'

Susan raised her hand. 'Where's Nettie?' she asked.

'Reassigned. Now, I am here to talk about a pattern of mind that has recently been resurrected by the women of Artemis. We call it the half fuse.'

'The half fuse? Like Half-fused City?'

Half-fused City was the old quarter, it lay not that far from the making rooms. The women tended to avoid it. It was against the rules to talk, but the women were regarded as mothers of Artemis now, and that gave them some leeway. There was a buzz as they discussed the half fuse: what did it mean? Was it moral? All of them but Susan, who was gazing at the metal floor, wondering about Nettie, wondering about her friend.

'The half fuse,' said Gretel. 'Maximum power and

longevity backed up with *just sufficient* intelligence. Imagine the robot that would power! Strong, capable of following orders to the glory of Artemis . . .'

This was the mind that Nettie had begun to show them, realized Susan. *But why would anyone want to make such a mind? What sort of society would this be? Strong, but nearly unthinking? What would be the point in it?*

She couldn't hold the thought, because another truth was forcing its way into her mind. First Axel and Karel, and now Nettie. Everyone she had loved had been taken from her. And she just sat here, in this room, accepting it.

She remembered a robot she had met, what seemed like a lifetime ago, back in Turing City. Maoco O, the City Guard. He had known of the Book of Robots, and had thought that Susan did too. He had asked Susan a question:

When the time came, would you be strong enough to twist a mind in the way you knew to be right?

He had been talking about the coming war, talking about Turing City's defeat. It had been easy to be defiant when City Guards such as Maoco O still patrolled in their sleek, over-engineered bodies. But now she was here, alone, in the middle of the enemy city, she was confronted with the real answer.

No. When the time had come, she had sacrificed her principles in order to stay alive.

And so what? Was that anything to be ashamed of? Wouldn't any other robot do the same in her position? A remnant of her old life as a statistician came to her aid. Yes, most other robots would. At least, all the ones who had lived to make new robots. So why did she feel so guilty, if that was the way that robots were made?

At the front of the room Gretel was talking about the half fuse, and Susan realized what she was doing. She was hiding from the new reality. Circumstances had changed. She was no longer the frightened, dented woman who had been led into this room those months back.

She was a mother of Artemis, she had something like respect in this city. She was free to come and go as she pleased, within reason. So what was keeping her here now?

Nothing. Nothing but fear and momentum.

Nettie was gone, reassigned. Reassigned where? To what purpose? Nettie wasn't allowed to make children, was this the final reassignment?

And that wasn't all.

Karel was out there somewhere. Her husband was alive, somewhere in Northern Shull. So she had been told, anyway. What would she tell him, if he ever found her? That she just sat here and waited for him? That the one friend she had here had vanished, and she had just let her go?

That decided her.

She was going to get out of here. If it was too big a step to leave the city for the moment, then at the very least she would find Nettie.

And then, if he hadn't come to her by then, they would go look for Karel.

Karel

South of Blaize, the valleys were full of dead towns. Hollow shells of stone buildings, long stripped of any metal, shedding their flat slates across the grass-grown road.

'What are they doing here?' wondered Karel.

'Perhaps they mined the surrounding hills to make robots, and the robots just walked away down the road, leaving these buildings behind them to rot.'

'Could be,' said Karel, looking down yet another narrow valley crowded with dead buildings. Grey slate held together with green moss, all crowded higgledy piggledy together.

'They remind me of something . . .' began Melt.

'What?' asked Karel.

' . . . nothing.'

'Were you remembering something about your past?'

'I remember lots of things. Morphobia Alligator told me this would happen. The metal of my mind is pushed together.'

'I would have thought that would short it out,' said Karel, suspiciously.

'You would have to ask Morphobia Alligator about that,' said Melt.

'I'd like to ask Morphobia Alligator about a lot of things,' snapped Karel, and he immediately felt bad about it. He had never seen a robot in such pain as Melt. He had tried to imagine himself trapped in the body, and had failed. He couldn't have even stood up in it, he was sure.

Melt stumbled, a hiss of static pain briefly escaping from his voicebox.

'Do you need a rest?' Karel asked.

'I'm fine.'

'No, you're not. You can't go on much further.' Karel scanned their surroundings. 'That building over there looks like it used to be a forge. Come on. We can sit in there for a while. There may be some coal or metal remaining.'

'The place will have been stripped centuries ago,' said Melt. 'You can feel the emptiness in this land. Let me keep on walking.'

Karel felt it too. There was nothing here but wind and grass and stone. The echoes of whatever life had once hammered metal here had long since faded. Then, up there, on the hillside, shaking green hands at the wind he saw . . .

'Trees! They burn! I saw that in the Northern Kingdom. I could climb up there and cut some pieces from them. We could make a fire and dry our electro-muscle at least. Heat some metal and bend it—'

'It's too wet,' said Melt. 'The wood will be too green.'

'So you know something about trees?' asked Karel, who knew nothing. There had been virtually no organic life back in Turing City.

'I remember forests, and wood and carving,' said Melt, gazing at the floor. Once more Karel had the impression he knew more than he was saying. It was as if the robot was deciding just what it would be safe to reveal. 'But I don't think it was me who did it. I remember that you need a sharp blade to cut into wood.'

'Are there forests at the Top of the World?'

'The Top of the World?'

'You say that Morphobia Alligator brought you here, Melt. Do you think it was from the Top of the World?' He gazed at the strange half-melted body of the other robot. Even before it had been damaged it would have been nothing like his own.

'The Top of the World,' repeated Melt. 'I don't know. I don't remember.'

Liar, thought Karel, and then he immediately felt a surge of shameful panic as he watched Melt freeze in place. Slowly, the great lead and iron body toppled forward, landing on the ground with a crash that sent Karel's own body rattling.

'Melt!' he called, 'Melt! I'm sor—' He stopped himself just in time. He was being ridiculous. Thinking that Melt was a liar hadn't caused this failure. He knelt down and looked into the other robot's eyes. They barely glowed, such was Melt's exhaustion.

'I'm okay,' he said.

'No you're not!' said Karel, and the sky unfolded a fall of rain that began to patter upon their metal shells.

'Bullets,' said Melt.

'Rain,' said Karel. 'Just a shower. Come on, let's get you into shelter.'

'Soon pass,' said Melt.

Karel took the robot by the shoulders and began to drag him awkwardly to the nearest building. He weighed so much! Melt said he had once been a soldier. What sort of a soldier would fight in a body like this?

Slowly, painfully, he dragged the other robot to shelter, metal grinding and scraping on the wet ground. Finally, he pulled him across the threshold and let him go.

Karel looked around the ancient room in which he found himself. Nothing but dry brick and stone and crumbling mortar. Green organic life grew around the cracks where water had made its way in. The place was long stripped of anything useful: he could feel the hollowness of his surroundings, empty of all metal.

'Melt, I'm going out to look around. There must be some dry wood or something somewhere.'

Melt gave the faintest hiss of static in reply.

Karel re-emerged into the long grey street, huddled under the dull green hill beneath a wretched grey sky. The rain plinked on his shell, and he felt utterly miserable. A noise, the sound of shifting stone. He turned, but there was no one there.

Something had changed. Karel scanned the blank faces of the old buildings. Something was out there, he could feel it. A flicker of movement to his right and he swung round. Nothing.

'Hello?' he said, his voice lost in the pattering rain. 'Morphobia Alligator?'

He sensed something behind him.

He turned around and saw two robots walking towards him, their hands raised in greeting. His feeling of pleasure at the sight of help quickly turned to disgust as he saw the state of the robots that approached.

Their bodies were dented and in poor repair, the

squeaking and grinding noises they made as they walked showed what little care they took of themselves.

Worst of all though, and the sight of it filled him with utter revulsion, they were covered in rust.

Wa-Ka-Mo-Do

Wa-Ka-Mo-Do looked around the Emperor's Palace in deepening awe, trying to put his emotions into order, trying to make sense of the odd trepidation that he felt. It wasn't the sight of the high, polished ceilings of brass and titanium; it wasn't the paper scrolls that hung down over the brushed aluminium walls, a few strokes of paint evincing autumnal scenes, a bough of cherry blossom or elegant robots from times past dressed in copper bodies. It wasn't even the sound of the robot gamelan that played in the corner of the room, and this was unusual, for Wa-Ka-Mo-Do, warrior and poet, understood the music of the metallophone and the gong, and those instruments cast in Sangrel were famous throughout Yukawa for their clarity and tone.

No, what truly moved him to silent wonder was the sight of the animals that moved through the building. Humans everywhere, their soft brown and pink and muddy-yellow bodies covered in bright fabrics. That the Emperor should give this place up to the animals was hard enough to believe, that they could accept this gift seemingly without understanding its significance was beyond comprehension. Yet it was so, for the animals had pushed aside the busts and vases and screens of the palace, with no regard for the harmony of the place. And then, insult upon insult, they had brought in their own furniture. Plastic chairs; long tables covered in cloth; ugly white lights. Everything they used had function but little form. Their artefacts were plain and ugly, an insult to the Emperor. And everywhere they had draped the long black wires that snaked through the rooms and corridors, singing with the strange electricity that the humans used. Rectangular screens hung on walls, flickering with pictures of other places, they made Wa-Ka-Mo-Do's head buzz if he looked too closely.

Wa-Ka-Mo-Do and Ka-Lo-Re-Harballah entered the Great Hall together. Wa-Ka-Mo-Do's scarlet body was polished beyond its usual shine, it seemed to glow with a deep red light this evening. The ceremonial blades at his hands and feet sharpened to a razor's edge. His electromuscles were freshly straightened and his joints lubricated with fine oil. He looked just how the commander of Sangrel should look. Or so he had believed, until he saw Ka-Lo-Re-Harballah. He had forgotten that fashion of the nobility: to wear another body to events such as this. Ka-Lo-Re-Harballah's dress body was built in the imperial style, a stylized representation of a warrior, a sweeping arrangement of fins and blades, of quicksilver motion captured halfway through an attack. Impressive to look at, but so thin and fragile, it would crumple almost at a touch. Of course, that wasn't the point. The nobility could afford to wear bodies such as this, protected as they were by their position. Wa-Ka-Mo-Do knew that some of the animals in the room would mistake Ka-Lo-Re-Harballah for the commander of Sangrel. He didn't mind. The robots were here to put on a show. Tonight, Ka-Lo-Re-Harballah at least, outshone the humans.

The humans wore virtually no metal. They covered themselves either in plain black fabric or exotically coloured silks. It took Wa-Ka-Mo-Do a few moments to realize there was a system to their dress. He had seen quite a few of the humans by now: he was at the stage where he could distinguish the sexes without having to look for the two swellings on the chest that signified a female (so gauche). Now he realized that the men all wore black cloth. They were the ones who most resembled robots, if black fabric tubing pulled up around the arms and legs could ever be said to resemble panelling. But as for the women, they looked like no robots Wa-Ka-Mo-Do had ever seen before. They wore long flowing envelopes of silk that seemed to start just above their chests, to hug their strange bodies down past the waist and hips and then to flare out to touch the floor. They gave the females the strange appearance of not having any legs, so that they seemed to move across the floor as if they were on wheels.

Ah, but Wa-Ka-Mo-Do was mistaken. Not all the females were dressed in that fashion. Those soldiers who stood around the walls were dressed in the same grey and green uniforms regardless of their sex. Yet these soldiers were not like his own Copper Guard. They didn't seem to maintain the motionless stance his own Guard would have done were they here and not marking their time in Smithy Square. These humans turned this way and that, they nodded and chatted to each other. That wasn't to say they weren't well trained. Wa-Ka-Mo-Do could tell by the way they were always scanning the crowd, despite their easy posture. And yet they seemed to regard the people at the party with something like amused derision, not like their superiors whom it was their honour to guard.

Ka-Lo-Re-Harballah appeared at his side.

'Mr Ambassador, may I present Wa-Ka-Mo-Do, commander of the Emperor's Army of Sangrel.'

Wa-Ka-Mo-Do found himself face to face with a human a little taller than he was. The animal's skin was a shiny black colour that reminded Wa-Ka-Mo-Do of anthracite. His hair was grey, his eyes a deep brown. He reached out one shiny black hand and Wa-Ka-Mo-Do stared at it.

'The Ambassador wishes to shake your hand,' murmured Ka-Lo-Re-Harballah. Wa-Ka-Mo-Do remembered his instructions, and reached out and took the anthracite hand in his, looking at the pale pink tips at the end of the fingers. The hand was warm and soft. Wa-Ka-Mo-Do moved it up and down.

'And how do you like our city, Mr Ambassador?'

'I find it both spectacular and beautiful, Commander. It is a wonderful testament to the culture of the Yukawan robots. The sense of history and tradition is written in the very stones themselves.'

'Thank you.'

'But I understand that this is not your own city, Commander? I have been told that you represent a very, ah, different culture?'

Wa-Ka-Mo-Do felt a skitter of current up and down

his hand. How on Penrose would the Ambassador know this? Was this La-Ver-Di-Arussah's doing?

'I represent the Emperor, Mr Ambassador,' replied Wa-Ka-Mo-Do carefully. 'However it is true that I come from another province, some distance from here. You may have seen its mountains from your ship?'

'How fascinating. You must tell me about it sometime. Now, forgive me, I must circulate.'

And at that the Ambassador shook his hand once more and headed off around the room.

'What just happened there, Ka-Lo-Re-Harballah? I feel as if I've just been dismissed. Doesn't he realize who I am?'

'I fear he realizes all too well, Honoured Commander. I don't think it would serve either of you to engage in anything but small talk. Do you really wish to mention what happened this morning in number three mine?'

'I don't know! What happened in number three mine?'

'You mean you haven't been told?'

'Obviously not.' Wa-Ka-Mo-Do's voice was cold with fury. Ka-Lo-Re-Harballah looked at the floor, embarrassed.

'The robots refused to work, Honoured Commander. They said that they would only follow the commands of the Emperor's robots, not animals.'

Wa-Ka-Mo-Do held his face immobile.

'And what did the humans do?'

'Nothing, Honoured Commander. They chose to pretend they could not understand what was going on.'

'Is the matter resolved?'

'Of course. La-Ver-Di-Arussah led a detachment of the Copper Guard there and killed one in ten of them. Half of them children, as is customary.'

'What!'

'Children cannot work as efficiently, Honoured Commander. Plus the effect on the parents is remarkable. It is the logical thing to do for so many reasons.'

'You know that's not what I mean! How dare you take such action without my permission?'

Wa-Ka-Mo-Do realized that he had spoken too loudly. Animals and robots were looking in his direction. At that moment he saw La-Ver-Di-Arussah, standing with three humans, resplendent in a body of gold foil. She was staring towards Wa-Ka-Mo-Do with a look of amused condescension.

'Bring her here, Ka-Lo-Re-Harballah,' said Wa-Ka-Mo-Do. 'At once!'

La-Ver-Di-Arussah strode up, the gold of her body swaying in the wind. Long sheets had been stretched out and soldered back on themselves, giving her a flouncy, puffed up appearance that reflected the dress of the human women.

'Honoured Commander,' she said. 'I hardly think this is the place—'

'Silence, La-Ver-Di-Arussah. I've just heard about number three mine! How dare you take such action without my permission?'

'Honoured Commander, it is neither custom or practice that you are informed of every action that takes place within the city. I acted according to precedent.' She moved, and Wa-Ka-Mo-Do heard the sweet singing of current perfectly tuned in to her golden body. He was more than aware of the deadly force that lurked beneath that fair construction. 'However,' she continued. 'In future I will inform you of all activities, if that is your wish?'

'Don't try that dumb insolence with me, La-Ver-Di-Arussah. We are not playing court games here. My orders are clear. Punitive actions on civilians will only take place with my express permission. Do you understand me?'

'Of course I do, Honoured Commander,' La-Ver-Di-Arussah smiled sweetly. 'Now, if you will excuse me, I left our guests rather suddenly. I fear I am being rather rude . . .'

At that she turned and made her way back to the waiting humans.

It was all Wa-Ka-Mo-Do could do to remain still. The urge to kick her to the ground was surging through every electromuscle in his body.

Karel

Sometimes Karel felt as if he lived in a ghost story of the north. He stood in an empty town under a grey sky, watching two robots that had succumbed to rust walking towards him through the rain. He felt nothing but disgust at their state. Good metal left to flake away, joints squealing for lack of oil, sluggish current dulled by dirty contacts . . . How could a robot have so little self-respect?

'Greetings,' said one. Her voice was so badly tuned

that it sang with harmonics. 'My name is Gail, this is Fleet. May we help you?'

She held out a hand, as if to support him. Karel took a step back, as if rust was something that would spread from her body onto his own.

'Please, don't look badly on us,' said Gail sadly. 'There is precious little metal in this place. We do our best with what we have.'

Karel felt a mixture of shame and anger at this.

'I'm sorry,' he said, carefully. 'One forgets how lucky one is sometimes.' Even so, surely there was always something one could do to prevent oneself falling into this state of disrepair? 'My name is Karel.'

'We saw your friend collapse,' continued Gail, and her voice wobbled up and down the registers, harmonizing and burbling. 'We have a fire and some metal. Perhaps we could help?'

Some metal? Then why not use it on themselves?

'There are always those worse off than ourselves,' said Gail, guessing his thoughts. 'We can still move around.'

Karel looked back towards the forge where he had left Melt.

'Maybe we can at least dry him out?' she suggested.

'How far is your place? We will have trouble moving him.'

'A little way into the hills. We cannot stay in this town. Other robots are about. Soldiers. Silver Scouts. They carry sharp blades on their hands and feet. They would tear us apart.'

Gail was right, realized Karel. Although, he felt a little like doing the same himself. And yet, there was pity mixed with his contempt. Karel realized that Fleet had not spoken yet. Gail noted his look.

'Fleet cannot speak, his voicebox is long decayed. Yet he will still do all he can to help.'

Pity moved Karel, that and embarrassment. How could he refuse such an offer of help from those who had so little?

'Thank you,' he said.

There was a narrow path leading up into the hills from behind the buildings of the old town. They dragged Melt along it with less difficulty than Karel had expected: Fleet, though badly warped and rusted, was stronger than he looked. He took a firm hold of Melt and dragged.

'So much metal,' said Gail, in wonder, looking at the melted mass of lead and iron.

The path split into two. Karel looked down the left-hand branch. There was something inviting about it, the way it curved around the hillside, disappearing into the rain. A wide path, well trodden in the past . . .

'Don't follow the left branch,' said Gail. 'Robots who take that path never return.'

Karel looked along the track of the path to where it vanished around the green hillside.

'Why not?' he asked.

'That's a story for later,' replied Gail. 'Come on, up here.'

The right-hand branch of the path led further up the hill. The rain was growing harder, it made metal slippery, made it harder to grip Melt. Below them, Karel caught a glimpse of the old town, snaking through the hills, and he had a sudden urge to return there. What was he doing up here, following these rusty strangers?

'Almost there,' said Gail, and she pointed to a stone arch built into the hillside, a thin trail of smoke emerging from it. 'This is the last entrance to the mine that made the town below rich. But all the iron is gone now.'

The path they followed widened as it approached the opening, and Karel wondered if he could make out the faint imprints of sleepers on the level ground before it.

'In here,' said Gail. Karel hesitated. He turned for a moment and gazed back down at the town. You got a good view of the Northern Road from up here, he realized. This was an excellent place to watch for robots approaching. Robots like him and Melt.

'In we go,' said Gail. 'Nice fire inside.'

The sky chose that moment to let fall a further tumult of rain. It slipped into Karel's panelling; it was cold on the electromuscles. That decided him. Despite his misgivings, he followed Gail into the mine.

Wa-Ka-Mo-Do

The west side of the Great Hall resembled a waterfall of iron arches, set with glass. The windows in the lowest, largest arches had been opened up to allow the robots and humans access to the terrace beyond. Wa-Ka-Mo-Do followed the evening breeze outside, the sound of the robot gamelan diminishing as he left the room.

The stars were bright above. Their light, and the light

streaming from the open windows of the Great Hall, made the surrounding lands that much darker by comparison. Wa-Ka-Mo-Do could just make out the flatness of the lake beyond and below the edge of the terrace, then the hills that lay in the distance. The orange glow of fires could be seen, dotted here and there across the hills, and he moved forward to get a better look.

Rachael, the young human woman from the Street of Becoming, was there, covered in lengths of long green fabric. She wore a set of polished gemstones around her neck in a setting of crudely made silver.

'Hello, robot,' she said. 'What are you going to do now? Order up an airstrike because I'm blocking your view of the lake?'

Wa-Ka-Mo-Do smiled. 'I don't know. What's an airstrike?'

She waved a hand at him. 'Never mind. Hey, while you're here perhaps you can tell me what that is?'

She pointed out across the lake to the low mound, barely visible on the opposite shore.

'That?' said Wa-Ka-Mo-Do. 'That's the Mound of Eternity.'

'Thank you!' Even coming through the little speaking machine she wore, Wa-Ka-Mo-Do could hear the frustration in her voice. 'You know, I've asked just about everyone here about that place and no one would give me a straight answer.'

'They wouldn't,' said Wa-Ka-Mo-Do. 'They don't speak of the Mound here in Sangrel.'

'Why not?'

'Ah,' said Wa-Ka-Mo-Do. 'I'm not sure if this is really the time to tell you. We're supposed to be on our best behaviour tonight, after all.'

She liked that answer, he could tell by her smile. Maybe he was getting used to humans after all.

'Perhaps I'll tell you later,' offered Wa-Ka-Mo-Do. 'Perhaps I could do something else for you first?'

'Like what?'

He reached out and touched the silver chain that hung around her neck.

'May I?' he said.

'Go on.'

He undid the tiny metal clasp, resisting the temptation to press down on the exposed flesh of the human, to get a feel of the structure underneath.

'This is good metal,' he said, 'but badly formed.' He began to work on the tiny links of chain, bending out the imperfections.

'Wow!' she said. 'How are you doing that? Your fingers don't seem to touch it.'

'It's just twisting metal,' said Wa-Ka-Mo-Do. 'You know, this would be stronger and more attractive if you put a half twist in the loops, like so . . .'

He held a length of adjusted chain before her eyes.

'Oh! That's beautiful!'

'Or how about making it into a flexible band, like so . . .'

He worked the chain again, flattening the silver loops and stretching them and forming them into a plait.

'Of course, if I had a little copper in the mix—'

'No! No! It's perfect just the way it is!'

He adjusted the settings for the polished gemstones and then handed her back the reformed necklace.

'Are all robots such craftsmen?' she wondered, turning it this way and that in her hands. 'Hold on, how am I supposed to put it back on?'

'Sorry! I forgot that you were a . . .' his words trailed away.

He retrieved the necklace and quickly formed a clasp into it. He showed her how it worked.

'That's so clever,' she said, fastening it back into place. 'Thank you, Wa-Ka-Mo-Do.'

'It was my pleasure. It looks beautiful on your neck now.' He wasn't just saying that. There was something oddly attractive about the sight of the silver chain against the white curve of her neck.

'I feel as if I owe you a favour now.'

'Certainly not. You humans are our guests.'

She grinned at that. 'Actually, you are the guests in our embassy tonight. So I *do* owe you a favour.'

Wa-Ka-Mo-Do wondered if, despite her smile, he detected a note of bitterness in her words.

'Well,' he said carefully, 'maybe you could tell me what you are doing here? I mean here, on Penrose. You're not like the other humans.'

'And you're not like the other robots. I like your smooth, shiny body. You look like a classic car, not like those other kitchen utensils.' She waved a hand in the direction of Ka-Lo-Re-Harballah. She was angry.

'Rachael. Have I said something to upset you?'

'It's not your fault.'

'I couldn't help noticing. I'm so sorry, but you do

seem different. You're . . . well, younger. I wondered why you were here. Why no one else like you—'

'What am I doing here?' Even in the dim light, Wa-Ka-Mo-Do noted the way that Rachael's face changed colour. 'What am I doing here?' she repeated. 'Well, my father is the controller of ———.'

Wa-Ka-Mo-Do looked at the human in confusion. She had spoken, he had heard her, but for some reason the device that she wore clipped around her head had not translated her final words.

'What happened there?' asked Wa Ka Mo-Do. 'Your machine didn't speak properly.'

Wa-Ka-Mo-Do was fascinated to see the red colour deepen in Rachael's pale face.

'I'm being censored, that's what's happening.' She raised her voice. Some of the other humans were looking in her direction. 'I'm not allowed to say what I think! What do you think of that, robot?'

'My name is Wa-Ka-Mo-Do, and there's no need to shout.' He lowered his own voice. 'I don't call you human, do I, Rachael?'

Her eyes flicked to the ground for a moment.

'You're right. I'm sorry, Wa-Ka-Mo-Do.' She smiled weakly. 'Hey, that's a mouthful. Maybe I'll call you Wacky.'

'That would be an insult, Rachael. A Yukawan robot earns their full name.'

'I'm sorry, Wa-Ka-Mo-Do.' And then her face flushed again. 'But maybe you'll understand how I feel. I've been dragged here from ———, made to leave home and travel ——— ——— ———, all for the sake of my father's job.

And the time has gone all funny on Earth, you know that? I won't be ——— for ———. ——— ——— ———.'

Wa-Ka-Mo-Do held up his hands.

'Rachael, you're cutting out. I don't understand what you're saying.'

'That's what happens when you grow up surrounded by fascists.' She clenched her fists and rolled her eyes, and Wa-Ka-Mo-Do had to force himself not to laugh. It seemed such a strange thing to do.

All of a sudden she calmed down. 'I'm thirsty, Wa-Ka-Mo-Do.'

'Thirsty?' the word confused Wa-Ka-Mo-Do for a moment, but then he remembered what Ka-Lo-Re-Harballah had told him. 'Oh yes. I understand.'

'It's polite for a gentleman to fetch the lady's drink,' added Rachael.

'Is it?' said Wa-Ka-Mo-Do, puzzled by this custom, but pleased for the opportunity to watch a human drink. 'What do I do?'

'You mean you don't know? I suppose you wouldn't. Well, you call across one of the waiters, ask him for a glass of champagne, and then you take it from him and hand it to me, and then I drink it.'

'Champagne,' said Wa-Ka-Mo-Do, carefully. 'Very well.' There was a black-clad human nearby holding a tray. Wa-Ka-Mo-Do signalled to him, as he had seen the other humans do.

'Champagne, please.'

The light flickered on the waiter's headset as Wa-Ka-Mo-Do spoke the words, but if the human thought there was anything odd in the request, he didn't say so.

Wa-Ka-Mo-Do took the champagne and turned to see Rachael had walked off along the terrace's edge, as if she didn't know him. This seemed a very strange custom. Wouldn't it be easier if human females fetched their own drinks? He carefully carried the glass across to her, noting what a ridiculous design the vessel was. The yellowish liquid that it contained seemed to be always about to spill over the rim of the wide bowl. Surely it would be more sensible to make the glass taller and narrower?

'You did it!' said Rachael, sounding impressed. She seized the glass and took a sip. Immediately, she began to make a harsh hacking sound.

'What is that you are doing?' asked Wa-Ka-Mo-Do. 'Does that mean you are enjoying the drink?'

'Just a cough,' said Rachael, her voice strangely modulated. 'It went down the wrong way.' She made the hacking noise once more, and then took another sip of the drink. Wa-Ka-Mo-Do watched fascinated, seeing the way her throat moved as it went down.

She turned to lean against the stone balustrade, seemingly unperturbed by the sheer drop below her. She was looking out at the green mound opposite.

'Now, Wa-Ka-Mo-Do. You said you'd tell me more about the Mound of Eternity.'

Wa-Ka-Mo-Do looked around, wondering if he was doing the right thing. Ka-Lo-Re-Harballah and the rest of the robots and humans still circulated in the Great Hall. He could see the Ambassador, talking to two robots in copper skins. Mine Chiefs, he guessed. He should really be in there himself, but he couldn't face returning to that room just yet. Besides, he was enjoying Rachael's company.

'Do you want to hear a story about a story?' he asked.

'A story about a story? Is this a robot thing?'

'It's supposed to tell you something about yourself.'

'I'd rather know about the Mound of Eternity.'

'This story is about the Mound of Eternity too.'

'Then I'd like to hear it.' She took a drink of champagne, and Wa-Ka-Mo-Do began to speak.

The Story about a Story

'A long time ago, the robots who built this city ruled the world, or at least all the land that they could see, which in those days was the world. They were proud and clever.

'They mined this hill for iron and copper, and built the walls from the stone that they excavated. They built forges and presses and foundries, and the city waxed strong. And all would have been well, but for the streak of cruelty woven into the minds of those who led, and they treated those in their charge badly. When they wove their children, they wove a little more cruelty into their minds. And so cruelty deepened with each generation.

'Now, you need leisure to be truly cruel, and these robots had leisure. Do you want to hear more?'

'Yes,' said Rachael.

'But I warn you, the story of the Mound of Eternity is not a pleasant one.'

'Go on.' She took another sip of the champagne. Wa-

Ka-Mo-Do was a novice in the ways of humans, but it seemed to him she wasn't really enjoying her drink.

'Very well,' he said. 'So the metal of this land was twisted into patterns of exquisite cruelty, and the people of this city suffered under the hands of the rulers—'

'Hold on,' interrupted Rachael, waving a hand airily in the darkness. 'It couldn't be that bad.'

Wa-Ka-Mo-Do felt disorientated to be put off his flow so.

'Well . . . Why not?'

Rachael took hold of the balustrade and looked out over the orange fires, burning in the dark distance. She seemed to be a little uncoordinated, her speech a little slurred.

'Because robots have it easy. If someone damages your leg or arm you can always build another one. If a human is tortured they can be damaged for life.'

Wa-Ka-Mo-Do wore a tolerant expression. 'That's why it's better to be a human.'

'No way! Really? Why?'

Wa-Ka-Mo-Do gazed at her face. He could barely read human expressions; even so, he got the impression that this wasn't bravado. Rachael really hadn't thought this through.

'It's better to be a human,' he repeated, 'because once a human's body is destroyed the pain ends. With a robot they just fasten on another limb and start the torture all over again.'

He leaned closer to her; he heard the strange rasping noise she made as she blew wind into and out of her mouth.

'You know that if you cut the coil of a robot it cannot control its body?' he said. 'It's cast into a world of darkness before it dies?'

'I had heard that.'

'Not that long ago, here in Sangrel, they cut the coils of robots. They cut the coils of children. They made mothers watch as their children were brought forward and their coils broken before them. They made mothers weave minds knowing they would be destroyed immediately they were finished.'

The human's eyes widened. Wa-Ka-Mo-Do saw the intricate patterns woven in the blue circles that acted as focussing mechanisms.

'But that was awful!'

'That was just the start,' said Wa-Ka-Mo-Do. 'I told you, as the years passed, the cruelty of those robots increased. Cruelty is a sport that must be constantly reinvented lest it grow dull. Look at this.'

He led Rachael to the end of the terrace, to where the exhibits lay.

'So? It's a suit of armour. What's so bad about that?'

'Not a suit of armour. A robot body. Doesn't it look odd to you?'

'A little. Why? What is it really?'

'I can't tell you. You're too young.'

'Too young? I'm fourteen!' She picked up her empty glass. 'I need more champagne,' she said. Wa-Ka-Mo-Do signalled to another waiter who replaced the glass with a full one.

'Cruelty was once written throughout this state,' he said. They moved back to the edge of the terrace and looked back over the lake to the dark shape of the Mound of Eternity. The rhythm of the gamelan had changed, now the slowly ringing gongs spoke of stillness and calm.

'The robots of this city were tortured and crippled and melted and bent. Voiceboxes were amplified so that the screams of the suffering could be heard across the countryside. Ever more inventive ways were found to torment the populace. Do you want to hear more?'

'Yes! Go on!'

'Very well. Know then, that in the end, the robots of Sangrel wove fear directly into the minds of their subjects.'

Rachael frowned. 'I don't understand.'

She wouldn't. She was a human.

'They were made to be afraid. They were, what is the word you use? Born? That's it, they were *born* to be afraid of everything. Of the changing of the weather, of patterns in the stone, of the forge and the flame. Even of the very touch of metal itself.'

He gazed down at the mound below.

'Wa-Ka-Mo-Do?' said Rachael. 'Wa-Ka-Mo-Do! Speak to me. You still haven't told me about the mound!'

'The mound? Oh yes, the mound. It was raised at the very end. Just before Sangrel was made a part of the Empire.' He lowered his voice. 'It was there that the last of the old race performed its most unspeakable acts.'

'Like what?' She leaned close, concern etched on her face.

Wa-Ka-Mo-Do lowered his voice.

'I can't tell you,' he said, in grave tones. 'They were unspeakable.' And then he laughed, loudly.

'Hey!' Rachael forgot herself and slapped him on the chest. They both looked at each other in surprise, Rachael sucking at her fingers.

'Sorry,' she said. 'But don't tease me like that.'

'I won't.'

'So what's in the mound now?'

'No one goes there. It's the property of the Vestal Virgins.'

'What are the Vestal Virgins?' asked Rachael, eyes wide. 'They're mentioned in Earth stories.'

'Have you heard of Oneill?'

'Yes! He's the mythical creator who's supposed to have made the first robots, isn't he?'

'Sort of. Well, the Vestal Virgins were supposed to have tended the fire of the first forge where Oneill made all the robots. One night, when Oneill was out searching for more iron ore, they took one of the men that Oneill had made that day and they began to twist his wire. You understand what I mean? They were making a new mind.'

'I understand,' giggled Rachael.

'Good. But Oneill returned and found them and was angry, so he declared that the Vestal Virgins would never twist fresh metal, but rather would only be able to work on minds that had already been made by other women.'

Rachael was nodding. 'The Vestal Virgins were keepers of the sacred flame on Earth,' she said. 'This translator is a clever piece of kit. It seems to understand stories as well as individual words. But what do you mean, they can only work on minds already made?'

'They twist the metal of other creatures to their own

ends. They form the lengthening caterpillars, for example. The Emperors keep them as pets and for sport. In the wild caterpillars have ten segments. The Vestal Virgins twisted them so that they fight. The winning caterpillar takes the segments of the loser. There are pictures of them hanging in the Great Hall.'

She nodded. 'I think I've seen them. I wondered what they were.'

'It's not my favourite of the royal sports. The longer a caterpillar, the more power it has to stun the weaker competitors. The Emperor has caterpillars more than a mile in length. They have trouble moving . . .'

They weren't the only ones. Rachael had drained her second glass of champagne. Wa-Ka-Mo-Do saw she was having real trouble standing up straight. She swayed as if her gyros were incorrectly tuned.

'Anyway, enough about caterpillars. You said you were going to tell me a story!'

'I said I was going to tell you a story about a story, and I did.'

'When?'

'Just now. The story of a story is the story of a robot, or a human, I should say, wanting to hear about cruelty.'

She shook her head.

'I don't get it.'

Wa-Ka-Mo-Do laughed.

'This is a game that is played on young robots. Asking them if they want to hear about cruelty, in order to reveal the fascination with cruelty that's woven into their own minds. What pure person would wish to hear about such evil?'

'But you told me you were telling me a story! You tricked me!'

'I didn't trick you, I asked you repeatedly if I should go on, and I warned you each time that the next step held worse cruelties, and yet still you wanted to know more. Humans are like robots: they have a fascination with evil woven into their minds.'

'Humans can't help the way they are made. Robots must be worse because they chose to put such things into the weave.'

'Minds need a mix of emotions. Or so the women say. This is something that men can never understand.'

'Yeah! You never do understand!' She swayed as she spoke. She seemed angry and more uncoordinated than ever. Did champagne affect all humans in this manner? Then if so, why drink it?

'I'm sorry, Rachael, I didn't mean to offend. The point of the story is to show that cruelty is everywhere, and it's in you. Weren't you aware of this?'

'*Weren't you aware of this?*' she mimicked. 'Look at you, so smug. Think you know everything. And yet, you're the ones who don't realize . . .'

'What?'

She raised herself up. 'You *don't* realize, do you?'

'Realize what?'

'The way you make yourselves. Like humans. Two arms and two legs and five fingers. You have a head and two eyes. You even have mouths to smile with. You're just like us!'

'Or you could say that you are like robots,' replied Wa-Ka-Mo-Do.

'Don't try and be clever. You're not thinking. Why do you need mouths, anyway? Why not just communicate by radio?'

'There's all the different frequencies, and the trouble with metal and—'

'No, you're not listening to me, are you? I stand here in front of you, breathing the air of an alien planet unaided and you don't think that's strange?'

'Should I?'

'Of course! Look at me. What about ——— and ———.'

There they were again, those strange discontinuities. She was speaking, he could hear it, but the device that she wore wasn't translating her words.

'Rachael, I really don't understand.'

'Look!' she said, and she pointed up into the sky. 'Look at that!'

He looked up. Zuse, the night moon, was there, a perfect metal sphere, reflecting the sunlight down upon the world.

'I don't understand,' he said. 'That's just Zuse.'

'*Just Zuse?*' she mimicked. 'It's a metal moon! And none of you think there's anything wrong with that?'

'Well there isn't,' said Wa-Ka-Mo-Do, puzzled. 'Why should there be?'

'You don't even know what we're doing here, do you? About ——— the ——— ——— ——— ———'

'Rachael!'

The words came from behind Wa-Ka-Mo-Do. He turned to see a human male hurrying up. In the light cast from the Great Hall, he had the same copper colouring as Rachael. Was this her father?

'Rachael! Why are you shouting? Have you been drinking?'

The man looked from Rachael to Wa-Ka-Mo-Do, and something about his gaze caused the robot to rise on his toes a little and prepare a fighting stance.

'Did you give her champagne? Don't you know that she's too young?'

'Honoured guest, if I have made a mistake I apologize . . .'

But the human had an arm around Rachael's shoulder and was already leading her away from the terrace.

Ka-Lo-Re-Harballah appeared at Wa-Ka-Mo-Do's side.

'Are young humans not supposed to drink, then?' asked Wa-Ka-Mo-Do, genuinely puzzled.

Karel

Karel turned up the brightness of his eyes. Just inside the mine entrance was a wide chamber, the only illumination the glow from the small forge in the centre of the room. The air was filled with smoke, and through the haze he made out the shapes of three other robots. Peering closer, he found them to be in a poorer state than Gail and Fleet.

'Don't be like that,' said Gail, noticing his reaction. 'Or are you afraid of us? Come on, what could we do to harm you? Look at us! Too weak, too far gone. Here, let's drag your friend to the fire.'

They dragged Melt closer, and Karel took a look at the forge. There was a bucket of coal next to it; he weighed a piece in his hand.

'This is good quality,' he said. 'Where do you get it from?' No one answered.

'What happened to him?' asked a very thin robot, half crawling, half dragging herself up to Melt's great cast-iron body. She ran a hand over Melt's chest, feeling the metal there.

'He won't say,' said Karel. 'He seems to have been permanently joined to that body somehow.'

'Levine will be able to help you,' said Gail. 'Would you like metal?' She brought forward two strips of iron. 'We have some oil, too.' Fleet came up, carrying brass and tin.

Karel gazed at the iron that Gail held. Like the coal it was of good quality. He turned his gaze to her rusted body.

'There is more to life than metal,' said Gail, answering his unspoken question. 'Come, take this. Perhaps it will help your friend.' She pushed the metal towards him. Five pairs of eyes gazed through the smoke at Karel, and he felt a growing sense of unease.

'We don't need metal,' repeated Gail. 'We repaired ourselves not that long ago. Come, use this metal on yourself. Look here . . .'

She crossed the room to another robot lying on the floor, arms and legs so bent as to be useless. Her steel plate was punctured by crumbling circles of rust.

'Look at her chest,' she said. 'Look at her electro-muscle, how kinked it is. She's draining her own lifeforce away.'

'And yet she's happy,' said Levine, and the woman who lay on the floor increased the glow of her eyes by way of confirmation. 'She understands the truth: that metal is not the sum total of a robot's life. Look at your friend. He understands the trouble that metal can bring.'

They all looked at Melt, who was stirring feebly on the floor, trying to sit up.

'Relax,' said Gail. 'Lie back and let the fire dry you. Let Levine take away some of the metal that troubles you.'

Levine was still running her hands over Melt's body, feeling the metal there.

'I can do something for him,' she said.

'Levine is a great craftsrobot,' said Gail. 'She was a princess in one of the mountain states, born to a body of steel and silver and gold. She walked here dressed in the finest metals, bent into patterns that you would marvel to see.'

'I realized that such things are nothing but vanity,' said Levine, and she ran her hand over Melt's body, peeling away the finest shavings of iron. Karel was impressed. His wife had been a great shaper of metal, too. The skill that Levine evinced showed her to be at least her equal. And this was in that poorly constructed body.

'Is this something to do with the Book of Robots?' asked Karel, suddenly.

'The Book of Robots?' asked Levine. 'No? What is that?'

'The Book of Robots is a fallacy,' said Gail.

'Then you've heard of it?'

'I read it once, or at least part of it.'

'You read it? When? Where?'

Gail smiled and shook her head.

'It doesn't matter, Karel. Don't you see, that such things are not of interest? The Book of Robots simply shows another way of twisting metal, and metal does not concern us here.'

Levine continued to scrape thin flakes of iron from Melt's body. It didn't seem to be hurting him.

'I've travelled in the north,' said Karel. 'I heard many robots talk of the Book of Robots. I never met anyone who actually read it.'

'Karel,' smiled Gail. 'It doesn't matter. Let's not speak of it.'

'But I want to,' said Karel. He felt uncertain and uneasy, and when Karel felt like that his anger kindled. His mother had woven that into his mind.

'Who are you all?'

'I'm Gail, I come from the north. Fleet walked the Northern Road. Levine and Carm came from the mountain states, and Vale came from sea. We help travellers who come into difficulty on the Northern Road.'

Fleet bent and collected together the scraps of metal from the floor that Levine had scraped from Melt; he rolled them together into a ball.

'Why don't you take that metal and use it to repair your voicebox?' asked Karel in frustration. Fleet just shrugged and handed Karel the metal.

Karel still felt uneasy, but his anger was slowly passing.

These people were different, but there seemed to be no harm in them. And Levine definitely seemed to be doing Melt some good.

'There's lead inside him,' she said. 'Why would anyone fill a robot with lead?'

'Can you remove it without hurting him?' asked Karel.

'Not all of it,' said Levine. 'But I'll do what I can.'

'Are you sure you don't want any metal?' asked Gail, pushing the strips of iron towards him once more.

'I'm fine,' said Karel.

Time passed to the slow scraping of metal. There was something strangely satisfying about this place, a sense that things no longer mattered. All the pain, all the exertion: wouldn't it be easier just to sit back and let the world pass by?

It was with some surprise that Karel looked out of the mine entrance and noticed that night had fallen. Fleet had gone, he realized. But when? And where to? He realized then just how sluggish his thoughts had become.

There was a hum of current and suddenly Melt sat up. He looked around at the circle of swarf in which he sat.

'I feel so much better,' he said. 'Thank you.'

'I could do so much more, if you gave me the time.'

'I'm sorry, we have to move on.' Melt flexed his arms and shoulders.

'We understand.'

'I want to thank you for your help,' said Melt. 'If there is anything we can do for you?'

Through the smoke that filled the chamber, Karel saw how Gail and the rest of the robots smiled at that.

'You could accept a gift from us,' said Gail. 'Would you do that?'

'We would be delighted,' said Melt, not seeming to notice the look that Karel directed towards him.

'Then, please, take these, as a token of our respect for you.'

Gail held out both hands. A scrap of silver wire lay on each palm.

'Thank you,' said Melt, reaching out to take one. Karel pushed the leaden robot's hand away. He leaned forward suspiciously, to get a better look at the gifts. Two pieces of metal, two scraps of silver wire.

'What's the matter, Karel?' said Melt. 'It's only metal . . .'

Karel peered closer. It *was* only metal. So what was wrong? And then he saw it. *They were moving.*

'No!' shouted Karel, slapping Gail's hands away. The two twists of metal flew somewhere in the room.

'Oh Karel,' said Gail, in such disappointed tones that Karel felt ashamed of himself. 'It was a gift!'

Melt lurched to his feet, heavy body at the ready to fight.

'What is it, Karel?'

'Worms!' said Karel. 'No wonder they care so little about metal!'

'Worms?' said Melt, confused.

'A story from the Northern Lands. Worms that creep into your head whilst you are sleeping, they twist themselves into the metal of your mind. They work on your thoughts, twisting the wire in your head into copies of themselves.'

'They bring peace and happiness and understanding,' said Gail. 'How can you condemn what you haven't tried?'

'And you did say you would accept our gift,' reminded Levine, the former princess. She had retrieved the two twists of silver from where they had fallen. Now she held them out on one thin, bent palm. Karel saw them wriggling, sensing the lifeforce in his mind, turning their little blunt upper ends in his direction.

'We're leaving now,' said Karel turning to go. Something was blocking the mine entrance. Fleet. There were four other robots with him. These robots were nowhere near as badly rusted as Gail and the rest. Two of them wore the bodies of Artemisian infantry.

'All the robots who take the worms return here in the end,' said Gail. 'They come back to the spawning ground.'

'Try it,' said Levine. 'You promised.'

Melt swung a heavy cast iron arm and smashed her hands away.

'Stop that!' shouted one of the infantryrobots by the door.

'Peace,' said Gail. 'Metal doesn't matter, Kerban. You will see that in time.'

Kerban? That was an Artemisian name! To think that an Artemisian would come to believe that metal was not important! They had to go, now.

'Let us past,' he said.

Fleet moved to push him back into the chamber. The two infantryrobots stepped forward to help.

'Hold them down,' said Gail. 'Once the worms enter

their minds we will let them go as they please. They will return here in the end.'

The two infantryrobots seized Karel's arms. He tried to tug them free.

'Easy,' said one of them.

Karel kicked down, dented a robot's shin. It didn't care.

'Melt!' he said. 'Run!'

Run? The word was ridiculous. Even scraped of metal as he was, Melt could barely walk. He knew it. Gail knew it. She hadn't even bothered to try and restrain the heavy robot.

'Let him go,' said Melt.

'Melt, don't be stupid! Get away!'

'Are you suggesting I have so little honour?' said Melt. 'I used to be a soldier.' And he reached into the fire with both hands and pulled out two burning coals. The robots in the chamber watched, frozen, as he pushed them into the neck of one of the infantryrobots, screwing them back and forth, squeezing hot coal past the panelling. The robot let out an electronic squeal and Karel pulled his arm free of its grasp. Now Melt clasped his hands together and brought them down as hard as he could on the head of the other robot, badly denting the metal skull.

The other robots moved forward. Melt took hold of one of them and pulled backwards, using his considerable weight against it. He swung the robot around and slammed it into the others with a ringing crash.

'Now we run,' said Melt.

Out of the cave, into the darkness, sliding down the rain-soaked grass.

Karel and Melt tumbled down the slope, rolling back towards the town, scraping on stones, slipping on the turf.

They reached the bottom in a tangled clash of metal. With some difficulty, they got to their feet, bodies badly dented.

'They're not following us,' said Karel, looking backwards.

'They won't. We're too much trouble.'

'Where did you learn to fight like that?' asked Karel, eyes bright so he could see Melt in the darkness.

'I . . . don't remember,' said Melt, and again Karel knew he was lying. But that was for later.

'Thank you,' he said. 'Maybe Morphobia Alligator was right.'

'In what way?'

'Sending you to look after me.'

'I wish he was,' said Melt, and Karel could hear the longing in his voice.

Wa-Ka-Mo-Do

Wa-Ka-Mo-Do crossed to the Copper Master's house, his head spinning with questions. The sky was clear, and he gazed up at the night moon, wondering at Rachael's words. So Zuse was made of metal. What was so strange about that?

The Copper Guard stood to attention as he passed through the doors into his residence. A nervous looking aide was waiting in the hallway.

'Honoured Commander, your presence is requested in the Copper Room.'

'Later,' said Wa-Ka-Mo-Do, 'I have work to attend to.'

'I'm sorry, Honoured Commander, but your presence is requested.'

The aide looked terrified at having to contradict Wa-Ka-Mo-Do, and no surprise. Wa-Ka-Mo-Do himself was growing irritated by the constant directions he had been given since he arrived here. He was beginning to realize that the post of Commander offered more restraints than it did freedoms.

'Who wishes to speak to me?' he asked, but the aide had retreated into the depths of the house.

For a moment Wa-Ka-Mo-Do considered ignoring the summons, but curiosity got the better of him.

He padded past robots, their eyes glowing in the dim light, heading for the heart of the building.

The Copper Room was in the centre of the Copper Master's house. It had no windows and only two doors. One led out into the main building. The other was concealed and led down through the rocks upon which Sangrel was built; a secret passage, an escape route built in less enlightened times. The Copper Room was the ideal place for holding private meetings. Wa-Ka-Mo-Do stepped into the room and felt his gyros lurch. No wonder the aide had looked so nervous.

Three robots stood in the middle of the room. Female, so obviously female that Wa-Ka-Mo-Do felt the wire stir within him. They were the most beautifully constructed robots he had ever seen, their bodies bent into curves of perfect symmetry. He could feel their metal from here, the mix of platinum and gold, steel and aluminium shone like starlight across his senses. He wanted to move closer to them, just to touch them, just to have them touch him, to pull his metal from his body . . .

He suppressed the thought. What would they want with his metal? They were Vestal Virgins; they only worked on minds that had already been twisted by others!

But it was so hard . . . Look at them, so beautiful, they seemed to shine all by themselves. Their faces were so delicate. Look at those smiles, so knowing, so calculating, so pretty . . .

'*Wa-Ka-Mo-Do*' said one, and her voice was the sweetest notes of copper bells. '*Honoured Commander of Sangrel. We wish to speak to you.*'

'Really?' said Wa-Ka-Mo-Do. 'Is it important? I am very busy.'

'*Are you?*' said a second robot, her voice a little deeper than the first, still it resonated in Wa-Ka-Mo-Do's chest. '*Zil-Wa-Tem is dead and yet the market place runs as normal.*'

Zil-Wa-Tem, thought Wa-Ka-Mo-Do, and he remembered that was the name of the robot who had been found stitched into the animal's skin in the market.

'*I would have expected the city to ring with the cries of the grieving,*' said the third woman, her voice the deepest of all. '*I would have expected to see the minds of men and women arranged in a circle by the entrance, their coils crushed. I would have expected to see the smoke of a hundred fires filling the air, the bare electromuscles of the captured held over them in order that confessions be extracted.'*

'*Or maybe we misjudge our Commander,*' said the first of the Vestal Virgins. '*Maybe we underestimate his cruelty. Perhaps he intends instead to play the silent game, to raise fear by remaining still for a time before making a move?*'

'*Perhaps you are right,*' continued the second. '*Perhaps he wishes to request our help? To ask us to steal children away in the night and to work on their minds. Twist them so that they don't recognize their own parents. Or maybe to make it so they are filled with the urge to disassemble themselves slowly whilst their mothers look on in despair.*'

'*That must be it,*' said the third. '*Then the word of the Honoured Commander's displeasure would quickly be spread and the names of the perpetrators of the crime brought to the Copper Guard—*'

'Silence!' said Wa-Ka-Mo-Do.

'*Silence?*' said the first, her tone one of laughing delight. '*He orders us to silence? We think he must have forgotten his place.*'

'I have not!' said Wa-Ka-Mo-Do. 'I am the Commander of Sangrel, and it is my prerogative to decide how to handle this situation.'

'*Handle this situation? Perhaps we misunderstood? Are the perpetrators already caught, their bodies filled with molten lead as an example to others?*'

'You know they're not,' said Wa-Ka-Mo-Do. 'But what you have described won't achieve anything. There are robots out there who have already lost everything.

It won't take much to push them over the edge into full-scale insurrection. What then?'

'*Then the Commander of the Emperor's Army will have no choice but to order the death of all the robots of this province.*'

'Of course. And if some humans get caught in the fighting?'

'*Then the Commander of the Emperor's Army will be held accountable.*'

Wa-Ka-Mo-Do spoke with an authority he did not feel.

'Humans will get killed if we pursue your course of action. I know this. I come from the poor lands, far from the Silent City and the court of the Emperor. I've seen what happens when robots have nothing to lose. Believe me, my methods are the right ones.'

One of the Virgins held up something for inspection. Wa-Ka-Mo-Do gazed at the object in fascination. It was like a mind, but twisted into the wrong shape.

'*This is the neighbour of Zil-Wa-Tem. She sells cleansed oil,*' said the woman.

'You mean she's still alive?' said Wa-Ka-Mo-Do, unable to hide his horror.

'*She will live as long as we decide.*'

'But what has she done?'

'*Nothing.*'

'Then why punish her?'

'*Because she did nothing. She did not defend her neighbour, or the honour of Sangrel.*'

'Is she in pain, her mind twisted like that?'

'*Agony.*'

Almost too fast to follow, Wa-Ka-Mo-Do drew his sword and sliced it through the twisted metal. The Vestal Virgin holding the former mind looked at the two pieces, the cut ends of wire shining like little mirrors, and then dropped it to the floor.

'*You interfere with our work?*' said one of them, in the softest, most beautiful voice.

'This is my city. You interfere with mine.'

The three women exchanged glances.

'*Perhaps you are right, Wa-Ka-Mo-Do.*'

'Perhaps I am.'

'*There is to be an attack tomorrow night. That mind that you destroyed told us this.*'

'Where?'

'*To the south of the city. Robots with blades and oil and petrol. They mean to destroy the crops the humans have planted as a signal to the Emperor of their displeasure.*'

'*The Emperor will be humiliated indeed if his guests were to witness such an occurrence.*'

'I realize that.' He drew himself up. 'Thank you for bringing this to my attention, fair ladies. You can trust me to deal with this.'

The three women gave him smiles of such sweetness.

'*Of course we trust the Honoured Commander of San-grel,*' said one. '*We trust him at all times to remember his duty to his command. We know he will never abandon that duty.*'

'I will not.'

'*And he will do what is required to maintain the harmony of the Emperor?*'

'I will.'

'*Then we shall allow him to continue with his duty.*'

And at that, the three Vestal Virgins left the room by the concealed door.

Wa-Ka-Mo-Do held his poise until they were gone, and then he released the current he had been building up in his electromuscles in one long shudder.

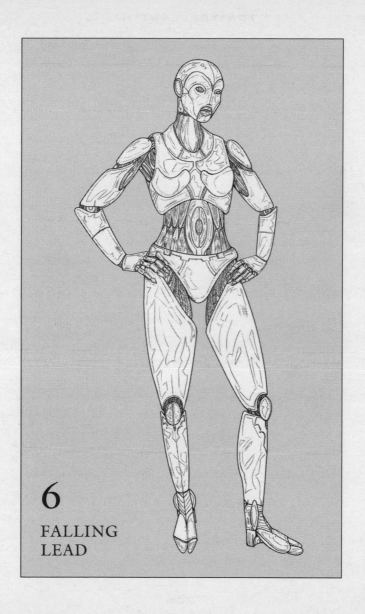

6

FALLING
LEAD

Kavan

Kavan and the Uncertain Army marched down from the mountains onto the plains of Artemis. They marched from the cold remnants of winter that clung to the peaks into the warming summer of the plains, they marched from the petty guerrilla conflicts towards the decisive battle.

They walked out from the shadows of the mountains, towards the bright plains, the rock sheets giving way to stones, then pebbles, then sand. The temperature rose, the glare of the sun ever present in the daytime, the stars clear and cold above at night.

The plains of Artemis vibrated to the stamp of robots. Straggling companies of infantryrobots who had managed to evade the Artemis retreat came to join Kavan and his army. A silver stream of robots in the distance was a garrison from Raman heading south to reinforce Artemis City.

But by far the most numerous, Kavan knew, would be those robots that chose not to make themselves known. They were the ones who would be waiting in the distance, waiting to see which way the forthcoming battle would go. The ones who would emerge to pick over the shattered corpses before blending once more into the background, or who would perhaps come and join the winning side.

So much metal flowing across the plains of Artemis,

swirling and eddying like currents in a pool, with Kavan buoyed along in the centre.

'You know, this battle has been written in the Book of Robots many times before,' said Goeppert. He marched with Kavan for the most part, a group of his robots nearby. Calor and Ada and Goeppert. Kavan's staff.

'There is no such thing,' replied Kavan evenly.

'Of course, there is no *book* as such,' agreed Goeppert, 'but the stories that twist around this planet will be collected into a volume some day, and that will become the Book of Robots.'

'Ah. Verbal trickery. I believe in nothing more than Artemis and metal.'

'Someday Artemis itself will be written in the Book of Robots. You know, Kavan, you should not ignore the stories. They are the verbal equivalent of the patterns twisted into our minds. What is a robot but a story that a mother has woven?'

'Given the choice between a story and a rifle, I would take the latter anytime.'

'Yet you don't seem to carry a rifle, do you?'

Kavan waved a hand at the surrounding army. 'They carry them for me.'

Goeppert laughed.

'Still, Kavan. Nicolas the Coward, Janet Verdigris, Eric and the Mountain. All these stories mean something.'

'Eric and the Mountain?' said Kavan, suddenly interested. 'You know that story?'

'Only the first half. Do you want to hear it?'

Kavan looked at the surrounding army.

'Maybe another time,' he said.

Susan

The midnight streets were filled with light and sound. Electric light, burning flares, the shriek of arc lights all heard over the marching of robots: grey infantryrobots running to their positions; the stamp of Storm Troopers, shouldering all aside as they headed to the front. Only the Scouts passed by unheard, a half-seen flash in the night. The pounding of hammers, the rumble of trains: the city was busy building its defences in readiness for Kavan's attack.

Susan passed amongst the preparation, lost and uncertain where to go, but always moving. It had been so simple to slip away from the making rooms. It was only when she had done so that she realized she had no further plan. She had no idea where Nettie was or how to find her, but she was nonetheless filled with a determination not to return. She kept to the back streets, the narrow alleys, heading vaguely for the centre of the city.

'Hello there.'

The robot moved unusually quietly for a Storm Trooper. He towered over Susan, his matt black panelling only half seen in the darkness. His body looked newly made, but Susan sensed the mind that rode it was old, and cynical, and evil.

'A Turing Citizen, I think,' he said.

'I'm a mother of Artemis,' said Susan.

'Possibly. You're certainly dressed that way. Shouldn't you be down in the making rooms?'

'That's none of your business,' she snapped.

The robot leaned closer to her, the lights of its eyes reflecting from her face. She could feel the current from its strong body.

'You sound angry, but I sense nervousness. I don't think you should be here at all.'

He moved so quickly, seizing Susan by the hand before she had a chance to jump back.

'Let go of me,' she demanded.

'No,' it said. 'That's not real anger. Too frightened. You shouldn't be skulking here, in the back streets, should you? And even if you should, who's going to miss you? As far as I'm concerned you're just metal for me to do with as I will.'

Susan grabbed his hand and feebly tried to prise his fingers free. The Storm Trooper laughed.

'Don't bother! You're not as strong as I am!'

She was cleverer, though. She unsnapped her wrist and ran, leaving the big robot holding her hand. Brief laughter sounded behind her, and then the clatter of metal feet on the stones as the Storm Trooper ran after her. Where to? Where to? She veered towards the bright lights of the wide street ahead. She could see robots moving there, grey infantryrobots, marching along in ranks. Something grabbed her foot, she tripped and slid into the light, her body sparking on the stones.

She came to a halt bathed in electric streetlight, the stamp of marching feet all around her, a steady stream of infantryrobots marching past in perfect time. And, in the centre of all that motion, stillness. Five faces looking down at her. Infantryrobots.

The Storm Trooper loomed above her, still holding her hand in his.

'He tried to rape me,' said Susan. 'Help me.'

'Leave,' said the Storm Trooper. 'She's mine.'

It was the wrong thing to say. Five rifles swung from shoulders and pointed at the black robot.

'Are you telling us what to do?' asked one of the infantryrobots. The Storm Trooper raised itself up, then it seemed to notice the faces of the other soldiers. Susan got the impression that these were experienced fighters. Their bodies were well worn, covered in a fine tracery of scratches.

'What's a mother of Artemis doing roaming the streets with the city preparing for attack?' asked the Storm Trooper.

'I was trying to get back to the making rooms and he captured me,' lied Susan. 'He dragged me down there. He took my hand . . .'

'Give it back to her,' said the lead infantryrobot.

'She's lying!' The Storm Trooper seemed more amused than angry.

A rifle pointed directly at his head.

'Give her back her hand!'

The Storm Trooper dropped the hand to the ground. Susan quickly snapped it back into place.

'I must get back, right now!' she said, and before anyone could stop her, she turned and ran up the street, losing herself in the crowd of marching robots.

The Storm Trooper's voice followed her up the road,

deep and growling, it cut through the sound of the marching.

'I'll be coming for you . . .'

Susan ran up the street, dodging through the moving ranks. Ahead of her she saw a black phalanx of Storm Troopers, and she dodged down another side alley. She was quickly lost in darkness, the lights of the city vanishing as the buildings enfolded her.

Where was she? This was like no part of the city she had been to before. It seemed so empty, and it took Susan a moment to realize that the area in which she walked was almost completely devoid of metal. Stone buildings ran in every direction. Tall and short, wide and long, crammed together higgledy-piggledy, they seemed ancient and modern and everything in between.

It seemed so strange, so un-Artemisian, in a city that prized utility above all else. She walked through an area without purpose. The current in her body seemed to pulse. Somewhere behind her was the Storm Trooper. She imagined him looking for her now, creeping through the darkness, reaching out to seize her shoulder . . .

She spun suddenly around. Nothing. Only darkness. She started at a sudden movement, and then relaxed. Just her hearing and vision turned up full and responding to every stimulus.

She walked carefully on, her path defined by the bright stars above her, irregular patches of light over the dark world.

It was so silent, the sound of the hammering and marching had faded to nothing and for the first time in months Susan felt utterly alone. It was a new sort of fear, different to that instilled by her capture by Artemisian troops. This was the fear of the strange, the unknown. The fear of asymmetric streets under starlight, the fear of empty windows and hollow buildings.

Ahead of her two towers climbed into the night, so tall, their shapes only seen where they occluded the stars. There was something so unsettling about them, she wanted to avoid them, but now all the side roads seemed to have vanished. She could either walk towards them, or back into the arms of the Storm Trooper.

The two towers seemed so sinister, but there was nowhere else to go. They rose higher into the sky as she approached them; they loomed over her.

She found herself walking between them.

'I'm coming . . .'

The Storm Trooper! It was almost a relief to hear the words, their distant menace a thread of familiarity to lead her from this strange night. *Keep away from him, but don't get lost in this empty, silent place.*

She felt the metal door to her side. In the middle of all this stone, its presence seemed amplified. She found herself walking towards it without thinking. It was a stupid thing to do, she realized later. Where else but in here would the Storm Trooper think to look for her? But nonetheless she found herself placing her hand on it, feeling for the catch through the metal, opening it.

She edged into the darkness beyond and pushed the door closed, shutting out the city beyond.

As she did so she heard the movement in the room behind her.

She turned around.

Yellow eyes illuminated the darkness.

Wa-Ka-Mo-Do

Wa-Ka-Mo-Do summoned two dressing women and made his way to the Copper Master's forge. There he stripped away his panelling and allowed the women to clean him, to adjust his electromuscle, to work smooth the roughened bearings, to gently oil him. Red coal light filled the room, white flame flared, pumped by the leather bellows. There was the gentle knock and clank of metal on metal.

The armourer was summoned; she opened a black metal case before him. Inside was a display of pistols arranged in order of colour, alloys running from grey to black.

'May I recommend this one, Honoured Commander?' she said, lifting a black snub-nosed specimen from the case. The grip was smooth, it would be moulded to the shape of Wa-Ka-Mo-Do's hand should he choose it. 'I supervised its construction myself. It is made of steel, obviously, but there is a version in red brass, should you prefer.'

'No, thank you, Ging-Lan-Keralla. Do you have a shotgun?'

The armourer could not quite conceal her look of hurt surprise.

'My apologies, Ging-Lan-Keralla. I did not mean any insult to your craft. But I think a shotgun would be the most suitable weapon within this city. Less lethal, for one thing. And easier to aim at close quarters.'

'The commander is perhaps not used to firearms?'

Wa-Ka-Mo-Do gazed up at the armourer. There was no insult intended, he was sure.

'I am competent, Ging-Lan-Keralla, however I prefer the blade. I would be most pleased if you would sharpen my sword, and the blades of my body.'

At that he extended the blades at his wrists and fingers. He caught the change in the electrical hum of the dressing woman nearest to him and noted how she immediately looked away from his naked form, blades extended. Ging-Lan-Keralla, however, gazed down at him with a look of approval that was entirely down to her craft.

'It will be my pleasure, Honoured Commander. And I shall arrange for a shotgun to be delivered immediately.'

Wa-Ka-Mo-Do was a self-made robot, and his form caused a little confusion to the dressing women, but they worked efficiently enough. Despite the pressure he was under, Wa-Ka-Mo-Do allowed himself to relax: this was one of the arts of a warrior.

Eventually, he was cleaned and fixed and tuned. A dressing woman brought him the first of his panelling, freshly polished.

'My mistake,' he said, taking it from her. 'I should have told you that I was dressing for the field, not the ballroom,' and he showed her how to hold the gleaming scarlet-painted metal in the flame of the fire, blackening it. As he did so Ging-Lan-Keralla returned with a short, black shotgun.

'Thank you,' he said, admiring it. 'But why the wooden stock? Surely that will make it harder to repair?'

'It will. But the Commander of Sangrel is known as a poet as well as a warrior, and that is both a weapon and a thing of beauty.'

'It is indeed,' he replied, turning it in the light.

'Excuse me, Honoured Commander,' said the armourer, taking the gun. She fastened a long leather strap to it, and then slung the gun over his shoulder.

'There. It suits you.'

Wa-Ka-Mo-Do looked at himself in a sheet of polished copper. It did.

'Thank you, Ging-Lan-Keralla. You are a master of your craft.'

Her eyes glowed briefly.

His body oiled and humming sweetly beneath blackened panelling, Wa-Ka-Mo-Do stepped out into the midmorning daylight.

His company was waiting for him in the Street of Becoming, just beyond the Ice Gate.

Eighty robots, in red-brass bodies, their swords sheathed in wood at their left sides, their rifles slung over their right shoulders. They were lined up in compact formation, each robot pressed against the robot in front, a mass of metal pushed together so that virtually no inch of space was anything but robot. Only their eyes moved, following him as he walked to meet them.

Ka-Lo-Re-Harballah was waiting, too.

'Honoured Commander, I wish to be allowed to accompany you on this mission.'

'No, Ka-Lo-Re-Harballah, I want you to remain here. I need you to watch La-Ver-Di-Arussah.'

Ka-Lo-Re-Harballah was visibly shocked.

'But Honoured Commander, she is my superior!'

Wa-Ka-Mo-Do chose a different tack.

'Forgive me, Ka-Lo-Re-Harballah. You understand I am a robot of the High Spires. I do not always express myself as well as robots such as yourself. What I meant to say was that La-Ver-Di-Arussah will find her attention drawn to many events. I wish you to maintain the peace whilst she is otherwise engaged, not to raise the tension.'

'Surely you would be better placed to do so, Honoured Commander. Let me lead the troops instead.'

He was right, realized Wa-Ka-Mo-Do. But the Vestal Virgins had been most insistent that he leave. More than that, Wa-Ka-Mo-Do wanted to see what was happening outside the city.

'No, Ka Lo-Re-Harballah. A good commander should walk the extent of his command. Now, return to the Copper Master's house. I will lead these robots.'

Ka-Lo-Re-Harballah saluted, obviously torn between what he believed to be right and what he believed to be his duty, then turned and made his way back up into the city.

'Captain,' called Wa-Ka-Mo-Do, and a captain detached himself from the crush of robots. He wore bronze flashes on his shoulders. 'Get the robots ready to march.'

'Commander.'

Wa-Ka-Mo-Do watched as the ranks of robots opened up like a bellows. Arms unfolding and legs shuffling free. The company expanded before him, filling the street. He took his place at the head, told the captain to give the order, and the company began to march.

Outside the Ice Gate, Lake Ochoa shone with the healthy blue of copper salts. Wa-Ka-Mo-Do turned his gaze away from the Mound of Eternity, imagining the eyes of the Vestal Virgins upon him. It was a fine day, lit by a yellow sun that warmed the metal of the robots moving busily back and forth around him. He heard the singing of the nearby rails: a train was approaching the station.

'Wa-Ka-Mo-Do! Wa-Ka-Mo-Do!'

The voice came from over towards the lake. A human was running towards him. Rachael. She was wrapping a piece of cloth around herself as she came, concealing the pink-white skin of her body.

'Wa-Ka-Mo-Do! Wait!'

Couldn't she see that he was marching at the head of eighty armed robots? Didn't she realize that he wasn't going to bring the troops to a halt, just for her? It dawned on Wa-Ka-Mo-Do that she really didn't. Humans didn't seem to consider the Empire's work as being important. It wasn't even a considered insult; it was just a simple lack of awareness.

'Wa-Ka-Mo-Do! I know you can hear me!'

He remembered her father's attitude the night before. He didn't want to be seen to insult Rachael again, even unknowingly. Maybe in human terms it was just as wrong to ignore a young woman as it was to give her something to drink. Frustrated, he ordered the captain to call a halt. Beyond him he felt the discharge of electricity, heard the clank of metal as the soldiers stopped.

He turned and waited for Rachael as she ran past the red-brass robots, their bodies warming in the yellow sun.

'Wa-Ka-Mo-Do! You stopped! Thank you!'

Rachael was in front of him, wrapping that strange piece of cloth over her body. It was almost transparent. Through it he could see the two dark strips of cloth she wore around her chest and the top of her thighs. She realized that he was looking at her, and she clutched the cloth tighter. Then she looked straight at him with those copper-blue eyes.

'Wa-Ka-Mo-Do, I wanted to apologize.'

'For what, Rachael?'

'Wa-Ka-Mo-Do, what I did last night was wrong. Tricking you into giving me drinks. I was taking advantage and I shouldn't have. I'm sorry.'

'I accept your apology,' said Wa-Ka-Mo-Do. He was uncomfortably aware of the captain standing by his side, gazing straight ahead.

'I hope I haven't got you into too much trouble?'

'Trouble?' said Wa-Ka-Mo-Do in surprise. 'I'm the Commander of Sangrel.'

'I know that,' said Rachael. 'Listen, I explained everything to my father. It should be okay.'

Again, Wa-Ka-Mo-Do was struck by the humans' attitude to the robots. They certainly did not act like guests of the Emperor. He dismissed the subject.

'All is harmony, Rachael. Now, if you will excuse me . . .'

She finally seemed to notice the soldiers, lined patiently in the sun behind him. The contrast between her soft pink body, barely wrapped in thin cloth, and their hard, steel bodies was marked.

'Oh! I'm sorry! You're busy. I'll get back to the beach. The sun is the best thing about this place. Shame you poisoned the lake.'

'Poisoned? That's copper!'

But she was already gone. He watched her running back towards the lake, the strange cloth flapping behind her.

Susan

'What are you doing in here?'

Yellow eyes gazed at her out of the darkness. Susan turned up her own eyes to get a better look at the stranger. She made out the grey shape of an infantryrobot.

'I'm looking for my friend. She's called Nettie. Have you seen her?'

Susan stepped forward, the other robot moved away, keeping the big stone bowl at the centre of the room between herself and Susan.

'No! She's not here. Now go away. Leave me alone.'

Susan gazed thoughtfully at the other robot.

'You're hiding in here too, aren't you? Have you run away from the battle as well?'

'That's none of your business! Get out of here!'

'I should keep your voice down if I were you. There's a Storm Trooper out there, hunting me.'

The other robot looked at her, trying to decide if she was telling the truth or not.

'I'm Susan. I was from Turing City, I'm now a mother of Artemis. Who are you?'

The other robot's eyes glowed brighter for a moment, and then they dimmed just a fraction.

'Vignette,' she said. 'I'm from Lankum in the central mountains. I was conscripted into the Artemisian army along with the rest of my kingdom when Spoole fled south. We were brought to help in the construction of the trenches they're digging around the city. We were to have been stationed between Kavan's army and the walls of the city, showered by the cannons and the guns of both sides. I wasn't going to have that happen to me, so I slipped away as we marched through the city.'

Vignette's voice echoed oddly in the building. Susan raised a hand.

'Too loud!' she said, 'He's out there, looking for me.'

'Then why did you lead him here to me, you selfish *Tok*? I was safe until you turned up!' Her eyes flashed, more in fear than anger. Susan was patient. She knew what it was like to be frightened.

'There is no safety here in Artemis City. You can only hide for so long. In the end they'll find you, and then . . .'

'You must have been safe,' said Vignette, the envy thick in her voice. 'The mothers of Artemis work beneath the ground, away from danger.'

'Raped twice a night.' Susan laughed bitterly. 'I'd rather take my chances in the trenches.'

Vignette gazed at her, eyes glowing in the darkness.

'I'd rather shelter in the making rooms.'

'That's immaterial. What is done is done.'

Susan spoke with bitter finality.

'No it's not,' said Vignette. 'Change places with me. Swap your body for mine.'

The idea brought Susan up short. Swap their bodies? It had its attractions. Surely an infantryrobot would fare better in the city at the moment? She would certainly be less noticeable in that grey body. Would that aid in her search for her friend?

'But how?' she said, slowly. 'We'd need a third robot to unplug our coils.'

'The robot at the top of this tower would do it. We could ask him.'

Susan felt as if she had wandered into a children's story.

'What robot at the top of the tower? Where are we? What is this place?'

'You don't know? Have you never seen a shot tower? We used to have one in Lankum like this, only ours was taller. We carved a groove in the side of the mountain, and then built a tower on the top of it. There was a copper sieve at the top through which molten lead fell in drops. It formed into spheres as it fell and then landed in a basin of water at the bottom.'

Susan looked up, the light of her gaze lost in the darkness. The tower was a spiral of stone. A robot could walk up the interior wall to the top, she realized.

'Who is he, the robot up there?'

'He's the robot who built this tower. His wife built the one opposite.'

'How do you know this?'

'He told me.'

'Why is he still here?'

'He's waiting for lead. Sometimes Artemis needs more spherical shot than it can produce elsewhere.'

Susan looked down at the stone bowl. She saw the water inside, as still as the night outside.

'You know that if you leave this tower in my body, the Storm Trooper out there will rape you?'

'Better than dying in the trenches,' said Vignette.

Susan looked up again, up to the top of the tower.

'Very well,' she said. 'Let's exchange bodies.'

They climbed the tower's interior and emerged into the night. Susan found herself standing on an island of darkness in the middle of the illuminated city. Up here the night sky billowed with stars. In the distance, around the edge of the dark sea of this strange, forgotten collection of buildings, light bloomed. It blossomed in yellow flames from chimneys, it glowed deep red from forges, it reflected in gold and silver from metal towers and aerials. Beyond it there was the darkness of the Artemisian plain. Susan gazed out, wondering if she could see the lights of Kavan's army out there, moving to surround the city. Was Karel somewhere out there too, separated from her by two armies? Was Nettie trapped in here with her?

'Bouvan?' called Vignette. 'Are you there?'

Susan gazed into the darkness at the centre of the tower. She was standing on a circle of stone that surrounded the three hundred foot drop. Something was moving, something was rising from the centre of the tower.

'Bouvan?' said Vignette again. 'This is Susan.'

Bouvan had the longest arms and legs of any robot Susan had ever seen. She realized he must live wedged in the space at the top of the tower.

'What do you want?' Bouvan spoke in the flat tones of an unfused robot.

'We want you to swap over our minds,' said Vignette.

'Very well,' said Bouvan. Susan recoiled as a hand reached towards her on the end of an impossibly long arm, felt a surge of current as she realized how close she had come to stepping back over the edge.

'Hold on a moment!' she shouted, suddenly uncomfortably aware of what she was agreeing to. Allowing another robot to unplug her coil, leaving her perfectly helpless. 'How can I trust you both?' she said. 'How do I know that you will reattach my mind?'

'I'll go first,' said Vignette.

'Hey, you!'

The voice came from behind her. Susan turned and looked out over the darkness to the other shot tower. Down on the street they had seemed so far apart. Up here, in the stillness beneath the twinkling stars, she almost felt as if she could jump from one to the other. Ridiculous, of course. They must be sixty feet apart.

'Yes, you!' Sound travelled easily in the clear air, that voice could have come from a robot standing just by her. She looked and saw another robot standing at the top of the other tower. She looked just like Bouvan, and

Susan realized that this must be the wife Vignette had talked about.

'Listen, lady! You don't want to trust him! He'll fumble and break your coil! Come over here, I'll change your minds!'

Bouvan's eyes flashed in the darkness and he spoke with an emotion that completely contradicted Susan's first assessment of him as being unfused.

'Shut up, Appovan!' he shouted across the night. 'Why do you always have to interfere? This is my tower, they came to me.' He turned back to Vignette. 'Come here, I'll be gentle.'

He was too. Susan saw the way that he felt around the infantryrobot's neck and gently opened up the head and pulled the mind clear, unplugging the coil as he did so. He laid the body carefully down on the top of the tower.

'There,' he said, holding the twisted metal of a mind towards Susan with his incredibly long arm. She looked to see the coil intact. A sense of vertigo overcame her.

Be careful not to drop it! The words never made it to her voicebox.

Bouvan could see the look of satisfaction on the robot's face at his successful removal of Vignette's mind. 'Your turn,' he said. She hesitated.

'He'll drop you!' called Appovan from her tower. 'He's always been the same. Clumsy! It took him for ever to build that tower, he was always dropping stones. He hit a soldier once! Flattened her! It's a wonder they didn't melt him down for scrap . . .'

'Shut up, woman!' shouted Bouvan, eyes flaring.

This was all so unreal, thought Susan, standing here above the world, listening to the two of them argue.

'You built the tower?' she said.

'Oh yes. It took me nearly thirty years. Don't listen to *her* talking about me being clumsy. It took *her* longer. Couldn't find the right sort of stone, always trying to make patterns, like that was going to make the shot any better.'

'But that can't be right,' interrupted Susan, 'this tower looks so old. How old are you?'

'One hundred and fifty years old,' said Bouvan.

'Don't listen to him!' called Appovan. 'I'm not a day over twenty!'

'No robot lives that long,' said Susan.

'They do if they're half-fused,' said Bouvan, 'like me and her. This is Half-fused City you're in. Didn't you know that?'

Half-fused. Suddenly it all made sense to Susan. Robots of limited intelligence, but robots that lived longer and were stronger. Robots like the ones Nettie had told her about, the sort of minds that Susan would soon have been twisting, had she stayed in the making rooms.

'Come on, lady. I'll swap your head with hers.'

'He'll drop it!' called Appovan. 'He dropped a block of half-melted lead once. What a waste! They were looking for bits of metal for weeks afterwards! Weeks!'

Susan wanted to run back down the steps of the tower, down to the streets below.

Down to where the Storm Trooper searched for her. That thought brought her up short.

She looked back at Bouvan, the half-fused robot. She had had the plan for a half-fused mind explained to her, and she understood something: such a robot would be too stupid to lie. In that sense, she could trust it.

'Okay,' she said. 'Do it. Swap my head with hers.'

She carefully lay face down on the floor. She felt something touch the back of her head, then her sense of the world vanished, leaving her in darkness and silence. She waited for sensation to return.

And waited.

What if it were a trick?

It was a trick! How could she have been so stupid? To give her mind to a complete stranger, a mad robot who lived on a tower high above the city. Maybe he *had* dropped her? How would she know? Would there just be sudden oblivion, her thoughts ceasing to exist? Or would her mind be damaged, twisted out of shape? Would she begin to imagine strange places, strange thoughts? Trapped in a twisted world of her own mind?

Then, just like that, sense returned. She could see darkness again, and a long hand moved and she was gazing at the stars.

'Careful!' called out a voice. Her own. That was confusing. She hadn't spoken, she was sure of it.

She remembered where she was, and she realized who had spoken. That was Vignette, now in her old body. She lay still for a moment, getting the feel of her new body. It was really quite well made, she realized. She moved her hands, felt for the edge of the ledge on which she lay, sat up slowly, and she recognized a fellow crafts-robot's work. This body was made of cheap materials, it was true, but an expert job had been made of the construction.

She looked across the other side of the circular chimney to see Vignette gazing back.

'You build well,' said the other robot.

Susan felt a sudden stab of jealousy. Vignette was wearing her old body, now she had the use of all the good metal that had gone into its making. Now Vignette looked well made and attractive, a true mother. And she, Susan, was just another infantryrobot.

But this is what she had wanted.

'You build well, too,' she replied. The two robots exchanged a look of mutual respect.

Susan got to her feet.

'Are you going?' asked Bouvan.

'Of course they're going,' shouted Appovan from across the way. 'No one ever stays up here, do they?'

'I used to know other robots,' said Bouvan. 'Back when I lived on the ground, but I had to go higher and higher. It's always been in me to beat Appovan. So they brought me stones and I started to build. Now I live up here, all alone.'

'You've got me, haven't you?' called Appovan.

'But I don't like you.'

'And I don't like you.'

'Please don't leave me alone,' said Bouvan.

'Come down with us,' said Susan.

'I can't. I have to stay up here. That's the way my mind was made.'

Susan hesitated.

'Listen,' she said. 'I have to find my friend. I don't

know where she is, but I need to find her. But when I do, I'll come back here, if I can.'

She was lying, and she knew it. She couldn't imagine how she could *ever* return here. Not with Kavan about to attack the city. Not with her a fugitive, fleeing from the making rooms, but she had to say something.

'Thank you,' said Bouvan, and he seemed so pathetically grateful that Susan felt ashamed.

'Come on,' called Vignette, already descending the steps.

Susan gave a last wave to Bouvan and then followed her. As she went she heard Appovan's voice.

'She's never coming back, you old fool. She was lying so she could get away from you.'

'She wasn't,' said Bouvan. 'I did her a favour! She'll repay it!'

Susan turned her hearing right down, shame building within her, and followed Vignette down the stairs.

They reached the bottom of the steps and Vignette made to open the door.

'Hold it!' called Susan.

Vignette turned back to look at her. Silence. Susan remembered she had turned down her hearing.

'What is it?' repeated Vignette.

'Don't forget, there's a Storm Trooper out there looking for me. He'll be looking for you, now, given that you're wearing my body.'

Vignette looked down at herself.

'So what do we do?'

'Let me go first. Let me do the talking if we meet him.'

Susan pushed the door open and peered out into the night. There was nothing, just the starlit street, the eerie, empty buildings.

Silently, she signalled to Vignette, and the two of them slipped from the tower, pushed up against the shadows. Susan was impressed at how the grey paint of her new body blended into the surroundings.

She began to move down the street, but Vignette put a hand on her arm.

'Wait,' she said, so softly. 'They trained us in this when I was conscripted. Take a few moments to tune in with your surroundings.'

Susan did so.

The dark buildings around her seemed to solidify into view, partially illuminated by the dark sky above. She wondered if any of them housed others of the half-fused, ancient and forgotten. Strange, it was so un-Artemisian, leaving metal in a place without a purpose.

'Okay,' said Vignette. She began to move down the wall, heading back the way that Susan had come earlier.

'Not that way!' said Susan. 'He's back there some-where.'

'There's nothing the other way,' said Vignette. 'Just the Centre City. We don't want to go there . . .'

Her words were lost in a flurry of movement. Susan saw something big and black hurtle past, she heard the clatter of metal on metal, of metal slamming onto brick and stone.

'Stupid, Stupid, Stupid!'

It was the Storm Trooper, it was on top of Vignette,

had both her hands clasped in one of his. He was sitting on her chest, his big body humming with power.

'Only two places to hide. Through this door or that one. I only had to sit and wait to see which you emerged from. But hold on . . .' He looked closer, looked into Vignette's eyes. 'You're not the woman I found earlier. Who are you?'

Susan brought down both her hands as hard as she could on the back of the Storm Trooper's neck, hoping to break the coil there. There was a dull thud and pain shot through the electromuscles of her hand.

The Storm Trooper moved so fast, his arm swung back and caught Susan's head, cracking an eye and sending an electric snowstorm fizzing across her sight.

Vignette had twisted one hand free, but she wasn't fighting, she was patiently fiddling with the Storm Trooper's wrist.

'Hey, stop that!'

The Storm Trooper turned his attention back to Vignette, and Susan dived for his free arm, grabbing it through the storm of electricity that danced across her broken vision. It was enough time for Vignette to finish what she was doing: she had unshipped the Storm Trooper's hand. He let out an electronic roar and brought his other hand down on her head, denting it.

Now Susan grabbed him around the neck again and set to work finding her way through the panelling there, trying to locate his coil. Bright lights swirled around her, she wasn't sure if it was feedback or the stars above.

'What are you doing, you rusty *Tokvah*? Get off me!'

The Storm Trooper wasn't shouting at her. Her world lurched as he got to his feet, and Susan saw Vignette there on the floor, a wicked smile on her face, twisted metal around her hands, and she realized that Vignette had pulled it from the Storm Trooper, *pulled it from between his legs.*

'You little *Spartz!*'

Vignette giggled, tugged harder at the pliable blue wire. The Storm Trooper yelled again, stamped down hard on Vignette's thigh. She let out an electronic squeal of pain, but she tugged harder on the wire. The Storm Trooper jerked back and Susan, still clinging to his neck, fought to keep her grip. She scrabbled again at the panelling there, but he was too well designed, there was no easy access to his coil.

Now the Storm Trooper reached back with his one remaining hand, and Susan saw her chance. The panelling at his shoulder lifted a little as he raised his arm, and she took hold of it, jerked it upwards, stabbed up into exposed electromuscle and smiled grimly as he shrieked. Vignette kept pulling more wire from the Storm Trooper, wrapping it around his legs, tangling him up, sending him mad with rage. He kicked at her, catching her full in the chest, denting it badly, but still she fought on. Susan wriggled her fingers in the electromuscle at the shoulder, trying to get a grip, trying to tangle it, squeeze it, short it. She sent as much current through her hand as she could, there was a blue flash and the arm fell to his side, useless.

And that was the beginning of the end for the Storm Trooper. He fought viciously, he had strength and power on his side, but he was fighting two women who were in the grip of a passion that had lain dormant all this time they had been in Artemis. It was a hatred that had grown in muffled darkness, repressed and compressed whilst the women struggled to survive. Now it arose with a vengeance, with a spitefulness and a loathing that was taken out on his metal body. They didn't kill him: they tore off his metal panelling and removed his electro-muscle in strips, they humiliated him, tying him up in his own wire. Then they left him, a mind marooned in a broken body whilst they stripped parts from him to repair themselves. Vignette removed one of his eyes and used it to replace the one of Susan's he had broken. Susan bent some more of his metal with her own hands and used it to patch Vignette's broken chest.

'Go to the making rooms,' she said. 'They will fix you up there. You will make a good mother of Artemis. You handle metal well.'

The Storm Trooper watched them with his one remaining eye. Occasionally, he let out an electronic moan. Eventually, Vignette detached his voicebox so they didn't have to listen to him.

'You seemed so afraid when I first saw you in the base of the tower,' said Susan.

'I was,' said Vignette. 'I ran away for too long. Perhaps now is the time to fight. First, though, I will go to the making rooms. And then, who knows? What about you?'

'I'll head for the Centre City,' said Susan. 'Perhaps my friend was taken there.'

'You'll only get so far dressed in that body.'

'Then perhaps I will find myself on the front line. There are worse things that could happen.'

'Will that help find your friend?'

'No.'

Vignette reached out and touched Susan's shell, pulled loose a piece of swarf.

'Stay smart,' she said, suddenly practical. 'Listen. I heard that the Generals are in disagreement. My advice, find one of the weaker ones and attach yourself to their staff. They'll be grateful for your support. And you'll be closer to the centre of power.'

'Find a General? I don't know anything about them.'

'Learn. Go in search of Spoole, he's isolated now.'

'Spoole? He's the robot who had my city destroyed. If I were ever to meet him, I think I would kill him.'

Vignette smiled.

'So you say. I always thought I would fight to the death, and yet look at me now, running away to hide in the middle of the enemy's city. Until you live the reality, you can never be sure the way your mind is woven. It turns out that my mother wove my mind to place my survival above all else. Would killing Spoole help you find your friend? Would it help you find your husband?'

Susan said nothing. She knew the way her mind was woven: her mother had made her mind to look after her husband, first and foremost. It was a current-draining moment, to realize that her thoughts of revenge meant nothing compared to this truth: that she could calmly work with the man who was ultimately responsible for her child's death if it brought her closer to Karel.

'You understand what I'm talking about, don't you?'

They gazed at each other for a moment. Vignette looked down at the broken body of the Storm Trooper.

'He'll have heard everything we said.'

Whatever cold hatred had filled Susan's mind in the middle of the fighting was suddenly gone.

'We have to kill him,' said Vignette.

'I know,' said Susan. 'But I don't think I can.'

'I can,' said Vignette.

She bent down said something so softly that Susan didn't hear it. Then she reached around behind his neck and broke his coil.

'What did you say to him?' asked Susan.

Vignette wore a nasty expression.

'I told him that his wire was weak and of low quality.'

'That was cruel.'

'He would have killed us!'

'He was only acting the way he was woven.' Susan was suddenly sad.

'Then so am I,' said Vignette, coldly. Her eyes glowed for a moment and then faded back to normal level.

'Good luck, Susan,' she said.

'You too.'

The two women turned and headed off in opposite directions. Back to the lights of Artemis City.

Back to the approaching war.

Wa-Ka-Mo-Do

Wa-Ka-Mo-Do and the rest of the troop waited amongst the tall shapes of the human crops. The plants were so strange. Where robot plants were thin and fibrous, ideal for making paper and other useful materials, these human crops were mutants, the yellow fruits at the top of the stalks hugely oversized, so heavy they threatened to topple the whole plant. No wonder the farmers out here were so angry! What use would plants like this be to the robots of Sangrel?

He raised himself up and peered north through the top of the stalks.

From this distance, Sangrel was a scene of golden radiance set on a black throne. The city was a collection of jewelled lights beneath the bright stars. Wa-Ka-Mo-Do wondered what was happening back there. Was La-Ver-Di-Arussah following his orders? There was nothing he could do about it out here, that was certain.

He thought back over the past few days, wondering at the events in this province: his presence in Sangrel, the death in the market place, the trouble in Ell, the trouble that threatened here tonight, the humans.

The humans were more powerful than the Emperor had led him to believe. Yet there was something more . . . He thought of Rachael, the night before. Her father's behaviour, the way that her translator had kept cutting out.

What was it they were holding back? Did the Emperor know?

He remembered the Emperor's insistence that this had nothing to do with the Book of Robots.

It was funny, robots like La-Ver-Di-Arussah mocked him, questioned out loud if he believed in the Book of Robots.

How could they be so stupid? Of course he didn't. Wa-Ka-Mo-Do had the knowledge woven directly into his mind by his mother. He didn't *believe* in the book, he *knew* it to be true. He knew that there was a pattern of instructions for the first robot mind. He knew that there was a way robots were supposed to be.

What terrified him was the thought that he may have met his makers. He hoped that it wasn't true.

Someone tapped him on the shoulder, and he turned to see the captain beckoning. He followed him through the tall plants, pushing aside the mutant stalks until they came to a path trampled through the centre of the crops. Wa-Ka-Mo-Do bent down to examine the trail. It was recent. Quickly, silently, he followed it until it came to a fork. He listened carefully. He could hear a sound in the distance. Robots trying to move quietly.

Wa-Ka-Mo-Do pointed to one path after the other, indicating that the troops should split up. The captain nodded and gestured to some of the red brass soldiers behind him. Wa-Ka-Mo-Do watched them lope quickly down the path, impressed. These soldiers were well built and well trained. A few civilians should present them with no problems.

He signalled to the remaining soldiers to follow, and led them silently down the path. Up ahead he could hear the sound of splashing. Petrol. They were going to set fire to the crops, just as the Vestal Virgins had predicted. He unslung his shotgun and swept it in a wide circle, indicating that the soldiers should fan out.

Somewhere in the distance he heard the crackle of gunfire, and he realized it was the captain attacking.

'Now!' he shouted.

The soldiers jumped forward, surprising the saboteurs, firing once, twice. They dropped their petrol canisters. Wa-Ka-Mo-Do drew his sword and slashed down at a third robot. The saboteurs were efficiently dispatched.

'Stop!' he commanded, holding the blade of his sword before a soldier's raised gun. 'We need at least one to question.'

The hum of current died away, leaving the robots standing amongst the broken stalks. Broken bodies lay around them, the living still squealing in electronic pain. As for the dead: twisted metal uncoiled across the ground. Wa-Ka-Mo-Do suddenly realized just how pathetic these people were. Their panelling was of cheap tin, they hummed and buzzed as they moved. They sounded as if their electromuscles were full of dust and dirt. He could see how poorly repaired they were, and he wondered when they had last seen the inside of a forge.

'On your knees,' shouted a soldier, pushing the captive down. She reached out and unfastened one arm, whilst another soldier did the same on the other side.

'Please don't kill me,' begged the saboteur on the ground. 'My husband, my children—'

'Silence,' said Wa-Ka-Mo-Do. He didn't feel any particular anger towards this being. Rather he felt pity; pity at her circumstances, at what she had been reduced to.

'How many more of you are there?' he demanded.

'There were twelve of us, Honoured Commander.'

'Why do you act in this fashion?'

'We have no land, Honoured Commander. We have

no purpose, no place to go. We wanted someone to heed our situation. The Emperor is merciful and wise and just. He will surely act when he is aware of our plight!'

'You seek to sabotage his lands!'

'We meant no harm to the Emperor! You must believe me! We only harm the humans' possessions.'

'And risk the Emperor losing face in doing so?'

The saboteur looked at the floor in shame.

'Honoured Commander!'

One of the soldiers was holding up a metal canister. There was something very peculiar about its shape.

'Is that of human construction?' asked Wa-Ka-Mo-Do.

'I think so. It's what they were using to carry the petrol.'

Wa-Ka-Mo-Do turned back to the captive.

'More dishonour! Where did you steal that from?'

'Honoured Commander! I swear we did not! It was waiting for us at the edge of the fields, as we were told it would be.'

Wa-Ka-Mo-Do took hold of the can and felt the metal with his hand. It reminded him a little of the chain Rachael had worn: good quality metal but poorly constructed.

'Who told you it would be there?'

'We never got to see our intermediary.'

'No, you wouldn't.' Wa-Ka-Mo-Do was silent. He looked down at the woman before him. She had mentioned a husband and children. 'You realize the penalty for your crime is death?'

The woman said nothing. She looked so pathetic,

kneeling there, her arms removed, her tin body filled with dust and dirt.

'Though it gives me no pleasure to carry out the execution, I have nothing but sympathy for you.'

Wa-Ka-Mo-Do was merciful indeed. His sword had struck as he spoke these last words. The saboteur was dead before she was even aware of it. Wa-Ka-Mo-Do gazed down at her.

'Bring the metal back to the city,' he said.

'What about the petrol canister, Honoured Commander?'

'Bring that too. But conceal it.'

He looked at it again, puzzled.

'Someone is using these people. There is more to this than a few upset farmers, I am sure. Who is behind all this?'

'Commander?'

'Nothing.'

They waited at the edge of the fields for the rest of the soldiers to rejoin them.

'All this way for a few peasants,' said Wa-Ka-Mo-Do as the captain took his place at his side.

'It could have been serious had they caused any damage, Honoured Commander.'

'Perhaps. I can't help thinking that was not the primary reason I was brought here.'

He looked northwards, back to Sangrel. It looked so beautiful, a copper sculpture beneath the silver stars.

'Why am I here?'

'Commander?'

'All that is happening in Sangrel at the moment. In Yukawa . . . What's that?'

It took a moment longer for the captain and the rest of the army to hear it: a thrumming, drumming noise.

'It sounds like an army attacking the sky with their swords,' said Wa-Ka-Mo-Do.

A low droning sounded, and then a pattern of lights awoke in the night.

'Human machines,' said the captain. 'I've seen them before, in the distance.'

The noise grew louder, Wa-Ka-Mo-Do's body reverberated to it.

'They're coming towards us.'

'Not us,' said Wa-Ka-Mo-Do. 'They're heading for Sangrel.'

Now he could make out dark shapes against the bright stars. Lumpy objects that hung sullenly in the sky, bristling with spikes.

'They're carrying guns,' he realized. 'Have these craft ever been seen around Sangrel before?'

'No,' said the captain.

'You know,' mused Wa-Ka-Mo-Do out loud. 'All is harmony in the Empire . . .' He knew it was a lie, but he wanted to follow this thought to the end. 'But there are other lands on Penrose. Primitive, backward lands. Each inhabited by their own race of robots.'

'Yes, Honoured Commander?'

They watched as the craft droned slowly past. The cockpits were illuminated by faint light, and they could just make out the shape of the animals sitting in there.

'Even in the Empire there are those robots who dissent,' continued Wa-Ka-Mo-Do . 'Look at the events this night. The humans arrived here and we naturally assumed they are all of one tribe. But why should they be any different to us?'

He almost had it. The answer was almost there. The thought of Ell sprang into his mind, of the train taken over by the Silent Wind. What did the Emperor know that he wasn't telling? It was obvious now.

'What if there are several tribes of humans here?'

As he spoke, five flares lit themselves at the same time, five streaks of flame leaped from the flying craft, streaking forward towards the illuminated city on the mound to the north.

'What are they?' asked the captain. But they both knew the answer. Five explosions rumbled in the distance.

'They're attacking Sangrel,' said Wa-Ka-Mo-Do.

Kavan

Artemis City sat in the middle of the wide plain of Artemis. The city was visible from miles away, its great bulk a brooding presence in the distance, a constant reminder of the ultimate power on the continent of Shull.

There was no avoiding the fact of its existence. By day, the sunlight reflected on the windows of the Centre City, black streamers of smoke pumped from the chimneys of the forges trailed across the sky. By night the lights of its streets sparkled like a diadem around the red and gold flames of the fires that burned hot in the brick foundries.

Artemis City, the biggest concentration of power and metal and force on the entire continent.

It seemed that most of the robots of Shull were converging on it, marching by day and night.

The city had become the target for every grievance, grudge and dream on the continent. Even the railway lines seemed affected: where once they had seemed to spread across the land, carrying Artemis across the continent, now they seemed to converge upon the city.

Kavan had divided the Uncertain Army into two wide columns. It had been his original intention to plunge the army straight into the heart of the city, but, in consultation with Ada, that plan had changed. Calor and the other Scouts had brought him word of other troops, also marching. There were robots heading towards the city from all directions. The remnants of Stark, armoured divisions who had long waged guerrilla war against Artemis from the central mountain range, were approaching the city from the west. A company had emerged from the sea near Turing City State and were marching north. And then there was Goeppert and the robots who had joined them from Raman and Born . . .

Kavan spoke a lot with Goeppert and Ada as they marched south, the Uncertain Army raising trails of dust into the bright sky. They were discussing tactics, constantly updating their plans on the basis of information brought to them by Calor and the rest.

It looked like it was going to be a siege, not that Kavan

should have expected anything else from Spoole and the Generals. Actually, it was a sensible tactic on their part. They held the advantage. This land had long been stripped almost bare by Artemis. The little metal that remained was now being removed too. Kavan saw the last trains retreating ahead of them, loaded up with coal and ore and the disassembled parts of the few scattered forges and factories that had lain on this plain. After they had passed by, the railway lines themselves were taken up and pulled back into the city.

'How much further?' Kavan asked Calor.

'One day's travel. You'll be there tonight.'

'What will I find?'

'There are three huge moats dug around the city, one inside the other. They have left troops marooned on the banks of the trenches, conscripts mostly.'

'Good. If we lay bridges to them, then they will join us.'

'There are Storm Troopers amongst them, Kavan. They will make them fight to the death, one way or another.'

'Is there no way around the moats?'

'None. The city is completely isolated. Beyond the trenches, they have built a wall of iron. One hundred feet high and twenty feet thick.'

'It won't be solid iron,' laughed Ada. 'That would be ten and a half million cubic feet of iron per mile!'

Calor glanced at Ada and buzzed in frustration.

'Go on, Calor,' said Kavan.

She turned back to Kavan. 'Every three hundred feet

there is a guard tower, and on each tower there are cannons.'

'I wonder how the people within the city feel about that? They will know that hiding behind walls is not Nyro's way.'

The morning was bright and still cold from the night. It felt good to march across the flat plain, electromuscles pleasantly cool, the ground firm beneath his feet. Despite the fact he had rarely been there, Kavan felt as if he was coming home. The other robots felt it too, he was sure. There were so many of them, they were marching with a purpose towards Artemis City. They could see it in the distance, like a ship sailing across a calm sea, trailing smoke behind it.

'There are already soldiers taking up positions around the city,' said Calor.

'Where have they come from?'

'Some of them are your own troops, Kavan. Scouts and infantryrobots who have gone ahead of the pack. Some of them have just turned up on their own.'

'And what have the people in the city done?'

'Nothing, as yet. A few stray shots, the odd cannon shell.'

'Then they've lost already,' said Kavan. 'If I were in that city I would have sent out a party of soldiers to wipe out small concentrations of the enemy before they had a chance to set up their positions. Why make things easy for them?'

'They can't come out,' said Calor. 'They are trapped behind their own moats.'

'There are no drawbridges?'

'There isn't even a gate in their iron wall.'

'Then they've not only locked us out, they've locked their own robots in.'

'They're not true Artemisians,' said Calor.

'No,' said Kavan, but he was experiencing something very rare. Doubt. Spoole wasn't a fool. Why would he trap himself like that? What were they planning in there?

Kavan had travelled a long way. Starting alone on the northern coast of Shull, he had walked over a thousand miles, through hills and valleys, over the mountains, and finally over this vast plain, all the while picking up an army as he went.

Well, an army of sorts.

It lacked discipline and organization, but to Kavan it was just another tool to Nyro's purpose. All that metal would end up in the forges and furnaces of Artemis City one way or other. Even himself.

And now he was finally arriving at his destination, just as night approached. He walked near the centre of the army, as he had done all the way here, not quite a leader, not quite a prisoner.

Ahead of him two streams of metal were flowing around the city. The sparks and flames from the distant chimneys danced, half seen, against the darkening sky. The tiny figures of robots could be seen on the top of the iron wall, rushing this way and that, getting themselves into position. Kavan thought he could hear sirens sounding from inside the city.

Closer and closer, he became aware of something that

had been a growing presence in his life these past few weeks, something he had put from his mind: the sound of marching feet. The hum and spark and crash of so much metal, striking the ground as one. He realized something else: that over time these robots, this ramshackle array of men and women, had gradually begun to march in time with each other. Order had arisen from the chaos, and Kavan felt an incredible sense of inevitability as to what was to follow. He looked at Goeppert, marching nearby, strange elongated body keeping perfect time, and he was struck by a sudden insight. He, Kavan, was in the middle of a story, a story that would maybe one day find itself written in the Book of Robots – if indeed such a thing existed.

Now he had reached the place where the columns divided, and he followed the left-hand stream. To his side he saw, not four hundred yards away, the edge of the first moat. And beyond that, the grey bodies of infantryrobots, marooned there to fight him and his army. They just stood and gazed at the seemingly endless stream of robots that marched past them. No one on the moat raised a gun in challenge, nor did any members of the Uncertain Army.

Kavan marched on, following the length of the iron wall to his right. From the ramparts, more robots gazed down at him, their gradually darkening silhouettes lit by the golden light behind them.

A flash of silver, and Calor appeared at his side.

'Something's up, Kavan. They just stand there, watching us.'

'They'll be hoping to settle this by words,' replied Kavan.

The robots ahead were coming to a halt; a wave of stationary metal seemed to travel back through the moving stream.

Kavan, Ada, Calor, Goeppert and the rest stopped. They turned to face the city.

'Now what?' asked Calor.

Kavan looked to the left and right, searching for any signs of weakness in the seemingly impassable wall. There were none. For the moment.

'Now what?' repeated Calor.

'Is there any question about it?' said Kavan. 'Now we attack.'

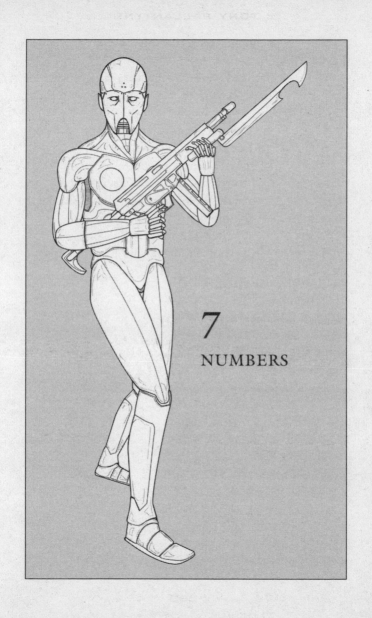

7

NUMBERS

Susan

Years ago, Karel had told her about the Centre City, long before the war had come to Turing City State.

'It's the *utility* of the place, Susan,' he had said, eyes glowing as he remembered his recent trip. 'Everything is just iron and steel and brick. There is no decoration, no paint, save what they use to keep the rust at bay. I walked down streets surrounded by grey and green and blue robots, and I saw nothing there that didn't have a purpose.'

'They'll be making a point,' Susan had said. 'It won't be the same inside the buildings, you can trust me on that!'

'No, you don't understand! That's not the way they think in Artemis City. To them, everything is bent towards Nyro's purpose.'

'That will be what they say,' laughed Susan. 'There will be some variation in the way their minds are twisted. There always is! Listen to me, I'm a mother. I know what it's like to make a mind. There'll be decoration somewhere in that city. And even brutal utilitarianism is a sort of aesthetic statement.'

'I realize that. But it's different there, Susan. They really believe in what they're doing!'

'Most of them will,' Susan agreed. 'But anyway, I don't like you going there Karel. I don't like what Artemis City is doing. They say they are going to attack Wien!'

'They may do.' Karel had been suddenly serious. 'But that's the way they think. It's the way their minds are twisted. That's what I'm trying to explain!'

'Then I don't like the way their minds are twisted.'

'Well, at least they are true to themselves. You can see it in their Centre City. You'd understand if you could see it for yourself.'

'Well, I don't think I ever will . . .'

But she had been wrong on both counts. Here she was now, thought Susan, and look, Karel had been right.

The Centre City was well made, but it was utilitarian from top to bottom. The road was constructed of good brick, as were the walls. There were steel and iron pillars and doors, steel window frames and guttering and copper tiling, and that was it. It wasn't like the centre of Turing City, where metal had leaped in loops and arches, and stained glass and copper and brass chasing had decorated every surface. The paint in Turing City had been of all colours; here, if paint was used at all, it was the same standard red lead, splashed onto the metal with little waste but little care.

There was a stillness in the middle of the Centre City. Occasionally she would see a figure, hurrying along in the distance, or a door would open and shut further down the street, and a clerk of some kind would come dashing past.

One of them had called out, 'Kavan is here!' as he hurried by, three rolls of foil tucked beneath his arm. The panelling around his legs was loose, as if he had been suddenly called away while tending himself. She watched him go, and then turned and resumed her wandering through the streets.

This was where the computers worked, she knew. This was where the calculations were performed that balanced metal coming into the city with robots walking out. All the numbers that modelled the Artemisian State were brought here on sheets of foil: tons of coal mined, yards of railway line laid, gallons of petroleum refined, number of robots built, number of robots conscripted . . . All of these were added and multiplied, means and standard deviations calculated, regression lines plotted on yet more sheets of foil, and then reports were compiled, the mass of data reduced to a few lines of figures and graphs, and then those results inscribed on yet another sheet of foil that would be passed to the leaders of Artemis, that they could better decide their future strategy.

Susan understood all that, it was what she used to do back in Turing City, though for very different reasons. There it had been about maximizing happiness. There they hadn't exactly tried to put a number on beauty, but they had at least attempted to model curves both on foil and in actual steel that were pleasing to the eye.

Even so, Susan was confident of this: that whatever had happened to Nettie would be logged here somewhere. Somewhere amongst the millions of sheets of foil that resided here would be the record of what had happened to her friend. Find Nettie, and then maybe she would be ready to look for Karel. If he hadn't found her first.

All she had to do was find the correct sheet.

Another robot came hurrying towards her, his shell painted the green of a computer.

'Hey,' she called. 'I'm looking for Spoole. Where is he?'

'In the Basilica, I should think. You should try the Main Index, two blocks over,' said the robot. 'Though you won't find anyone to help you there. They're on a stripped-down staff what with Kavan and everything.'

'That's okay, I've got my orders.'

'Really?' said the other robot, suddenly suspicious. 'And what are they? Shouldn't you be on the walls with the other infantry?'

'No,' said Susan. 'And my orders are none of your business. I've been sent here on an important job.'

Susan had killed another robot not half an hour ago. At the moment she felt as if she could do anything. Facing down a computer was the least of her worries. She held his gaze.

'Okay,' he said, 'fine. We've all got our jobs to do.' And he hurried off down the road.

Susan set off in the direction he had indicated. The streets seemed hollow, empty of life and movement. Nothing but steel doors set in red-brick walls. One of them opened and another computer appeared. Her courage had not yet deserted her; she decided to bluff it out.

'I'm looking for Spoole,' she said.

'Only one of you?'

'How many did Spoole expect?'

'It's not for me to say,' replied the computer. 'But I

suppose a robot in his position will be happy with what support he can find. You'd better come this way!'

Vignette had been right, she realized. The Generals really were in disarray. The city was not being properly led at the moment, and that left scope for robots such as herself to move between the spaces.

She followed the computer through the door, down a corridor, into a huge room, past lines of desks. A few green-painted robots still sat working at them. Steel styli scratched shapes into the metal foil.

Up one flight of stairs, and then another. She passed more rooms where robots still worked.

'The sheets pass up the building,' said the computer, conversationally. Susan had the impression that, to him, the coming war was nothing more than a reason for more foil to be written on. His true world existed in here, all else was just pale shadows. 'The figures are analysed and reduced on each floor. As they approach the upper levels all that data is changed to information.'

'Oh,' said Susan.

The computer touched her elbow, the current in his hand weak.

'I thought you might like to know,' he said, smiling all the time, 'while you're here and all. People look at Artemis City and all they see is train tracks and infantry-robots, but there is more to this state than that!' He squeezed the grey metal of her elbow harder. 'No offence intended, of course.'

'None taken,' said Susan as they climbed yet another flight of steps. The robots on this floor seemed slightly better built than the ones below. The foil they worked on was of higher quality, judging by the colour of the metal.

'These offices are what makes Artemis possible!' said the robot proudly. 'Those robots are producing the information that will enable Spoole and General Sandale and the rest to make decisions. But decisions are only part of the story. Okay, there are tactics involved in attacking a city, but that's not all. You wouldn't believe what it takes to move guns and troops and supplies and ammunition to the right place! Logistics is the key to Artemisian success!' His eyes glowed as he spoke, but that glow suddenly faded. 'Saving the contribution you and the other infantry make of course,' he added.

They had left the building now. They were walking out across a glass and metal bridge that stretched over the street far below, connecting the computer office with the building opposite. Susan's gyros lurched when she realized where they were going.

'Is this the Basilica?' asked Susan, in wonder.

'Oh yes!' said the computer, proudly. 'This bridge is part of the information superhighway that connects all of the Centre City! Hundreds of sheets of foil a day travel this way!'

They entered the Basilica, and Susan looked around at the decoration that had appeared. Maybe it wasn't as ostentatious as that of Turing City, but it was there. Gold, silver, platinum, titanium, tungsten, all wrapped around each other, moulded into the walls. Always discretely, austerely, but there nonetheless.

She had been right. The Centre City was a statement after all, and the thought filled her with sadness. She doubted she would ever be able to tell this to Karel.

But these thoughts were pushed from her head as the robot opened a door and led her into a sparsely furnished room. A steel-clad robot stood inside, gazing out of the window. So simple was his appearance that Susan did not realize who it was until the computer spoke.

'There's an infantryrobot here to see you, Spoole.'

Kavan

They'd built trenches and walls, thought Kavan. They'd lost already. What would be in those trenches, he wondered. Petrol? Hot oil? What would he put in them?

Kavan knew the answer to that: he wouldn't have built them in the first place.

'The trenches can be bridged,' said Ada.

Kavan looked at the engineer, her blue body streaked with oil. She was loving this, he knew. He could hear it in the rich hum of current that rose from her body.

'Not yet,' he said. 'We'd be cut down by the troops in the middle if we funnelled ourselves in that way.'

'Well, when you're ready, just say the word.' Ada didn't seem to mind. She was gazing eagerly at the iron wall. 'Just get me close enough to that. Let me get to work on it.'

'I will.' Kavan felt a curious sense of satisfaction. This was what he was made for. He was back in his element again. Something caught his attention.

'What is it?' asked Ada, unscrewing the end of a metal cylinder, checking the explosives inside.

'That Scout.'

'Yes?'

'You don't see many male Scouts, do you?'

'Something to do with the pattern of the mind,' said Ada, glancing at the silver robot nearby. 'It works better when it's female.' The robot's body was as graceful and feminine as any other Scout's, but there was something about the way that he went through his warm-up movements that was unmistakeably male.

'Why do you ask?' said Ada. 'It's a funny thing to wonder about, just before a battle.'

'I don't know,' said Kavan. 'We take things for granted, don't we? Did you ever have children, Ada?'

'No. That's a job for the mothers of Artemis.' She gazed at him. 'Did you ever have children, Kavan?'

'No. We are all woven with our own purpose.'

And this is mine, he reflected.

'Okay,' he said. 'It's time to begin.'

Susan and Spoole

'Come in,' said Spoole.

Susan walked into the room, her gyros spinning.

'Turn down the power,' said Spoole, 'I can feel the current in your electromuscles from here.'

With an effort, Susan forced herself to relax.

'What's your name, soldier?'

'Susan.'

'Susan. And how many robots do you represent, Susan? How many infantryrobots do you bring to follow me?'

'How many?' said Susan. 'There's just me.'

'Just you?'

If Spoole was disappointed, he didn't show it. He looked more closely at her.

'Who are you? You don't wear that body like an Artemisian. Are you a conscript?'

'My name is Susan. I'm a Turing Citizen.'

'There is no such place any more.'

Susan looked at Spoole. 'I thought that you would be at the front line, leading your troops.'

'Artemis is no longer led in that manner,' he said. 'Besides, there are other plans in place . . .'

His voice trailed away.

Susan stared at the robot standing by the window, his body reflecting the yellow glow of the lights beyond. This was Spoole, the leader of Artemis. She was standing not five feet from the man who was ultimately responsible for the death of her child, the loss of her husband and the destruction of her home.

Spoole had turned and was looking out of the window again, gazing at nothing. His body seemed simply constructed, but Susan recognized excellent metal work when she saw it. She could feel best-quality steel, her fingertips almost tingled at its presence. Spoole was an expert at bending metal, his handiwork had a cold sort of humour about it: his body was austere at first glance, but elegantly made when you took a closer look. It was the same joke that the Centre City had played on the rest of the continent, as they had taken it apart.

One of the perpetrators of that joke was standing right in front of her. If she brought down her hand hard enough, she could break his coil. So what was stopping her?

And she knew the answer. Vignette had been right. *Until you live the reality, you can never be sure the way your mind is woven.* This wasn't the way she was made.

'You can't see Kavan's troops from here,' said Spoole, conversationally. 'The wall obstructs their view.'

'Really, Sir?' said Susan.

'You *are* from Turing City, aren't you? We don't say "Sir" in Artemis, Susan.'

'Very well.'

'You didn't build walls around Turing City either, did you, Susan?'

'No, Spoole.'

'Nor did we in the past. But things have changed. I remain here whilst others lead.' He turned suddenly to face Susan. 'They leave someone to guard me, and I don't know whether it is an insult or a subtle threat. What do you think, Susan?'

He was testing her. Or was he teasing her?

'I don't know,' she said.

'And what would you do if they attacked me now, Susan. Would you defend me?'

'If who attacked you?'

'Though they forget I used to be a soldier too,' continued Spoole, not appearing to notice her question.

'If they do come in here, they'll have the two of us to fight.'

'Who will attack us, Spoole? You mean Kavan, right?'

'Kavan?' laughed Spoole. 'Kavan is the least of my problems.'

Kavan

The attack was the culmination of Artemis's hundred-year climb to supremacy on Shull. It was the greatest so far of Kavan's career. And yet its beginning was strangely low-key.

The orders radiated out from Kavan's position, they circled the iron walls, passed on from robot to robot. When the metal circuit was complete, the attack began.

Kavan formed two groups of infantry, two hundred yards apart, and set them firing on the robots between the first two moats. Copper and lead and cupronickel formed an almost solid wall in the air, it thumped into the earth of the mound, riddling the soil with metal.

The robots on the mound were trapped between the two groups of infantry that Karel had formed, and those groups now started to move towards each other, cutting down the robots opposite, riddling them with holes, piercing electromuscle, shattering plate, cutting through the wire of the mind.

'Then you simply repeat the process all around the mound,' said Goeppert, delighted. 'Whoever commands that army has trapped their soldiers there with no means of support.'

'I know,' said Kavan. 'And that worries me. Spoole is not a fool.'

Goeppert looked at the wall of robots who stood behind the two firing groups.

'What are they for?'

'To capture the metal that is fired back at us. It will lodge in their bodies, ready to be used again.'

The glow of portable forges could be seen, way back from the lines. Robots would be waiting there to melt down the metal reclaimed and recast it as minié balls and spitzer rounds that would be passed back, still warm, to the troops on the front line. Ada was back there too, directing the robots who were now at work on the wide platforms they would use to bridge the moats.

Kavan gazed at the two groups of infantry, shuffling towards each other as they fired. The night was lit with the flash of powder from the older guns, the spark of electromuscle suddenly punctured, the blue glow of a mind suddenly pierced, expending its life force in one flash.

'It seems to me,' he began, 'that Spoole is trying to slow us down, not stop us completely. Why else would he build his fortifications in this manner?'

The defenders on the iron wall finally understood what was happening. They brought their cannon and mortars to bear on Kavan's infantryrobots. A staccato tattoo travelled down the walls, and heavy canister rained down upon Kavan's lines.

Clouds of dark chaff exploded amongst the troops, glittering silver as the scraps of foil caught the light of the battle. Kavan's vision began to blink with interference.

'The chaff is electrified,' said Calor. 'They'll follow it up with iron filings next.'

More canisters rained down, and Kavan saw, through flickering vision, black lines drawn by the magnetized iron on the bodies of his and the other soldiers.

Engineers moved in, laying a magnetic perimeter to draw off the chaff, but the defenders switched to shrapnel bombs. Corkscrews of metal spun through the air, burrowing their way into bodies and limbs. A nearby robot froze, and the light in its eyes faded. It fell forward, to reveal the shaft of iron that pierced the back of its head.

'Gather the metal!' called Kavan. 'Pull it back to the forges!'

No one heard him in the crackling confusion caused by the chaff, but his command was unnecessary. Already Scouts, frustrated by their lack of input to this kind of battle, were dashing back and forth, carrying what metal they could find. Even the long black tails of iron filings that followed them like whizz lines would be reclaimed.

The magnetic perimeter was in place. Already the air was getting clearer, as it pulled chaff and iron filings towards itself. A pattering, ringing noise started, and Kavan realized it had begun to rain.

'Good,' he called. 'This will clear the air further!'

Now he could see the two firing groups once more. They had almost met up. Beyond them, on the section of the mound, nothing moved.

'Some of them flung themselves into the far trench rather than be shot,' said Calor, peering through the distorted air with her enhanced vision.

'We'll capture their metal later on,' said Kavan.

'Set up two groups again, this time four hundred feet apart. We're clearing a path straight through here, right now.'

'Very well, Kavan.' She looked beyond the trenches. 'Then there will only be the wall to pass.'

Was she being sarcastic? Kavan said nothing. Behind him he could hear Goeppert and the rest of the Borners checking over their bodies, ready for the ascent of the wall.

Susan and Spoole

Somewhere in the distance, the sky began to flicker.

'The battle has begun,' said Spoole. 'Kavan has returned at last.'

'Are you worried?' asked Susan.

Spoole turned and gazed at her. He didn't seem concerned. He turned back to the window.

'We take conscripts too easily,' he said. 'These past years we have placed too high a value on expansion at all costs. We have forgotten Nyro's way.'

He stared at the flickering in the night sky.

'No, Susan, I'm not worried, at least not in the way you think. If Kavan were to lead this city, it would at least be according to Nyro's way.'

The window was vast, squares of glass set in a metal frame. It curved at the edges, the top and bottom. Again Susan was struck by how Artemis could make such an austere statement of power and beauty, so totally different to those formerly made in Turing City.

Drops of rain began to streak the window. Other than their pattering on the glass, there was no sound.

The silence unnerved Susan.

'Well,' she said, 'do you think Kavan will win through?'

'No. Kavan will not win this time.' He spoke the words with some sadness.

'You're not an infantryrobot, are you Susan?' said Spoole suddenly. 'I wonder what you are. I sent out messages asking for support days ago. I thought I would have heard from the Storm Troopers at least. But nothing. Maybe Sandale and the rest have got to them. And then you turn up . . .'

He leaned closer, looking into her eyes.

'What are you? Just another robot jumping on the best opportunity for safety? Well, you're wasting your time coming to me! Go and see Sandale and the rest, if you want to be accepted as an Artemisian!'

'I never claimed to be an Artemisian,' said Susan angrily. 'I was a Turing Citizen. Your state kidnapped me and had me brought here. Forced me to work in your making rooms.'

Her current surged. She could feel it filling her electromuscles, drawing them in. This body was getting ready to fight. She fumbled for the rifle she carried slung over her shoulder, pointed it towards Spoole. He didn't seem to care.

'Ah,' he said, eyes glowing, '*Now* I understand! You are a mother of Artemis. That explains it. You don't walk like a soldier. You're too precise; you have a different sort of thoughtfulness. I was a soldier, I know these things. Who did you swap bodies with?'

'Like you would know! You took my husband from me! You killed my son! Do you know that?'

'I killed your son? I don't think so.'

'Maybe not directly, but your rusting state attacked mine.'

'Yes. That's what we do. And your state crumbled and ran away, rather than fighting. Just like you're doing now.'

'Not at all,' said Susan with angry dignity. 'I came here by choice. I'm looking for someone.'

'Who?'

'My friend.'

'What about your husband? I thought you said I took him from you. I would have thought you wanted him back?'

'He's out there somewhere, on the other side of that wall. Tell me a way through and I'll take it.'

'What was your friend's name?'

'Nettie.'

'Should I know her? Another mother of Artemis, I suppose?'

'Nettie wasn't a mother. Nettie never twisted a mind. She was our teacher.'

'Your teacher?' said Spoole, and his expression changed. 'What sort of minds were you making?'

Susan moved her grip on the rifle. It felt odd and comfortable at the same time, made to fit this body.

'New minds. Minds full of power, minds that barely thought.'

'Ah, then I think I understand.'

He turned back to face the window.

'Understand? Understand what?'

'Susan, have you ever heard of the Book of Robots?'

Susan laughed bitterly.

'Oh yes. It doesn't exist. But the idea of it causes people to do things and weave minds that only bring misery.' Of course Susan knew that. Her own mind had been woven that way.

'I never believed it existed either, Susan, but lately I wonder. The Book of Robots is supposed to contain the plan of the original robots. It is supposed to have the template of the way that minds should be woven.'

'I know that,' said Susan. 'I don't see the need for the book. Any answers there are can be found by looking at the world around us.'

'I think you're right, Susan,' said Spoole, delighted. 'We live in this world and we take its form for granted. We don't see what is right in front of us.'

His words were like a shock to her body. Spoole wasn't the first person to tell her this. She remembered Maoco O, the Turing City Guard, how he had stood on the mound by the city fort beneath the light of the night moon and spoken almost exactly the same words to her.

It was just coincidence, she told herself.

'I've heard that before,' said Susan. 'The trouble is, no one can ever tell me what the answers are. They don't tell me *what* we are taking for granted.'

'Oh, but I know,' said Spoole. 'I can tell you.'

Kavan

Kavan's troops had completely encircled the city. Now they moved to join the bulges that were growing at five positions around the encircling moats, getting ready to cross at the points cleared of enemy troops.

'They can't get out of there,' said Kavan. 'They've trapped themselves behind metal and earth.'

The first of the platforms constructed by Ada and her engineers had been dragged forward and used to bridge the first moat. Storm Troopers charged across and fanned out, left and right, pushing back the enemy troops marooned there by Spoole and the Generals.

They were followed by infantryrobots who went to the edge of the first mound to repeat the tactics Kavan had used earlier, firing into the enemy who were stranded between the next set of trenches.

More chaff and iron filings rained down, shrapnel and high-explosive canisters fell amongst the tightly packed troops, killing Artemis' friends and foe alike. The air was filled with smoke and metal and rain, so full of motion that there was barely any untouched space there amongst the darkness. Silver Scouts cut through the confusion, pulling metal back to the growing number of forges glowing red on the Artemisian plain behind them.

Calor appeared, silver panelling badly scarred.

'The troops marooned between the moats have pulled away, Kavan. They're caught between our fire and that coming from the walls.'

'Conscripts, the lot of them,' said Kavan, and he

looked around at his own, Uncertain Army. 'How many of these are loyal, do you suppose?'

'All of them, when things are going well,' said Calor, and she gave a brittle laugh. 'At the moment, about half of them.'

As she spoke, there was a huge explosion in the centre of the first bridge, splitting it in two. Twisted metal, shrapnel and robots tumbled into the moat. Already a second bridge was being pulled into position.

'There are enough troops,' said Kavan. 'We will make it into the city. That is, if we need to. They know we are here. There will be robots in there who will be on our side.'

Susan and Spoole

'What's the difference between an animal and a robot, Susan?'

'A robot is made of metal, an animal is organic.'

'But what about the robot animals? We don't think of them as being like us, do we? Think about beetles. They forage for scraps of metal with which to build their young. Think about snakes, wrapping themselves around small robots and killing them with a shock of current. Think about smaller robotic life forms. We lump them in with the organic animals, don't we?'

'I suppose so. What point are you making?'

Spoole's eyes flashed.

'What's the difference between us and a porphyry worm?'

'We're intelligent, we have arms and legs . . .'

'And what else? Come on, you're a mother of Artemis.'

Susan already knew the answer.

'Only robots twist the minds of their young. Animals don't, whether they are metal or organic.'

'Haven't you ever wondered why this should be?'

'No. It's twisting minds that makes us intelligent.'

Spoole laughed. 'That's what I thought, at least until a few days ago. Tell me, what other differences are there, between us and animals? Organic animals, I mean.'

'I don't know. There wasn't much organic life in Turing City. We kept the place clean.'

'What do organic animals do that robots don't?'

'I don't know. I'm not that interested in organics. It wasn't twisted into my mind, I forget what I hear about them.'

'They eat,' said Spoole. 'They eat each other.'

'Well, we take metal from each other to build new robots.'

'Yes, but organic animals need to eat each other to stay alive. They consume plants and animals for fuel. Didn't you know that?'

'I knew that. Is it important?'

'It's a clue, Susan. If the Book of Robots exists, then this should be written in there. Robots don't eat, they don't breathe. They're not like animals, they're not even like the machines that we make. Locomotives need fuel to propel themselves, fires need air to breathe or they fail to burn. Robots don't. A mother weaves a mind, and there is sufficient power there to power a body for thirty or forty years!'

'That's the way that things work. Is there something wrong with that?'

'Well, yes, apparently there is.'

Kavan

The area before Kavan was filled with carnage, it was covered with smoke, it was watered by rain, it was lit by the flare of the guns on the wall that poured high explosive down on the advancing wall of robots, it was lit by the incandescence of minds discharging their life force into the night in one flash, it was rocked by explosions, it was distorted by chaff, it was pounded and twisted and thumped.

Beyond the line of attack, the night was strangely still. The glow of the forges on the plain, the area of quiet expectancy along the rest of the wall lent the scene before Kavan an air of the surreal.

Goeppert appeared at his side.

'Not long now,' said Kavan. 'We're almost at the wall. You realize you'll be climbing under heavy fire all the way?'

'We know that,' said Goeppert. 'We were twisted in the mountains, we're used to fighting on vertical planes.'

'You have sufficient weapons?' asked Kavan, looking at the rifle and knives that Goeppert carried. 'Would you like some grenades?'

'No use on a wall,' said Goeppert. 'Don't throw them far enough and they fall back towards you.'

A new noise rose above all the rest.

'Machine guns,' said Kavan. 'Titanium-tipped bullets, I would guess. We must be almost there—'

And then there was a huge explosion, bigger than any they had heard so far. It didn't come from the ground though . . .

'Look,' said Goeppert, pointing, 'its magazine must have blown up.'

One of the guard towers built into the wall had erupted in flame. The long barrel of a gun appeared over the edge and began to slide slowly, slowly, downwards, slipping into the second moat. A tremendous cheer went up from the attackers, and for the first time that night, the Uncertain Army began to stamp on the ground.

Stamp, *stamp*, stamp; stamp, *stamp*, stamp.

A wide tear spread down from the top of the guard tower, the metal of the iron wall split apart by the force of the explosion.

'It's begun,' said Kavan. 'The soldiers in there *know* we are here. They know who I am, they'll know what I represent. They'll come back to Nyro.'

The gunfire from the top of the walls increased, only it was no longer all turned outwards. Now the city was fighting amongst itself. Just a tiny flame at the moment, but it would spread as it burned, Nyro's fervour gradually overcoming the whole city.

Calor reappeared, her scratched panelling covered in drops of melted lead.

'We're there, Kavan,' she said. 'We're at the walls. The defending troops are in dissarray. They are fired upon by their own side. They leap into the moat for safety.'

Goeppert stepped forward.

'Then we are ready to attack. Kavan?'

'Go,' said Kavan.

He watched with Calor as Goeppert and his troops ran forward, their elongated bodies picking their way amongst the twisted wreckage of the battlefield.

'And now we follow,' said Kavan, and he followed the Borners as they made their way to the wall. Bullets rained down around him, they ricocheted from the bodies of the fallen. So many bodies, so many of them still alive. Kavan saw the glow of their eyes, heard the pleading of robots trapped in shorting bodies, waiting to be dragged away from the battlefield and to be rehoused in new machines. There would be time for that later.

Kavan's feet rang on metal bodies. The smoke formed a roof above him through which the rain fell, the spark and crackle of the injured illuminated the enclosed scene.

Through a gap in the smoke, Kavan saw that Goeppert and his troops had reached the wall. The rest of the Uncertain Army watched as the Borners ran up to the base, placed their feet on the sheer surface, and then began to run upwards.

A cheer went up from the assembled troops; the Borners ran up the wall, they unslung their rifles, they began to fire on the few defenders who realized what was going on. Racing closer and closer to the top.

'They're almost in,' said Kavan. 'We've returned to Artemis.'

Susan and Spoole

'We never even noticed, Susan! It wasn't right in front of our eyes, it was right behind them! Our minds, Susan. The wire that a male produces has such power in it. Where does it come from?'

'I don't know. I'm not a male. I don't understand what you do, any more than a male understands how a female twists metal!'

'That's not what I mean! You want to power a loco-motive, you need to burn oil or diesel. You want to heat a forge, you burn coal. But to power a robot, all you have to do is twist a piece of metal. There is power there, it lasts for thirty or forty years, and then it is exhausted. Why is that?'

'I told you, I don't know. I'm not male!'

'You can't just twist the same piece of metal. Even males know that, don't we? We've seen dead minds. The metal is brittle and lacking in something. You have to mix it with new metal to make a new mind.'

'Which metals?'

'That depends upon the mind, but iron and copper are the most important. And palladium and platinum, always a little palladium and platinum.'

The flashing lights beyond the window were building to a climax. Just on the edge of her hearing, Susan could hear the thump and shake of distant explosions.

'So a mind does need to be refuelled. That would seem to make sense. After all, that's what an animal does.'

'Yes, but there is nothing like a robot mind, the efficiency with which it creates power! And we never even noticed! We built atomic bombs and nuclear trains, and we thought we were clever. We never realized that there is an engine like that running in our minds, a source of power produced purely by twisting metal. Imagine if we were to turn minds purely to the production of power? Imagine the energy that would create.'

Susan didn't have to imagine it, she had already done it.

'Is that what was going on in the making rooms? Is that why we were making those minds? But that's . . .' she struggled for the word, '. . . it's *obscene*. It's treating robots like, like *animals*, not like metal!' A thought struck her. 'Does this have something to do with Nettie? Is this why she vanished?'

'I don't know, it could be,' said Spoole. 'You still don't understand, Susan. What might have happened to Nettie – that's just the start!'

Susan walked away from the window, mind reeling. To see a mind as nothing more than a source of power. It was obvious when Spoole mentioned it. He was right, the answer had been behind their eyes all this time. Was that why no one had ever seen it before? Why had they seen it now?

The floor of the room was covered in a pattern of metal tiles, half of them polished to a shine, half roughened for traction. It was all steel, and yet some of the tiles reflected the light, and some of them were dull. She gazed at the pattern, thinking.

'Maybe what you say is true,' she said, eventually. 'Maybe the Book of Robots does exist after all. Maybe this is written in it.' She looked up suddenly. 'It does, doesn't it? You found the book! Artemis has found the book, and you, Spoole, have read it. That's how you know, isn't it?'

Spoole lowered his head.

'No,' he said, sadly. 'I wish that were true. I wish that was the way that I found out.'

'Then how?' shouted Susan. 'How did you figure this out? Which robot finally saw the truth?'

'Ah,' said Spoole. 'If only a robot had done. You see, Susan, there are other minds at large on Penrose . . .'

Kavan

Goeppert and his robots were in. The bullets and shells directed at the bridgehead of troops who crowded at the base of the iron wall were already reducing in number as the Borners went to work inside the city.

Calor suddenly began to laugh. Kavan was used to this, he almost expected it: Scouts pumped current around their bodies at a high frequency, they usually died young and half mad.

'What is it, Calor?' asked Kavan.

'It's Goeppert. I've just realized why he followed you here! The Borners have just taken your city!'

'Not yet they haven't,' said Kavan.

'But they're in there, and you're out here! What if they take it over and don't let us in? That would be so funny!'

'Go on Calor. Go and fetch Ada. I want her supervising the work here.'

'It will take time, Kavan. She could be anywhere back there on the plain.'

'Then fetch someone who knows what to do! She'll find her way here, I'm sure.'

Engineers were bundled to the base of the wall. Standing on the bodies of the fallen, they began to supervise the stripping away of the iron, forcing a path through into the city. A huge explosion sounded to their left, and the second of the guard towers was blown apart.

'Goeppert works well,' said Kavan. 'That, or more Artemisians are returning to our side.'

'Kavan, what's that?'

Calor tilted her head, listening. Now Kavan heard it too. A low drone, and under it a thumping noise.

'It's coming from behind us,' said Kavan.

The other robots turned to see. There was nothing there. Somewhere beyond the noise and the gunfire they could just make out the glow of the forges and nothing else. The droning noise grew louder, the thumping became more insistent.

'There's something up there,' said Calor, 'shapes in the sky.'

'Shapes?' said Kavan. 'What shapes?'

As he said it, golden flares ignited amongst the raindrops, they drew straight lines towards Kavan and his troops.

'What are they?' asked Calor.

'Into the trenches!' called Kavan.

The golden lines streaked towards them and struck the ground between the first and second trench. Fountains of earth sprang from the resulting explosion.

Kavan and Calor tumbled down into the inside moat, landing on the gravelled bottom with a jolt that shook their metal frames. Something snapped in Kavan's right arm, and he lost partial control over his hand.

'Look!' shouted Calor. She had landed on her feet, like any true Scout, and was pointing upwards. The top of the trench was a line in the sky, beyond it, something dark moved. A huge shape, lights blinking on its underside.

'What is it?' called Calor.

'I don't know!' called Kavan. 'I've never seen anything like it before!'

A second shape moved over the top of the trench. There were machines up there, huge flying machines that groaned and thumped the air. Where had they come from? Were they of Spoole's invention? Surely not.

Golden flares streaked from one of the craft. One fell into the moat, a few hundred yards from where Kavan and Calor sheltered. It exploded in a wash of soil and sand that rattled on their damaged shells.

'Go towards it!' yelled Kavan, 'See if it's blown down the walls enough for us to get out of here.'

Calor ran awkwardly along the trench bottom. She had lost her usual light gait, her body was failing due to the damage it had taken.

Another craft flew by overhead, and more robots tumbled into the trench. An infantryrobot landed near Kavan. He heard the splintering crack that disabled her legs.

Calor was coming back.

'Kavan!' she called. 'The last bomb blew out the

walls clear to the next moat. We can make it through there.'

He followed her awkwardly down the trench. It was hard to move his right arm properly; his whole body was off balance.

The humming drone of the strange craft had increased. No, realized Kavan, it was rather that the noise of gunfire and shelling from the walls had lessened. The robots of the city wouldn't want to open fire on their own craft.

He stumbled down the trench, cut through the gap in the walls to the next moat along. There were robots there already, clambering up the walls. Another huge explosion shook the ground behind Kavan, shaking the climbing robots free of their handholds.

'They know we're in the trench!' called Calor. 'They're aiming for us down here!'

'Good!' called Kavan. 'Their bombs will shatter the walls and make it easier for us to climb out!'

'And if they hit us?'

'Then we will die. We're only metal.'

Kavan and Calor ran, the patterns of explosions reflecting in the rain water that flowed down their mud-spattered shells. Kavan and Calor and the rest of the robots, infantryrobots, Scouts, Storm Troopers, even some engineers, all seeking a way out of the confusion. All the while, those heavy craft droned and hovered somewhere above, sending down golden tongues of fire.

'Here, Kavan, here!' called Calor. She had found a sloping bank of earth, up which she led Kavan, both of them scrambling up into the night above. They emerged near one of the bridges that led away from the mounds onto the plain beyond.

Kavan turned for a moment and looked back towards the city. The gunfire there had almost ceased, bright yellow lights had been turned on to illuminate the walls. Before the walls, the dark craft hovered, sending down streaks of light that burst in golden fountains on the blackened ground. Fires leaped into the sky, fires fell from the night, and the battleground was picked out in bars of light.

'What about Goeppert?' asked Calor.

'He's on his own now,' said Kavan. 'We need to retreat and reassess.'

'Retreat to where?'

'Scatter across the plain,' said Kavan. 'It will make it harder for those craft to pick us off.'

'What about Artemis City?'

'It will still be here tomorrow. We need to understand what is happening!'

The command went out, and the Uncertain Army broke up into hundreds, thousands of little companies that scattered into the night.

A new sound fell out of the night, a piercing whistle that sang from high above. A second noise joined it.

'What now?' asked Kavan.

'Two more craft,' said Calor, gazing up into the night. 'Small craft, I think. No. Or are they large craft, but further away?'

'Never mind that,' said Kavan, 'look!'

The humming, droning machines were turning their attention away from the trenches and instead moving towards Kavan and the rest. They began to chase the robots across the plain, golden tongues of fire chasing them into the night.

Susan and Spoole

Spoole was ashamed. Susan could tell. He may not be part of what had happened, he may not have made the decision, but he was still ashamed.

'Other minds?' she said. Then she remembered what Nettie had told her, out by the radio masts. The creators had come. The writers of the Book of Robots had returned to Penrose. 'Is it true?' she asked. 'Have our creators come?'

'No!' said Spoole. 'No! They never claimed that. At least not at first. But they pick things up so quickly. They know how to manipulate people, how to win robots over. They know when to lie and flatter, and when to threaten and to tell the truth and when to just ignore the question. Oh, they're clever.'

Susan gazed at him, a massive potential building inside her.

'Is it true that they are animals?' she asked.

'Humans, they call themselves. Yes. It's true.'

'Have you seen them?'

'No. Only heard their voices, and then I wasn't supposed to. They've been speaking to the Generals these past two months using the radio. They kept it a secret from me for so long.'

'I thought you were in charge!'

'It doesn't work that way, Susan. Not in Artemis. The humans have been speaking to the Generals, making promises, making deals. And the Generals have been listening. The humans have promised to defend the city in return for certain considerations.'

'What considerations?'

'Robots, Susan. The humans are clever, but they can't work metal like we do. That's how I know they didn't write the book. Do you understand that? They don't know enough about us.'

'I understand.'

'They want robots to come and work for them. They want us to weave them robots that they can take back to their homes as slaves.'

'And the Generals agreed to this? They are willing to sell your children to animals?'

'Why not, Susan? Children are nothing more than twisted metal. We all are.'

'That's only what you think!' Susan shouted with frustration. 'This state is riddled with rust from top to bottom!'

Spoole just smiled.

'You're part of this too, Susan. More than you know. You realize what else the humans want? Minds full of lifeforce that can't think. The minds that your friend told you to make.'

'Nettie!' said Susan. 'Then she knew?'

'I don't know. The Generals have been so good at concealing their actions. They know that the robots of the city will not see this as Nyro's way.'

'Well, surely it isn't!'

'Who knows? The Generals defend the city against attack; perhaps they believe they are defending it for Nyro's sake.'

'And do you think they are right?'

Spoole was silent.

'I thought not.'

To Susan, master craftsrobot, sometimes the metal of a room would sing with the potential inherent within it. Sometimes it would appear as if it had achieved that potential. This room now seemed empty and devoid of purpose. Whatever life had once filled it was long gone. Spoole seemed to feel it too.

'I can't leave here,' he said. 'My mind was woven to lead Artemis. There is nowhere else for me to be.'

Much to her surprise, Susan understood Spoole. She had been woven to love her husband. Hers was an arranged marriage: it didn't make it any less real.

'Why are you still here, Susan?'

'I told you. I came looking for my friend. I want to find out where she was taken.'

'Why should I help you?'

'You don't believe in what the Generals are doing. And maybe Nettie knows something. Maybe she has spoken to the animals. You're a leader, get to speak to them, maybe you can negotiate a different deal!'

'That won't work,' said Spoole. 'If you were a leader you would understand that. And yet . . .'

'And yet what?'

'Nothing. Your friend has probably been melted down and recycled to stop her telling what she knows.'

Spoole went back to the window. A high-pitched whistling impinged on the edge of Susan's hearing.

'Then the records will be in the next building. Help me find them.'

'Why should I?'

Spoole just went on gazing out of the window. The flickering and percussive thump of the battle was still present, but overlaid on that was the descending noise of the whistling.

'What is that?' asked Susan.

'I think that will be the humans,' said Spoole. 'The Generals said their ships were large. They're dropping down from space. They're coming to take their city.'

Kavan

Kavan and the rest ran across the plain, kicking up sand and grit, dislodging the glowing coals from the over-turned forges, tripping and stumbling on the bodies of the fallen. Behind them the thrumming craft still fired, only now they had changed ammunition: the shells exploded in a low circle, parallel to the ground. They sent out razor shards that sliced off legs just above the ankle, tumbling a robot forward into the secondary blast that ripped bodies and minds apart.

'I think they've stopped following us!' called Calor. She was running backwards, looking back at the city. 'They seem to be maintaining a perimeter around the city.'

Kavan's electromuscles were aching now. He needed

to rest, give them a chance to cool a little, let the life-force replenish.

'Should we stop?' asked Calor, loping along at his side.

'Not yet,' said Kavan. 'When day comes we'll be exposed on this plain. Those craft will be able to pick us off at their leisure. We need to get well clear.'

'Where are we going, Kavan? There is no shelter until we get to Stark! Or should we head north, back to the mountains?'

'No. We need to spread out, make it harder for them to find us.'

'Let's stop here.'

Kavan was so tired.

'Very well,' he said. 'Five minutes.'

They stopped. Kavan looked around. Ten of them. Himself and Calor, seven infantryrobots and one other Scout. All of them scratched and pierced by shrapnel.

'We need a forge,' said Kavan.

'Look,' said Calor. She pointed up into the sky over the city.

The piercing noise had been there all the time they had been running. Now they stopped they had time to notice it again. It shrieked through the metal, it set the inside of the head ringing. They watched the two dark shapes that descended through the rain clouds. They looked like rolls of hot lead, long tubes rolled in the hands by a child and then flattened.

'That can't be right,' said Kavan. 'My eyesight needs recalibrating.'

'No,' said Calor. 'The larger craft is over nine hundred feet long. The smaller one is six hundred.'

'What's holding them up?'

'I don't know.'

What must it be like for the robots in the city, wondered Kavan? To look up and see those vast shapes hanging above. Expecting them to fall at any moment.

The front of the larger craft began to flicker, and the effect was taken up by the smaller.

All around the great plain, Kavan sensed the stillness as robots that had been running moments before came to a halt and turned to watch what was happening.

The two craft seemed to be speaking to each other using yellow, green and white lights. First the front of the larger craft would flicker, then the smaller craft flickered in reply. The conversation went on for a few moments, and then, in a series of shining bands, the lights spread backwards over the surface of the two craft, now joined by red, orange and yellow, the glowing pattern gradually encompassing the whole extent of the two ships.

The lights increased in intensity, their brightness lighting up the plain, sending dark shadows streaming out behind the watching robots.

Kavan saw the way that Calor looked at them, her shell reflecting the patterns, and he realized something. The craft were big and they were bright, and though they were much smaller than the city, they seemed to dwarf it. Whoever was flying those craft, it seemed to Kavan, was sending out a message.

We are here. And we are in control.

Susan and Spoole

Susan and Spoole stood by the window, gazing up at the enormous craft that floated overhead. The room was illuminated in red and green, the patterns of light played across the chequered floor.

'It's bigger than the Basilica,' said Spoole. 'What have the Generals done?'

'Made peace with a bigger bully,' said Susan. 'You were right, Spoole. It's too late to fight these people. The other Generals have outmanoeuvred you.'

'You're giving up so easily?'

'It makes no difference to me,' said Susan. 'I don't care who's oppressing me.'

'You don't mean that,' said Spoole.

'Spoole, I don't care. Welcome to my forge. Welcome to the world I have lived in since you and your *Choarh* state destroyed mine.'

Spoole couldn't take his eyes from the vast shape hanging overhead. Every surface in the room danced to the movement of its lights.

'Maybe the Generals were right,' he said, softly. 'What else could they do?'

'I think they were right,' said Susan, and a vicious pleasure welled up inside her. 'What does that say about Nyro, Spoole?'

Spoole didn't answer.

'She's dead, Spoole!' Susan couldn't keep the savage joy from her voice. All the suffering she had endured, now was the time she could pay some of it back. 'Nyro has gone, Spoole. If not now, then in a few days or a few weeks. The Generals have given the city away to a greater power, and from now on you'll be playing by its rules!'

She laughed.

Spoole turned and looked at her, and his eyes were bright.

'What now, Spoole? What will you do now?'

He didn't reply, he raised his hands slightly, as if he was going to attack her. She didn't care. She was having her revenge.

'Well, Spoole? What now that Nyro has gone?'

He lowered his hands.

'What now?' he repeated. 'Susan, you're right. Nyro has no place in this city any more. This is not the place I was made to lead. I'm free to go.'

The vicious smile faded from Susan's face as he spoke.

'Yes,' said Spoole. 'Free to go.'

'No,' said Susan, disappointed to be cheated this easily of her revenge, poor though it was. 'No you're not. Stay here, Spoole. Stay here and see how pointless it all is. Everything that you fought for, everything that you did to me and my family. All for nothing.'

But all the doubt had gone from Spoole. He was his old self again, calm and assured.

'Would that make you happy? Don't be so silly Susan. No. We need to go now. Both of us.'

'Both of us? But why should I come with you?'

'Because this is wrong. The Generals are wrong. You asked me for help not two minutes ago. Well, I'm offering it. Come on, we're going to find out what happened to your friend. And then, maybe, we will have some proof of what it is that the Generals have done. We're going to show Artemis City that this is not Nyro's way.'

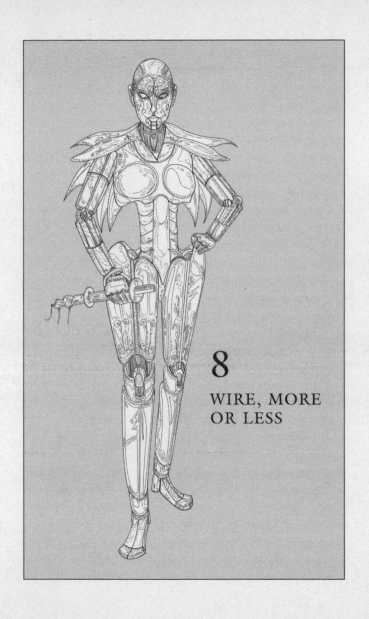

8

WIRE, MORE
OR LESS

Wa-Ka-Mo-Do

The dark surface of Lake Ochoa was flecked red with burning mirrors of the rising sun. Wa-Ka-Mo-Do and the robots ran along its shore, metal feet slipping on the pebbles, kicking them, sending them dancing across the water. To their left a railway train burned: long tanker wagons were torn apart; they belched black diesel smoke into the sky. Wa-Ka-Mo-Do saw the line of bullet holes down the side of them. Those wouldn't have caused an explosion, he reflected. Those strange craft must have also been firing incendiaries.

Past the burning train, metal moving to a steady pulse, they turned from the lake shore and headed to the City Gate, clearly visible before them now, wide open and guarded by four humans wearing green panelling. They carried rifles, but not like the ones Wa-Ka-Mo-Do had seen before. These weapons were shorter and constructed mainly of plastic. What little metal there was, was of an odd alloy that felt strangely transparent to Wa-Ka-Mo-Do's senses. Those guns made him feel uncomfortable. They were different – alien. Just like the humans.

Their attitude and demeanour had changed since yesterday, he noted.

The running troop slowed to a halt, Wa-Ka-Mo-Do coming to attention before one of the humans.

'Thank you for your service here today,' he said. 'May I respectfully ask, where is the Imperial Guard?'

The human made an odd motion, and Wa-Ka-Mo-Do realized he wasn't wearing a translation device.

'Come on,' he called, and stepped forward. The humans stood to one side, allowing him to pass, and Wa-Ka-Mo-Do headed into the city, his troops marching along behind him. Inside his gyros were spinning. What would he have done if the humans had tried to prevent him from entering Sangrel?

The Street of Becoming was littered with broken tiles and rubble. Bullet holes stitched the upper parts of the buildings. Dark cracks spread across their walls, and a fine sprinkling of dust fell on the robots.

There were four more humans guarding the top gates of the Street of Becoming, each of them holding the same strange new weapons as those at the bottom. Behind them, Wa-Ka-Mo-Do noted with some relief, were ten warriors of the Emperor's Army. La-Ver-Di-Arussah stood at their head.

'Honoured Commander,' she said. There was a scratch on her brightly polished body.

'La-Ver-Di-Arussah, there are humans guarding the entrance to the Emperor's city of Sangrel. Did you not, perhaps, feel this to be an insult to his name?'

'These are the Emperor's orders, Honoured Commander,' replied La-Ver-Di-Arussah coolly.

I don't believe you! The words died in Wa-Ka-Mo-Do's voicebox. It seemed that things had gone so wrong here in Sangrel she probably was telling the truth.

'How badly damaged is the city?' he asked.

'The flying craft fired missiles that hit the Emperor's Palace. Several humans died. Furthermore, they have destroyed some of the buildings that the humans erected by the lake.'

'What about robots? How many citizens are dead?'

'We haven't yet had the time to find that out. The Emperor instructs us that the humans must be assisted first.'

'Surely you questioned these orders?'

'One does not question the Emperor, Wa-Ka-Mo-Do. We are to secure a passageway from Smithy Square to the Gate of Becoming to allow the humans to bring in new equipment.'

'No! I don't believe it! How do you know this is what the Emperor wishes?'

'His orders were relayed here by radio not one hour ago.'

Did he believe her? He didn't know.

Wa-Ka-Mo-Do looked down at his hands. His body was covered in grime, a thin patina of dust from the human crops. He felt dirty and disconnected from this city. Nothing seemed to be making sense.

'La-Ver-Di-Arussah. Think on this: there was already tension in this city before the attack. Imagine the feelings of the citizens now! If we go out and are seen helping to rebuild some of the damage caused by the human craft we may calm things a little.'

'It is not our job to calm things. The Emperor wishes any rebellion to be quashed in the most brutal manner possible, as an example to other cities.'

She was smiling as she spoke. The *gar* was actually smiling. 'After all,' she added, 'the Emperor has many more robots. He doesn't have that many humans.'

'He has no humans! The humans have him!'

Seldom had the silence of robots been so deep. La-Ver-Di-Arussah's troops stared forward blankly.

'Surely, if you must speak treason, it would be better away from the troops?'

'Where's Ka-Lo-Re-Harballah?' demanded Wa-Ka-Mo-Do.

'Up in Smithy Square, helping the humans.'

'I'm going up there.'

'Take your squad with you, Wa-Ka-Mo-Do. You will need them to protect you from the robots of Sangrel. They're angry.'

'Was that a deliberate insult, La-Ver-Di-Arussah?'

Her smile widened.

'No. Only advice.'

Wa-Ka-Mo-Do set off alone. He looked through the entrance to the Copper Market, and saw that the stalls in there were still open. The place was a lot emptier than usual, it was true, but there were still robots selling metal and oil and coal. It made sense, he supposed, robots would need materials with which to repair themselves.

He continued up the hill. Where was everyone else, he wondered? He feared he knew the answer. In houses and buildings, in the caves at the back of the Copper Market, stoking up the fire of their grievances.

There were two peasants up ahead, raking the rubble from the street.

'What happened here?' he demanded.

'Silversmith's house got hit, Honoured Commander.'

They looked at the ruptured wall of the nearby building. Melted silver droplets were spattered across the road and the rubble.

'Was anyone hurt?'

'Silversmith's family were all killed. Melted.'

'Melted?'

'We don't understand it, Honoured Commander. Whatever hit that building sent a jet of liquid metal into it. The family's minds burned like flares. If you go in there you can see their bodies welded to each other, the whole family turned into one lump.'

Wa-Ka-Mo-Do examined the ground. Mixed among the rubble were droplets of iron and aluminium.

'What are you doing now?'

'Clearing a path for the humans. There is a transport craft coming. They will need to bring their own weapons up into the city if they are to defend themselves from further attacks.'

'What about defending us?' asked Wa-Ka-Mo-Do.

'Honoured Commander?'

They didn't understand. Wa-Ka-Mo-Do was already gone, heading up the hill. If the humans wanted to inflame the robots of the city to rebellion, they couldn't go a better way about it.

It wasn't until later on it occurred to him that that may have been their plan.

Finally, he reached Smithy Square, and he felt as if the current had drained from his spongy-feeling electro-muscles.

The rising sun had bitten through the roof of the Emperor's Palace.

At least that's how it seemed. Half the roof was gone. Blue tiles hung broken from the torn edges, aluminium was burned to white oxide. The red sun cast a rusted, decaying light over the scene.

'It's still burning inside,' said Ka-Lo-Re-Harballah, appearing at Wa-Ka-Mo-Do's side. 'The humans won't let us in to help extinguish it. They say they have the situation under control.'

Wa-Ka-Mo-Do looked at the thin black smoke curling into the air through the broken roof. He imagined the ballroom burning, the ancient engravings warping in the heat, the paint flaking from metal.

'No,' said Wa-Ka-Mo-Do, 'we go in now, and rust the humans. Get me six robots.'

Ka-Lo-Re-Harballah didn't move.

'Did you hear me, Ka-Lo-Re-Harballah?'

'I'm sorry, Honoured Commander. The Emperor says that we are to obey the humans.'

'How do you know that, Ka-Lo-Re-Harballah?' flared Wa-Ka-Mo-Do. 'How do you KNOW that?'

'The Vestal Virgins commanded it, in his name.'

'You've seen them?'

'La-Ver-Di-Arussah did. Honoured Commander, you must be aware that she is part Vestal Virgin herself. Her family is known to have connections to that line.'

'There is no Vestal Virgin lineage, how could there be?'

Ka-Lo-Re-Harballah did not answer. He was staring shamefully at the ground.

'Am I alone?' wondered Wa-Ka-Mo-Do aloud.

Still Ka-Lo-Re-Harballah was silent. Wa-Ka-Mo-Do looked around. The Copper Master's house stood across the square, seemingly undamaged.

'Is the radio room untouched?' wondered Wa-Ka-Mo-Do, an idea forming in his mind.

'Yes, Honoured Commander.'

Wa-Ka-Mo-Do came to a decision.

'Good. I'm going to contact the Emperor. I will make him aware of what's going on here.'

'Honoured Commander, the Vestal Virgins were quite explicit. So La-Ver-Di-Arussah said. You are to aid the humans in every respect.'

'And that I shall, Ka-Lo-Re-Harballah, once I have spoken to the Emperor.'

Ka-Lo-Re-Harballah looked horrified. 'Honoured Commander, are you suggesting that the Emperor is ignorant of events?'

'I am not suggesting anything. Look, I am to aid the humans, am I not? Why don't you go and let them know that I would be pleased to speak to their ambassador at his earliest convenience?'

'But Honoured Commander—'

'Thank you, Ka-Lo-Re-Harballah.'

Before Ka-Lo-Re-Harballah could speak again, Wa-Ka-Mo-Do turned and strode across the square, heading for the Copper Master's house. It glowed red in the morning sun, and Wa-Ka-Mo-Do felt as if he was stepping directly into the forge.

The Copper Guard by the door stood to attention as he entered the building. He strode past into the hallway.

A polished robot hurried up to meet him.

'Honoured Commander, allow me to escort you to your quarters.'

'Take me to the radio room, Lo-Kel-Gollu.'

'Honoured Commander, the Vestal Virgins left specific instructions—'

'The Vestal Virgins do not command this city.'

'Honoured Commander . . .'

Ignoring the robot's cries, Wa-Ka-Mo-Do strode through the building towards the radio room.

What was going on here, he wondered. *Why didn't they want him to know what was going on?*

'Honoured Commander!'

'Not another word! Go back to your post!'

He mounted the green cast-iron stairs that led up to the radio room, the sound of his feet echoing from the tiled walls.

There was another guard waiting outside the radio room, his sword drawn.

'Cho-Lee.'

'Honoured Commander, the Vestal Virgins have ordered that you should not enter here.'

Wa-Ka-Mo-Do looked the guard up and down. He was a big man, buzzing with lifeforce.

'Let me pass.'

The robot raised his sword a little, but his voice buzzed with emotion.

'I'm sorry, Honoured Commander. Shame lies at the end of whichever path I take. Please turn around now, that I may not fight you.'

'Cho-Lee, I must enter the radio room. You've seen what's happening outside. This is not right.'

'Honoured Commander, please. Leave, or if you must stay, draw your sword that we may fight as equals.'

Cho-Lee had a well-made body, reflected Wa-Ka-Mo-Do. Polished and humming with energy. He was a good fighter.

'Cho-Lee, please remember, I am one of the Eleven. Step aside and allow me to pass. This is the order of the Commander of Sangrel, the ultimate authority in this city.'

Cho-Lee looked down at the smaller robot.

'You are in charge, Honoured Commander?'

'Of course I am.' Wa-Ka-Mo-Do saw Cho-Lee's expression clear. 'You know that, Cho-Lee.'

Cho-Lee lowered his sword.

'Then I apologize for my actions.'

'Apology accepted. You serve in good faith Cho-Lee. Now, I have new orders for you. No one is to pass these doors while I am in this room. Do you understand, Cho-Lee?'

'I understand, Honoured Commander.'

The guard drew to one side, and Wa-Ka-Mo-Do pushed open the iron door.

He entered the radio room.

Karel

Karel and Melt were walking south into the summer. The grass was changing, little yellow and white faces emerged from amongst the green stalks. They watched them as they passed by.

'The mountains look so beautiful in the sun,' said Karel, deliberately ignoring the organic life.

Melt said nothing. Never the most talkative of robots, he spoke even less as they approached the central mountain range. Karel guessed he was exhausted by his travels. Despite her madness, Levine had done a good job of scraping away metal in that mine up near the village of Klimt, but he was still too big and heavy. Melt had walked nearly five hundred miles. Karel doubted he himself could walk one mile in that heavy body.

'I last saw these mountains when I was driving a train,' he continued, pleased by the sterility of the stone ahead. It would be so good to leave behind the feel of soil beneath his feet. 'Artemis placed my mind inside a locomotive, you know. I could only see straight ahead. It was winter then . . .'

'It will be winter somewhere now,' said Melt. 'Down in the real south, below the equator. Everything balances out in this world. When summer approaches in the north, winter approaches in the south. When there is happiness in the spring, there is sorrow in autumn.'

Karel was intrigued. Melt rarely admitted to anything.

'Does it?' asked Karel. 'Do you really believe that?'

'I wish it were true,' said Melt, sadly.

Karel waited, wondering if Melt would add anything else. Nothing.

'Have you been to the real south?' asked Karel. 'Have you been below the equator?'

'There's been fighting ahead,' said Melt. 'Look.'

They saw the scars in the ground ahead, ragged gashes of earth amongst the green grass.

'Kavan,' said Karel. Their journey to Artemis City was along a path of rumour built on the words exchanged with robots heading north. Those deserters from Spoole's and Kavan's armies had told them of this battle, warned them of the destruction, the unexploded shells, the booby traps. Karel and Melt had tried to keep their own company, but more than once they had found themselves hiding with other robots, watching the newly formed militias and bandits that now stamped and bullied their way across the land. Those other lone robots had told them of the little armies and forces that had set up camp in the mountains, each ruling and fighting over their own tiny territories.

Now they were almost there.

'This must be where Spoole and Kavan faced off, here at the edge of the mountains,' said Karel, looking up at the distant ledges. They would make a good place to set guns.

'The road beyond here will be booby trapped,' said Melt. 'That's what I would have done, if I were Spoole, fleeing the battlefield.'

'And you were a soldier,' said Karel. 'So what should we do now, then?'

'We should leave this path. There are still bodies ahead. So much metal will attract attention, especially in these empty lands.'

Indeed, there was movement in the distance. Peering ahead, between the flanks of the mountains, they saw robots moving about.

'Why would they bother us, when there is so much metal freely available?'

'Probably they wouldn't. But they could capture us, enslave us.'

'Then we'll have to fight them. This path is the only one that I know of through these mountains.'

They walked on. Into the battlefield proper. The ground here was torn apart, the earth and vegetation and stones mixed together in an uneven mush. Metal was strewn everywhere. Broken, abandoned. Parts of bodies, some of them covered in a light patina of rust.

'There must have been so much easy salvage,' said Melt.

'These pieces will go too,' said Karel. 'These mountains were full of little tribes and kingdoms. They'll all come creeping back now that Artemis has withdrawn.'

On and on they walked, approaching the pass. They joined the course of a set of railway lines, stepping from sleeper to sleeper.

There was a robot standing in the middle of the tracks. He stood, waiting for them as they approached.

'Hello,' he said. 'My name is Simrock. Which way shall I go?'

'Whichever way you like,' said Melt, making to push his way past. Simrock held out his arms.

'I don't know which way I like.'

'You're Spontaneous, aren't you?' said Karel. 'Where did you come from?'

'From the mountains. I walked up from the depths, following the paths of those who had gone before me.'

'Spontaneous?' said Melt. He seemed angry. 'There is no such thing!'

'Of course there is,' said Karel, puzzled at the big robot's reaction. 'I used to work with them, back in Turing City. I was an immigration officer . . .'

Simrock's eyes glowed.

'Turing City,' he said. 'Yes. I know about Turing City.'

'Then you have taken a long time coming to the surface. Turing City was destroyed by Artemis five months ago.'

'He's a liar,' said Melt. 'How could he know about Turing City, if he was formed deep down?'

'I don't know,' said Karel. 'They just do. Melt, what is the matter? I've never seen you so angry.'

It was true. The leaden man had clenched his fists, such was the power running through him.

'Nothing. I'm okay. I'm fine.'

'Very well,' said Karel, doubtfully. He turned to the other robot. 'What do you do, Simrock? What's your purpose?'

'What do I do? I look for the body of Nicolas the Coward. It will be useful in these times.'

'Nicolas the Coward was just a story,' said Karel. 'If he ever did wear an adamantium body, then it would have been found long ago. Anyway, how did he swap his mind from one body to another without any help?'

Simrock tilted his head. 'There was more than one person there, obviously. When Nicolas's wife wove the story into their child, she altered the details.'

Melt tugged at Karel's arm.

'Why are we wasting our time with this robot? Come on, your wife is waiting for you.'

'Hold on, Melt. What's the matter with you?'

'I told you, nothing!'

'I don't believe you.'

'Then don't. But why waste your time with this robot?'

'Maybe we can help each other. Simrock, do you know a way through the mountains?'

'He doesn't even know where he is!'

'No, he doesn't know which way to go. There's a difference. Where are you now, Simrock?'

'Just north of the central mountain range.'

'Apart from this road, do you know another way through the mountains?'

'I don't know this road. I only know the Northern Road.'

'Would you take us to it?'

'I will. Perhaps Nicolas the Coward will be there.'

Karel didn't bother to disagree. You couldn't change the way a robot's mind was twisted.

And after all, who was to say what was the right way to twist a mind?

Wa-Ka-Mo-Do

The floor, walls and ceiling of the radio room were covered in blue and white tiles that reflected the sound and made listening to transmissions harder than necessary. But this was the room of the Nine Virgins, built by the original Copper Master, and the paintings upon those white tiles must be preserved.

Two desks sat in the middle of the room, the focus of a tangle of wires and cables plugged into the piled black transceiving equipment that stood in marked contrast to the rest of the room. Two robots were on duty, they stood up as they realized Wa-Ka-Mo-Do had entered the room, pulling jacks from their heads as they did so.

'Honoured Commander, you should not be here . . .' The robot who spoke had the sign of the knot embossed on his shoulder, signifying he was one of the family of La-Ver-Di-Arussah. He was dressed almost entirely in copper in order to reduce sparks and possible interference.

'I am the commander of Sangrel, and I have decided to enter here,' said Wa-Ka-Mo-Do. 'I wish to speak to the Emperor himself. Arrange it immediately.'

The two robots exchanged looks.

'Honoured Commander,' said the second robot. 'The Emperor is not a servant to be summoned so . . .'

'The Emperor's city of Sangrel was attacked by humans last night. Are you suggesting that the Emperor would not wish to make his Honoured Commander aware of his feelings on this matter?'

'No, Honoured Commander. But we have been in contact with the Silent City earlier this morning and they made no attempt—'

'I believe I gave an order?'

Again the two robots looked at each other, then the second of them sat down and plugged a jack directly into his head. He reached out to one of the transceivers before him and turned a dial slowly around.

'This is four oh one Sangrel calling oh one one Silence.'

'*Receiving you, Sangrel.*'

'Silence, Wa-Ka-Mo-Do, of Ko of the state of Ekrano in the High Spires, Commander of the Emperor's Army of Sangrel, requests an audience with the Emperor.'

'*We will consult the Emperor's Secretary immediately. Tell the Honoured Commander he will be notified of his audience within the next few weeks.*'

The radio robot turned to face Wa-Ka-Mo-Do, but the light of satisfaction in his eyes faded on seeing his commander's expression.

'I want to speak to the Emperor immediately,' said Wa-Ka-Mo-Do. 'On the radio.'

The poor robot looked terrified as he swung back to face the equipment.

'I'm sorry, Silence. The Honoured Commander insists that he speak to the Emperor immediately.'

There was a pause, and Wa-Ka-Mo-Do could imagine the consternation at the other end of the line. He could see the current surging through the radio operator's body.

'*Sangrel, your commander is displaying a remarkable lack of understanding of the protocols of court. We suggest you relay this to him.*'

'There is no need!' wailed the terrified man. 'He is standing beside me now!'

Another prolonged silence followed. Wa-Ka-Mo-Do looked at the second operator.

'What's your name?' he asked.

'Li-Kallalla, Honoured Commander.'

'And I am Go-Ver-Dosai,' said the one who bore the knot insignia. Wa-Ka-Mo-Do ignored him as the voice on the radio said:

'*Sangrel, this is Silence. Your commander is indeed honoured amongst robots. Prepare to receive a message dictated by the Emperor himself, as relayed by the Silver Guard.*'

Li-Kallalla looked around in astonishment.

'Such a thing has *never* happened in the past, Honoured Commander.'

Wa-Ka-Mo-Do lowered his head and waited for the response, doing his best to appear dignified, but all the time feeling waves of relief surging through his body. At last the Emperor had been made aware of the situation. At last he understood what was happening to the robots of Sangrel.

The radio crackled, and a voice spoke.

'*Wa-Ka-Mo-Do, of Ko of the state of Ekrano in the High Spires, Commander of the Emperor's Army of Sangrel. Hear the words of the Emperor, dictated to his servant.*'

Out of respect, the two radio operators stood to attention. Wa-Ka-Mo-Do found himself doing the same.

'*The Emperor wishes it to be known that the situation in Sangrel is in harmony with his wishes. Wa-Ka-Mo-Do, his commander of the army of Sangrel, is to continue in his duties, and to offer all support to the humans that the Emperor has been pleased to welcome within his province. The wishes of the humans are paramount, and the Emperor would not wish himself to be disgraced in the eyes of his guests by being seen to place the needs of his subjects above those that he has welcomed into his lands.*'

Rank and roles were forgotten for just a moment as Wa-Ka-Mo-Do and the two radio robots looked at one another.

'*To be specific, the Emperor wishes his commander to understand that he is to place himself under the command of the Emperor's guests and to aid them in any way they request. Any actions otherwise would be deemed treachery to the Emperor. Is this understood?*'

The two radio robots gazed at Wa-Ka-Mo-Do, who remained motionless, staring at the black mouth of the speaker.

'*I repeat, Sangrel, is this understood? We wish to hear this from the mouth of the commander himself.*'

Li-Kallalla flicked a switch and looked up at Wa-Ka-Mo-Do.

'*Is this understood, Commander?*'

Wa-Ka-Mo-Do felt the current building in his electromuscles.

'*Is this understood?*'

'Yes,' said Wa-Ka-Mo-Do. 'I understand.'

'*Very well. Continue with your duty, Honoured Commander. Silence out.*'

Li-Kallalla flicked some more switches, and then turned back to gaze at Wa-Ka-Mo-Do.

'Do you have any more orders, Honoured Commander?'

Wa-Ka-Mo-Do was lost in thought.

'Honoured Commander?'

'What is going on?' said Wa-Ka-Mo-Do. 'What is going on, Li-Kallalla?'

'I do not know, Honoured Commander.'

The two robots were nervous and embarrassed by Wa-Ka-Mo-Do's behaviour. No wonder. He was addressing them as equals. He couldn't help it.

'If we follow the Emperor's commands then the robots of this city will all be killed,' he said.

'If those are the Emperor's wishes . . .' began Go-Ver-Dosai.

'Don't you understand, their deaths would be my responsibility.'

'Honoured Commander! Please do not touch me!'

Wa-Ka-Mo-Do realized he had seized Go-Ver-Dosai's arm. Slowly, he let go.

'The only thing protecting the humans at the moment is my troops! If I pull them back the humans would be wiped out and peace and harmony would return to Sangrel.'

'Such talk is treachery!' Go-Ver-Dosai was horrified. 'You heard the Emperor!'

'I know. I know.' He turned to Li-Kallalla. The younger robot was nervous, trapped between two superiors. 'What do you think is going on?' he asked.

'I don't know, Honoured Commander,' burbled the young robot, his voicebox slipping out of phase. 'I wouldn't presume to understand the mind of the Emperor.'

'No. Nor would I. And yet perhaps it is the minds of the humans we should understand. They appear to be the new rulers of Sangrel.'

'More treachery! The Emperor rules all of Yukawa!'

'Be silent, Go-Ver-Dosai! I am one of the Eleven!'

'The Eleven are subservient to the Emperor. Or are

the stories true? Do you subscribe to some higher power? The heresy of the Book of Robots runs throughout the High Spires.'

'I subscribe to the truth, Go-Ver-Dosai. And we are not seeing the truth at the moment, I know it. Li-Kallalla. Tell me, where else are there humans on Yukawa? You operate the radio. You must know.'

'He doesn't know, Honoured Commander,' said Go-Ver-Dosai firmly. 'We do not speak of anything but what we are directed to.'

'*I* am directing Li-Kallalla to speak. You will be silent.'

The young robot looked from one superior to the other, terrified.

'I don't know for sure, Commander. But . . .' he hesitated.

'Yes, Li-Kallalla?'

'Well, there were said to be humans in Ell.'

'That is classified information, Li-Kallalla!'

'Go-Ver-Dosai, you *will* be silent! Li-Kallalla, I am your superior. Nothing you know is classified from *me*!'

Wa-Ka-Mo-Do felt the current begin to surge once more. Ell again. The robots of the city had written that name as graffiti. What was happening in Ell?

'You imply that there are no longer humans in Ell?' he said, carefully.

Li-Kallalla lowered his gaze.

'Well, Honoured Commander, no one is quite sure what is happening in Ell. They no longer speak on the radio, they are no longer mentioned at all in any of the official reports—'

'Li-Kallalla, be quiet!'

In one fluid movement, Wa-Ka-Mo-Do drew his sword and brought the point up beneath the chin of Go-Ver-Dosai. 'I am the commander of this city,' he said. 'This is the last time I will mention this. I will instruct my troops what to do.'

'We are not your troops!' said Go-Ver-Dosai.

'Then you are but a civilian, and will follow my orders or die. Li-Kallalla, go on. What do you know of Ell?'

'Nothing. Only that on the day before you arrived there was a blast of static across the radio frequencies that burned out half the equipment here. It came from the direction of Ell.'

Wa-Ka-Mo-Do thought for a moment.

'How strong a blast?'

'I don't know.'

'Strong enough to kill a robot?'

'I don't know.'

Wa-Ka-Mo-Do slowly lowered his sword.

'I don't like this,' he said. 'I don't like this at all. Who are we to trust?'

'Trust your Emperor!' said Go-Ver-Dosai.

'I'm not sure I do,' said Wa-Ka-Mo-Do. 'I no longer believe he is the true power here in Yukawa. And even if he were, then is it right that we should follow a man who would sanction the death of so many of his own people?'

'Hah! You are not of the high born, are you?' challenged Go-Ver-Dosai. 'If you were, you would not ask such questions!'

'Silence,' said Wa-Ka-Mo-Do, raising his sword once more.

'I will not be silent in the face of such treason, Honoured Commander. Your duty is clear. You heard the words of the Emperor himself.'

'I heard the voice of one claiming to speak for the Emperor.'

'So what? Since when does a low-born robot have the right to question the Emperor?'

'Since the Emperor proved he was not worthy of command. I will not place myself in the service of these humans!'

'Then you are a traitor!'

'Maybe I am!'

And as he spoke the words he felt the great drain on his current, which had sucked his energy these past few days, finally disconnect. Wa-Ka-Mo-Do felt as if he had cleaned the rust from his mind. He felt as if he was thinking clearly at last.

'Maybe I am a traitor,' he repeated. 'But at last I am doing what is right! There will be no robots left in this city unless I act!'

'They will send orders to have you relieved of your command!'

That silenced Wa-Ka-Mo-Do. Go-Ver-Dosai was right. What was he to do?

He looked at the radio equipment, and an idea dawned upon him. It was a terrifying thought, but he was already a traitor.

'Destroy the radio equipment,' he said.

'No!' That was Li-Kallalla. 'Honoured Commander, please, no!'

'We have no choice, Li-Kallalla. Destroy it.'

Go-Ver-Dosai stepped forward.

'I will not allow this.'

Wa-Ka-Mo-Do brought his sword up once more. Go-Ver-Dosai laughed.

'You are indeed without grace. You challenge me when I am unarmed?'

'Then you take my sword, Go-Ver-Dosai,' said Wa-Ka-Mo-Do, handing it over. As the other robot took it, Wa-Ka-Mo-Do pushed his arm, thrusting the sword into one of the amplifiers. White sparks crackled. Go-Ver-Dosai lashed back with one foot, but Wa-Ka-Mo-Do dodged easily.

Go-Ver-Dosai paused, getting the balance of the sword.

'No grace!' he scoffed. 'The fight had not even begun. And will you help me, Li-Kallalla? Or will you see the radio destroyed?'

'I don't know,' the young robot said, miserably.

Wa-Ka-Mo-Do reached out and pushed a stack of equipment to the floor. They heard the valves inside popping.

Go-Ver-Dosai laughed.

'And how long do you think it will take to rebuild that? A day at most!'

'A day may be all we have,' said Wa-Ka-Mo-Do, and he lunged as Go-Ver-Dosai thrust the sword at him, made to grab the robot's hand, was surprised as the sword was whipped around to drag a long scratch across the scarlet metal of his arm. Wa-Ka-Mo-Do sprang to the side, took hold of Go-Ver-Dosai's wrist and pulled him forward, sending him tumbling over the broken equipment that lay on the floor.

'You are not without skill, Go-Ver-Dosai, but I am clearly your superior.'

'Maybe so. But I will retain my honour. Can you say the same?'

'Perhaps not,' said Wa-Ka-Mo-Do, sadly.

And as Go-Ver-Dosai thrust forward again, Wa-Ka-Mo-Do took his arm and pulled him over, landed on top of him, his elbow pressed against the other's shoulder, an awl in his hand.

'You wouldn't dare kill me!' said Go-Ver-Dosai.

'I already have,' said Wa-Ka-Mo-Do, and they both heard the crackle of current discharging into the damaged radio equipment.

'What do you mean?' said Li-Kallalla, and then he understood what was happening. Wa-Ka-Mo-Do was shorting the coil. That crackle was the sound of Go-Ver-Dosai's lifeforce being expended in seconds rather than years. The surge was so intense the metal of the nearby transceivers was melting.

'Traitor!' screeched Go-Ver-Dosai, his voice way too loud, distorting the malforming speaker. Sparks wriggled their way down the length of this body. 'You will betray this city too.'

'I will do my best for its people,' said Wa-Ka-Mo-Do.

'You betrayed the Emperor. What's to stop you betraying the people too?'

The words struck home.

'I will be loyal to this city . . .'

'Will you?'

'Yes!'

He realized he was arguing with a dying man. This was not behaviour worthy of a warrior of Ekrano.

'Yes,' he repeated. 'I will. This city will be safe in my charge.'

'Will it?' asked the dying robot. His body was melting, the heat of his mind was radiating from the metal. 'Then what about Jai-Lyn?'

'Jai-Lyn?' said Wa-Ka-Mo-Do, confused by the sudden change of subject. 'Jai-Lyn? What has she to do with Sangrel?'

'Nothing,' said the robot. 'Yet she asks for your help. Three times now we have received messages from Ka, asking for you by name.'

'Jai-Lyn asked for me? Why didn't you tell me?'

'The Vestal Virgins ordered us not to.' His voice distorted. His mind was melting. 'They *buzzz* saw the *buzzzz* treachery in your *buzzz* mind.'

'Why did she want me?'

Go-Ver-Dosai just smiled. He reached up and placed a finger to his head, prised open the broken panelling there and pushed the finger inside. There was a blue flash and three loud cracks. He convulsed and died. Smoke came from his head.

Li-Kallalla looked as if his own mind was melting.

'You killed him . . .'

Wa-Ka-Mo-Do looked at the young robot.

'Li-Kallalla,' he said urgently, 'whose orders will you follow. Mine, or the Vestal Virgins'? Will you speak of what happened in here?'

'Will you kill me too?'

Wa-Ka-Mo-Do didn't answer. He didn't know.

Li-Kallalla spoke, but Wa-Ka-Mo-Do wasn't listening, swamped by thoughts. Go-Ver-Dosai lay dead and smoking in the middle of the wreckage. He had betrayed the Emperor, betrayed his command, all for what he hoped were the right reasons. Could he be trusted?

Jai-Lyn was asking for help. She had summoned Wa-Ka-Mo-Do. He had promised to go to her aid. But he couldn't. He had to stay here in this city.

First Ell, then Sangrel. And now Ka.

What was happening on Yukawa?

Karel

'How long will he stay with us?' asked Melt, looking at the Spontaneous robot walking the Northern Road ahead of them.

'There's no telling,' said Karel. 'The Spontaneous are like this, especially when they first emerge.'

'What happens to them then?'

'Some of them assimilate into the prevailing society. Some of them wander to the borders. They seem to be driven by imperatives according to the knowledge they are born with.' He looked around at the high mountain views, thoughtfully. 'Just like us, I suppose. I wonder how he knew about this road?'

'There have been others here before us,' said Melt. 'An army has marched this road. Kavan's, I suppose.'

Karel hummed in agreement. The high passes of the

Northern Road were littered with the ash of portable forges, the stones worn further by the many feet that had passed.

'The views are amazing up here,' said Karel, looking at the streams of snowmelt that wet the grey rock beyond the low wall. 'The sky is bluer. The rocks seem more alive.'

'I know,' said Melt, and Karel thought he heard a touch of sadness there. What was he remembering?

'Why don't you like Simrock?' he asked.

'No reason.'

'Yes there is. You don't have to tell me if you don't want to.'

'I'll tell you why. His mind is twisted around a story. How can we trust him?'

'All of our minds are twisted around stories,' said Karel. 'Who is to say which ones are the right ones?'

'I need to rest,' said Melt, suddenly. He sat down, leaning his heavy body against the low wall by the side of the road.

'Simrock!' called Karel. The Spontaneous robot was up ahead, looking over a ridge at the road's descent beyond. He came back to join them.

'We need to rest.'

They remained in silence for a while, the blue sky deepening to black above them.

'Did you have a wife, Melt?' asked Karel.

'No,' said Melt.

'Karel does,' said Simrock. 'She's in Artemis City.'

Metal scraped on rock as Karel turned to stare at the other robot.

'How do you know that? I never mentioned that to you.'

'I know about you, Karel,' said Simrock.

'How?'

'How did he know about these mountains?' asked Melt. 'I thought that was the way of the Spontaneous.'

'What do you know of me?' said Karel, eyes glowing uncomfortably.

'I know about your mind.'

'What about it?'

'I think it's probably useful for the present time. It's not the way for regular robots though. Your moment will pass.'

Karel's gyros had begun to spin, seeking a balance he did not feel.

'So many minds,' said Melt. 'I once heard a saying. A robot is just a mind's way of making another mind.'

'Is that supposed to calm me down?' wondered Karel.

'I don't think that applies to the Spontaneous, though,' continued Melt, following his train of thought. 'Where do their minds come from?' He looked suspiciously at Simrock.

'We're all probably descended from the Spontaneous,' said Karel, also staring at Simrock. How many other robots knew who he was? It was an unsettling thought. Here he was in the mountains, and across the world below him there were maybe robots who even now were looking towards him, and pondering his moves.

'I know a story about where robots come from,' said Simrock, brightly. 'The story of Alpha and Gamma.'

'I never believed that story,' interrupted Karel,

before the story even began. 'Anyway, what happened to Beta?'

'That comes later,' said Simrock. He began his tale.

The Story of Alpha and Gamma

'Alpha and Gamma lived in the mountains at the Top of the World. They were the first two robots. No one knows where they came from, and no one knows why they decided to make a child. Some people say that the urge was woven into their minds, as it is in all robots' minds to differing extents, but that would imply there were robots before Alpha and Gamma to do the weaving. Others say that as Alpha and Gamma grew older they desired a robot to look after them in their old age, but that implies they knew of death, and how could the first two robots know of something they had never seen before? And some people say that Alpha and Gamma wove a child because they simply had the idea to do so.

'So how was the first mind made? For even though there is disagreement about *why* Alpha and Gamma made a mind, all agree that they did not have the knowledge at first about how to make such a thing. This is something that they learned for themselves.

'Where to begin? First they opened up each other's heads and they examined the metal inside. They saw iron and copper, gold, silver, platinum and palladium, and so they went away and they mined ore and they smelted it and they made wire, just like that in their own heads.

But the wire they made was straight and smooth and unthinking.

'"How do we twist it?" asked Gamma, holding the wire in her hands. "Where do we begin? This is just a piece of wire. I see nothing here. No sense of love or fear, no happiness or sadness or yearning or satiety . . ."'

'But Alpha looked at the wire in another way.

'"I see none of those things," he said. "But I can do this . . ." and he bent the wire around, twisting it over itself.

'"Now a current flows," he said, and he twisted again, "now it doesn't." And he repeated the movement over again. "Off and on," he said.

'"Life and death," said Gamma. "But there is no emotion there . . ."

'"Maybe not," said Alpha. "But emotion is not all there is to a mind. I can do this . . ."'

'He twisted the wire some more, making two living twists, one larger than the other.

'"Now it recognizes, more or less," he said.

'"More or less?"

'"Five twists are more than four. Seventy is less than one hundred. More or less."

'"More or less? What sort of a mind is that? That's just numbers. Does it understand that love is more than justice, or that sorrow is more than pain?"

'"No, but . . ."

'"Then stop wasting my time!" And she walked from the mountain ledge where Alpha worked, out into the golden sunset. (For I should say that in those days all sunsets were golden, and the world was beautiful and that metal ore littered the ground.)

'Alpha sat for some time, but the idea had taken hold of him, as such ideas do with men, and he worked through the night, twisting the wire back and forth. He found he could twist the wire to one hundred positions by rotation around the axis of the wire, and a further one hundred positions by pitch. He could make it add, subtract, multiply and divide; it could look at different parts of its own extent; it could loop around itself and remember. He found that he could string these functions together, but he could do no more than that.

'And in the end he saw that Gamma was right, that the task was pointless, and as morning dawned, he threw the wire to the floor and walked off in search of his wife so that he might apologize.

'He looked for her to the north and south, to the east and west, but could not find her. In the end he returned to the ledge to see Gamma sitting there, the length of wire in her hands, and she looked up at Alpha, her eyes shining with awe and wonder.

'"How did you do it?" she asked.

'"I did nothing," he bitterly replied.

'"Did nothing? You brought life to this wire! It doesn't feel, it doesn't know, but the rudiments are there!"

'"The rudiments? It does nothing but add and take away!"

'She stared at him.

'"Alpha, please, don't be like that to me. I am sorry for the way I spoke."

'"Be like what? I did my best, but I failed."

'"Failed?" She looked deeper into his eyes, and saw no deceit there. "Alpha, you did the hardest part! It is almost finished! Look, twist it here, twist it back on itself, see, and it will *know* itself. Twist it again, and it will know others . . ."

'Alpha stared at her.

'"I don't see what you mean."

'So she showed him again, but he still didn't understand.

'And it has ever been thus, that men and women work together to make a child, but neither understands what the other has wrought, nor shall they ever.'

'And that is the story of Alpha and Gamma and how they made the first child.'

Simrock beamed at them, delighted.

'Hold on,' said Karel, 'what about Beta?'

'Oh yes, Beta. In some stories, it is said there was a third robot, Beta, who sat between Alpha and Gamma and placed the extra twists in the metal that moved it from the male understanding to the female understanding. Some say that Beta crept to the ledge in the night and added the extra twists. And some say that Alpha and Gamma never existed, there was only Beta.'

'How do you know all this?' asked Melt. 'You're Spontaneous, you have only just arrived here. How do you know all this?'

'I don't know.'

Karel was wondering aloud. 'Where do these stories come from?' he asked. 'Stories of Four Blind Horses, of

Valerie of Klimt, stories of Alpha and Gamma, of Nicolas the Coward. This world is built on stories, some of them we know, some of them we don't even understand! Where do they come from?'

'I don't know!'

'Why does no one ever ask?'

'It's not woven into people's minds to ask,' said Melt. 'Why should it be? They're only stories.'

'I'm asking!'

Karel was suddenly shaken, as if by a bolt of electricity. Morphobia Alligator had spoken of this. Robots like Karel, robots who could choose to do things that weren't woven into their minds.

Robots who saw things that other robots did not.

Karel looked around. Melt, the robot who claimed to have forgotten his past, sat on one side, Simrock the Spontaneous robot on the other. All three of them on a forgotten road through the high mountains. He had once thought that that life in Turing City was liberal and edgy and cosmopolitan. Now it all seemed so safe and predictable, a tiny little island in a far corner of the world.

He had had to come up here to realize just how strange his world really was.

Was he the only one who saw it?

Wa-Ka-Mo-Do

Wa-Ka-Mo-Do made his way from the radio room and out into Smithy Square, his gyros spinning. What was going on? What had happened in Ell?

Wa-Ka-Mo-Do imagined walking through that city. Ell was a beautiful place, set with towers tiled in blue, green and gold. The city was famous for its ceramics, it was said there wasn't a surface in the city that wasn't tiled. The robots of Ell made a red iron oxide glaze of a colour unsurpassed throughout Yukawa.

Now he imagined those tiled streets filled with the dead bodies of robots. Bodies slumped on the ground, their arms and legs entangled, their eyes lifeless, and faint smoke emerging from their heads. What had the humans done there? What would they be doing in Ka? Jai-Lyn had asked for his help. There was something so pathetic about that request. They had only met for a few hours, and yet she had turned to him. Was that a surprise? Wa-Ka-Mo-Do was probably the most important robot she had ever met.

He walked from the Copper Master's house into the daylight. The sun was bright, it thinned the black smoke, it threw the scorch marks across the tiled square into harsh relief.

The sight of the humans clustered around one of their cannons at the edge of the square irritated him. La-Ver-Di-Arussah was there, speaking to one of them.

She beckoned him to join her.

'Honoured Commander, the humans have requested that we remove ourselves from the Copper Master's house and relocate lower down the city.' La-Ver-Di-Arussah was buzzing with energy. 'I've already sent Ka-Lo-Re-Harballah down to secure an area around the Copper Market.'

Wa-Ka-Mo-Do looked at the broken roof of the

Emperor's palace, looked at the strange cannons that the humans were erecting all around the perimeter of the square. They seemed to move of their own accord, their strange metal muzzles constantly scanning the sky.

'How are the robots of the city?' asked Wa-Ka-Mo-Do.

'They remain under control.'

'What does that mean?'

'Honoured Commander?' Her face was innocent. He saw the knot insignias on her panelling and thought of Go-Ver-Dosai, lying dead in the radio room. What would Li-Kallalla do, he wondered? Who would the young robot betray, Wa-Ka-Mo-Do or the Emperor?

Either way, it was out of his hands now.

Wa-Ka-Mo-Do looked up again at the broken roof.

'Have the humans apologized for what happened to our city?' he asked aloud.

'Honoured Commander?'

'Nothing.' Wa-Ka-Mo-Do straightened up. He had chosen his path, now he had to walk it. 'La-Ver-Di-Arussah, fetch me the human commander.'

'Honoured Commander, he is far too busy at the moment. He is co-ordinating other troop movements, preparing a counterattack on those who came here last night.'

Too busy, thought Wa-Ka-Mo-Do. *He is too busy to speak to me.*

'So, Honoured Commander, shall I organize the withdrawal from the Copper Master's house?'

'No, La-Ver-Di-Arussah. No. I don't think so. We will remain where we are for the moment.'

'But the humans said . . .'

Wa-Ka-Mo-Do felt the current begin to hum inside him.

'The humans are no longer in charge here. I am. And I received my orders from the Emperor, not ten minutes ago.'

'But—'

'No buts, La-Ver-Di-Arussah. Tell the human commander I will be pleased to see him at his earliest convenience, here, in the middle of Smithy Square. Tell him that I will be pleased to discuss his continued presence in my city.'

'But—'

'Tell him that *now*, La-Ver-Di-Arussah. And whilst you're doing it, get me Ka-Lo-Re-Harballah. He will no longer be required to secure quarters for us in the Copper Market. We're staying here. Quickly now, La-Ver-Di-Arussah.'

She didn't move quickly. As slowly as possible, La-Ver-Di-Arussah turned and moved away. He wasn't overly surprised when he saw her head, not in the direction of the Street of Becoming, but back towards the group of humans. Wa-Ka-Mo-Do didn't watch their hurried conversation, but made his way instead to look out across Lake Ochoa towards the Mound of Eternity.

There was a lot of movement down there today. Human machines – those boxy green and yellow shapes that spent much of their time in the fields to the south of the city – had been brought back here to the very edge of the city and set to excavating holes, moving soil and gravel.

Human craft flew above them. They were lifting up machines on cables, carrying them to new locations. Wa-Ka-Mo-Do watched as a craft headed up to the terrace, one of the strange guns swinging on a cable beneath it.

Wa-Ka-Mo-Do ignored it. He was still scanning the area around the lake. Amongst all the humans he saw robots. Many, many robots. More robots than had business being there. It was happening already. All the resentment that had been building up over the past weeks had found a focus. Sangrel had been attacked. To make matters worse, the humans were withdrawing from the surrounding land. Whatever pressure had been holding those farmers and miners in their place was being released. They were coming towards the city. For the moment, they were only watching. But for how long would that be true . . .

'Wa-Ka-Mo-Do!'

Wa-Ka-Mo-Do turned to see a human female. She wore grey cloth panelling; her face was dappled with dew, like metal in the morning.

'I'm Gillian.' The female held out a hand, and Wa-Ka-Mo-Do took it in his own, the way he had seen other humans do, and moved it up and down.

'My official title is Honoured Commander.'

'I'm sorry, Honoured Commander. Blame the trans-lating machine.' Wa-Ka-Mo-Do watched the little blinking light as the female spoke. 'Listen, we have a problem. You saw the attack last night? You saw the machines that came here? Well, our intelligence suggests that the next attack will be with much faster craft. Craft that use rockets for propulsion, not propeller blades. Do you understand those concepts?'

'I understand.'

'Good! Now, do you see our cannon? They're fully automatic. They can track moving objects many miles away, they can turn and fire in a fraction of a second.'

'They are impressive devices indeed,' replied Wa-Ka-Mo-Do, politely.

'Thank you, Honoured Commander.' Gillian seemed pleased at the compliment. She was not at all like Rachael, Wa-Ka-Mo-Do noted. Her hair was grey, her face had far more lines upon it. 'But there is a problem,' she continued. 'You see, the enemy has equally fast devices. We need to give our cannon enough time to see and react to an attack.'

'I understand this.'

'Good! Then you will understand why we need to occupy the Copper Master's house.'

'I understand.' Gillian beamed. 'But there is another solution, you realize? A much simpler one.'

'Yes?' Gillian leaned forward, listening carefully. 'And what's that?'

'If you were to leave this city, there would be no reason for an attack to take place.'

There was a moment's silence, and the human adopted an expression that Wa-Ka-Mo-Do could not quite read. She moved her head from side to side. Wa-Ka-Mo-Do knew from Rachael that this meant disagreement.

'Sadly, Honoured Commander, it would just make the attack more likely. The attackers will seek to take control of this city themselves.'

And would that be any worse than your presence? wondered Wa-Ka-Mo-Do.

'So, you will give your permission?'

'I'll think about it.'

Wa-Ka-Mo-Do was suddenly flushed with self-doubt. What had he done? By destroying the radio he had completely isolated himself. He had placed himself in charge of this dreadful mess, and he didn't know what to do next. What if removing the guns left the city open to worse attack? How was he to know?

'You'll think about it?' said the woman, and something in her attitude hardened. 'I thought it was understood, this city is a gift to the humans from the Emperor.'

'A gift?' said Wa-Ka-Mo-Do, and he felt a double lurch of betrayal, one by his Emperor, one by himself. 'I wasn't told about that. I was only told to command the Emperor's Army of Sangrel.'

'Robot, there—'

'My title is Honoured Commander. You will show me respect by using it!'

Her eyes widened at the tone of his voice. Even through his annoyance he saw the way her animal body tensed, and then relaxed.

'Fine. Honoured Commander, there will be another attack tonight. Would you hinder it? What would your Emperor say?'

'I don't know. Nor have I the means to find out. The radio is destroyed.'

'Destroyed? How?'

'Just destroyed. I said I will think about your request. You may go.'

The woman looked at him for a moment, and he caught a hint of Rachael in her expression.

Rachael! thought Wa-Ka-Mo-Do. *Where is she? Did she live through the attack?* He hadn't thought of her since returning to the city; he had been too busy dealing with the fallout. Jai-Lyn, Rachael . . . He hadn't exactly promised the human he would look after her, but even so . . .

But, to his relief, here she came now, there amongst a group of humans that had just emerged from the western gate. She wore different panelling today, something of a heavier cloth, it showed very little of her skin, it concealed the shape of her body rather than displaying it to the world, as had been her style in the past. The other humans were dressed in the same manner; they were almost like the soldiers that guarded them, the long black spikes of their rifles held not quite pointing at the ground.

Rachael was marching with her father, part of the group of the more important humans. Wa-Ka-Mo-Do looked for the anthracite-skinned ambassador, with his iron skin, but he couldn't see him.

'Honoured Commander!'

A woman stepped forward. Wa-Ka-Mo-Do recognized her as Captain Littler, La-Ver-Di-Arussah's equivalent amongst the human soldiers.

'Captain,' said Wa-Ka-Mo-Do. He watched the little light on her headset flicker as he spoke, translating his words.

'Honoured Commander, we must apologize for what has occurred in this city last night! I hope you understand that we are not ourselves without losses. Ambassador Mbeki died in the Emperor's Palace.'

'That is a great sadness,' said Wa-Ka-Mo-Do. 'Many robots also died last night.'

'We're sorry, truly we are.'

Wa-Ka-Mo-Do couldn't read her face. Was that expression one of genuine sorrow? Whatever it was, it vanished immediately.

'But Honoured Commander, you must understand, this is not the end. Our intelligence tells us that we will be attacked again tonight. We must take appropriate defensive action!'

Wa-Ka-Mo-Do asked the question that no one else seemed yet to have asked.

'Why was this city attacked by other humans?'

He saw Rachael staring at him, her copper sulphate eyes willing him on. Willing him to do what?

Captain Littler had lost her voice. She was speaking to the other humans, but the light on her headset stayed dark. The unpleasantly wet organic sounds she made annoyed Wa-Ka-Mo-Do unduly. Now she turned to him and that little light began flashing once more.

'I am sorry, Honoured Commander, that we did not tell you the full truth earlier, but you will understand our embarrassment. You see, one of our units has gone rogue. A company of soldiers have broken away from our command; they seek to overthrow the legitimate government of Sangrel in order that they might exploit your land.'

Wa-Ka-Mo-Do watched Rachael as Captain Littler spoke. He tried to read the expression on the young woman's soft face. She was trying to tell him something, he was certain of it.

'A company of your soldiers?'

'You must sympathize, Honoured Commander. After all, your own robots seek to rebel against you.'

Only since you came here, thought Wa-Ka-Mo-Do.

'I am sorry to say some of this rebellion was fuelled by humans.'

Wa-Ka-Mo-Do thought of the petrol cans back in the fields. The human-made cans.

'But believe me, Honoured Commander, once captured, they will be made to pay for their actions. For now, though, we need your help.'

'And you may have it, Captain Littler. Only not at the expense of the robots under my command.'

He saw La-Ver-Di-Arussah and Ka-Lo-Re-Harballah approaching, hurrying across the square. Ka-Lo-Re-Harballah was wearing another robot's arm.

'I was pulled into a crowd,' he explained. 'They wrenched my own from me.'

'I took that arm from another robot,' said La-Ver-Di-Arussah. 'Honoured Commander, is there discord between you and the humans?'

'There is no discord, only misunderstanding,' said Captain Littler, smoothly. 'I'm sure that the commander will aid us to his fullest ability.'

'Of course I will.'

'Honoured Commander,' said La-Ver-Di-Arussah, 'I know your feelings on this matter, but may I strongly suggest we open fire on the crowd below in order to encourage their dispersal? They are getting angry.'

'Of course they are! Their city was attacked!'

'It is, of course, the Emperor's city,' corrected La-Ver-Di-Arussah.

'I thought it belonged to the humans now?' replied Wa-Ka-Mo-Do.

'Then obey their orders, as the Emperor commanded.'

'I told you, the Emperor has issued new orders.'

'So you said. Ka-Lo-Re-Harballah,' she turned to face the young robot, 'go and bring confirmation from the radio room.'

'You dare to question my authority, La-Ver-Di-Arussah?'

'No, Honoured Commander, but confirmation is appropriate in these circumstances.'

'Sadly, that will not be possible. The radio is destroyed.'

La-Ver-Di-Arussah gazed at him, and he could feel the surge of the current through her body even from here. She was angry.

'How did that happen?'

'Go-Ver-Dosai lies dead amongst the debris. He did not like the Emperor's words.'

He felt such shame. He hadn't lied as such, but what he had implied was not the truth.

'You're saying that Go-Ver-Dosai destroyed the radio?'

La-Ver-Di-Arussah stared at him. He knew that she was wondering whether or not to challenge him, here and now. Even the humans felt it. They were listening to the exchange in silence, their wet eyes wide.

'Ka-Lo-Re-Harballah,' ordered La-Ver-Di-Arussah.

'Go and see what must be done. Find out how long it will be until the radio is repaired.'

'Ka-Lo-Re-Harballah is under my command,' warned Wa-Ka-Mo-Do.

'It was a reasonable request, Honoured Commander.'

It was. He directed Ka-Lo-Re-Harballah to go.

'And so, Honoured Commander,' pressed La-Ver-Di-Arussah. 'What of the robots who approach this square? Shall we open fire?'

'Not yet. Order the robots to disperse. Tell them that I am controlling this city now, and that there may be another attack tonight.'

Captain Littler stepped forward.

'And that's why, Honoured Commander, it is of the utmost importance that the guns are set up in the Copper Master's house!'

'Then set them up,' said La-Ver-Di-Arussah.

Wa-Ka-Mo-Do drew his sword.

'You undermine my authority for the last time, La-Ver-Di-Arussah. I challenge you to a duel.'

'What? Here in the middle of preparations for battle?' She laughed. 'You are being ridiculous, Wa-Ka-Mo-Do.'

'Fight, or I will cut you down where you stand.'

Rachael ducked under her father's arm and ran forward from the group of humans. She paused just short of where Wa-Ka-Mo-Do stood, his sword gleaming sharp, La-Ver-Di-Arussah looking up at him, taunting him.

'Stop this!' she called. 'This is so stupid!'

'Stand back, Rachael,' said Wa-Ka-Mo-Do, voice low.

'Rachael, get back here!'

The young woman rounded on her father, face red.

'You're going to get them all killed! Don't you care?'

At a nod from her father, one of the humans dressed in green stepped forward to pull Rachael back.

'You get a soldier to do your dirty work now?' she said in tones of disgust. 'Wa-Ka-Mo-Do,' she called, turning those blue eyes upon him. 'Stop her! You've got to listen to me!'

Slowly, Wa-Ka-Mo-Do resheathed his sword, and he saw the humans relax a little. Then he held up a hand. He flexed the blades at the ends of his fingers. The green human saw them, looked to Rachael's father for instructions.

'Let her speak,' commanded Wa-Ka-Mo-Do.

'Would the Emperor be pleased that you threaten his guests?'

'Be *quiet*, La-Ver-Di-Arussah!'

Rachael's face had changed colour, became chalk white, and again Wa-Ka-Mo-Do recognized something in common with her. They were both at the edge of something. Wa-Ka-Mo-Do had just crossed a boundary, Rachael was about to.

'Speak, Rachael,' said Wa-Ka-Mo-Do. And Rachael took a deep breath and did just that.

'It's the people here, Wa-Ka-Mo-Do,' she began. 'The people of —— ——. Don't you see, that they're just —— ——. There are —— —— ——.'

She gradually became aware that her words were not being translated, and she pulled the headset from her head and rounded on her father.

'SSSSSSSWWWW WWSSSWSDSDD,' she shouted at him. 'OOO SSSSS SSKKSKKS WWWSSKKS.'

Her father recoiled at her words.

'You can't have it,' he said.

'SSSKKK SSSKKK WWWWWKKKW.'

'What they do is nothing to do with us!'

'WWKKK SSKKKS SSSSSWWWKKK.'

She was winning, Wa-Ka-Mo-Do could tell. He was no expert at human body language, but he could see that Rachael was winning the argument. Her father gave in, pulled the headset from his head and passed it to Rachael. She took it, and when she spoke now, it was with her father's voice.

'Don't you see, Wa-Ka-Mo-Do,' she said, in deep tones that were at odds with her appearance. 'We're not part of one human tribe or Empire, come here to deal with you.'

'I guessed that.'

'No! You don't know how bad it is! They kept this planet a secret for as long as they could, but there are so many different concerns back on Earth, and they're all rushing here to exploit this place. Dragging whole families along if it's more convenient that way . . .'

Her father shouted something to her, something not translated.

'No, Father, you never did care about anything except your precious job.' Her face had changed colour again, it now glowed red.

'Wa-Ka-Mo-Do, you're wasting time arguing, you don't know how bad it is. We're only the first, but there are more humans coming. Better equipped and better armed! They'll take this planet from you!'

'We won't let them,' said Wa-Ka-Mo-Do, with a confidence he didn't feel.

Rachael laughed bitterly.

'Won't let them? You haven't a choice! Look at what happened to Ell!'

And at that her father stepped forward and grabbed the headset from her.

'That's enough, Rachael,' he said, but he said it in Rachael's voice.

'What happened in Ell?' said Wa-Ka-Mo-Do, the blades on his hands extended.

'That wasn't us,' said Rachael's father. 'It was ——
——'

He pulled a face, put his own headset back in place. Now he spoke in his own, uncensored voice.

'It was another organization that attacked Ell. The one that attacks us now. They are bigger and stronger than us.'

'Good! Then we'll throw you out of this city and let them deal with you. Perhaps they will leave us in peace.'

'Don't be a fool! We're the best you'll ever get. We're half sponsored by the SEAU University, they want us to research your society. All the other organizations are interested in is profit! They will exploit this city just like they exploited Ell. And if you get in their way, as the robots of Ell did, they will destroy you too.'

Wa-Ka-Mo-Do felt as if his lifeforce was draining away. He looked at La-Ver-Di-Arussah struggling to hide her uncertainty.

'And the Emperor permits this?' he said in despair.

'The Emperor does not,' said Rachael's father. 'Not any more. The Emperor lost control of Yukawa months ago! Back when he first made a deal with us. Hah! He thought he was being so clever. He didn't have a clue. Not a clue.'

Wa-Ka-Mo-Do brought his hands up, blades extended.

'I should kill you now!' he said.

Rachael was there, standing between the two of them.

'Wa-Ka-Mo-Do, no! That's my father!'

Slowly, Wa-Ka-Mo-Do lowered his hands.

'What would you do now, *Honoured Commander?*' taunted La-Ver-Di-Arussah. She had regained her composure.

'You heard what he said,' replied Wa-Ka-Mo-Do. 'The Emperor no longer rules Yukawa.'

'Human lies. The Emperor will always rule.'

'Then how do you explain that!' He pointed to the smashed roof of the Emperor's palace. La-Ver-Di-Arussah ignored it. She was constructing her own reality. One where she was still an important robot. She ignored anything that didn't fit in with that world view.

Wa-Ka-Mo-Do turned around.

'Captain Littler, you may liaise with my staff as to the placement of your guns, however the Copper Master's house remains under my control. La-Ver-Di-Arussah, you will assist Ka-Lo-Re-Harballah in warning the robots of Sangrel of tonight's attack. Tell them they may leave the city if they wish, though I cannot guarantee their safety, no matter where they go.'

'Yes, Honoured Commander,' said La-Ver-Di-Arussah. 'And the humans?'

'After you have followed my orders you will find them quarters in the middle city.'

'Certainly, Honoured Commander.'

He watched her cross the square. He couldn't trust her, but if he kept her here he would have to fight her, and he didn't have time for that. He turned to Rachael, who gazed back, blue eyes looking from a white face. His copper girl.

'Are you frightened?' he said.

'No,' said Rachael. But she was, he knew it. He was too. He was lost, isolated, cut off from his Emperor, severed from his command, and diverging from the path he had followed since childhood. Then something else occurred to him.

'Ka,' he said. 'What do you know about Ka?'

'Ka?' said Rachael. 'That's the city on the coast, isn't it? The one with the whales?'

'Yes.' He thought about Jai-Lyn, so similar to this human, if such a thing was possible.

'Ka,' said Rachael. 'They occupy it, the ——. The ones who —— Ell.'

Her headset was censoring her again. It didn't matter, he had got the gist of the conversation.

Either way, Jai-Lyn was on her own. He had problems enough of his own here in Sangrel.

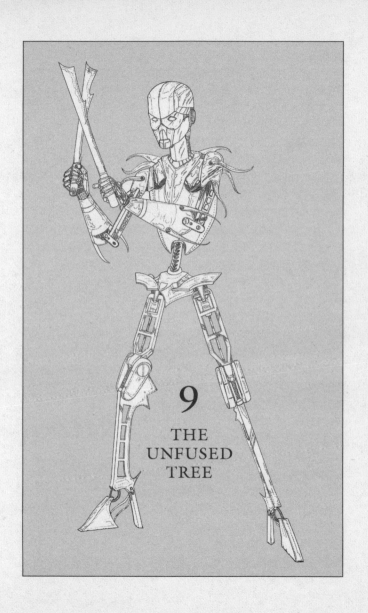

9
THE
UNFUSED
TREE

Susan

The robots of Artemis City strained for a view of the animals, but they were too far away to be properly seen. They were building themselves a compound to the south-west of the city. Susan watched it growing from the windows of the Centre City, following Spoole from room to room. She had seen the construction as a series of separate pictures, each framed and viewed from a slightly different vantage point. In a room of computers, busily calculating figures relayed to them on foil sheets, she had watched as the larger craft had settled on the plain, the smaller craft hovering above it all the while, standing guard. The two ships were so alien, painted in bright, unrobotlike colours, covered in strange symbols, and so, so large. When the sun passed behind it in the evening, the smaller craft cast a shadow across the whole southern part of the city, and Susan saw robots standing in the streets, gazing up and pointing to it.

They had spent a day in an index room, Spoole asking questions, sending green robots scurrying this way and that, bringing back still more sheets of foil on which answers were written, and Susan had watched through the window as yellow machines with huge shovels on the front had dug great trenches into the plain. Other machines set to work erecting the metal skeletons of buildings whilst yet more drove around them, spilling black tar across the plain, making roads and squares for still more machines to run across. The humans seemed to have a machine for everything!

Susan could see the blue-painted shells of the engineers in the distance, watching from the newly constructed iron walls of Artemis City, noting everything they could about the animals' devices.

Spoole seemed to be getting nowhere.

'I'm being given the runaround,' he said to Susan, as they rested in a forge one afternoon, Susan idly rubbing a file across her seams. 'Sandale and the rest don't dare get rid of me, at least not yet, but they're not going to help me. Don't worry though. We'll find your friend somehow. Here, take some of this.'

He handed Susan some platinum wire that lay bundled on a shelf near the fire. Susan accepted it with bad grace. He didn't seem to get it. He thought they were both friends now, rather than just two people united in a common cause. She looked at the wire, felt it. It was very pure, as good a quality as anything she would have found back in Turing City. She looked around and realized that everything in this room was superior. The plate iron, the chrome steel alloy, the choice of solders in a range of thicknesses. Truly, in Artemis City, not all robots were quite so equal as they would have you believe.

'I can't believe that Sandale and the rest would betray Shull to the humans,' she said.

'They claim to still follow Nyro. They have gained more metal than they have lost. The animals have presented the city with iron and gold. There are rumours . . .' He looked around the room. No one else was present, any robot who entered swiftly withdrew when they saw Spoole there. 'There are rumours that they have presented Artemis with *aluminium*.'

'Aluminium?' said Susan. She felt a tingle of current in her hands. She was a craftsrobot. What would she give in order to feel the mythical element? 'Still, even if it were true, you sell your principles cheaply. The animals are taking more than they give. You've seen that base they are building. Do you think they will be content to stay there when all of Artemis City is on their doorstep? The whole of Shull will be connected to their base by railway lines.'

'I know that,' said Spoole complacently. He was too busy twisting a sheet of copper into shape.

Susan looked at the other robot. She hated him. And yet she followed him.

The next day they had walked the corridors of the Main Index, and Susan was sure she saw robots ducking out of their way as they approached. Spoole was right, she decided, they *were* giving him the runaround. The clerks were helpful, but only up to a point.

Outside, the animals were at work again, erecting a perimeter of guns around their base. Strange guns, almost like robot women, they moved by themselves in a kind of dance, spinning this way and that as they looked across the wide plain. They reminded Susan of the Turing City Guard, the way they too had danced in the night whilst patrolling the city.

That evening there was a shift in the light, lines of shadows moving across the city, golden and dirty in the setting sun, and Susan saw the second craft, the one that had hung there these past few days, descending slowly to the ground, settling within the perimeter of guns.

Blue and silver and black and grey robots crowded the walls, watching the spectacle. The ship came to rest, and a stillness settled over the city.

'They're here,' said Susan, spite in her voice, 'they have really arrived. I don't think this is our world any more.'

'It was never *your* world,' said Spoole, 'it was always Nyro's.'

A week passed, and Spoole was no closer to their goal. Worse, they were starting to be noticed. Infantryrobots seemed always to be present, standing in rooms, passing them in corridors, repairing themselves in forges they would not normally frequent.

'The Generals will only tolerate me as long as they think I am not a threat,' said Spoole. 'Fools. They always seek to avoid direct confrontation as long as possible. Still, it would be wise if we were to try something else for the moment.'

They left the high rooms of the Basilica and the Centre City, and descended to street level.

'Where you taking me now?' asked Susan.

'The Old City.'

'Look at the stars,' said Susan, pointing. 'They're falling.'

'No,' said Spoole. 'They're taking down the wall. They don't need it now that Kavan has been defeated.'

Susan looked at the stepped shape to the west. She could make out the robots working quickly to disas-

semble the structure. She guessed they would be ship-
ping it to the forges and factories at the northern end of
the city, to be turned into more soldiers for Artemis.

'You really think Kavan is defeated?' she said.

'I don't know,' said Spoole. 'The Generals always
underestimated him, as did I.'

He looked towards the stars that shone in the gaps
where the wall had been.

'I wonder if the animals have done so as well,' he
murmured.

Kavan

Kavan felt the downdraught from the human ship as it
flew overhead. It scattered dust and sand across the plain,
blowing yet more inside his metal body.

'It's landing,' said Calor, excitedly. 'It's landing!'

They lay beneath a thin covering of sand with their
heads pressed together, using vibration more than sound
to communicate.

'How far?' asked Kavan.

'Just under a mile.'

'Do you think you can make it, Calor?'

'I *know* I can.'

Kavan wondered if he should make her wait, but no.
One day's grace was the most they could hope for, after
that the humans would have learned and rethought their
tactics.

'Do the best you can,' he said, and he felt the current

surge as she charged her electromuscles. She held it there, held it, letting it build to peak and then . . .

She eased her way slowly from the ground, her silver body gritty where the sand had stuck to the thin film of oil with which she had covered herself. Kavan raised his own head above the level of the earth, and saw the luminous green craft in the distance, the big blades on the top of the craft spinning, beating up the dust. Half seen through the haze, two humans were unloading a yellow crate from a hatch in the side of the craft. The robots had watched the humans at work on these crates before. They contained a mechanism that unfolded itself from the box like a robot climbing to its feet. A skeleton of metal that stood up and held out its arms. The Artemisian plain had been studded with pylons over the last few weeks: this would be the next in line. The humans were taking over the land, mile by mile, relentlessly imposing their machinery on Shull. Even the earth itself was not left untouched: out near the western coast, great areas of land had been churned up by human machines that crept back and forth on their hands and knees, turning shiny brown swathes of soil over to face the sunlight.

The advance was remorseless and logical. It was this very logic that Kavan was hoping to exploit: it was so easy to predict where they would be next.

Calor moved forward. The humans had the crate on the ground now; they were unfolding its sides, unaware of the Scout creeping up on them.

She had covered barely one hundred yards when a proximity signal rang out from the craft. The animals' heads jerked in Kavan's direction at the same time as Calor sprang forward, releasing stored current through her electromuscles at an incredible rate. She tore forwards, a sandy silver flashing pattern of light, her arms and legs pumping away as she closed the distance.

The humans froze, they stumbled towards their craft, hesitated, returned to the crate, then ran back into the craft. All the time Calor was closing the distance. The humans were inside now, the pitch of the engine increased.

Calor was still too far off, Kavan saw the dust whirling in a pool as the rotors' speed increased, he saw the black turret at the front of the craft swivel towards the Scout. The craft began to lift, and a line of explosions travelled towards Calor. She easily sidestepped the jumping path that cut across the plain, giving that last desperate burst of speed as the craft lifted higher; she jumped, claws extended . . .

She plunged the blades deep into the side of the machine.

Kavan realized he had just been standing, watching. He remembered his own role and began to run towards the craft himself. The line of explosions turned and began to pick its way across the plain, heading in his direction. Closer it came, and he prepared himself to jump to the side, just as he had seen Calor do, but the line suddenly swung off erratically. The craft was spinning wildly across the sky.

Calor had made it inside.

The luminous green craft twisted this way and that, headed downwards, pulled up at the last moment, lost height again, and dived into the ground, ploughing a furrow of sand. The great blades on the top touched the earth, and Kavan ducked as they tore themselves apart in a reckless fury of metal. Fragments of the blades flew across the plain, tearing more grooves in the sand.

Smoke emerged from the stricken ship. Kavan was running towards it again, going to the aid of Calor. If she had survived.

His muscles hummed as he loped forward, watching for movement from within. Yellow flames slowly slid their way down the rear of the craft.

Nothing. No! A jagged hole was torn open in the front of the craft and something emerged. Something blackened and twisted. Kavan caught a glimpse of silver and realized it was Calor. She fell to the ground, struggled to get up again.

Her body was burned and twisted, the left side of her chest riddled with bullet holes.

'Get away, Kavan,' she said. 'That thing is full of petrol.'

Kavan thrust a shoulder beneath her arm, and half walked, half carried her away from the craft.

'It might explode,' she said.

'You're too valuable,' said Kavan.

'Now I know I'm mad,' said Calor. 'Metal must be twisted out of true. I just heard Kavan say that I was too valuable. I'm nothing but metal.'

'At the moment you're one of the few robots who know about human craft,' said Kavan. 'You're more valuable than mere metal for the next few days at least.'

The noise of the flames behind them died away. They

turned to see white foam oozing from all the cracks in the stricken craft, saw it smothering the flames.

'Clever,' said Kavan. 'Very clever.'

'Not if you're stuck inside the craft with it. Not if you need to burn oxygen to make energy like the animals do.'

'It looks safe to go in now,' said Kavan.

'How long do you think we have?'

'Half an hour at most.'

Kavan raised a hand. A mile away on the plain, the sand and grit began to stir. Ada emerged from the ground, followed by three other blue-panelled robots. They hurried towards the craft.

While the engineers got to work on the craft, Kavan helped Calor strip away the damaged panelling from her chest. They both worked on the mechanism inside.

'You keep yourself in good repair,' said Kavan, approvingly.

'Thank you. I wish I had some oil.'

'Here,' said Kavan, producing a small canister. 'I'll do it.' He squeezed a couple of drops onto the mechanism in her chest, and the part that had been scorched by flames resumed its regular motion.

'You know they will send other craft to destroy that one? They don't want us finding out their secrets.'

'You said we had half an hour.'

'They may come sooner.'

'Then we'll run.'

Time passed as the pair of them worked on, the engineers busy nearby.

'You'll be okay, I think,' said Kavan finally, looking at the streaks the acid had burned into the chest panelling they had carefully slid back into place.

'I'll be fine. It's only metal.'

'I know that.'

Ada appeared at his side.

'Kavan, we're ready to go.'

The other engineers were moving away from the stricken craft, carrying various parts they had salvaged from the machine. Two long cylinders, about half the height of a robot; a metal canister that sloshed with liquid, two thick cables emerging from one end; several smaller pieces of equipment. The engineers held them carefully, reverently. All of the pieces had that overly complicated design of human machinery, too many wires, too many parts.

'Come on,' said Kavan. 'Back beneath the ground.'

'Too late!' called Calor, looking up into the distance.

Kavan followed her gaze. He couldn't see anything yet, but he wasn't a Scout. 'Should we run?' he asked.

As soon as he said it he saw a straight line, ruled across the sky, foreshortening. No noise. It was travelling faster than—

The missile hit the human craft with less noise than he had expected. More of a crack than a bang. Kavan realized that Ada was still standing, watching what was going on.

'They use depleted uranium for the shell tips. I know that. I think there is a magnesium charge inside, but there is something else there as well, I'm sure. Look how it burns!'

The craft was already glowing white hot, the metal collapsing in on itself. She took a step towards it. Kavan pulled her back by the arm.

'Look out, Ada!'

Two lines of jumping sand ran towards them. Ada watched them approach, then stepped out of their way, quite unconcerned.

'They have too little control at that distance,' she explained. 'You can tell by the spacing between the bullet impacts.'

'Ada, you mad *Tok*, get down.'

'They won't come closer,' said Ada. 'They'll be worried we'll bring them down too, just like we did the first craft.'

Kavan got to his feet, wondering at what was happening here. It wasn't like him to shelter whilst others walked around calmly. Two more lines of bullets tore across the sand, and the blue robots stepped around them once more. Behind Kavan the burning craft was collapsing into a molten pool, fusing the sand around itself. Thin smoke rose into the bright day.

'What did you find?' asked Kavan. The bullets were curving around again, coming back towards them, then suddenly, they just stopped.

'It's hard to say,' said Ada. 'The mechanisms make sense, up to a point, but there are parts missing, or parts that shouldn't function as they do. I'm certain it's all down to this.'

She held out a flat square object. Fine gold wires were arranged in patterns around the side.

'I think it's the human equivalent of a mind. A metal

mind, I mean, a robot mind. It's made of stone and metal.'

'It's like a mirror on the top.'

'If you look at it under a lens you can see incredibly complicated patterns there. Finer than a woman could weave, more complex than a man could make.'

Kavan turned the object this way and that.

'We can copy most parts of the human craft, but without a suitable mind, I don't think we can make it fly.'

Calor had little interest for the alien machinery. She was built to run and fight and look into the distance. She was doing so now.

'Kavan,' she said. 'Something's coming.'

Kavan saw it too. A dark craft with wide wings, two large engines mounted at the tail. It moved slowly but deliberately, flying low over the surface of the plain.

'What do we do?' asked Calor.

'I'd like to try something,' said Ada. 'Would you mind?'

Kavan looked on as two of the engineers stepped forward. Things were changing so quickly. For years he had barely paid the blue robots any attention. The engineers had always arrived after the main attack. But now, with the arrival of the humans, they were taking on a new role, stepping forward and taking the lead whilst he and his robots stood and watched. Just like now. Two of the engineers were handling one of the cylinders they had retrieved from the stricken craft, pointing it towards the approaching aeroplane. Kavan could see the animal in the clear glass cockpit at the front of the craft, he heard the whistling of the two engines, saw the dark holes of the guns as the front of the craft turned to face him, heard the rippling smack and crack as bullets stitched a line towards him.

'Ada, are you sure about this . . .'

Then there was a snap, a flare, and a whoosh of flame. A missile crowning a line of light, it travelled from the cylinder the two robots were aiming and connected with the craft just below the cockpit. The glass bubble filled with orange-yellow flame; there was an explosion all along the fuselage. The wings of the craft folded down and the whole thing fell to the ground, skidding towards them.

'Well done, Ada,' said Kavan, genuinely impressed. 'Well done, all of you.'

He turned to see one of the engineers lying on the ground, most of the area below the chest burned away. Ada was carefully removing the head and the coil from the body.

'He's okay,' she said, 'but it means we can carry less.'

'Never mind. There will be more craft, I'm sure.'

'Come on,' said Calor, dancing from foot to foot. 'We *really* need to get away now.'

'Sure. But you can carry something, too,' said Ada.

Kavan was impressed at the way the engineer had assumed command. He didn't mind. Whatever was best for Artemis.

He wondered if Sandale and the rest of the Generals would see it that way.

Susan

'This way,' said Spoole, leading Susan deeper into the Half-fused City. When the Storm Trooper had chased her through here before, the place had been deserted. Now the area was teeming with robots.

'What's going on?' Spoole asked a passing infantry-robot.

'We're relaying the railway lines,' said a soldier. 'Now that Kavan has gone, the wall is coming down and we're plugging ourselves back into the continent. Artemis is getting ready to march again.'

'Kavan is gone? You're certain of that?'

'The animals cleared the area, didn't they?'

'And you're happy about that?' said Susan.

'There is neither happiness nor unhappiness,' replied the infantryrobot, 'there is just Artemis.'

'They're laying the lines into the animals' base,' said Susan. 'You could see them putting down the ballast from the Basilica.'

They picked their way through the streets, the yellow flares and lights not quite holding back the darkness of the old buildings, the march and stamp and hurry of the troops not quite dispelling the feeling of stillness around them. In the distance, rising over the other buildings, Susan caught sight of the tops of the two shot towers.

'Why do they keep this place standing?' she asked. 'It seems so out of place, here in the middle of Artemis City. Surely there is no sentimentality for the past in Nyro's world?'

'None,' said Spoole. 'This is where the unfused and the half-fused work. Robots that live indefinitely. They serve their purpose. But this place shrinks a little every year, as we find new ways to do things. Down here.'

He led her down a narrow side street. Ahead of them was a small building, one storey high, barely big enough to hold a family forge. Its red-brick walls were dark and shiny in the dim light. It had no other features save for a plain steel door and a small smoking chimney. The other buildings around it were taller, they seemed to have edged away from it, their windows gazed distrustfully at their smaller cousin.

'What is it?' asked Susan.

'The database,' said Spoole. Susan followed him to the door. She noticed how well trodden the cobbled road was; there was a smooth path worn into the round stones, heading for the door ahead.

'There is frequent talk about shutting this place down, of recycling the metal that lies inside, but they have yet to come up with a better way of storing records.' Spoole laughed suddenly, a hollow sound in that still place. 'Who knows, the database may outlast even Artemis City. All that we have been will still be recorded here, even when the rest of the metal of Artemis is spun into shape and carried to the stars by the animals.'

And at that he knocked upon the steel door. There was no handle, Susan noticed.

'Open up,' he commanded. 'It's Spoole!'

For a moment, Susan wondered if Spoole would be obeyed. What would he do if not, she wondered? The door without a handle was pushed open from inside and

Susan looked into a single room, dimly lit by a yellow bulb. A Storm Trooper waited there, body humming with power.

'Hello, Spoole.'

'Hello, Geraint.'

Susan followed Spoole inside. She felt trapped in this tiny space, she wanted to be safely outside, under the bright stars that filled the night above.

'You bring an infantryrobot, Spoole? That's not allowed.' He looked at Susan. 'Wait outside.'

Susan looked coolly back at the Storm Trooper, intimidated though she was by his heavy black body. She could feel his current even from here.

'I am leader of this city,' said Spoole. 'Stand aside.'

'*A* leader of the city,' said Geraint, but he stood aside anyway. Behind him a set of iron steps spiralled into the ground.

'How many people are down there at the moment?' asked Spoole.

'Only a couple of filing clerks. Things have been quiet since the animals arrived. Who wants to look to the past, when the future is setting up base right outside the city?'

'Who indeed?' said Spoole.

With the tap, tap, tap of metal feet on iron treads, he began to descend the stairs.

'Haven't we met before?' said the Storm Trooper, looming over Susan. 'You're a conscript. I can tell. What body did you used to wear?'

Susan had a memory of the making rooms, kneeling before robots like this. Had she made a child with him? The thought filled her with loathing.

'Aren't we all Artemisians?' she replied, following Spoole down the steps, resisting the urge to strike the huge black brute.

The steps spiralled through three turns and deposited Susan in a brick room, about the same size as the one above. There were two facing doorways leading through to similar rooms. An iron pipe led from a small stove up into the ceiling. A robot stood in the middle of the space, eyes glowing a weak grey. Unfused, she realized. Here was a robot whose mother had tied the end of its mind into a knot, making a mind doomed neither to die in forty short years nor to ever properly think or feel.

'Nettie,' said Spoole. 'We're looking for a robot named Nettie.'

The robot pointed to the right-hand door.

'If that robot exists, its record will be through that door.' The robot lowered its head, losing all interest in them.

Spoole was already walking through the right-hand door. Susan followed to find a similar room with two more exits, this time, though, one went down another set of stairs. A second unfused robot waited. It looked up as Spoole approached.

'We're looking for a robot named Nettie.'

'If that robot exists, its record will be down the steps,' replied the robot, pointing. Spoole was already descending. She followed him, only to see the robot in the next room pointing down once more.

'How far down does this go?' she called.

'I've heard fifteen levels,' said Spoole.

Susan calculated.

'That's 32, 768 robots down here. That is if this is a true binary tree we're traversing. That's almost as many robots as lived in Turing City!'

'There are only three hundred and two, I think,' said Spoole. 'Each node robot holds several thousand records in their mind.' He was facing another unfused robot now. 'I'm looking for a robot named Nettie,' he said.

'If that robot exists, it will be through that door.'

They followed the direction that was indicated, and continued their descent beneath the Half-fused City.

Back in Turing City, Susan had been a statistician. She understood that she was walking through a concrete example of what she had previously thought of as an abstract concept. Artemis City had made a binary tree. She imagined a robot walking from the Main Index, carrying foil sheets to this building. She imagined the information it brought being passed down the tree of robots buried beneath the ground, each sending the sheet left or right depending on where it lay in the index. A tree. Susan had seen branching examples of organic life named after this structure.

'This is bizarre, Spoole. Are you always so literal in this city?'

'I don't understand what you mean.'

'Do you build every abstract idea you come across?'

Spoole still didn't understand. 'Everything that Artemis has done ends up here eventually,' he said.

Down and along they went, traversing the data construct. Robot after robot pointed across or down, and they followed the direction indicated. Every so often they passed a little stove, its chimney leading up to the ceiling, and Susan guessed this was where the robots repaired themselves. And then, something new. Piles of soil in the corners of the room. Stacks of fresh bricks.

'They build new rooms as the database gets bigger?' she wondered aloud.

'It used to be once every few years. Now it's once every six months. The rate of Artemis's expansion increases.'

'We're coming to the end.'

'Inevitably. The newest data is stored at the farthest nodes.'

Susan moved deeper into the earth, the piles of bricks became more frequent, until eventually they stood before a robot, its body shiny and freshly made.

'I'm looking for a robot named Nettie,' said Spoole.

The robot gazed back with its grey eyes. Susan felt the current build within her muscles. The unfused robot spoke.

'I know of three robots by that name,' it said. 'Scout, Infantryrobot and Making Room.'

'She worked in the making rooms!' said Susan eagerly.

'Making Room,' said Spoole.

'Nettie,' said the robot. 'Mother Kinsle, Father Jaman. Constructed in—'

'Hold,' said Spoole. 'I don't want her history. Where is she now?'

'Assigned to Making Room 14, temporarily seconded to Barrack 245, awaiting transfer to Aleph Base pending its construction by the animals.'

'What?' said Susan. 'They're sending her to the humans? Why?'

The unfused robot said nothing, just stared forward with those dull grey eyes.

Spoole spoke.

'State her new assignment.'

'Nettie is to commence training of batch Aleph of the new mothers of Artemis under the direction of the animals.'

'What?' Susan looked at Spoole, eyes burning brightly.

Spoole said nothing. He was gazing at the unfused robot, his eyes glowing brightly.'

'What, Spoole? What is it?'

'Sandale! Don't you see what he's done? He's a traitor!'

'Traitor to Artemis? Good!'

'Don't be so stupid! Do you think the animals will still have to deal with Artemis City when they have robots with minds woven to serve them directly? Sandale has betrayed Nyro!'

'All for a few tons of metal?' said Susan.

'This isn't Nyro's way,' said Spoole, his voice crackling with static. 'This isn't about Artemis, this isn't about Kavan, this is about robots keeping themselves in power by any means! This is what happens when robots' minds are woven to think of leadership above all else!'

He was so angry, Susan could feel the flash of current through his electromuscles, see the way his eyes were glowing.

'This is wrong!' he said. 'I have been distracted, I've allowed Sandale and the rest to cloud my thoughts! Sulking down here when I should have been out in the city, alerting the true Artemisians to what was happening!'

He looked around the small room. He looked down at his own body.

'I should be out there with Kavan, helping him to fight against this heresy, not standing here in this over-styled body, of no use to anyone but myself.'

'Okay,' said Susan, frightened by his sudden passion, nervous to be so far underground, trapped in the middle of the city. 'Let's get out of here then. Let's go and find Kavan.'

'Yes,' said Spoole. He made to climb the metal steps to the next level, and then paused. Susan heard it too: the sound of more feet on steps, the sound of voices.

'This way!' shouted someone. 'Down this way! Spoole is trapped!'

Kavan

The clock tower in the centre of Stark rose to nearly eight hundred feet. Kavan could see it in the distance, rising over the horizon, and he wondered why Artemis had left it in place when they conquered that state. It served no purpose now. Back when Stark was an independent force, it had spread its influence throughout eastern Shull by ensuring each town and village had its own timepiece. It was a form of control far more subtle than that practised by Artemis City, but just as effective.

Kavan had passed through many villages on his way

here, each with their brick clock tower empty and broken or turned to the business of Artemis. No longer did every town click and advance to the radio-synchronized tick of the Stark clocks. But then again, nor did they move to the glory of Nyro and the advancement of the Artemisian State.

Out here towards the eastern coast the land turned to rocky rills wound with rivers of sand and gravel. The Artemisians had laid railway lines that followed the lie of the land. Those railway lines were now subtly altered.

'The humans have done a lot of work in a very little time,' said Ada.

'I don't think so,' said Calor. 'They were here already. The animals were in Shull before they came to Artemis City. I've spoken to the other robots from round here.'

'Spoole and the General must have given them this land as a staging post,' said Kavan.

'There was an Artemisian refinery to the east,' said Calor. 'The humans have taken it over. They must have been there for some weeks. You can see the changes they've made to it. They've modified the railway lines out here too. Straightened their courses.'

'Then the fact they have been here for some time makes me feel a little happier,' said Ada. 'Perhaps they are not so different to us.'

'What do they use the railway lines for?' asked Kavan.

'They're taking refined oil to Artemis City. Their trains can move at incredible speeds.'

'They plan well,' said Kavan. 'They're not stupid.'

'Train approaching now,' said Calor.

'I can hear it,' said Kavan. That high-pitched whistle.

He could see it, too. So much metal moving through an electrical field, it lit up in a rainbow of colours, an elongated raindrop that drew a shrieking line across the countryside.

'It's the way they put all their technology on display,' he mused. 'Don't they realize what they are doing?'

'I don't think they do,' said Ada. 'But they think so very differently to us. Comes of being organic, I would guess, comes of being a statistical fluke. They don't design themselves, like we do. They accept the good and the bad in their bodies, they can't omit the flaws when they make themselves, like a robot would.'

'I know,' said Kavan. 'But look at that. How can they be so stupid and so clever at the same time? It's like they've handed us a loaded gun.'

And then the train was upon them. It made far less noise than Kavan had expected, so smoothly did it cut through the air. There was virtually no engine noise, just that shrill whistling.

'If only I could examine one of those motors,' said Ada wistfully. 'It's impossible to stop one of those trains without destroying it. They move so fast. And as for the fuel it's carrying . . .'

There was a zip and the train passed. The engineer followed its course, thinking.

'No,' said Ada. 'We don't need it. We can make a good enough copy for our own purposes.'

'Very well,' said Kavan.

'Okay, time to get down there.'

Ada and her engineers were up and gone. Four of them ran down the tracks, measuring, touching the rails, looking up at the wires that looped overhead, talking all the while. Calor stalked up and down the gravel nearby, kicking stones, expending the energy that constantly built up within her.

'Okay!' called Ada. 'Bring it down.'

It took four engineers to carry the device down to the tracks. They pointed its nose towards distant Artemis City.

'Nice and straight,' said Ada. 'A good test.'

Twenty minutes until the next train. More than enough time.

'Do you think it will work?' called Calor, skittish with underuse.

'It doesn't matter what I think,' said Kavan. 'I'm not an engineer.'

They looked down at the device Ada and her team had put together. It was about as long as two robots lying end to end, and shaped like the blade of a knife.

'Ada, I'm impressed,' said Kavan. 'Barely two weeks since you first saw a flying machine, and already you've built this.'

'We wondered whether to place the eyes on top or underneath,' said Ada, modestly, as she lifted a flap and adjusted a lever inside. 'In the end we put them below. We thought that it could watch the ground, fly closer to it that way.'

Kavan crouched down to look under the machine. He saw two blue eyes there, midway along the smooth underside of the device.

'The engine design is our own. We tried to copy the animals' designs, but there are too many unknowns. We can't make the alloys they can, we can't refine fuel so well.'

'Are they cleverer than us, Ada?'

'I don't think so. But they've had to work harder than we have to stay alive. They've needed to develop faster than us: they are such fragile creatures.'

'Perhaps,' said Kavan, and he looked once more at the device. 'Still, you've done well. Out here on the plain, constantly moving, and you manage to build this.'

'That's the difference between us and the animals,' said Ada. 'I've been thinking about it. Animals need food and water. They will naturally congregate around sources of both. Rivers, fields. They will stay there, like young robots around the family forge. You've heard what the Scouts say. The animals have set up base near Artemis City.'

Kavan said nothing, but he was surprised. It was unusual for an engineer to even notice a Scout, never mind listen to what they had to say. Things were changing . . .

'Well, there could be good reasons for that.'

'Maybe there are, Kavan. You should know, you're the leader, you're the strategist. But staying in one place has never been your tactic, has it? You're constantly on the move, constantly on the attack. If you'd landed on this planet you'd be halfway across the continent by now, making new soldiers as you went.'

'Maybe . . .'

'Look at us! They chased us away from Artemis City. You didn't make a new base, you spread out your army! All those little cells across the land, planning, moving, waiting for the next assault.'

'You understand that, Ada?' said Kavan in surprise. 'You can see that?'

'Why not? The animals are here, and there are a whole set of new engineering problems to think about. Isn't it great?'

Kavan gazed at her. Sometimes he just didn't know what other robots were thinking.

'Ten minutes to the train,' said Calor, still dancing back and forth.

Kavan looked at the blunt arrow shape, lying on the tracks. 'Has your device seen enough?'

'I think so,' said Ada.

'Okay. Let's go,' said Kavan. 'We don't want the animals to get suspicious. Keep moving, keep preparing.' He looked at the device.

'Is it ready? Can we send the plans to the other engineers?'

'I think so,' said Ada.

'Yes!' shouted Calor, swiping her blades through the air.

'Take Mivan's mind,' said Ada. 'He's got as good an understanding as anyone.'

Mivan knelt down and another engineer carefully removed his mind from his blue body. He handed it to Calor, who turned without a word and sped off south, heading to another of the small groups that were dotted around the border of the Artemisian plain.

'What about Artemis City?' asked Ada. 'Are you sure about them?'

'Oh yes,' said Kavan, watching Mivan's former body being disassembled by the other engineers. They stored the parts in the large bags they carried around with them. 'You know machines, Ada, I know war. There will be many robots in Artemis City who are unhappy about the animals. Some of them will follow us when the time comes.'

'I hope there will be enough.'

Susan

The sound of stamping feet came closer. Suddenly they halted, and a voice called out.

'Spoole! We have an order for your arrest, authorized by General Sandale. You are hereby charged with treason against the Artemisian State.'

'Fools!' said Spoole. 'There's only one way out of this place. They should have waited at the top for us, and then captured us as we left!'

'What are we to do?' asked Susan, terrified.

'Use our minds.'

Spoole was already setting off up the stairs, heading towards the troops.

'Fools,' he repeated, eyes glowing with anger. 'This is what comes of never having fought for yourself!'

Up another flight of steps, the sound of voices and feet coming closer, and then, just when Susan thought she would meet their pursuers, Spoole headed into a side room and descended the steps in there, following a different branch of the binary tree.

'Quiet!' he said, holding up a warning finger.

Susan listened as the sound of footsteps came closer.

'We're looking for a robot named Nettie!'

She heard the colourless reply. 'If that robot exists, its record will be down those steps.'

They heard the clattering of footsteps receding.

'They know about Nettie!' said Spoole. 'The Storm Trooper must have overheard us. Now, quietly!'

Susan and Spoole retraced their steps, heading back to the surface, ears turned up full to listen for steps behind them, steps ahead of them. Spoole spoke so softly that Susan only heard the buzzing as she touched his metal shell.

'So stupid,' he kept repeating. 'So, so stupid!'

The unfused robots watched in silence as they passed, their grey eyes showing no interest or curiosity. The brickwork became older as they approached the surface. Spoole paused, listening.

'No one behind us,' he said. 'Only Geraint ahead. Come on.'

He climbed the last set of steps, up to the top. Geraint was waiting, rifle pointed at Spoole.

'You summoned them,' said Spoole. He sounded more disappointed than anything else.

'Sorry, Spoole. I was ordered to report if you ever came here.'

'Do you know what they're doing, Geraint? They are weaving robot minds to serve the animals. They are weaving minds that do not follow Nyro!'

Geraint hesitated.

'It's true,' said Susan. 'Go downstairs and ask the robot!'

'I'm sorry, Spoole. I am woven to be loyal to Nyro.'

'Loyal to Nyro, or loyal to the leaders of Artemis?'

Geraint thought about it.

'The second one.'

'That was a mistake.' Spoole looked at Susan. 'We have got things so badly wrong.' He turned back to the Storm Trooper, powerful black hands gripping the rifle. The bullet in there would pierce his skull and expand inside his mind, melting the wire as it tore it apart. 'What are your orders, Geraint?'

'Arrest you. If you resist arrest, I'm to kill you.'

'No, I can't let you do that! Come with me, Geraint, and hear the truth.'

'I'm sorry, Spoole.'

Geraint raised the gun.

'Your leaders never fought in battles, Geraint, you know that?'

'That doesn't matter.'

'It does, Geraint. They'd have known never to give a robot a rifle in a room as small as this.'

Spoole simply stepped forward, within the length of the barrel.

'I'm still stronger than you, Spoole.'

'But I was made to fight, as well as lead.' He slammed a hand forward into Geraint's chest, slammed the other up under the robot's chin. 'Knock your gyros out of sync for a moment,' he said, as Geraint wobbled unsteadily on his feet, and he snatched the rifle from his hands, placed the stock on the floor, the barrel pointing up beneath Geraint's chin, and fired. Blue wire expanded, slippery and sparking. Susan felt the percussion of the shot rattling inside her head: her ears were still turned up to their fullest extent.

'Sorry, Geraint,' said Spoole. Below them they could hear the pounding of feet. The other soldiers were coming towards them.

'Now what?' said Susan. Spoole told her what to do.

Susan flung open the door to the database. Three infantryrobots waited outside under the bright stars.

'This way!' she called.

The infantryrobots saw her grey body, saw she was one of their own, and ran into the building.

'Down there,' called Susan, pointing down the steps. She watched as they vanished from sight. Spoole emerged from the other branch of the tree.

'Made to lead,' said Spoole, emerging into the night. 'Strategy. It's all about strategy.'

'Well done,' said Susan with grudging admiration. 'Where now?'

'Barrack 245. Find Nettie and the rest. Get the proof. Raise an army and throw these animals out of the city.'

'What about the Generals?' asked Susan.

'I was talking about the Generals,' said Spoole.

Kavan

Calor couldn't help herself. She would run ahead of Kavan, then turn and wait for him to catch up. As soon as he reached her she was off again, another couple of hundred yards. Kavan hurried along behind her, his feet kicking loose stones into the little stream.

'Not far,' she said. 'Just around the bend.'

Kavan respected the animals. They didn't think like robots, it was true, but they had established themselves upon Shull with a ruthless logic he admired.

Their main base was close to Artemis City, but not too close. Any enemies approaching them would be seen from miles away across the plain, then either picked off by the Artemisians or the humans in their flying craft. Kavan hadn't actually seen the human base, hiding as he was amongst the broken landscape near Stark, but he had had it described to him by Scouts and engineers who had observed it from as close as they could manage, dodging the Artemisian patrols and hiding from the craft that criss-crossed the sky.

The base was well constructed, he understood. Two gigantic craft, surrounded by a perimeter of guns that moved of their own accord, turning to fire at robots that came too close. Even the Artemisians didn't dare approach those guns: the plain was littered with the shattered metal remains of the bodies of robots that had gone too close. So much metal left to go to waste was unheard of in Artemis.

Several buildings had already been constructed within the compound, and it was Kavan's understanding that the perimeter of the base was expanding as time passed and more and more materials were brought into the base. Materials taken from Shull.

Two railway lines led into the animals' camp; they

drew up alongside long platforms lined with cranes and other paraphernalia used to unload and load the trains that constantly ran back and forth between the camp and Artemis City.

Kavan had thought of a possible weakness at this point, he had asked his Scouts for further information. Two of them had died – picked off as they crossed the plain by missiles fired from high above – in order to bring Kavan the answer. The humans were well ahead of Kavan: the Scouts had confirmed that there were many guns at the point where the railway lines pierced the camp. Furthermore, their placement showed they were ready to be turned upon the trains, or indeed in the direction of Artemis City, should the current alliance break down.

'This way, this way,' said Calor, running back to meet him.

'I can't keep my feet on this loose stone like you can,' said Kavan, stumbling on a loose gravel bank. Stark had stripped this land of metal with devastating efficiency. The ground was a maze of pits and broken rubble, criss-crossed by hard packed roads. It was a great place to hide out, a difficult place to traverse.

'Nearly there!'

Yes, Kavan respected the animals. Yet he felt disgusted by them at the same time. They were so fragile. The robots had captured only three of them, so far as he knew, and each one of them had been broken and accidentally killed by its captors. The first had been trapped in the wreckage of a crashed flying craft. The Scout that had found it had cut off its limbs and lower torso to drag it free. According to her account, the creature had screamed horribly as she did this, and had sent masses of red fluid squirting in all directions before it had died.

A second pair had been captured almost immediately afterwards. They had been cut from their craft intact, and then sealed in an oil container whilst Kavan was sent for. It was a good plan; the idea had been the steel of the container would block any signals the prisoners might try to send to searching humans. Unfortunately, by the time Kavan had arrived there, the creatures were dead, their skin turned a strange blue colour, at least those parts that hadn't been burned red on contact with the hot metal, heated by the sun.

It was only after the second fatalities that Kavan had sent out a message asking for advice on the handling of animals. The advice that came back to him from the Wieners and the few conscripts from the Northern King-doms made him more aware than ever just how feeble these humans were. They needed water, grass and leaves to consume, they had to be kept within a narrow tem-perature range, they had to be exposed to the air. They couldn't be punctured, they couldn't be disassembled in any way. It made Kavan wonder if they were worth the bother.

But he persevered, and when the message came through that two Scouts had finally managed to capture an animal on the ground, one that had walked over a hundred yards from its flying craft, trusting to what turned out to be a faulty robot detector, Kavan had come running.

The animal had been hurried from the site of the craft by the two Scouts. They had followed standing orders and cut from the creature anything plastic or metal, all the while being careful not pierce any part of its fleshy body.

They had then led it at blade point across the rocky land to an old Stark village, abandoned after the invasion by Artemis over ten years ago. Kavan had been lucky; he was only fifty miles away at the time. He had immediately begun to travel towards the captive, hoping to reach it before the fragile creature died. It had taken him nearly two days, cutting across the broken ground, hiding from the aircraft that swooped back and forth over the land, desperately seeking their fallen comrade, but now Kavan was almost there. He could see, rising from behind the low hill ahead, the broken tower that would once have housed the village's clock.

'Come on, Kavan! Come on!'

Calor was singing with impatience, singing with too much current. Kavan slipped on broken stones as he made his way around the hillside and, finally, he was there.

The village was built of the incredibly hard, shiny red bricks that only Stark had been able to produce. Any metal had long been stripped away, but the robots of Stark built equally well with stone and metal alike. Tiled roofs remained intact, clear glass windows still stared at Kavan after all these years.

'In there, in there!' Calor was dancing, pointing.

Kavan passed through an empty doorway, the missing door no doubt now part of a robot or some other piece of machinery employed by Artemis, and he found himself in a dark space.

'No lights in here: turn your eyes up!'

Kavan did so. Two infantryrobots and an engineer stood nearby. And beyond them . . .

'Don't come too close yet, Kavan!' warned one. 'Your body will still be hot from the sun! You'll burn it!'

Finally, Kavan found himself face to face with an animal.

It was female. Kavan was surprised, but he could tell by looking that the creature was female. It was something to do with the shape of the body. She was looking at him with her blue eyes. She was frightened, Kavan could tell, but who could blame her for that? She was a fighter, though. Kavan recognized a kindred spirit, and he wondered that a creature so different, so alien, could have something in common with himself.

'Hello,' he said. 'My name is Kavan.'

The creature unleashed a string of gibberish. Kavan watched her pink mouth moving, saw the pink thing inside darting around as she shaped words with air and flesh.

'Why can't she speak properly?' he asked. 'Is she damaged?'

'I don't know,' said the engineer. 'I don't think so. If you listen carefully there is a pattern to what she says, like she's communicating, but with a different . . . protocol to the one which we use.'

'But why speak in a different way to us?'

Kavan was mystified. Speech was speech. It was one of the signs of an intelligent mind, that it could communicate with another.

'I don't know. Stefan here has a theory that maybe

speech isn't woven directly into their minds as it is with robot children.'

Kavan thought about it.

'It sounds plausible. But how are we going to communicate with her?'

'I've been working on that. Watch.'

He held up a hand.

'Hello,' he said.

'He-shhh,' replied the female.

'She can't make the feedback sound,' explained the engineer. 'Obviously her voicebox is organic, not electronic.' He turned back to the female.

'My name is Valve,' he said, placing his hand on his chest.

'Me shhh issh Luphanshh,' said the female, copying his gesture.

'Sounds a bit like Luvan,' said Karel. 'That's an Artemisian name.'

The female was still speaking. She was holding her hand to her mouth, the fingers curved, tilting her head back.

'That means she wants water,' said Valve. 'I sent the Scout to get some. She's fussy. Seawater is no good; it has to be from the stream.'

'Okay.' Kavan gazed at the creature, weighing it up.

'Four of you looking after her, the humans constantly searching for her. I wonder if it's worth the effort to keep her?'

'Oh yes, Kavan, I'm sure it is. There is so much to learn.'

'In other circumstances I may agree with you. I came

fifty miles hoping to question this creature, and now I find that I can't. The longer we hold her in one place, the more likely the animals will find her. We can't take her out of here now; they would spot her in minutes. You know, we would do better examining her body, learning how it works. We've never had a whole one before.'

The creature was looking at him. Her blue eyes were wider, he could see the whites around them.

'She knows,' said Kavan. 'Look at her; she knows what we're talking about.'

Kavan wasn't cruel, it wasn't woven into him. He was merely ruthless. 'I should make a decision quickly,' he said. 'To do otherwise would needlessly prolong this creature's agony.'

'Give me a day,' pleaded Valve. 'I'm sure I can find out something of worth.'

'Like what? How the flying craft work? I have engineers that can do that. What their plans are? We know that. They will continue to expand across Shull. I've already wasted two days on this. Kill her and put her out of her misery.'

'No!' said Valve. 'They're different when they're dead. They're not like robots! You don't understand, the whole body just stops working when the mind dies. I need to examine her whilst she's still alive. Let me block the mouth so she can't make any noise. I can cut her open, see how the parts move.'

Kavan held the creature's eye. She *did* know, she had some inkling about what was being said. She was terrified, and yet, she was fighting not to show it. He admired that.

'No,' said Kavan. 'That would be too cruel. We're robots, not animals. We kill for a reason, and we do it quickly. We don't torture. Shoot her in the head, do it fast so she doesn't know.'

One of the infantryrobots raised its rifle and fired. Grey gel, streaked with red, splattered over Kavan's body. The dead creature slumped to the ground.

'It's a pity,' said Kavan, stirring one of the creature's legs with his foot. 'Maybe later there will be a time to get to know more about them, once we've regained control of Artemis City.'

'*If* we regain control,' said Valve. He looked wistfully at the dead creature. 'I would have liked to have spoken some more.'

He brightened up.

'Still, at least now we get to take a look inside a healthy one.'

Kavan began to wipe the grey gel from his body.

'What now?' asked Calor.

'I think it's time,' said Kavan. 'We've spent enough time here on the periphery.'

He looked down at the dead animal. Strange to think that something so soft could cause so much trouble.

'Yes,' he said. 'I think it's time to return to Artemis City. Send out the word.'

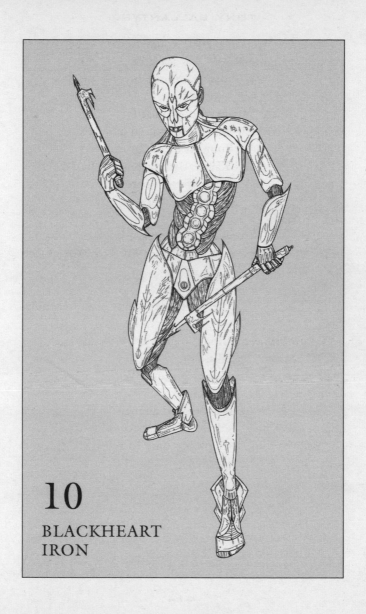

10

BLACKHEART
IRON

Wa-Ka-Mo-Do

The evening sky was flushing a deep red: it was the colour of the forge reflected on the roof of the world. The world was warping all around him, its struts and beams under pressure from the animals who had come from the stars.

The city was a slowly heating pyre, out there in the hot summer countryside robots were being moved to rebellion.

Wa-Ka-Mo-Do watched as the lake turned black, saw the red fire withdraw as the sun set behind the city.

The night was approaching.

Even as he waited for the enemy, there on the dark terrace, the stars switching on above him, even as he felt the fear that hummed in the city below, even as he struggled with that mix of boredom and anticipation of the coming attack, even then Wa-Ka-Mo-Do still found the human guns incredibly erotic.

There was something about the machinery, the way the impossibly smooth metal slipped seamlessly together, the dark sheen of the alien alloy, the way that it shimmered in starlight as if it were slicked in oil. Wa-Ka-Mo-Do had touched a barrel, revelled guiltily in the sleek smoothness, the absolutely zero static charge. What was it about these weapons? Did the humans deliberately build them to look so feminine? Were they even aware of what they had done? Wa-Ka-Mo-Do doubted it. It was obvious that the humans had little regard for what robots thought.

The land seemed darker in contrast to the brilliance of the rising moon, but the lake . . . The lake reflected the universe in curdled white clouds. Wa-Ka-Mo-Do looked at the stars, shining in the water. That was where the humans had come from, he thought. What else lurked out there? For that matter, what else was lurking here on Penrose, just beyond the horizons? The robots of Yukawa had lived in splendid isolation for so long. Now the universe had come looking for them.

He wondered how La-Ver-Di-Arussah and Ka-Lo-Re-Harballah were getting on. He had sent them down into the city to try and calm the population. The streets below sounded quiet for the moment, but he knew that wouldn't last with La-Ver-Di-Arussah down there. Still, if she had remained up here the two of them would probably be fighting each other by now.

It was peaceful for the moment, though. An island of calm under the stars. Somewhere out there humans were grouping to attack. Land ploughed up and covered in alien crops that poisoned the native life of Yukawa was being trodden by robots speaking openly of rebellion. And here he stood, in this square with humans on one hand and robots on the other, and somewhere in the Copper Master's house Li-Kallalla would be piecing together the parts of the radio, and for the moment keeping quiet about what he, Wa-Ka-Mo-Do, had done. How long would this suspended moment last? He was happy to have nothing for company but these darkly fascinating machines, singing with that strange alien electricity.

The guns suddenly raised themselves into the air and turned as one to face the same direction. A rapid pumping sound started up. There was remarkably little noise, it was almost a rippling of the air, but Wa-Ka-Mo-Do saw the electromagnetic field formed by so much metal being sprayed through the planet's own magnetic field. Orange light flared, out there in the distance of the night. The firing ceased, the guns turned their heads a little and then immediately resumed. Another orange explosion. The guns moved once more. Something was coming out of the night, so fast that one of the guns set up by the Copper Master's house was cut neatly in half. Now it was the turn of the house itself. Tiles shattered in a line of destruction that snapped off as suddenly as it had begun. The guns were firing once more, pointing at the third orange explosion lit up in the distance.

After that the guns seemed to lose interest, they lowered themselves, resting. Alien women, exotic and fascinating – they were moving! Up and turning to face the opposite direction, too late . . .

Wa-Ka-Mo-Do was tumbling over and over, clattering metal, scraping red paint on stone. The ground was shaking and cracking; Wa-Ka-Mo-Do's vision was filled with static, he felt his thoughts fold themselves around each other for just a moment, felt time jump forward a few seconds, as he moved from a scene of motion, dust and stones and tiles sliding and shaking through the air, to one of stillness, of the world recast after the explosion; the rubble and debris settled.

'What happened?' He was speaking out loud, to whom he didn't know.

The human guns were dancing around him, bobbing up and down in their bizarre dance, spinning this way and that, lighting up the sky in orange balls, lighting up the distant hills, the far horizons, casting deep, fiery reflections in the lake below.

Ka-Lo-Re-Harballah was running towards him, flanked by two humans, coolant water shining on their faces.

'What have they done, Ka-Lo-Re-Harballah?' cried Wa-Ka-Mo-Do. 'What have they done to the Emperor's city?'

'Half the west side of the city is gone,' said Ka-Lo-Re-Harballah. 'The Street of Becoming is buried beneath the houses that once lined it, the human weapon pierced through to the rock below!'

Ka-Lo-Re-Harballah had lost most of the panelling from his body. His grey electromuscle was smeared in carbon: he sparked as he moved.

'I've failed, Ka-Lo-Re-Harballah,' said Wa-Ka-Mo-Do. 'I've failed in my duty.'

'No, Honoured Commander. The city still stands!'

From somewhere deep below them, half felt, half heard, came the sound of rock cracking, the shifting, sliding rumble as more of the city collapsed upon itself.

'Wa-Ka-Mo-Do!'

He turned to see Gillian, the human commander. The green cloth panelling that she wore was torn, her headset crackled as she spoke.

'They hit us with a mini-nuke, high radiation yield,' she explained.

'Do you understand those terms, Ka-Lo-Re-Harballah?' asked Wa-Ka-Mo-Do.

'No, Honoured Commander.'

'I do. It means that robots' minds are being affected.' Gillian wiped a hand across her brow.

'We're evacuating this city. There's a shuttle dropping towards us right now, we need to get all the humans up to this square so they can board it!'

Wa-Ka-Mo-Do was watching the human cannon, leaping and spinning all around him.

'Your guns seem to be holding off the enemy,' he observed.

'They will,' said Gillian. 'It's the radiation that's the problem,' her voice was still crackling. So was his own, he realized. 'And they may try another mini-nuke: go for an airburst, though if they do that they will irradiate the land. There'll be no crops here for—'

'Damaging the land? This is the Emperor's land.'

'Not any more, Wa-Ka-Mo-Do, not any more.' There was a sadness and finality in her words that the headset managed to translate.

'Honoured Commander?'

Wa-Ka-Mo-Do realized he was still staring, lost in the motion of the guns.

'Yes, Ka-Lo-Re-Harballah?'

'Shall I help escort the humans up here to the terrace?'

'Yes,' said Wa-Ka-Mo-Do. 'Yes, quickly.'

He heard, above the odd purring of the human guns, a new sound. One that was gaining in volume.

Wa-Ka-Mo-Do looked at Ka-Lo-Re-Harballah.

'What is it, Honoured Commander?'

Wa-Ka-Mo-Do knew what the sound was.

'Gunfire. Those are robot weapons. It's finally happened. The rebellion has begun.'

Karel

'We're going out of our way,' said Simrock. 'The Northern Road will lead us into Raman.'

'So?' said Karel. 'It's easy to walk. Better to take our time leaving the mountains than to rush and fall to our deaths.'

'No,' said Simrock. 'There is a better path. An older one. One from before the time that robots walked these mountains.'

'How do you know?' demanded Melt. 'How do you know?'

'He just does,' said Karel. 'The Spontaneous just do. He was right before, wasn't he?'

'Come on. Over this way.'

The Spontaneous robot stepped over the wall at the side of the road. He began to walk up a narrow ledge.

'Hold on!' called Karel. 'What do you mean, before the time that robots walked these mountains. Who could have made the path?'

'Robots, of course.'

He carried on, creeping along the ledge.

'Do we follow him?' Karel asked Melt.

'For the moment.'

'Are you sure? I thought you didn't trust him.'

'I don't. But we said we would follow him.'

And at that Melt heaved himself onto the ledge and began to follow Simrock along it. Despite the weight of his body, he moved with surprising grace through the mountains. He seemed at home here, up amongst the sheer slopes that tilted their faces to the sky.

Karel was not so comfortable as he brought up the rear, edging along the narrow path. It turned a corner, and he took a last look back at the Northern Road before it was lost from view.

The trail they followed was ancient and strangely constructed. Karel wondered at the mindset of the robots who would build a path that sometimes climbed near vertical cliff faces, cutting grooves with which to pull themselves forwards. More than once Karel and Melt found themselves lying on their fronts, fumbling in the darkness for the grooves that had been carved into the rock so they could pull themselves forwards. Karel's body was badly scratched and so full of grit: it constantly irritated his electromuscle. As for Melt, he didn't even have the comfort of looking forward to a chance to strip down and clean his body. Or was that such a comfort? It was all that Karel thought about now, and it made the irritation worse.

Still, they walked and climbed and crawled on, heading south all the while.

'What was that?' called Melt.

'What was what?'

Karel was too busy keeping both hands on the rocks. Despite his heavy body, Melt leaned back, one hand and one foot wedged into a wall.

'It's Simrock. He's speaking to himself. Is that what the Spontaneous do?'

'Ruth?' said Simrock. 'That's an unusual name. Where do you want to meet? The village? It's not that far.'

'What village?' asked Melt.

'It's just around here!'

'Who were you speaking to?'

'I don't know.' Simrock didn't seem concerned. 'I can't see anybody.'

Karel hurried to catch up.

'What's going on, Simrock?'

Simrock pointed. 'There is a village just around this corner. I know it's there!'

'Who is Ruth?' asked Melt.

But Simrock had already gone on ahead.

'I knew it! Just here! Can you see it yet?'

'No!' called Melt.

'He's not speaking to us,' said Karel.

They rounded a corner and halted, gazing down at the scene below in amazement.

Karel had never seen the village before, and yet he felt as if he knew it. He had the image woven into his mind, along with other tales and stories of childhood. This was how robots used to live, back before the villages had grown into towns and then states. Back when there was enough iron in the ground for all the robots on Penrose.

The village was a huddled collection of little circular buildings, all of the same basic design. Triangular sections of iron were riveted together to make bulging domes, which were fixed into place on stone foundations that rose to about the level of the knee. Flakes of orange rust peeled from the metal.

'It's not been abandoned for that long. No more than forty years, I would say.' Karel looked around in wonder. 'The village is set back on this ledge, it wouldn't be visible from below, the rock is too sheer above. But surely someone would have come up here?'

Melt said nothing, he pushed on, following Simrock towards the village. It was surrounded by a low stone wall; beyond the wall the ground was paved in wide, broken flags.

Karel followed him slowly, looking around in wonder. He felt as if he had stepped out of his own world and into another. At any moment he expected ancient robots to emerge from the antique buildings, waving to him with simply constructed limbs, peering at him through poorly focussed eyes. He imagined them coming forward and touching his body, admiring the metal, the smooth curves of its construction, scratched and damaged though it may be.

He heard Simrock's voice, calling out.

'Ruth? I'm here! Where are you?'

There was movement up ahead in the village. Two, three robots emerging from amongst the low, round buildings.

No, not robots! Karel halted in astonishment. Melt had recoiled, had clumsily assumed a fighting position.

They walked like robots, they had arms and faces like robots, but they weren't made of metal. They were animals!

Wa-Ka-Mo-Do

Once, when he was a young robot, Wa-Ka-Mo-Do's father had taken him to visit a tanning factory. He had seen the dead bodies of the cattle, flayed of their skins, lying in a pile, waiting for processing. There was something so exotic and other about the shapes of their internal frameworks, their *skeletons*, yellow bones smooth and curving in that weird way that suggested intelligent design. But what robot mind would bend and deform a structure in this fashion he didn't know.

'*You say that*,' his father had said, '*but I think we could learn a lot from such constructions. The material is light, but it's strong! Look at the way the curves give strength.*'

Organic life was like that, reflected Wa-Ka-Mo-Do. It looked so flimsy and soft, like you could squash it with one hand. But look at the damage it caused . . .

The west side of Sangrel reminded him a little of the tanning yard. The buildings had lost their roofs, their tiles blown away or shattered. Only the metal skeletons remained, twisted and blackened and illuminated by the fires that still burned orange and white below. One row of houses had been cut lengthways by the explosion, the further half collapsed; flames could be seen flickering through the broken windows. And beyond there, the centre of the blast, a crater punched into the very rock of the city itself, molten rock glowing red at its heart. Wa-Ka-Mo-Do knew about atomic weapons. Those robots close to the blast would find their minds subtly altered, their life spans drastically reduced. Not that anyone would care.

Columns of smoke held up the starry sky, cold and aloof above the damaged city.

'How many are dead?' wondered Wa-Ka-Mo-Do aloud. As he spoke, the crackle of gunfire sounded once more. Instantly he moved, searching out the sound. 'Over there,' he pointed.

A bell tower, the cap lost in the explosion, the bell still tolling slowly as it swayed in the night, and there, silhouetted by orange flames, two robots, firing down at the lower end of the Street of Becoming. Wa-Ka-Mo-Do looked closer. There on the ground was La-Ver-Di-Arussah, directing her troops to fire back. Successfully. First one, then the other of the two robots fell, the bell still tolling all the while, metal bodies smashing to the ground, shattering into fragments. They wore pig-iron bodies: cheap metal was all the poor of Sangrel could afford.

More shots, from further away, and La-Ver-Di-Arussah turned her troops towards the new attackers. Wa-Ka-Mo-Do saw how the robots were massing, saw how they were approaching the Street of Becoming in ones and twos, silhouetted bodies clambering over the rubble, carrying knives and guns, rocks and stones and metal bars.

He became aware of the slow throb of other bells ringing, all over the city, and he realized that the steady pulse wasn't the result of the after-effects of the explosion, but rather that the robots had picked up on that rhythm and had taken it for their own, a sign of their rising anger.

Now La-Ver-Di-Arussah and her troops were retreating, coming back towards Wa-Ka-Mo-Do.

'We need to hold this gate,' said Gillian, appearing at his side.

'Get back!' shouted Wa-Ka-Mo-Do, pushing her back with one hand as a bullet ricocheted from the wall nearby. More shots rang out. 'Get back into the square, you idiot!'

'Take your hands off me, robot!'

Gillian unholstered a pistol and raised it to eye level. She squeezed the trigger, and Wa-Ka-Mo-Do heard three faint pops as she fired at the nearest rebels.

'Get yourself a proper weapon,' she said, and she turned and stalked back into the safety of the square. She had a warrior's temperament, if nothing else.

The steady tolling of the bells was rising in volume. It seemed to Wa-Ka-Mo-Do he could feel a pulse of electricity behind it; the long pent-up rage of the robots of Sangrel building up to discharge itself in one lightning burst.

La-Ver-Di-Arussah and her soldiers came running up.

'They are approaching from every direction, Honoured Commander.'

'What about Ka-Lo-Re-Harballah?'

'He got through. The humans soldiers are already organizing themselves, getting ready to escort the civilians up here.'

'Good. We'll help bring them to safety and then hold

back the peasants until the humans have left. After that we will begin the job of restoring order to the city.'

'Get the humans to shoot them all for us,' said La-Ver-Di-Arussah. 'It will come to the same thing in the end.'

Wa-Ka-Mo-Do said nothing. He couldn't help thinking that she was right. Events had moved way beyond his control.

'Get up to the square and organize a defence,' he said.

'Very well.'

'We will do everything we can to help the humans. I want them out of my city as fast as possible.'

The slow tolling of the bells was increasing in volume, the fires burned on, the smoke climbed to the stars, cold and silent above. Wa-Ka-Mo-Do suddenly swept both his arms out wide, blades extended, expending so much built-up power in one crackling burst. He felt better for it. Centred, composed once more, he turned and made his way back up the hill to Smithy Square.

The humans had dragged one of their female guns to the top of the Street of Becoming. It sat there, looking down at him with that sleek, deadly expression.

'What's going on?' asked Wa-Ka-Mo-Do.

'We've reprogrammed it to only attack robots,' said Gillian.

La-Ver-Di-Arussah was watching the gun with interest.

'What about Ka-Lo-Re-Harballah?' he shouted. 'What

about the rest of the escort who will be bringing the humans back up here?'

'They'll turn it off when our troops approach,' said La-Ver-Di-Arussah. 'They'll turn it off now,' said Wa-Ka-Mo-Do coldly. 'Gillian! Move this gun away. You will not harm my citizens!'

'I thought they were the Emperor's citizens?'

'Rust the Emperor!'

The words were out before Wa-Ka-Mo-Do could stop them. A horrified silence fell between him and La-Ver-Di-Arussah. They gazed at each other, realizing that Wa-Ka-Mo-Do had crossed that final line. La-Ver-Di-Arussah recovered first.

'Very well, Wa-Ka-Mo-Do, if that's your wish.' She wore a cold smile.

'It's not *my* wish,' said Gillian. 'The gun stays on. I will not jeopardize the safety of my people.'

'Nor I mine,' said Wa-Ka-Mo-Do.

'You are outnumbered, Wa-Ka-Mo-Do,' said Gillian. 'Would you fight all my troops?'

Wa-Ka-Mo-Do looked around the green-clad humans, their guns swinging in his direction.

'I think I would,' said Wa-Ka-Mo-Do, blades extending at his hands and feet.

One of the humans did something, and the strange gun raised its head, turning round to face Wa-Ka-Mo-Do. They stood, gazing at each other. Wa-Ka-Mo-Do stared up into the round eye of the barrel.

'Shall I tell them to arm it?' asked Gillian, coolly.

To think was to move. He reached out, caught the human woman, pulled her before him, wrapped an arm around the middle of her soft body, placing her between himself and the gun.

'Tell them,' said Wa-Ka-Mo-Do.

They stood there, Wa-Ka-Mo-Do and Gillian, the female gun looking down at them, the slow tolling of bells pulsing in a night filled with the orange glow of burning, surrounded by bars of smoke, the stars cold above them. The human faltered first.

'Turn it off,' she said.

Karel

Simrock walked up to the leading animal.

'Hello. Are you Ruth?'

The animal smiled.

'I am! You must be Simrock! And who are your friends?'

'This is Melt, and here comes Karel now.'

Karel came forward, looking at the animal in astonishment. She was female, he knew it. She looked so like a robot woman. Her pink animal body was stuffed inside a padded silver thing that enveloped her body. Now he was close to her he could see animal eyes behind the dark glasses that covered half her face, he noted the white grease smeared around the rim of her mouth. It was bright but cold up here, and he wondered if these animals were at the limits of their tolerance.

'What are you doing here?' asked Melt, suspicion hard in his voice. 'Where are the rest of you?'

'Melt, what's the matter with you?' said Karel. The

animals unnerved him, the way they walked like robots, but so did Melt's attitude. He had never seen the robot so angry before.

'There are just the three of us,' said Ruth, answering Melt. She wore something over her head. A little light flickered as she spoke. 'I'm Ruth Powdermaker. The guy with the big feet is Brian Kovacs and the pretty young woman is Jasprit Begum.' The two other animals smiled as their names were mentioned. The male one waved a hand in greeting. 'We're ——————.'

Karel heard the sound of the word as it emerged from her mouth, wet and hissing.

'I'm sorry, there seems to be no robot equivalent. We study groups of people.'

'Did you make that talking machine?' said Karel.

'Never mind that,' interrupted Melt. 'Where are your weapons?'

'Here,' said Ruth, patting a holster at her side. 'Plus, Brian's got a rifle packed away on board the ship. But they're only for our own protection. We're not part of the group on the plain. We're here purely for research.'

'Research into what?'

'Life here on this planet. Contact with humans will change your society. It's already happening. We want to try and capture all that we can about conditions before we arrived. That's why we're up here. Plus, there are so many of the Spontaneous here.'

They all looked at Simrock.

'How were you speaking to him?' asked Karel.

'I hear her voice,' said Simrock. 'Like when I was below the ground.'

The animal called Jasprit was carefully examining Simrock's head. What was she looking for?

'And is that normal?' asked Ruth. 'Is that what you all experience?'

She was gazing at Karel.

'Hearing voices?' he said. 'No. Only the Spontaneous can do that.'

'Is that right, Melt?' asked Jasprit. She was smaller than the other two, her body a darker colour. Her eyes were dark and bright. Melt looked at her with undisguised hostility.

'I don't know anything about the Spontaneous. And I don't know anything about the three of you, either. Karel, I think we should go. Now.'

'Why?'

'Look at this place. These buildings. And then these *humans* turn up here.' Karel had never heard the word before, but Melt said *human* in the same way he might say *rust*. 'I say we go. Now.'

'The buildings!' said Brian with the big feet. 'They're strange, aren't they? Not at all like the other ones we've seen here. Why is that do you suppose?'

'Why do you keep asking all these questions?'

'Melt!' Karel looked at the big robot in astonishment. 'What's the matter with you?'

'These animals. Don't trust them.'

'You're suspicious. I can understand that,' said Ruth. 'Have you met humans before, Melt? We're not all the same, you know. We're not like those down on the plain.'

'You mentioned that before,' said Karel. 'What do you mean, the ones on the plain?'

'There is a big robot state to the south of these mountains. It controls the southern part of this continent. Do you know of it?'

'Artemis!' said Karel.

'Of course he knows Artemis, Ruth.' Brian stepped forward, and Karel noted the cloth panelling that covered him was streaked with grease and oil. 'He's wearing the body of one of their soldiers. Are you part of that state, Karel?'

'Me? No. They destroyed my home. Have you heard of Turing City?'

'Turing City? No. Where is that located? If I showed you a map, could you tell me? I'll just be a moment.'

Karel looked around in bewilderment as Brian dashed off around the side of one of the old-fashioned buildings.

'We could follow him,' said Ruth. 'There is an open area in the centre of this village where we have set up camp. All our equipment is there. Would you come with us? Would that be all right?'

She looked at Melt.

'If you've met humans before, you'll know what our guns can do. If I wanted to harm you, I could have shot you as you approached. I could shoot you as you leave. That wouldn't help me do my job though, would it? Come and speak with us! Please?'

'I think we should go with them,' said Karel. 'They might be able to tell us things we need to know.'

'What about your wife?' said Melt. 'Don't trust them, Karel.'

'Why not, Melt? What do you know about these humans? Why won't you tell me anything?'

Melt glared at him, eyes glowing.

'They said that there were humans in Artemis,' said Karel. 'I think we need to find out as much as we possibly can.'

'Very well,' said Melt. 'But watch out. Their words are lubricated in the finest oil. Don't trust the animals!'

Wa-Ka-Mo-Do

The night passed under the brilliant stars to the tolling of bells. The noise from the city was increasing, the steady stamping, the gunfire. More than once Wa-Ka-Mo-Do thought he should go to the aid of Ka-Lo-Re-Harballah, but each time Gillian had dissuaded him.

'They are coming,' she said, oblivious to Wa-Ka-Mo-Do's concerns. 'Our soldiers are more than a match for a few civilians.' Didn't she realize that, but for a lingering concern for the Emperor's authority and for the fact that he wasn't sure just what to do for the best, he would have given his robots the order to open fire upon her and her troops?

The gun at the top of the Street of Becoming was deactivated. The other human guns were mostly still now. Every so often one of them would twitch and send a brief stream of bullets into the night before lowering its head and resting once more. There was a sense of calmness and isolation up here at the top of Sangrel, a feeling of being temporarily removed from the trouble below. They all felt it, human and robot alike, staring into the surrounding darkness.

'Zuse is low tonight,' said La-Ver-Di-Arussah. 'Hiding behind the hills.'

Wa-Ka-Mo-Do looked at her in surprise, not expecting this sudden show of feeling. Was her confidence ebbing as his was?

'I heard that Zuse is mentioned in the Book of Robots,' she said.

Wa-Ka-Mo-Do couldn't be bothered to pretend any more.

'It is, La-Ver-Di-Arussah.' And he thought of Rachael. Rachael had told him that there was something significant about the metal moon. The humans seemed to know so much, he reflected, so much more than the robots did.

'What do you think of your creators now?' taunted La-Ver-Di-Arussah.

'They're not our creators,' said Wa-Ka-Mo-Do bitterly. 'The book says that we should look after each other. The humans don't even look after themselves: look how they are fighting each other.'

As if to prove his point, the nearest gun turned and fired a quick burst out into the night. He felt adrift, engaged in a war that he didn't understand, caught between opposing forces that had no interest in him, half following the remnants of orders issued by his former Emperor.

His former Emperor. Wa-Ka-Mo-Do felt a deep sense of shame at his treachery, but what else could he have done?

'They're coming!'

The words were spoken by robots and humans alike. He saw the remaining humans of Sangrel hurrying up the broken Street of Becoming.

The street was wider at the top, the houses there richer and more imposing. The humans moved quickly up the centre of the road, surrounded by green-panelled human soldiers, their feet slipping on the rounded cobbles as they headed for safety. The soldiers scanned the high windows and roofs, looking out for dark silhouettes against the stars. Every so often they raised a rifle to their shoulder and fired. Each time, a robot died. Still the bells tolled, but now, faintly behind them could be heard the chanting of electronic voices. Wa-Ka-Mo-Do peered into the darkness and saw the shapes of his troops bringing up the rear. Where was Ka-Lo-Re-Harballah?

The humans began to enter the square, walking three abreast, quickly but without haste, and Wa-Ka-Mo-Do felt a sneaking admiration at their grace under pressure. He scanned their faces for Rachael, but didn't see her. If they had any sense they would have put the young and weak in the middle of the line.

A shout came from the city below.

'The animals! They're escaping!'

How did they know? Did they guess the humans' plan? It didn't matter. All those little groups of robots out there, creeping through the rubble, searching for courage and direction, suddenly found a focus. The sound of gunfire increased.

The steady flow of humans became a stampede.

'It's started!' La-Ver-Di-Arussah drew her sword. 'Cover the humans! Don't allow any robot past!'

'No killing!' shouted Wa-Ka-Mo-Do.

La-Ver-Di-Arussah laughed.

'How else will we maintain order?'

She moved forward, the remaining robot troops forming up around her. More humans came running forward, tumbling over each other, and Wa-Ka-Mo-Do found himself struggling against the tide. It would be so easy to take his sword and cut through this all too yielding flesh.

'Where's Ka-Lo-Re-Harballah?' he called.

'Down there,' said La-Ver-Di-Arussah. 'At the rear!'

'Once the humans are past, bring all the troops up into the square!'

'I will!' She had resheathed her sword. Now she took out a pistol of human design and began to fire into the night.

'Where did you get that?' shouted Wa-Ka-Mo-Do.

'Gillian gave it to me!'

She wore a look of delight as she aimed the pistol down the street, picking off the civilians who showed themselves. There were more and more of them, the revolutionary crowd was growing all the time.

'I still can't see Ka-Lo-Re-Harballah!'

'He doesn't matter! Look at all these robots! We're not going to hold them!'

She was right. They were losing the battle.

Losing the battle? These were his own citizens he was fighting against!

And then he heard a noise behind him, and he turned to see the female gun at the top of the street raise its head.

Gillian had lied to him. The humans had set it working again!

He turned to run towards it, just as that odd rippling noise began. Just in time, he flattened himself to the ground, the air flickering above him as the gun fired down the road. He heard the shriek and clatter of metal being torn apart. Robots, the robots of his city, were being killed, troops and rebels alike.

From where he lay he saw Gillian and the soldiers looking down the street with empty eyes, eyes that did not light up with warmth or intelligence. Quickly, he began to crawl up towards the gun, hoping that it wouldn't fire upon him. It hadn't turned on La-Ver-Di-Arussah and the rest; he guessed that it was ranged beyond them.

It was a gamble, but a good one. Besides, better to die with honour charging the humans' weapon than to lie here while robots were being killed.

He sprang forward, sprinting up the street.

A human soldier pointed a pistol in his direction. Wa-Ka-Mo-Do glared at him, lighting up his face with the white glow of his eyes. The soldier hesitated, long enough for him to reach the gun, the shapely, curving machine that rippled death on the robots below. He could feel the power surging through it, that strange, singing current. He drew an awl and thrust it deep into the heart of the gun's shaft, heard the bang, felt the electromuscle in his right arm burn and die at the same time as the great gun did. Its head drooped, the rippling ceased. Wa-Ka-Mo-Do had killed it.

'What have you done?' shouted Gillian, running up to him. She had pulled her pistol from its holster and pointed it to his head as he stood there, arm hanging limply at his side. The gun wavered; the square was filling with humans all the time, behind them the noise of shooting was growing louder. The Street of Becoming echoed to the clatter of gunfire.

'Wa-Ka-Mo-Do!'

Rachael emerged from the crowd, face pale and smudged with soot.

'What happened to your arm?'

'Rachael,' said Wa-Ka-Mo-Do in a low voice. 'Get back.'

Rachael noticed Gillian, who lowered her gun and turned back to her troops.

'Get another gun across here, now!' she called.

Wa-Ka-Mo-Do saw that the last of the humans had entered the square. Now only the imperial soldiers remained, covering their retreat. La-Ver-Di-Arussah was forming them into a line at the top of the street, pouring fire down at the attacking rebels.

'What's happening, Wa-Ka-Mo-Do?' Rachael's voice sounded frightened. Wa-Ka-Mo-Do pushed the soft human gently away, and went forward to La-Ver-Di-Arussah.

'You should have left the gun alone,' she said. 'It would have kept them back. They'll overwhelm us soon.'

She was right. There were so many robots out there now. Thin, poorly constructed things, the light in their

eyes dim, their bodies made of tin and pig iron and whatever else there was to hand. They carried a few guns, a
few knives. Mainly they held metal struts and bars, ripped
from the broken buildings and quickly shaped into clubs
and spears. These were robots that had lived in poverty
for years under the Emperor's rule, only to have even
that taken from them when the humans had arrived.
Little wonder that tonight they had finally risen up.

Wa-Ka-Mo-Do felt the current draining from his
body. Everything had gone so wrong. La-Ver-Di-Arussah
had been right. He was nothing but a peasant, he was
not made for command.

He looked at the straggling remains of the Imperial
Army, joining the ranks of La-Ver-Di-Arussah's defence.

'Where's Ka-Lo-Re-Harballah?'

'Hit by the humans' gun.'

And at that the current flowed back through his body.
Stronger and brighter than before, humming with anger.

'The humans' gun?' said Wa-Ka-Mo-Do, softly. 'The
humans' gun? And you see nothing wrong with this? Our
soldiers cut down for the benefit of these *Sebol*?'

He spat out the words.

'We follow the will of the Emperor,' said La-Ver-Di-
Arussah, calmly.

'The Emperor is a fool! He has sold us to these animals!'

'We are his to sell. All of us. And none more so than
those pig-iron peasants down there.'

She waved to where the robots were moving in fits
and starts up the Street of Becoming, falling in ones and
twos before the volleys of the guns.

Something dark passed across the bright stars above, and a new sound could be heard: a descending hum.

'The humans' ship,' said La-Ver-Di-Arussah. 'Look, here it comes!'

Red lines leaped into being at the edge of the horizon, tracking a path through the night sky towards the descending craft. The female guns bobbed and turned, and high above more fire tracked out from the ship, intercepting the attack that had streamed from the distance.

'They're dropping the shuttles now,' said Gillian. 'Give us half an hour and we'll be gone.'

And then what about us?

His thought was cut off. Gillian gulped, gulped again. She spat dark oil from her mouth. No, not oil, blood. Blood was pouring from her mouth and her chest, staining her uniform. A second bullet struck Wa-Ka-Mo-Do in his dead arm. He heard the ringing noise through the night. Robots were pouring into the square. How had they got up here so fast? They hadn't breached La-Ver-Di-Arussah's line.

Wa-Ka-Mo-Do reached for his shotgun with his dead arm, realized his mistake and pulled it awkwardly from its sheath with the other. Across the square, humans were running towards one of the female guns, seeking no doubt to turn it on the robots.

'No!' called Wa-Ka-Mo-Do.

La-Ver-Di-Arussah was firing at the attacking robots, shattering a fragile head, sending blue wire tangling out. The sound of the bells, the humming of the descending ship, the rippling of the guns . . .

'Stop!' cried Wa-Ka-Mo-Do. He raised his voice. 'I

am Wa-Ka-Mo-Do, of Ko, of the State of Ekrano in the High Spires! One of the Eleven! Commander of the Emperor's Army of Sangrel! I command you to halt.'

It worked. For a moment. The peasants nearest to him paused and looked in his direction. Then one turned a gun towards him, but too slowly. Wa-Ka-Mo-Do fired his shotgun, shattering the front of its body.

He heard screams. Human screams. There was Rachael nearby, mouth wide open in a human expression of terror. Two robots had hold of her; they were pulling at her arms, trying to rip her apart. He leaped forward, kicked at the nearest with the blades at his feet, ripping the electromuscles in its leg. The second robot let go and ran. He shot it in the chest.

'Th . . . thank you . . .' said Rachael. She placed a hand on his arm. She looked as if she was going to hold him. At that moment she reminded him so much of La-Cor, his sister, he felt ashamed. Sangrel was burning, robots were dying, and he had paused to help a human. Would his sister understand that?

'Wa-Ka-Mo-Do,' said Rachael. 'Listen to me, as soon as we're gone, you've got to get away from here.'

'Can't. I've got the city to control!'

A knife flew out of the night. He held out the barrel of his shotgun and deflected it from Rachael. She didn't seem to notice.

'Wa-Ka-Mo-Do, listen to me! It doesn't matter! It will take us some time to get into orbit, but once we're clear, sometime tomorrow morning . . .'

Three explosions nearby. Shattered metal washed across the square. The first human shuttle descended from the sky. A widebodied craft, it landed near the terrace, light shining from its open doors.

'Go!' said Wa-Ka-Mo-Do.

'Wa-Ka-Mo-Do, you must listen to me! They're going to drop—'

But someone took hold of Rachael and dragged her away, off towards the shuttle. Wa-Ka-Mo-Do turned and rejoined the fight.

But the fighting was dying away. In the middle of the turning guns, beneath the explosions and flares that lit up the sky above, calm was spreading over the square. Humans retreated unmolested as robots were ceasing to fight, laying down their arms and kneeling down.

What was happening? And then Wa-Ka-Mo-Do saw what the robots had already noticed. He saw the three figures that had emerged from the Copper Master's house and who were now walking towards Wa-Ka-Mo-Do. He felt his gyros rattling, felt the current wobbling through his body. The Vestal Virgins had returned.

The electrical hum of terror affected everyone in the square, and Wa-Ka-Mo-Do remembered the stories he had told Rachael of how the old rulers of Sangrel had woven fear into the citizens. It was still there now, it was there in every subject of the Emperor. Subservience to the Vestal Virgins was woven into the mind of every robot.

The three women passed one of the human guns, their beauty rendering that of the alien machine strange and ugly by comparison. They halted before Wa-Ka-Mo-Do. He was swaying, he had discharged too much current that day. His arm hung useless at his side. He had never felt more powerless.

'Wa-Ka-Mo-Do,' said the first. 'You have failed the Emperor.'

She was as beautiful as he remembered her, but there, under the starry sky, with the fires of destruction leaping around the edge of the terrace, it was a terrible beauty.

'The Emperor has failed us!' shouted Wa-Ka-Mo-Do. His words rang hollow across the square.

'You have failed Sangrel,' said the second.

'The Emperor failed Sangrel.'

'You are relieved of your command,' said the third.

'By whose authority?'

'The Emperor's. There is a radio in the Mound of Eternity. Surely you must have realized this?'

He hadn't. He felt a shimmering whine inside himself, as if his lifeforce was dying away.

One of the Vestal Virgins turned to La-Ver-Di-Arussah. 'La-Ver-Di-Arussah, you are now in charge of this city.'

'No!'

'Be silent, Wa-Ka-Mo-Do,' said another.

La-Ver-Di-Arussah stepped forward, smiling.

'Put down this rebellion.'

He wanted to shout out, but he couldn't. He had been ordered to silence, and it was woven into his mind to obey the Vestal Virgins.

One of them stepped forward, she touched Wa-Ka-Mo-Do on the head.

'This way,' she said.

He found himself following her from the square. He had no choice. He looked across, saw Rachael's pale face looking across at him as she boarded the shuttle. She was shouting something to him, but he couldn't hear. The rattle of gunfire had begun once more, directed by La-Ver-Di-Arussah.

Wa-Ka-Mo-Do was led into the Copper Master's house, no longer the Commander of the Emperor's Army of Sangrel, no longer a warrior of honour.

He had failed, completely.

As he was meant to do.

Karel

The animals had set up a little roof made of flexible plastic in the middle of the village. Under it there was a table set with some electronic equipment and some more sheets of plastic covered in symbols and pictures.

Brian went straight to one of the sheets.

'Here,' he said, showing it to Karel, who took a moment to realize he was looking at green countries painted over blue seas. It was an odd choice of colours.

'Here's Shull over here,' said Brian. 'This is the large city to the south of these mountains. Can you show me where Turing City was?'

Karel was too taken by the rest of the map.

'What are all these other places?' he asked, pointing to two large islands, almost touching, to the right of the map. The two of them together were bigger than Shull.

'These? I believe you call them Yukawa. Those are the north and south islands. And over here is Gell.' He pointed to another huge island to the left of Shull. There was a scattering of smaller islands around it.

'I never heard of these places!' said Karel. 'Never, not in all my time in Turing City, never in all my time working in immigration. No one ever came from these places.'

'Really?' said Brian.

'Never mind that,' interrupted Melt. 'Ask them where they come from. I know these animals. They ask so many questions, and they give *nothing* in return.'

'How do you know so much about them, Melt?'

Melt leaned forwards. 'Go on, Brian, tell us. Where are you from?'

The animal laughed, his white painted mouth stretched in a wide smile. The dark glass he wore over his eyes reflected the surrounding peaks.

'We're from a place called Earth, Melt. Another planet. Millions and millions of miles away.'

'What are you doing here?'

'Finding out about you. On Earth, not so long ago, people like me and Ruth and Jasprit used to travel to other countries to find out how the people lived, what their customs and beliefs were.'

'Their beliefs?' said Karel. 'Why would you do that?'

'And what about the humans down on the plain below?' interrupted Melt. 'What are they doing here?'

'Trading.'

Ruth stepped forward. 'The trouble is,' she said, 'once one culture begins to interact with another they both begin to alter each other. That's why we are up here, in the mountains, where things are—'

'Yes, yes,' interrupted Melt once more. Karel was getting irritated by how rude he was being. 'Tell me about

Earth. Did countries trade with each other back on Earth?'

'All the time,' said Brian. 'They still do now. Tell me, Melt, where have you seen humans before? How long ago was it?'

Melt glared at the man.

'Could you show us on a map?' asked Brian, not giving up.

'It was the summertime, when I met you,' said Melt. 'Does that answer your question?'

Brian gazed at him. 'Yes, I think it does.'

'Here,' said Karel, feeling embarrassed. 'Here. This is where Turing City was.'

He placed a finger on the map, towards the southern coast of Shull.

'Odd,' said Brian. 'Our mapping software didn't pick up anything there.'

'It wouldn't,' said Karel. 'I told you, Artemis conquered my state. They leave nothing behind.'

'And you're going there now,' said Jasprit. 'Going to find your wife?'

'Yes.'

'And do you love your wife?'

'Yes. Of course.'

'Do all robots love their wives?'

'Usually. Often, when a child is being made, it is woven into their minds to love someone.'

'I know about that,' said Jasprit, ruefully, and the other two humans laughed, the machines they wore translating the harsh, juddering sounds they made into the sweet hiss of robot laughter.

'Tell me about him,' said Melt, suddenly, pointing at Simrock.

The laughter ceased.

'What about him?' asked Ruth, all businesslike.

'You spoke to him. How?'

'Don't you know, Melt?' asked Brian.

'I asked the question first. Answer me!'

'I'm sorry, Melt. We don't mean to frustrate you. That's our training. Often telling what we think to be true corrupts or changes the people we are trying to learn about.' Brian held his arms apart in a human gesture. 'But you must know how we spoke to Simrock. Don't you use radio to communicate?'

'Yes, of course we do . . .'

Then it struck Karel and Melt what she meant.

Ruth leaned forward, genuinely interested. 'Don't you find it odd that so few robots on this planet have exploited radio as a means of communication? I mean, the pilgrims, the whales, the hive insects do. That's about it. Why don't you?'

'Why should we?' blustered Melt. 'We build radios when we need them.'

'You have so little curiosity. All of you. You just accept things as they are.'

She was right, thought Karel. We do. He looked at Brian and Jasprit, saw the way they were looking at each other.

'You know about us,' said Karel. 'You know more about us than we do ourselves.' Something occurred to him. 'Have you been to the Top of the World?'

'Why?'

'No more questions!' shouted Melt.

'I'm sorry. Force of habit. No, we haven't. Why do you ask, Karel?'

'I've been to the top of Shull. There is a place there.'

'Can you show me on the map?' asked Brian.

'I'm sorry. No. But there is a building. I was forbidden to enter, but I looked inside anyway. There is an arrangement of robots in there, all lined up, showing how we evolved.'

Jasprit began to dance at this.

'Really? We've got to go, Ruth.'

'We will! What else is there, Karel?'

'A map of the stars on the wall. And the titles of three stories: The Story of Nicolas the Coward, The Story of the Four Blind Horses, and The Story of Eric and the Mountain.'

That had them.

'Really, Ruth, we have to go!' said Jasprit. 'We need to see that place!'

'We're interested in stories,' explained Ruth. 'They tell you a lot about a culture. I've heard the story of Nicolas the Coward. Simrock told us that as you walked here.'

They looked at Simrock, standing placidly nearby. He seemed to have lost interest in the conversation.

'I don't know the other two stories though,' said Ruth. 'Could you tell me them, Karel?'

'I'm sorry, no. I never heard them.'

Melt made a noise.

'Do you know them, Melt?' asked Karel.

'I thought everyone knew the story of Eric and the Mountain,' he replied.

'Everyone? No.' Karel gazed at Melt. 'Melt, where are you from?'

'Karel, do we have time for this?'

Karel was torn between Melt and the animals. To think he had walked all this way next to someone who knew one of the mysterious stories.

Melt spoke up.

'Ruth, maybe we can do a deal,' he said. 'We need to get down to the plain below. If you help us, I will answer all your questions.'

The three humans looked at each other.

'We could call up a craft,' said Brian. 'But I'm not sure it would take all three of them.'

'I'm staying here,' said Simrock.

'Why?' asked Melt.

'This is where Nicolas the Coward will be, not down on the plains below.'

'Two of us then,' said Melt. 'You must have flown up here in a craft. I can't imagine animals walking this far. Get us closer to Artemis City and we'll help you.'

'We can't take you too close,' said Brian.

'Why not?'

'It's another state's . . . trading area,' said Ruth. 'We have agreements.'

'I think I understand,' said Melt. 'Just take us down to the plains, then.'

'Very well,' said Brian, and he held out a hand. Melt took it and moved it up and down.

'You *have* met humans before,' said Ruth. 'In that case, if it's all the same to you, we will speak to Karel.'

Karel was too heavy for the humans' flimsy chairs. He didn't mind, he sat on the rocky ground amongst the curved iron buildings as these creatures from so far away asked him questions.

Such strange questions, at once so obvious but so difficult to put an answer to. Where did robots come from, how did they make children, what was the difference between a robot and an animal? Why were there two moons, why was there metal, how long do they live, what's the difference between a male and female robot?

And then, the oddest of them all.

'Take a look around the village, Karel. Tell us what you see.'

'Why?'

'We want to see this world through your eyes.'

Karel looked around. From here he could see nothing but sky, he was lost in the cupped hands of the mountain, watched only by the sun. No one knew of this place, but it still seemed odd that it had remained undetected for fifty years, if not the hundreds of years old that it looked.

'What do you think? Go on. Look around.'

He got up and, followed by Ruth, he wandered around the village. The buildings were just a little smaller than he was: he could not stand up inside those low iron domes. The doors were all low, no more than two feet high, and he ducked to enter one or two, to look around the empty interiors with glowing eyes. In one he found a shallow depression in the centre of the room that might once have held a fire. Looking up, he saw a hole in the roof, flames of rust licking through the iron towards him.

He ducked back outside and turned his attention to the collar of stone on which the iron dome sat.

It was green with organic life, he noted with some disgust. Green fur, yellow splats of lichen, even frills of some pale substance he had never seen before.

He reached out and dragged his finger across it. It felt so insubstantial, almost like it wasn't there. It was ironic. Up here, in this forgotten space at the top of the world, strong metal rusted, but weak organic life waxed wildly. Only in Turing City had the natural order reigned. Only in that state had the stones been scrubbed clean, the creeping tendrils of green life uprooted and burned, only there had metal walked pure and free. No more.

And then, as he stared at the obscene mush on his fingers, the world seemed to flip. For a moment, that mush was the true, vital life, and his metal body was cold and clean and sterile. Nothing but metal animated by thoughts.

Then the world flipped back again and he laughed. What did it mean to say 'nothing but metal animated by thoughts'? He was *exactly* metal animated by thoughts.

The world flipped again, and he looked at those low, wide doorways, and something else became clear.

Ruth was there, standing by him.

'What is it, Karel?'

'I think I see. The robots that lived here weren't shaped like me.'

He found the proof in the next building he looked inside.

Two bodies lay in there. Robot bodies of a sort. They were long, of many segments, two limbs, not quite arms, not quite legs, coming from each section. At one end there was an interface where Karel guessed another segment could be plugged. At the other there was a flat head containing two eyes of a similar design to his own.

The skull of one robot was broken open, and he peered inside at the blue wire in there, maybe not so much like in Karel's own head, but it was twisted enough to suggest intelligence.

Karel ran his hands over one of the bodies. He moved it, felt the articulation in the joints, saw the way the blue wire of the mind ran to the very tip of each limb. Then he noticed what was missing. No electromuscle. These robots controlled their bodies by lifeforce alone. They would be weaker than he was, a lot weaker.

It was good metal though. Steel with enough chromium to encourage passivation: these bodies would take a long time to rust. He noticed the traces of chromium in the dome structure too.

He took hold of one of the bodies, and crawled backwards out of the building, dragging it along behind himself.

'Have you seen robots like these before, Karel?'

'No. What are they, Ruth?'

'We were hoping you would tell us.'

He began to disassemble the body for parts, pausing for a moment.

'What's wrong?' he asked Ruth, hearing the odd noise that she made. 'It's only metal.'

He turned his attention back to the creature. Some of the chromium steel had welded together, and he had to tear the gelled parts from each other. Even so, it was a nicely constructed machine, and Karel was impressed by the craftsrobotship of the makers.

And a thought suddenly occurred to him.

Why was he shaped like he was? Why did robots have two arms and two legs? Why did they walk upright?

The answer was obvious, of course. That was a sensible shape for a robot. It was a sensible shape for a human. But was the obvious answer the right one?

Night was falling.

'We must take them down tonight,' Karel overheard Brian saying. 'They don't sleep, remember? Who is going to stay awake amongst us?'

'I'd do it. I want to know more about the stories! Melt knows more. You saw how he answered that question!'

'I don't care. I've summoned the craft already. There'll be other robots, Ruth.'

They were looking at him, Karel knew. He pretended not to notice. He was sat on the floor before Jasprit, looking at the patterns she drew on a piece of plastic.

'That looks like a child to me,' he said.

'But why?' asked Jasprit. 'What makes it look like a child?'

Ruth came up. She looked down at the pattern. 'I thought that was a man.'

'Apparently not,' said Jasprit. 'Not to a robot, anyway.'

'Karel,' said Ruth, 'the craft is coming. We'll need to head up the mountain a little way to the flat ground. Are you ready?'

'I am.'

Melt walked up. 'They say it will only take half an hour to get down,' he said.

'That will save us a lot of time.'

Karel looked around the three humans, at the strange village.

'I feel as if I should stay here . . .' he began.

'That's how it begins,' said Melt firmly. 'Promises and help, and before you know it you're dancing to their tune.'

'You know,' said Karel, 'you've remembered your past.'

'Later,' said Melt. 'When we're down.'

They said goodbye to Simrock.

'Good luck finding Nicolas the Coward,' said Karel.

'Thank you,' said Simrock.

'Goodbye Karel, Goodbye Melt,' said Jasprit.

They climbed from the village, accompanied by Brian and Ruth. Jasprit and Simrock waved goodbye.

'Not far up here,' said Brian.

They climbed to a little wind-whipped plateau. Brilliant white peaks surrounded them, framed by the deepening blue sky. Night was coming. Below them the slopes were greyer where the summer snowmelt had occurred.

'It's not too windy is it, Brian?' asked Ruth.

'They said it would be fine.'

As he spoke there was a low buzzing. Karel saw a flying craft approaching, a huge propeller turning on the top.

'A helicopter,' said Ruth.

The craft came closer; it hovered above them and then slowly settled on the plateau.

'Goodbye,' said Ruth, holding out her hand. 'I hope you find your wife.'

Karel took her hand. It was a delicate operation; not too hard so he crushed it, not so soft it slipped from his; he shook it up and down, the way he had seen Melt do.

'Thank you,' said Karel. 'I hope you find out all you need to.'

He shook hands with Brian and then moved towards the craft. The big propeller on the top was blowing down on them, pushing them to the ground. Something in the craft set up a singing resonance within his body. It was uncomfortable, but bearable.

Karel and Melt climbed on board. They were met by a human wearing something like a robot's skull over his head, a sheet of glass across the front. He showed them where to sit on the little metal seats. He seemed particularly concerned by the weight of Melt, moving him around the cabin until he was happy with his position.

Eventually they were settled. The note of the engine increased, and Karel gazed out of the window as they rose up into the air.

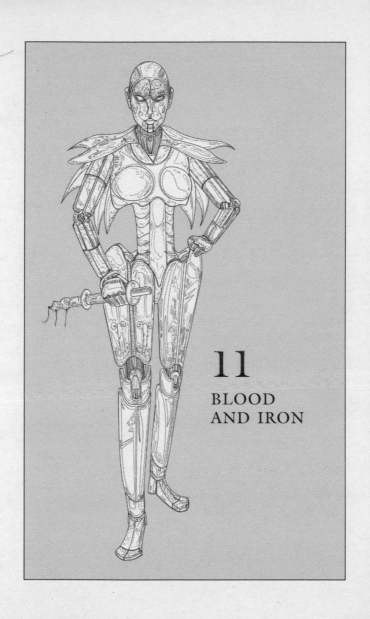

11

BLOOD AND IRON

Susan

Barrack 245 was one of twenty identical corrugated-steel buildings arranged in a four-by-five grid near the marshalling yards.

The windowless, rectangular constructions crowded together, keeping the narrow concrete paths running between them forever in gloomy shadow. Susan walked with Spoole, now also wearing the body of an infantry-robot, down one of the paths.

'There is fungus growing down here,' said Spoole. 'Here, right in the middle of Artemis City.'

'Fungus?' Susan looked at the soft white globes. 'They're obscene!'

'I saw them in Born,' said Spoole. 'They used to cultivate them.'

'Why?'

'I have no idea.' He looked up at the sheer wall of the building. 'This is the place. It's empty.'

Susan could feel it too. The building could hold one thousand, four hundred and fifty robots, packed in, arms and legs and bodies all pushed together. So many bodies combined would set up a faint hum. Spoole tapped at the wall. They heard the hollow vibration of the space beyond.

'They're gone,' he said.

'Not surprising,' said Susan. It had taken them days to reach the barracks. Days of dodging patrols and doubling back on themselves. The order had gone out that Spoole was now wanted for treason against the state. That was a difficult concept for the robots of Artemis, their minds woven from birth to think of nothing but Nyro's way. That conscripts should turn against the state, that they should only pretend to be Artemisians as a way of preserving their life, that was understood. But for Spoole, a robot whose mind was woven in the making rooms of Artemis, to turn traitor, that was almost unthinkable.

'What do we do now?'

Spoole had the answer already.

'Head for the Marshalling Office. Nettie will have been loaded onto a train. We can find out which one.'

They left the barrack area and followed the gloomy concrete paths back out into the sunshine at the edge of the marshalling yard.

Railway lines, their upper surfaces polished silver by the passage of wheels, swept across the ground in every direction.

'It's over a mile across,' said Spoole, proudly. 'Two miles deep, though some of the lines run back for five miles, almost into the heart of the city.'

Susan looked at the endless rows of the wagons parked on the lines before her. A diesel engine rumbled past, pulling a line of green tankers. She could hear the petrol sloshing around inside them. Only half full. Had the humans taken the rest?

'Where's the Marshalling Office?'

'Down there.'

Spoole pointed south, to the focus of the yard, the

place where all of the lines converged through a series of points and crossovers, the place where the hundreds of tracks joined together in ones and twos to leave just sixteen, running from Artemis City and into the continent of Shull. A gantry stretched across those sixteen tracks, a haphazard array of galvanized steel buildings erected upon it.

'Every train that leaves the city this way passes beneath the Marshalling Office,' said Spoole. 'Every train, every item of freight, is recorded there. If Nettie has been taken, they'll know it. Come on.'

They set off, jumping across the tracks, dodging between the trains that slowly rumbled past.

They found themselves keeping pace with a rake of open wagons, infantryrobots standing idly on board, watching the world go by.

'Where are you heading?' called Spoole.

'Stark!' one of them called back. 'They say Kavan is out there!' He took a closer look, and saw through the borrowed infantryrobot body. 'Hey, you're Spoole, aren't you!'

'I am!'

'Spoole!' Susan tugged at his arm. 'What are you doing?'

The infantryrobots all turned in his direction, pressing forward to the edge of the wagon.

'Spoole, what's going on?' they called. 'They say you're a traitor! Are you?'

'What do you think?' asked Spoole.

'I don't know. Why are you fighting Kavan?'

'I'm not sure I'm fighting Kavan. Are you?'

The train was speeding up. One infantryrobot began running back along the train, trying to keep level with Spoole. Jumping from wagon to wagon, pushing other robots out of the way. Spoole and Susan jogged forward to keep up with him.

'Would Kavan trade with the animals?' called the robot.

'You know the answer to that,' called Spoole.

'But . . .' The robot tripped on another.

'Hey!'

The train was accelerating now. Spoole watched as the infantryrobot receded.

'Spoole!' it called.

'It's going too fast,' said Susan, slowing to a halt. Spoole did the same. 'You took a risk there.'

'I don't know,' said Spoole. 'Look.' They both watched as an infantryrobot jumped from the train. Two more followed its example.

'Come on!'

They ran forwards, the end of the train passing them as they did so. More robots were jumping to the tracks ahead of them. Some of them lost arms and legs as they did so. Others helped put them back together.

Susan and Spoole arrived at the group.

'Spoole, I'm Copland. Do you remember me? Years ago, in Bethe?'

'Spoole, we can't believe you're a traitor.'

'I'm not. Treachery would be following the animals.'

Copland looked at the other robots.

'Listen, Spoole. There are others in the city who think the same as you. Hundreds of them. Thousands. All they need is a leader.'

Susan gazed balefully at Spoole.

'You're going to leave me, aren't you?' she said. 'You promised to help me!'

'I didn't, Susan. You are thinking like a Turing Citizen. An Artemisian follows Nyro. There are no other promises.'

Susan glared at him, hatred singing within her.

'However,' said Spoole, 'I bear you no ill will, and I will help you as best I can. Go to the Marshalling Office. Ask to see the freight records, under my authority.'

'Your authority? It means nothing to me. Nor to anyone else!'

'Apparently this is no longer the case,' said Spoole. Behind him, the other infantryrobots were finishing the repairs to each other and they were lining up in formation. 'Anger will get you nowhere, Susan.'

'Anger? After what your state did to mine? I can't believe I trusted you.'

'That trust is part of the reason why your city failed, Susan. Listen to me though, I'm trying to help you. Once you have access to the freight records, look for Nettie, find out where she was taken. The office staff will help you, they should see nothing unusual in your request. Such things happen all the time. Once you have found where Nettie was taken, note the service number of the train. After that, go to the timetable office and find when that service next runs. Get yourself on that train.'

Susan felt as if her gyros would break out of her at any moment.

'I hate you. I hate you and your rusting, badly twisted state.'

'That's the difference between us,' replied Spoole. 'I bear you nothing but gratitude, Susan. Which of us has the better mindset?'

At that he turned and began to march north towards the centre of Artemis City, the infantryrobots following him. Susan couldn't bear to watch him go. She couldn't bear to follow his advice.

She stood in the middle of the tracks for eighty minutes. Immobile, undecided as to which way to go. Trains rumbled by her this way and that.

In the end she did the only sensible thing. She headed towards the Marshalling Office.

Karel

The human craft flew down from the mountains.

Karel looked out of the window in awe. Though he had travelled up and down this continent he had never seen it from this perspective before. On his previous journeys he had been aware of a constantly expanding border, of Artemis pushing back its boundaries. Up here, though, sitting in the oddly soft human seat, he saw nothing but one land. Snow giving way to brightly coloured rocky cliffs, cliffs sloping down to fields of boulders, boulders shrinking to pebbles before giving way to the gravel plain beyond. More though, he was aware of the change in the colours of the rock, the way the bright profusion of ores faded to the grey of the Artemisian plain.

The helicopter swooped towards it, and Karel wanted to tell someone about what he was feeling, but he held back. He didn't want to speak to Melt. At least, not yet. More than ever he was convinced that the other robot was hiding something. The heavy lead man just sat there, gazing at nothing.

Karel looked at the human who sat in the back of the craft with the pair of them. It was looking at Karel with interest, examining his body, looking at the fingers on his hand.

'Hello,' he said, holding out his hand as he had seen the other humans do. 'My name is Karel.'

The animal smiled and took it, moved it up and down, then pointed apologetically at his head. He wasn't wearing one of the devices that would let him understand their words. Odd, thought Karel, that there would be different ways of speaking. He thought about what Ruth had said, how robots weren't very curious, and he wondered, should he be more curious? *The Story of Eric and the Mountain* ... That was meant to be important. Melt said he knew that story. Maybe when they landed he would get Melt to tell it to him.

The craft dropped lower. Karel saw railway lines in the distance; he saw a train shooting along at incredible speed. A human device. He leaned forward, twisting his head around the window, trying to follow its course. What was making it move so fast?

A voice crackled into life.

'This is the pilot. I'm afraid this is about as far south as I can go. Head a little to the east and you'll come across a railway line. Follow that to Artemis City.'

'Thank you,' said Karel.

The hum of the engine increased and the craft touched down in a cloud of dust. The human slid the door open and slapped Karel on the shoulder, sending the metal there ringing. Karel dropped to the ground, then turned and helped Melt do the same in his heavy body. They raised their hands in goodbye as the engine noise deepened, and the craft lifted and flew back north.

Karel and Melt watched it go.

'Okay,' said Karel to Melt. 'You've not been honest with me. Tell me now, I want to know the full truth!'

'I will tell you,' said Melt.

'I want to know everything.'

'Yes. But on the way. We need to speak to the robots of Artemis. We need to tell them what's going to happen to them!'

'Speak to Artemis? They won't listen to us.'

'They better had. Or they'll all be killed. All of them, and all of us. I've seen this before. I know what the humans are going to do . . .'

Wa-Ka-Mo-Do

Wa-Ka-Mo-Do followed the three women into the remains of the Copper Master's house. The few robots remaining there averted their eyes as he was led through the corridors to the Copper Room.

He wanted to turn and run, he wanted to head back into the square and wrest control back from La-Ver-Di-Arussah.

He couldn't. His shame cut too deep, and his mind was woven to listen to his sense of honour. He understood this. He had failed everyone, he deserved his fate. He had no choice but to follow the Vestal Virgins, and they knew it.

The previously concealed door at the rear of the Copper Room had been left open to reveal a rough corridor hewn directly from the rock. A set of steps spiralled down into the darkness, and Wa-Ka-Mo-Do raised the light in his own eyes to see.

Stepping from the Copper Room into the stone corridor, Wa-Ka-Mo-Do felt as if he was leaving his life behind. His last thoughts, oddly enough, were of Rachael. The pale-faced human, his copper girl. She had tried to warn him. Her words came back to him and he halted.

'Listen!' he said, urgently. 'Something's going to happen in the morning! We need to clear the city.'

'*That's no longer your concern, Wa-Ka-Mo-Do,*' said one of the women, sweetly.

'But what about Ell? What happened in Ell?'

'*Resume walking, Wa-Ka-Mo-Do,*' said another, '*and do so in silence.*'

They didn't have that power over him, the ability to command him to cease speaking, but Wa-Ka-Mo-Do was silent nonetheless. There was nothing to say.

Deeper and deeper they descended beneath the city. Ancient tunnels branched off from the corridor, most of them half collapsed with disuse, and Wa-Ka-Mo-Do remembered the copper mines upon which the prosperity of Sangrel was built.

They walked for some time through empty rock long stripped of metal, the perfect figures of the three women barely visible before him. They passed out under the lake, the waters dripping down from above.

Finally, they began to ascend.

'*Almost there*,' said one of the women, turning and smiling back at him, and Wa-Ka-Mo-Do felt his current wax and wane despite himself.

They reached a spiralling set of steps, cut in the stone, and ascended it. Wa-Ka-Mo-Do found himself in a small room, decorated in jade. There was a chair set in the centre, a small forge burning to the side.

'*Sit down, Wa-Ka-Mo-Do*,' said one of the women.

His body did as it was ordered.

One appeared at his side.

'*Your arm is damaged*,' she said, and he felt an electric thrill as she touched him at the shoulder. She did something, and he felt the loss of weight as the arm was removed. He forced himself to remain calm, to ignore the fear clamouring inside him. He was still a warrior.

'*This was well made*,' said the woman who examined his arm. '*Yet I'm sure I can improve upon it.*'

To his confusion, she began to carefully pull out the twisted, melted wire of the electromuscle. He flinched as the other two women knelt by him and began to unship his panelling. They set to work on his body, twisting and tweaking and shaping him. Fixing him and repairing him. He felt a sense of pleasure and well-being building up, all the while being pushed back by the terror that had lodged itself deep inside.

'*Is this nice?*' said one of the women.

'*Do we not tune and improve you?*'

Their voices were so sweet. He almost began to relax.

'*A healthy body will respond so much better to punishment.*'

The current surged through him, sending a crackling charge into the fingers of one of the women who knelt at his feet.

'*Naughty,*' she said, smiling patiently. '*Later. Relax for the moment. Enjoy the servicing! This will be the last time you will feel such pleasure.*'

'*Ever.*'

The three of them smiled at him so kindly, and Wa-Ka-Mo-Do felt a surge of horrified dread sing throughout his body.

He sat in the Jade Room, three beautiful women working on his body, on his electromuscles, on his metal skeleton, until it was morning.

Then, fully repaired, he was led through ornamented rooms and out into the sunlit dawn.

The air brushed his exposed electromuscle.

'*No panelling,*' said one of the women. '*You won't need it.*'

The Temple of Eternity was mostly open to the elements. White marble pillars separated the area into different rooms, some of them containing pitchers and vases, some of them containing robot bodies, frozen in positions of agony. Wa-Ka-Mo-Do turned away from them.

He was taken, electromuscle naked to the world, to a small terrace overlooking Lake Ochoa. Across the dark waters he saw the city of Sangrel, smoke still rising into the morning air. Apart from that, everything seemed so peaceful.

Then he saw what awaited him.

A small forge was set in the middle of the terrace, and by it lay a new body, warming in the rays of the rising sun. A thick body made of cast iron and lead.

'*Are you frightened, Wa-Ka-Mo-Do?*'

'Yes,' he answered, truthfully.

The three women laughed.

'*Not sufficiently, I suspect,*' said one. '*Otherwise your fear would have overridden your compulsion to obey. You would be running already.*'

'I deserve my punishment,' said Wa-Ka-Mo-Do.

'*You do. You realize, Wa-Ka-Mo-Do, that the Emperor hoped you would disobey his orders? He thought that one of the Eleven would fight back against the humans?*'

'No . . .'

'*Yes, Wa-Ka-Mo-Do. Don't you see that that way he could disown your actions, even though he was secretly proud of you?*'

Wa-Ka-Mo-Do could see it.

'*Or you could have obeyed his orders fully, and then the Emperor would have lost no face to the animals.*'

'*But instead you adopted this weak compromise. This half and half action that was suitable to no one. You neither fully rebelled nor fully obeyed. You truly have failed, Wa-Ka-Mo-Do.*'

For the first time, Wa-Ka-Mo-Do saw it was true. He

had failed. By the standards of the Empire, but worse, by his own standards.

One of the Vestal Virgins raised her voice.

'*Let it be known that the Emperor personally has judged this to be a suitable punishment for your failure.*'

'*And the Emperor has a fine judgement in these matters.*'

'*And your failure was spectacular.*'

'*Now, stand by the body.*'

He did so. Those three beautiful women moved around him, their delicate fingers picking away at Wa-Ka-Mo-Do's frame, unhooking the electromuscles they had so recently repaired and made whole, pulling out the rods of his skeleton, laying him back into the new leaden body, fitting the long electromuscles into place in his new housing. He watched in fascinated horror as first his legs, and then his hips, and then his left arm was hooked into place in that terrifying shell.

'*Move your right arm this way a little.*'

He obeyed, and then he felt that too being unhooked.

'*It's a beautiful morning,*' said one.

'*They say that, even when facing death, a robot should still take the time to appreciate beauty. Are you doing that, Wa-Ka-Mo-Do?*'

'Am I going to die?' he asked.

'*We all die,*' they laughed. '*But hopefully not for a long time yet. The Emperor wishes you to endure your punishment for many years.*'

They went to work on his neck and head, carefully pulling away the rods and panelling of the skull, peeling away metal until they held his mind and his coil, his eyes, voicebox and ears in their hands. They turned his eyes this way and that, showing him what they had done, and then laid him back so he was facing the blue sky, and the cold, heavy feel of this new body made its way up through his coil.

Then they tilted his head a little, so he could watch as they took all the metal remaining from his former body, all the metal and panelling that he had carefully formed and bent and knitted over his lifetime and they dropped it onto the little forge to melt before him. Scarlet paint turned black and flaked away.

Wa-Ka-Mo-Do felt some connection with his past sever, and bitterness overwhelmed him. It was about all he had left.

'The Emperor is a traitor,' he said. 'He has sold the Empire to the humans.'

'*The Emperor can never be a traitor,*' said one of the women, in the most delightful voice, '*for the Emperor's will is the Empire.*'

The words were spoken softly in his ear, and he wondered at how robots could be so fair but so cruel.

And yet so far he had felt no pain. They worked the metal of his body apart so gently and expertly that he had felt the wire stir within him. But no! That mechanism was gone, it was melting on the hot coal of the forge.

'The Emperor has sold his subjects,' said Wa-Ka-Mo-Do. 'He has sold his land and his livestock. And so the Empire is no more.'

'*Not so long as the Emperor's subjects do as the Emperor directs,*' said one of the women, kneeling down beside him. '*And now, it is time for the punishment.*'

Wa-Ka-Mo-Do watched as she took a pot of solder from the top of the forge and laid it on the ground next to him. She dipped a spatula in the pot and then applied it to something just beyond his vision. His right arm erupted with fire. The electromuscle, the connections that ran through his coil to his mind, all of them were singing to near overload with the heat and the current between the iron of the body and the metal of his electromuscle. The pain was incredible.

'*Do you have anything to say, Wa-Ka-Mo-Do?*' asked one.

He forced himself to speak. He was one of the Eleven, he would salvage what little dignity he could.

'The Emperor is a traitor . . .' he repeated.

'*You say that now, Wa-Ka-Mo-Do, yet the punishment has only just begun. Come, let us fix the other arm and then we shall see if you still feel the same way.*'

The surge of current and heat erupted in his left arm. It collided with the pain from the right arm at his coil.

'*And now how do you feel, Wa-Ka-Mo-Do?*'

'Traitor . . .' he managed.

'*Your voicebox is crackling with static after just two arms. We still have the rest of your body to work upon.*'

The women worked on as the sun came up, and the pain rose and rose, passing each supposed climax, until his body was fixed in place. Nearly all of his body. For there was one final act.

'*Finally, Wa-Ka-Mo-Do, the coil. You do understand what we are about to do?*'

A beautiful face appeared before Wa-Ka-Mo-Do, blocking the sun's rays for just a moment. The metal of her face was bent so smoothly. For the first time, Wa-Ka-Mo-Do noticed the fine holes that punctured the mask, tracing the shape of mouth and eyes. So fine. And behind them, the faintest glow of blue twisted metal. He could look directly at her mind. Such a twisted thing. How could a length of metal rejoice in such cruelty? What did cruelty mean? How could metal be cruel?

A ceramic pot was held before his eyes.

'*This is a mixture of platinum and gold and iron. Some copper and silver. Do you recognize the mix? This is the same alloy as your mind is twisted from. We will mix this with your coil, splay it out and flatten it against the metal of this body. The two metals will become one. To try and prise your mind free would be to break your coil. You will be trapped in there forever. Do you understand?*'

Wa-Ka-Mo-Do struggled to speak. His words were fighting against a static of pain.

'Traitor . . .'

'*I think you understand.*'

The face and ceramic pot withdrew. Suddenly, his coil, his mind, his body were on fire. The pain was unbelievable: nothing he had ever before endured had been like this.

And it would never cease, for the rest of his life.

Then came the final act. The three women had set crucibles of lead to melt. They came forward and stood over him, tilted the heavy bowls, and he watched as the metal, silver-grey and bubbling, spilled over the edge and poured into his body. And this time he couldn't hold it back any longer. An electronic squeal sounded from his voicebox. The Vestal Virgins looked at each other in satisfaction.

They left him. He gazed unseeing at the sun as it rose towards noon. The lead in his body was cooling, but the pain remained trapped there with him.

He saw movement. The Vestal Virgins returned.

'*Wa-Ka-Mo-Do,*' said the women in unison. '*Stand up.*'

'I can't,' he said, his voicebox buzzing.

They laughed.

'*What, Wa-Ka-Mo-Do the great warrior of Ekrano, defeated by this body?*' taunted one.

'*I have seen women with much less lifeforce stand up in much heavier suits. I have put them there myself,*' said another.

'*But we know that women can withstand more pain than men.*' said the third.

Wa-Ka-Mo-Do moved his arms. So heavy, each movement was agony.

'*Come on Wa-Ka-Mo-Do, great warrior of Ko. Try harder!*'

He flexed his arms again. So heavy!

'*Is that all he can do? The robots of the Silent City fare much better. But they have strength in their minds . . .*'

The pain threatened to short out his mind, still he forced himself onwards. Flexed his legs. Pushed himself onto his side, with great, heavy scraping movements. He held his balance for a moment, then he rolled forward heavily onto his front. The movement jarred, sent more pain surging through him. He felt the cooling lead shifting around him, thundering agony through his body, lances of fire and surging current. Slowly, inch by agonizing inch, he forced himself to his feet.

'I can . . . I can . . . do it . . .'

He saw the look in their eyes, just for a moment. They concealed it immediately.

'You . . . didn't, didn't . . . think . . . I could!' A surge of triumph, so weak against the pain.

'*Not at all. We're just surprised it took you so long.*'

'Liars!'

'*And now, Wa-Ka-Mo-Do, it is time for you to . . .*'

Her voice trailed away. She was gazing up into the sky. All three of them were. Gazing at something behind him, something out towards Sangrel. Wa-Ka-Mo-Do remembered Rachael's words . . .

Tomorrow morning. When we are far enough away . . .

Painfully, agonizingly, Wa-Ka-Mo-Do turned to follow the gaze of the Vestal Virgins. A small star was falling, it crackled with lightning.

'*What is it?*' said one of the women.

'It's a . . . human device,' replied Wa-Ka-Mo-Do. 'The Emperor has . . . betrayed you, too.'

The electric star fell, and as it did so a thin line of lightning flickered down to the city. It felt its way this way and that around the broken-roofed ruins of the Emperor's Palace, there at the top of the city. Then another strand of lightning flickered forth, and another. And then the air was filled with dancing lines, an electric rain storm of brilliant threads. They felt their way from the city, out across the lake, heading to the mound.

Wa-Ka-Mo-Do and the women watched as the threads of light climbed up the Mound of Eternity, seeking them out, touching the terrace, looking for something.

'*Look how it seeks my hand*,' said one of the Vestal Virgins, and she waved her arm this way and that, the strand of lightning following her movement.

'*And me*,' said another. '*Look it touches my foot*.'

She tilted back her head and let off such a lovely sound that it took Wa-Ka-Mo-Do a moment to realize that she was screaming.

'*What is it?*' called her sisters, and the threads touched them and they too screamed.

More lightning was dancing in now; it surrounded them like bars. The Vestal Virgins tried to run, tried to dodge. To no avail. The threads touched their hands, their feet. The air was filled with their cries of pain.

The electric threads found Wa-Ka-Mo-Do and he felt a muted ache, almost lost against the background of agony that already filled his shell.

'But it's not so bad . . .' he said.

The Vestal Virgins didn't seem to notice. One came to Wa-Ka-Mo-Do, her hands held out in supplication. He took them in his own and watched as the electric threads found their way into her mind.

He looked into her eyes as they glowed stronger and stronger, there was a buzzing thump and her mind exploded. The air was filled with white light. Two more thumps as her sisters died in the same way.

Now the threads felt their way to Wa-Ka-Mo-Do's head and . . .

Spoole

This is how Kavan had done it, thought Spoole. He hadn't so much commanded events as ridden them. The revelation had been a long time coming, but now he understood.

Spoole wasn't like Kavan: he had been woven to lead. He saw Artemis as something to be shaped and guided, something to be directed towards specific goals. Kavan hadn't been made that way. It had long been rumoured that he was made in Segre, that his mother had followed Nyro's pattern when she had made his mind. Finally, Spoole understood what that meant. Unlike Spoole, who sought to lead, Kavan saw Nyro's way, and he followed that path. It was a subtle distinction, but an important one. And now Spoole had learned to apply it.

As Spoole walked along the railway lines, following Nyro's way, heading towards the Centre City, the word spread. Robots who had wondered at the human's arrival here in Artemis. Robots who distrusted the motives of the Generals, robots who believed that all metal should be directed in Nyro's way. Robots looking for a leader to express their feelings.

Spoole and his growing army left the area of the marshalling yards. They began to walk the long mile by the cable walks, down the corridor of steel cable left piled by the sides of the road.

There was a rhythm developing to their tread. Faint for the moment, but growing.

Stamp, *stamp*, stamp.

Yellow-painted workers emerged from the buildings to join him.

Together, they marched on.

Wa-Ka-Mo-Do

Ka seemed fixed to the horizon. No matter how far Wa-Ka-Mo-Do walked, it remained dark and ugly in the distance. The sea wind blew thick ribbons of smoke inland. At night, their undersides were lit red with the burning fires.

All the while he felt the bitterness of defeat, the burning shame that was so great he almost welcomed the perpetual agony the Vestal Virgins had woven into his body.

Almost welcomed. The pain was too great. Every footstep sent a bolt of pain up through his legs to jar his body, a variation in the static agony that filled his shell, a counterpoint to the anguish that filled his mind.

He had failed completely. Failed the Emperor, failed himself, failed the robots of Sangrel.

Nearly every one of them was dead.

He had struggled through the streets and lanes of the city, painfully dragging his new body along, heaving his leaden prison past robots whose minds had been blown, but whose bodies remained untouched. Robots lay on the ground or sat on ledges. They collapsed forward, supporting each other in pyramids, they leaned back against walls. There was no movement, but there was a sense of motion about the scene, of activity interrupted.

Wa-Ka-Mo-Do almost expected them to come to life at any moment, to resume their angry insurrection, to pick up the knives and clubs that had fallen from their lifeless hands and resume their attack on the upper city.

It wouldn't happen. The life had gone from their eyes. Sangrel, poor, twisted, abused Sangrel, was at last at peace, lit by the yellow summer sun.

The only sound came from above, the plaintive bleating of animals in the copper market. What strange device had the humans used, to kill robots and leave organic life untouched?

Just how powerful were they? Powerful enough to have written the Book of Robots? Undoubtedly.

For a moment, just a moment, he had an understanding of the Emperor's position. What else could the Emperor have done in the face of such force? What else could he have done but negotiated and bought a few months' grace whilst he saved face and frantically sought some way of fighting this powerful foe?

But then Wa-Ka-Mo-Do moved that heavy body and the searing agony of current shorted across his back, and he was lost in pain once more.

It took him all morning to drag himself up to the Copper Market, pushing aside fallen bodies, crunching on the glass and broken tiles that littered the streets. He found the organic animals, and, not knowing what else to do, he unlocked their cages. He watched as the great beasts walked out amongst the fallen bodies, blowing hard from their noses, nudging at the metal remains of their keepers.

Wa-Ka-Mo-Do released all the creatures he could find,

a heavy fatigue building within him; then he stopped, exhausted. It took so long to build up the lifeforce to move this leaden body, and then it was expended in so little time. He looked around the broken market place as he rested; saw the stalls that had collapsed when their owners had fallen onto them. Their wares were strewn on the floor, slicked in oil and grease. Animals clattered over scattered metal plates, they knocked over displays, skittering away at the sound of ringing bells dying on the ground behind them.

He heard a noise and slowly turned around. Something metal ran from the market place.

'Wait,' he called, his voice heavy and badly tuned, but it was too late. Whoever it was had gone.

So he wasn't the only survivor.

He saw the remains of a soldier, over by the wall. The mob must have cornered it, torn it apart. The blue wire of its mind was pulled out and draped across the cobbled stones. Beside it, a child, a young boy, barely four years old judging by the size of the body he had built himself. His head was crushed, the wire exposed and deformed.

What had happened here, before the human bomb had fallen? Had there been a riot, the child crushed, the mob extracting vengeance upon the soldier?

Whatever it was, the two deaths weren't the responsibility of the humans. They weren't the responsibility of the Emperor. He, Wa-Ka-Mo-Do, had been in charge of the city. It was he who had failed utterly not only in his duty, but also in his mutiny. Despite his actions, his troops had still died, the people of Sangrel had still died.

Why couldn't the humans' weapon have killed him too? What was it that had protected him? Had the excess of metal in this body shielded his mind?

He contemplated walking to the very top of the city and flinging himself from the highest place. If that didn't shatter his mind, then he would walk back to the top and try again, and again and again until his body was broken.

That was when he remembered. There was still one to whom he was beholden, one who still sought his help. He remembered the message from Jai-Lyn, hidden from him all that time in the radio room.

Wa-Ka-Mo-Do still had one last chance to redeem himself. He had failed everyone else. Maybe it was not too late to save Jai-Lyn.

He had set out immediately for Ka, passing from San-grel and into the lands beyond, walking for mile after agonizing mile in that heavy body that sunk to the ankles in anything less than the firmest ground. He heard a low, static-filled hum and he realized it was his own voice; the agony he felt was leaking out through his speaker. With an heroic effort he stilled it and went on walking, pulling his feet, covered in clods of mud, from the soft earth, passing through the fields the animals had planted.

After a while he had the sense that he was being watched, and he turned this way and that, too slow in that leaden body, seeking other signs of life. How many other robots had survived the attack?

Eventually he found himself on a white stone path,

kicking up dust as he made his way to the coast. He saw smoke coming from a nearby forge, saw robots emerging from the doorway. They beckoned to him, but he kept on walking: outcast, pariah, unfit for the company of others. His shame and sense of failure glowed within him all the stronger for meeting company.

He saw the fire on the horizon after the third day. Ka was burning, he knew it. Still he walked on.

Other robots walked the road.

'What news from Sangrel?' called one, gazing in horror at Wa-Ka-Mo-Do's heavy body.

Wa-Ka-Mo-Do said nothing, he just kept on walking, still too ashamed to speak.

'Hey! What did they do to you? Let me help!'

'I don't deserve it.'

Slowly, he limped on.

That day he turned aside from the white stone road to avoid the other robots that walked it, and he made his way across the land, heading directly for the burning city and its black column of smoke.

The green hills gave way to flatter, marshy ground. To his right he saw the road, graceful white bridges arcing over the ditches and swamps. He ignored them, moving deeper and deeper into the saltwater-soaked land that bordered Ka. The sun burned red as it set, mirroring the flames of the city; it reflected in patches from the land, it stained the sky the colour of dull iron.

He passed into the swamp, and he sought out the rills of rock that lined the marshy bed, following the stone paths, the green water up to his waist, sometimes up to his neck. Occasionally he walked underwater, his vision a green blur, and the slippery shapes of organic life whipped around him all the time. He would emerge onto a soft bank and look ahead to see the city seemingly no closer, the despair within him no less, the pain as intense as ever.

Still he marched on.

Susan

Susan stood in the Marshalling Office. Through the window she could see the silver lines that spread out across the world, converging upon her. A line of wagons was passing beneath her right now and she found her eyes drawn to it, the regular flick, flick as the end of one wagon passed by and another rolled on.

The Marshalling Officer didn't seem to notice.

'Well,' he said, looking down once more at the piece of foil, 'this is the service you want, but it's not going to do you any good. It doesn't run any more.'

'Why not?' said Susan, frustrated. Another train rumbled by underneath, this time heading into the yards.

'Oooh, well, it was a special service, see? Only ran for about a month, straight into the humans' compound. They're not accepting direct services at the moment.'

'Why not?'

The Marshalling Officer laughed. He was painted a pale green, not quite the same as the computers of the Centre City.

'Why not? Susan, you're not on official business are you?'

'Yes I am, I told you—'

'Susan, it's okay! I don't care, see? All I want to do is to ensure that Artemis works. The way I do that is by making sure the railways run smoothly.'

'Listen . . .'

'Gresley.'

'Listen, Gresley, the robot in question used to work in Making Room 14. She has information—'

'Susan, I really don't care. Half the information on this continent flows through here. I know what's really going on. I know that Kavan is out there on the plain somewhere, building an army. I know that he is getting ready to attack this city again, and I know that he is coming closer. He might even be here by now. Troops ride in and out on these trains all the time. If I were Kavan I would have simply hopped on board one of them.'

'Yes but—'

'No, Susan, listen to me. I know that the robots in this city are growing more and more unhappy about the way Sandale and the rest have made an alliance with what are no more than a bunch of animals. I know that unrest is growing all the time. They say that we are receiving metal from the humans in return for land, but I've examined the lading bills and I know that we're giving away more than we're receiving.'

'And you think this is wrong?' said Susan, eagerly.

'Susan, you misunderstand! I don't care!'

The pale-green robot sat down on a seat by the metal desk that overlooked the yard and spread the foil out before him.

'I keep trying to explain, I don't run this city. I don't make decisions about which lands we should conquer, or about where we build our forges, see? My mind wasn't twisted to do that. What I do is make sure that the goods on the railways are picked up, and that they are deposited at their destination. If anything passes beneath this gantry, then it is my business to know about it. Do you understand that?'

'Yes, I understand.'

'Good. Then understand this, Susan. I don't care who you are, I don't care if you work for Kavan or Sandale or Spoole. I don't even care if you're in this for yourself. In a few weeks' time such things will probably all be irrelevant anyway!'

'Yes, so—'

'So, ask me anything you like, and I will be delighted to answer!'

At that Gresley sat back in his seat and smiled.

'This state has rust in the mind,' said Susan.

'It may well do,' said Gresley, 'but as long as the railways run properly, I am a happy robot.'

Susan took the piece of foil from the desk.

'My friend was taken into the human compound on this service,' she said. 'I want to follow her in there.'

'There we are!' said Gresley. 'Why didn't you say that at the start?'

He leaped to his feet and walked to the other side of the room, where he examined a piece of foil pinned to the wall.

'Now,' he said, examining it carefully. 'As I said, there are no direct services to the human compound planned.

However, there are a number of troop trains being prepared for a direct attack on the compound.'

'They're going to attack the humans?' said Susan, in astonishment.

'I didn't say that,' said Gresley, 'but you can't just call up a train from thin air. These things have to be prepared. Someone is obviously planning ahead.'

'Who?'

'I don't know. It could be Spoole, it could be the Generals. It could even be Kavan. Like I said, he may be in the city already.'

He pulled a sheet of foil from a book and scribbled something on it with a stylus.

'Here you are,' he said. 'Line 4 point 16 point 3. The lines are numbered from the right. That's line four down there, the one with the ore hoppers passing by at the moment.'

Susan looked down at the yellow stone-filled hoppers that rumbled by beneath them.

'Just follow it up and count the branches. You should be able to join the train, dressed like that. I'm sure another infantryrobot would always be welcome.'

'What do you mean dressed like that? I *am* an infantry-robot.'

'Of course you are,' said Gresley, and he turned back to his desk. 'Now, if you'll excuse me . . .'

At that he picked up a pile of foil sheets and began to read his way through them.

Susan watched him for a moment, and then turned and headed out to find her train.

Wa-Ka-Mo-Do

Ka was a city caught between worlds, a city built half on sea and half on land, a city caught between the harsh realities of whaling and the culture and civilization of the Empire.

It was a shifting, animate city. Whales were dragged from the sea, their bodies taken apart and separated into piles of metal. That metal was taken to plate the bodies of robots, robots who would then strip the metal from themselves and use it to construct new buildings, buildings that would then be dismantled and rebuilt elsewhere as more robots flowed into the city, or taken to line the new roads that were built into the sea. Metal would be formed into cranes and used to construct the little ships that carried metal up and down the coast, then the ships themselves would be dismantled and the metal used to construct new buildings.

Ka had moved up and down the coast over time; it waxed and waned like the tide. It was anchored only by the Whale Road, running as it did from the long-unused jade and stone buildings of the Emperor's Sea Palace, all the way back through the provinces and cities of Yukawa to the Silent City itself.

Not that many of the Emperor's robots travelled to this harsh town, grey and utilitarian as it was, lashed by the sea rain and choked with the smoke of forges.

This place was left to the strong and uncultured robots that worked there. Mostly male minds, full of lifeforce that powered big, heavy bodies, suitable for pulling whales down to the sea bed. Minds that thought nothing about ripping open the panelling of the huge creatures, and reaching through to disable the electromuscle beyond.

Robots who had fought back.

Wa-Ka-Mo-Do saw the signs almost immediately he entered the city.

These robots had fought against the humans.

With guns and harpoons, with swords and spears and anything else that came to hand. Rocks and stones and metal bars lay discarded all around. The ground was still soaked with the red blood the humans carried within them. He saw the bloated remains of their bodies, long stripped of any useful materials, the yellow-white bones poking through the bare flesh.

The robots of Ka had swatted the flying craft with cranes. Wa-Ka-Mo-Do wandered through the docks, the grey sea splashing beside him, and he saw one of the human craft lying broken on the ground. Close up, it seemed so fragile: metal skin as thin as gold leaf, the transparent plastic cockpit bubble bulging and torn by the metal girder that had pierced its length. Two humans lay dead behind it, the fluid that had once filled their bodies dried and rusted around them. Wa-Ka-Mo-Do held out a hand near the red patch. There was iron there, just a trace. So these creatures had a little in common with robots. He inspected the face of the dead human. Had it felt pain or fear as it had died? He couldn't tell.

But the dead humans were only part of the story.

There were dead robots, too. Dead robots lying everywhere in the streets. The humans had dropped one of their electric bombs here, too, though it hadn't been anywhere so near as effective as in Sangrel. Many more robots still lived. Going about their work, clearing the streets, sorting the body parts into piles for re-use.

When they saw Wa-Ka-Mo-Do pass by they obviously recognized the handiwork of the Vestal Virgins, but this didn't seem to bother them so much. If anything, his slow fight against the agony within his leaden shell seemed to grant Wa-Ka-Mo-Do a certain respect.

A man came running up to him.

'You have one of these?' he asked, handing Wa-Ka-Mo-Do a flexible metal mesh. 'No? I thought not! Put it around your head and shoulders if the humans return. If they drop the electric bomb again, I mean.'

'Thank you.'

The man hesitated. He gazed at the dark metal of Wa-Ka-Mo-Do's body.

'That is, if you can reach up to your head. Will your hands move that far?'

'I can manage.'

The man's eyes glowed.

'Spread the word, brother. I say, let the animals return. We'll be ready for them next time.'

With that the robot turned and dashed off.

Wa-Ka-Mo-Do dragged the heavy shell around the city, looking for Jai-Lyn. It was a pointless task, he knew, slowed further by his constant need to rest and recharge. She wouldn't have stood a chance in the fighting, not wearing that thin, delicate body. Even if she was spared death from some human gun, then the electric bomb would have surely caught her. Only the heavy-duty bodies had survived, that and those robots who had later emerged from the sea, fresh from the hunt. Those robots found a city much changed since they had set off in search of whale metal.

He came to a set of making rooms. An old building, made of stone, chased in copper and lead. There was a forge inside, cold in the middle of the floor. The rest of the room was so neat and tidy. Bundles of wire and piles of plate, tins and tins of paint of all colours, neatly arranged on shelves around the walls. Doors led from the main area to the little rooms where the robots of higher rank would go. A dead woman lay in each, hands clutched to her head, the metal of the skull deformed and crushed by her own dying strength. None of them were Jai-Lyn.

Wa-Ka-Mo-Do looked at the last woman, full of silent shame. Somewhere in this city, Jai-Lyn would no doubt be sat, her hands clutched to her head in just that posture.

He emerged from the making rooms back into the red daylight. A robot was sitting by one of the stone tables in the middle of the square, waving at Wa-Ka-Mo-Do.

'Hello, stranger,' he called.

Wa-Ka-Mo-Do moved towards the robot. He was sat on an iron seat, the stone table before him crawling with life, both metal and organic.

'Pull up a chair.'

'It will break beneath the weight of this body.'

'You know, I think it will. Perhaps you can kneel instead?'

Wa-Ka-Mo-Do did so, and felt the pain in his feet move to his knees. There was no relief to be found in any position.

The table was marked with a seven by seven grid of squares. Metal beetles, worms and lice wandered at random across its surface, all of them contained by the stone lip that ran around the table's perimeter. Half of the creatures had a blob of red paint on their back.

'Have you played chess before?' asked the stranger.

'Not like this. Not with animals.'

'Really? This is the true game.' The stranger reached out and quickly placed the creatures on their starting positions. Slow creatures, worms and placid beetles on the back row, skittering lice in the position of pawns.

'They're moving around already,' said Wa-Ka-Mo-Do. 'They won't hold their position.'

'That is why you must make your moves quickly, or your strategies will be of no use. You can be red, you begin.'

Wa-Ka-Mo-Do fumbled for one of his lice pawns. His hand was too clumsy.

'It's no good. I can't take hold of it.'

'You give up so easily?'

The man's words stung Wa-Ka-Mo-Do. He tried again. With a feeling of tremendous satisfaction he managed to take hold of one of his lice pawns and move it two spaces forward. As he did so it began to rain. Dark spots appeared on the stone table.

'Interesting opening,' observed the other robot, 'but, alas, it is undone already. Your pawn has wandered away . . .'

The stranger picked up a pawn of his own and moved it onto a square currently occupied by one of Wa-Ka-Mo-Do's.

' . . . so I take your piece.'

'What is the point of this game?' said Wa-Ka-Mo-Do, irritated. 'I can barely move in this body.'

'Then you will have to be cleverer than me, won't you?'

With difficulty, Wa-Ka-Mo-Do seized his own pawn, but the piece he was aiming to take had walked out of its range. Frustrated, Wa-Ka-Mo-Do set the piece down on an empty square.

'This is like life, no?' said the stranger. 'Like robots. Our parents twist our mind, set us on their path, but after that they can do nothing more than watch how their children interact with the other players in the game.'

'There is no logic to the motion of these creatures,' replied Wa-Ka-Mo-Do, in frustration.

'Of course there is,' said the Stranger. 'They act as such creatures will. It's just that the logic is not apparent to us.'

'It would be easier if we just used regular pieces,' said Wa-Ka-Mo-Do, watching as the robot captured another of his pieces, and dropped it, legs moving, in a stone cup at his side of the table. 'Or if we could predict which way the pieces would move.'

With a major effort, Wa-Ka-Mo-Do took hold of a beetle. He waited a moment as one of the stranger's creatures hesitated on the edge of a square, and then brought it heavily down.

'Check!' he said.

'No longer,' said the robot, and sure enough, his emperor walked from its square.

'This is pointless!' said Wa-Ka-Mo-Do.

'Not at all! In life there are many moments when things seem final, then everything shifts and the game resumes. Just like now. The pieces are shifting. This is your moment, Wa-Ka-Mo-Do.'

Wa-Ka-Mo-Do gazed sharply at the stranger.

'How do you know my name?'

'I was told it by a robot on the sea shore. He is waiting there for you now.'

'Waiting for me? How does he know about me?'

'Through listening. Some minds speak to each other, Wa-Ka-Mo-Do. You know that the whales talk to each other?'

Wa-Ka-Mo-Do looked at the stranger, looked at his thin, delicate body.

'You don't look like a whaler.'

'I'm not. I was brought here by the robot on the sea shore. He thought there might be a place for me here in Ka with the humans temporarily defeated.'

'Doing what?'

'Studying them. Finding out more about them. Deciding how best to fight them.'

'Should we fight them?' asked Wa-Ka-Mo-Do, deep in shame.

'Why not? Your Emperor no longer rules this continent. It is not his *real* wishes you follow by serving the humans. You know, despite everything, you did well in Sangrel, Wa-Ka-Mo-Do. Maybe the best anyone could have done.'

The praise did nothing to lift Wa-Ka-Mo-Do's mood. The weight of his body was not the heaviest part of his prison.

'I could have done more. I could have followed the Emperor, or followed my own beliefs. Instead I did neither.' He looked around. 'Maybe I can succeed here. Join the fight with the other robots . . .'

'There is nothing for you here, Wa-Ka-Mo-Do. You know that.'

Wa-Ka-Mo-Do felt the last vestige of hope slip away.

'Then my life is over.'

'You know that isn't true. Anyway, isn't despair forbidden by the Book of Robots?'

'You know of the book?' asked Wa-Ka-Mo-Do, but with no eagerness.

'The knowledge wasn't woven into my mind at birth, but yes, I know of it.'

'What does the book mean now? You've seen the humans.'

'Who said that they wrote the book? There is no reason why they should have done. Even if they did, does that give them the right to treat us in this way?'

'Do you know what it is like to have your core belief thrust in your face and then twisted out of shape before your eyes?' asked Wa-Ka-Mo-Do, his voice full of pain.

'No,' replied the stranger, and he picked up a beetle and dropped it on a square, taking another of Wa-Ka-Mo-Do's pieces.

Wa-Ka-Mo-Do felt suddenly empty, drained of all emotion.

'What do you want with me?'

'Me? Nothing. But there is a robot waiting for you by the sea shore. I think you should go to him.'

'I'm looking for a robot. She's called Jai-Lyn.'

'She's dead. You know it, Wa-Ka-Mo-Do. There's nothing for you here in Yukawa.'

'There's my sister, my family.'

'Would you shame them by returning to them in that body?'

Wa-Ka-Mo-Do said nothing. He moved another pawn across the board.

The stranger lifted a piece of his own: the forge. He waited a moment in the pattering rain, then placed it on the grey board.

'Checkmate. Come on, Wa-Ka-Mo-Do, it's time to go.'

He stood up. Wa-Ka-Mo-Do got to his feet and followed the robot through the streets, down through a forest of crane legs, human craft tangled in the cables and lines above him. He followed the stranger down to the sea.

A robot waited by the water, his body like none that Wa-Ka-Mo-Do had seen before. His arms were way too long, his face and body inverted drops of water.

'His name is Morphobia Alligator,' said the stranger, 'and he is a pilgrim.'

'Where is he taking me?'

'North, to the top of another continent. When summer approaches in the north, winter approaches in the south. Where there is happiness in spring, there is sorrow in autumn.'

Wa-Ka-Mo-Do gazed at the stranger.

'Winter is ending, the humans have just arrived there. From one perspective, you will have a chance to live the last six months again.'

Wa-Ka-Mo-Do moved forward. Something was rising up from the water beyond. Something huge. It was opening its mouth.

'Wa-Ka-Mo-Do,' said Morphobia Alligator. He gestured towards the whale's mouth. 'Shall we go inside?'

Spoole

Artemis City was locked in a dynamic equilibrium of busy preparation for the next war. Like a storm cloud, the potential was continually rising, and all the robots were waiting to see where it would discharge itself.

The robots were forming into clans: infantryrobots, Storm Troopers and Scouts, computers and engineers, all forming their own groups, all waiting to see where to move next. On the edge of the city, the human compound sat in silence, its guns constantly scanning the surrounding area.

Rumour was rife. It jumped from robot to robot. The humans were leaving, they were going to attack. Sandale and the rest were arming themselves with human weapons; Spoole had taken the north side of the city; Kavan was about to attack the city, attack the humans; Kavan was already here, inside the city . . .

And at the centre of this maelstrom of uncertainty, Spoole marched into the largest of the forges, surrounded by a group of infantryrobots and Storm

Troopers that were not quite escorting him, not quite following him. Kavan wasn't the only person with presence, he noted with satisfaction.

He saw the Generals in the middle of the floor, just as he had been told to expect, and he felt a surge of relief. So that information at least was true.

'Sandale!' he called. 'Why do you and the other Generals hide in here?'

They had been expecting him. All those Generals in their new bodies, all of them sporting the metals the humans had brought. Their bright, flashing panel work was in marked contrast to the dull greys and blacks of the soldiers who had followed him here.

He noticed the way they had arranged themselves: the younger Generals had moved to the back of the crowd. It was the older ones like Sandale who had the courage to challenge him.

What have we done? thought Spoole. *What have I done? To think, if the animals had never arrived we may have carried on in this way, tearing Artemis apart through our constant jockeying for power. Robots like Kavan marching across the surface of this planet, conquering all, robots like these Generals, making copies of themselves, making robots to lead, robots that have never done anything else . . .*

Sandale had stepped forward. 'What are you doing?' he demanded. 'Why do you bring these troops into this place?'

'As witnesses, Sandale.' And he raised his voice so it could be heard within the forge.

'General Sandale. Generals. I accuse you all of

treachery! You are traitors to Nyro!' Silence fell in the forge. All were listening. 'Robots!' he shouted. 'We have made a grave mistake in Artemis City. We see it standing here before us. Where we should have built robots to fight and to build to the glory of Nyro, we chose instead to weave minds to *lead* us. That was a mistake! Because to them, leadership has become all! They have never walked a battlefield, they have never constructed a bridge or a forge or an engine. Worse than that, they don't see any reason why they should do so! Instead, they believe that an ability to lead is all that is required. And so they do anything they can to continue that leadership, even if it means betraying us and Nyro to the animals! Better that, in their minds, than have Kavan return here to oust them!'

The forge was filled with silent attention. The crackle of the fires burning, the gentle pulse of the magnetic motors, the distant hammering, all seemed to fade into the background in the ringing of this greater truth. So many robots looking on, their rifles and knives and awls so far untouched. There was unresolved tension, waiting to be dissipated one way or the other. Of all the Generals, only Sandale seemed untouched by the building current. His low voice carried across the room.

'You accuse *us* of treachery? It is *you* who do not follow the will of Artemis. Artemis's leaders did not request your presence in this forge.'

Spoole walked forward, his simple, elegant body an eloquent contrast to the over-engineered machine that Sandale wore.

'You no longer have any authority, Sandale. Not since

you gave over part of Artemis to those who do not follow Nyro.'

Sandale smiled.

'Spoole, did not Nyro herself say that land is not important? Only Artemis. The animals rendered a service to Artemis; they took the land as their payment.'

'What service, Sandale?'

'They rid us of Kavan, Spoole. Have you forgotten that was also your wish?'

'Not in that manner, Sandale, never in that manner!'

But Sandale's words had achieved their intended effect. Spoole sensed the change in the mood, he felt the scales tilt against him. Still, he pressed on.

'The animals have taken their payment and more, Sandale! They are spreading across our land!'

A buzz of current ran across the room, jumping from robot to robot. Sandale raised his arms for attention.

'You exaggerate, Spoole,' he said, once silence had returned. 'The animals remain within their compound.'

'They remain within their compound? Except for their flying craft! Except for the railway lines they convert to their purpose and then use to take metal and fuel from us! Day by day the number of trains that ride the rails to their base increases, trains laden with refined oil and good plate steel, all carried from their bases in Stark and Raman and Wien!'

The point struck home, as Spoole knew it would. Taking metal away was like taking children away. All those unmade children that were the future of Artemis. Still, Spoole knew he should not underestimate the Generals. They were of a different manufacture. The newer minds may not be prepared in the ways of the battle-field, but they were twisted to rhetoric and the art of debate. Already, one young General clad in the lightest of bodies was stepping forward to speak.

'Indeed, Spoole is right!' she declared. 'The humans do take oil and steel, but what you seem incapable of realizing is that they return more than they take! And what they return is of a higher quality, or better than that, of materials previously unknown to us. Look at the metal that is scattered around this forge, given to us by the humans! Look at the aluminium they have brought!'

The entire room gazed at the body of the General, regarded its lustre, felt with their senses its strange but natural essence.

'Aluminium!' said one robot, near to Spoole, and the wistfulness in its voice was almost painful to hear.

'Yes!' called Sandale, delighted at how the point had struck home. 'Aluminium! Look, all of you, look at the metal that lies to the far wall of this assembly room. Look, too, at the copper and the platinum, the gold and the electrum that the animals have exchanged with us!'

A buzz ran around the room. Sandale stepped forward, and, old soldier that he was, Spoole saw the titanium beneath the aluminium that he wore.

'You call us traitors, Spoole?' called Sandale. 'Why? Artemis has traded in the past, it will continue to do so in the future!' He moved to face the crowd. 'Listen, all you who have come here today, following this relic of the past. The world may be transforming, but *we* remain true to Nyro! If Spoole and his philosophy are no longer in keeping with the new reality, as they so clearly are not, then what do we do but build new leaders? Leaders such as those you see before you. Leaders who understand the need to twist new minds suitable for the continuation of Artemis!'

At that some of the robots around the room stamped their feet in agreement. Stamp, *stamp!*

Sandale turned to face Spoole.

'See, Spoole? We are not traitors.'

Spoole was not built to feel uncertainty under most conditions, and so it was for the first time that he wondered if he had made a mistake. What if Sandale was right? What if he really were a relic of the past?

He pushed the thought aside. He wasn't made to be indecisive under any circumstances.

'What about the mothers?' he said.

'What of them?' asked Sandale.

'Yes, what of them?' called a nearby infantryrobot. Spoole spoke to him directly.

'The mothers of Artemis, Olivier, didn't you know? Sandale has given some of them to the animals, he has ordered them to weave minds that will serve the animals, to weave minds according to the animals' designs.'

The assembled robots didn't like that. The thought of minds being woven in any way but that of Nyro's was abhorrent to them. Spoole saw the glow of their eyes, he felt the mood swing back towards him. But once again the young General dressed in aluminium stepped forward.

'"Minds according to animals' designs"?' she said. 'And what of it? The metal will still be metal. It will run for forty years or so in the humans' service, and then it will die, and it will still be metal. Eventually it will return to Nyro's cause. And just think what we may have gained in trade from the humans in the meantime.'

That calmed the robots a little. They were still unhappy, but they were willing to listen. They wanted to listen. It was built into them to trust the Generals. Spoole felt the balance swinging this way and that. He saw the Generals ranged against him, one robot against the many. He would lose this argument in the long run, he knew it.

He realized his mistake then, coming here and arguing like this. He had walked onto a battlefield advantageous to his enemies. He should have fought them directly instead, using guns and knives. Too late to realize this now.

Then someone spoke from the back.

'This metal is from Turing City State!'

The robots turned in the direction of the shout.

'Turing City State is no more!' called Sandale, but Spoole noted the hum of current that had arisen within the General.

'Hold,' called Spoole. 'Speak, robot. What metal is from Turing City State? What do you mean?'

'This electrum! This metal that is said to be a gift from the humans! I would recognize the mix anywhere! It's from the coastal mines. I used to assay there, before the invasion.'

'From the coastal mines?' called Spoole, and he saw the reaction of the Generals.

'You knew that, didn't you?' he said, realization dawning.

'No . . .' said the young General, her current humming audibly.

'You did!' he said, anger rising within him. 'You knew that already! Yet you continued to deal with them! They are trading us our own metal! They take metal from us and give us back our own!'

'Why would they do that?' replied Sandale, desperately.

'The mothers of Artemis! They want the mothers! And you've given them to the animals!'

Rifles were gripped more tightly now, awls and knives were drawn.

'The aluminium!' said the young General. 'What about the aluminium? That doesn't exist upon Shull.'

'Not on Shull,' said Spoole. 'But maybe elsewhere on Penrose! We never looked that far abroad, did we? Too content on keeping ourselves in power!'

'No!'

The current in the room was building to a peak, ready to discharge. The Generals felt it. They saw how guns and knives were turned in their directions. Their reign was coming to an end.

Spoole's followers turned towards him, awaiting the order.

'No!' he shouted. 'Not now. Save your anger for the true target! It lies outside our doors, it lies just outside this city! Robots of Artemis, take back your land! Take back your metal! Take back your mothers!'

The young General stepped forward once more.

'No!' she exclaimed. 'NO!'

And the robots were silent for a moment.

'Listen! Just listen to me.' The robots were still, they looked at her. They wanted to hear what she had to say. Anything was better than the near certain death that would likely result from attacking the humans.

'Listen,' she repeated, and her voice was calm now. 'You're angry. I understand that. But you must trust your leaders. Yes, we were lied to. Yes, the humans misled us. But which one of you could have done better? Who here has any experience of negotiating with animals? None of us! So now we find ourselves in a situation not of our choosing. Well, what would you do now? Follow Spoole as he leads you into the human guns? What good would it do Artemis if we were all to die this day?'

Spoole laughed.

'What good would it do to follow the humans?'

'We would live a little longer, and so would Artemis. I say we think about where we are. I say we follow the humans for the moment. Then, when we understand them better, that would be the time to attack!'

'No! No longer. We attack now!'

But once more the robots in the forge were undecided. The young General pressed home her advantage.

'And there it is, Spoole. That is the sticking point. Is there really any robot here that we would trust to lead us in an attack on the humans? Is there any robot here capable of defeating them? I don't think so.'

And a voice called out from the rear of the crowd.

'There is one.'

They all turned to look in the direction of the robot that had spoken. It was a Scout, her silver body scratched and battered.

'There is one,' she repeated, and she turned towards the door. They all followed her gaze and saw the robot who stood there. An electrical thrill surged through the crowd.

Kavan had returned.

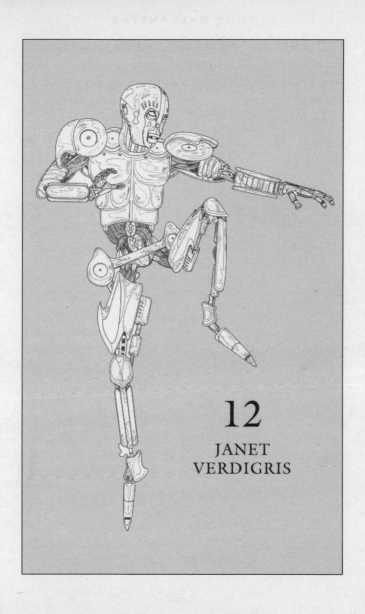

12

JANET
VERDIGRIS

Kavan

'Fight until your coil is broken,' said Kavan. 'If we lose, our metal will be taken from this planet, never to be reclaimed. Shull will gradually be drained of all metal, and the diminishing number of robots who remain will be left to fight over ever decreasing resources.'

That was it. No more speeches.

The attack began at night, when the humans slept like children.

The guns that surrounded their compound suddenly lifted their heads and turned to look at the night. The railway lines began to sing, bright white flares rose into the sky, electricity began to hum, and the ground shook as thousands of feet stamped down in unison.

The human guns began to ripple, tearing apart the leading edge of the train that sped down the tracks towards them, bullet holes travelling its length, perforating the metal, peeling it away into the night. A fire glowed white at the heart of the locomotive, it caught and spread backwards, and the train flared into a metal comet streaking onward.

Explosion!

The first atomic bomb detonating at a speed of nearly two hundred miles an hour, the explosion bouncing forward, wiping out the human guns closest to Artemis City . . .

The rest of the guns were already refocussing on the

second and third trains, racing up behind, the massed firepower much reduced by the first explosion, but the tracks were now ripped apart and there was no road through. The second train exploded further away from the compound, the third train further still.

Scouts running across the plain, their bodies shattering as the human guns saw them, more Scouts coming up behind, watching the paths of those ahead, seeking out the lines where the firepower was weaker or non-existent. Engineers poured from the city, laying new lines; they were followed by the wagons that rolled down the newly laid tracks, bringing more rails and sleepers. Infantryrobots walked the corridors picked out by the Scouts, Storm Troopers aiming heavy weapons into the night, firing bazookas in the direction of the guns, the shells picked off and detonated by the compound's defences when they were still half a mile distant.

'Concentrate your fire on one gun!'

'Fire on one gun only!'

'Aim for the nearest! Your shells will have less distance to travel!'

'Less chance for their guns to get their aim.'

The sergeants called the orders, the troops obeyed, and then, there in the distance, there was a bright yellow flare as the first of the human guns was destroyed by Storm Trooper fire.

'Good! And again! And again!'

More Scouts were running forward. The human defences had less of a field of fire now. The massing troops began to move forward. Scouts exploded in silver fragments, cutting into their sisters running up behind them. Some of them dragged themselves from the front, their legs cut away, heading back to find fresh bodies in order to resume the attack.

Now the human guns began to fire upon the infantry-robots. Their cheap grey bodies were shattered by just one bullet, and random patterns of disintegrating fragments jumped back and forth amongst the ranks as the human guns turned frantically back and forth, covering an ever-expanding front. And then another gun exploded, and another, picked off systematically by the Storm Trooper weapons.

'It's working!' shouted Spoole, watching with the rest from a point just inside the marshalling yards. 'It's working!'

'It's only the first phase,' observed Kavan. 'The humans will have awoken by now. They'll begin their counterattack soon. That's when we'll see the weapons they've been holding back.'

'We should launch Ada's devices now,' suggested Sandale.

'No,' said Kavan. 'Not yet.'

'Then let's not launch them at all,' said Sandale. 'It would be easier to let the humans go, if it comes to that.'

'You're not leading this attack,' replied Kavan.

The infantryrobots continued to push forward, gaining ground on the enemy guns. The new railway lines grew, bringing the engineers within range of the enemy. They exploded in blue fragments, their peers working on around them. Behind them in the marshalling yard, the troop trains revved their engines.

The human compound was coming alive. Lights

flicked on, dark shadows moved between them. Helicopters were rising into the air; they turned towards the attacking robots and yellow lines speared the night, connecting with a group of Storm Troopers that had just succeeded in destroying another of the guns. The helicopter fire shattered their bodies in an incandescent explosion. Grey infantry boiled forward and the human craft tilted their noses down and flew towards them, their drone filling the night, their firepower filling in the gaps in the field of fire where the human guns had been destroyed.

'Sensible,' said Kavan. 'Just what I would have done.'

With the additional support of the helicopters, the guns were able to halt the advance. Now two of the craft peeled off and began to fly towards the city itself.

'What now?' asked Spoole.

As if in answer, the night lit up in brilliant white once more. More atomic weapons, these detonated beneath the helicopters as they crossed over into Artemisian lines. The two closest craft were destroyed immediately. In the distance, the others fought to remain in the sky.

'Just as you said, Ada,' said Kavan.

'That will keep the others back for a while,' observed Ada with satisfaction. 'They won't know where we'll do that again!'

The area between Artemis City and the human compound was filling with craters, invisibly glowing with radiation, but still troops and engineers poured forward, running over the bodies of the fallen, turning their fire on the human guns. Everywhere there was movement, light, explosions, dark shapes running in lines this way and that.

And then, to the left, another explosion.

'Ours or theirs?' wondered Spoole.

'Ours,' said Ada. 'There are more railway lines being laid over there, hidden by the darkness. They must have got another train close enough to the compound.'

'They're being attacked on two sides now!' called Calor in delight, and she swiped the air with her claws.

'What's that?' called Spoole.

Three lights flared in the human compound. Then three more, then three more. Something bright streaked towards the city.

'Missiles!'

Three explosions to their right. So loud and bright. It filled the head with static, their vision blurred with white noise.

'Atomics!' shouted Ada, and her voice bent as three more explosions came from the left.

'Launch the first devices,' instructed Kavan.

'They'll take forty seconds to get heeeerrrrr!'

The third set of three explosions was the closest yet. Kavan saw three more lights flash in front of him. They instantly dissolved in a brighter explosion.

'The Storm Troopers,' whooped Calor. 'They hit the launcher!'

The order of the battlefield was breaking down as the Artemisian soldiers charged forward indiscriminately, dropping into shell holes, cut down by guns, shattered by nearby explosions, picked off by the bullets of the helicopters that hung in the distance, afraid of more weapons, but all the time gaining ground, all the time advancing on the human compound. The area before them erupted.

'Mines!' said Spoole. 'How did they do that without us knowing? Do they burrow up from underground?'

'Ineffective,' said Kavan, dismissively. 'A mine can only blow up once. The metal of the soldier that it disables can be used again and again.'

'What's that buzzing?' asked Sandale, and Ada spun to look behind them, her face filled with delight.

'Here they come!' she exclaimed. 'We had to launch them from trains in the end. The engines don't work unless the device is already up to speed, so we set them on trucks and got the train moving to ninety miles an hour. There is enough of a flow of air into the inlet then to keep the reaction going . . .'

Kavan wasn't listening. Ada had to explain everything she saw. All he was interested in was the application. He saw the first of the streamlined devices as it flew overhead, so low that Kavan could make out the eyes set in its underside.

'. . . pulse bombs!' Ada continued. 'We wove the minds to aim for anything hanging in the air. Look! It's seen the helicopters!' Ada's eyes flashed blue with delight.

First one, then two, then a whole pack of the devices streaked past, heading towards the human craft, rolling through the air to dodge their fire. The first one hit a helicopter and exploded in yellow flames. Up ahead, the robots stamped the ground, three times. Stamp, *stamp*, stamp.

'And more,' called Ada, looking up. 'And more! Oh, give me more time and I will make you missiles like the humans build! I will build a device that will carry Artemis to the stars! Then Nyro's voice will be heard across the galaxy!'

The pulse bombs rumbled overhead, the strange buzzing noise of their engines resonating against each other.

'We had to tune the combustion chambers to a precise pitch for each one,' explained Ada. 'Listen, how they each sound a different note. Listen to how they build chords in the sky! The harmonies resonate against each other! We are building a symphony from the battlefield.'

'Oh yes!' shrieked Calor, slashing her claws once more. 'Oh yes! I can hear it!'

Mad, thought Kavan. *They're all mad.*

More human guns detonated around the perimeter of the compound. More Storm Troopers moved forward, more bazookas firing. More infantryrobots running forward, closer to breaching the perimeter.

'Nearly there,' said Spoole, the excitement in his voice. 'And then the second offensive begins! Are you ready, Sandale? Are you ready, Generals?'

The Generals had scratched wire wool across their bodies, dulling the shiny surfaces. They carried rifles and blades, they wore grenades and determined expressions.

'We're ready!'

Kavan was impressed to note the steel in their eyes. They were going to attack, he was sure of that much. After that . . . he would just have to wait and see.

More of the pulse-bomb devices buzzed overhead.

But now white tracer was streaming up from the smaller of the two human spaceships lying there in the middle of the compound. The tracer caught the missiles, exploding one of them overhead, the force of the blast knocking Kavan and the rest to the ground. Some of the robots didn't stand up again.

'Lights,' said Calor, peering into the night. 'All over the human compound. They are running this way and that. Climbing into vehicles. Coming to meet us.'

Yellow and red flames flared up inside the compound, they arced up and over the perimeter fence to drop down on the infantryrobots just beyond, disintegrating their bodies, flinging shrapnel everywhere, damaging the fence itself.

'Now,' said Kavan. 'Generals! Redeem yourselves!'

The Generals stamped the ground. They began to march forward, they broke into a jog, and then they ran. All around them, shuffling forward through the marshalling yard, the infantryrobots and Storm Troopers and Scouts saw them and began to do the same. A grey and black flood, flecked in silver, was unleashed towards the compound, rolling forward to the accompaniment of the buzzing symphony in the sky.

Kavan and his entourage began to walk forward too, following the advance.

'Something new,' shrieked Calor. 'Can you hear it?'

They all picked up on it. A rising note, engines spinning to life.

'Something's moving!' called Calor. 'The ship! One of the ships is taking off!'

'That's their gun platform,' said a nearby robot.

'That's the one that attacked us back when we first tried to take Artemis.'

A dark shape was rising from the centre of the compound. As Kavan watched, lights moved across the shape.

'Ada! Bring it down! Bring it down now!'

Ada was speaking into a radio.

'Ninety seconds!' she said. 'We have to bring the next trains up to speed.'

'Will it work?' shouted Kavan. He could hear the roar of the diesel engines in the distance.'

'It'll work,' said Ada. 'Will your troops be ready?'

'They'll be ready.' And, in an uncharacteristic moment of doubt, Kavan added, 'Let's hope what Goeppert told us about the whalers is right!'

The human craft rose higher. White flame spurted from its nose, missiles slamming down on the attacking troops beneath. The pulse bombs that dodged and rolled in the sky, chasing the helicopters, now turned their attention towards the rising ship, flinging themselves towards it, running themselves into the needle missiles it fired, exploding in balls of flame that illuminated the grey and black battlefield below. The humans were also bringing new guns into position: mobile guns on vehicles, they poured their fire into the solid mass of troops that crept inexorably towards them.

'Sixty seconds!' called Ada.

The ship was turning as it rose, sliding towards the city. Black and gold bands travelled slowly down its length, and Kavan recognized the meaning. It was signalling a warning. Two hatches opened beneath the craft, and smaller craft, very much like Ada's own pulse bombs, fell from them. Their tails ignited as they fell and with a lurch they streaked towards Kavan, passing over his head in a blur of flame. Heading for the Centre City.

'Get down,' said Ada. They fell to the ground just as the repeated percussion of the explosions shook the earth. White light glowed so hard it burned into the eyes, dark shadows tore the brightness apart.

'Atomics,' said Ada. There was a moment's pause on the battlefield. Robots looked back to the clouds that rose, dark above the centre of the city.

'They hit the Centre City,' said Calor. 'Wiped it out . . .'

'Thirty seconds,' said Ada.

The noise of the battlefield was increasing. Even with hearing turned right down it rattled the shell: the rumble of diesel engines, the noise of trains on tracks, thunder of explosions, chatter of gun shots, the drone of pulse bombs, rippling of human guns, pulsing of pressure, crackle of the first of the Tesla towers discharging. The night sky was alive with dancing devices, trails of tracer, and now, rising higher and higher, launched from the trains, the remainder of Ada's devices. The ones that Kavan had held in reserve, streaking towards the human craft, each trailing a long cable behind it.

'Rocket engines,' said Ada with satisfaction. 'Harder to build. Harder to manoeuvre.'

They moved fast. But not fast enough. The human ship rippled with light as its weapons picked them off, the guns on the ground turned upwards to destroy them.

The infantryrobots took advantage of the lull and surged forward, breaching the compound perimeter, and the guns turned their fire back to earth again. And so the first of the new devices finally saw a pathway and struck home, piercing the human craft. The long wire trailing from it looped down to the ground.

'The barbs should extend on impact,' said Ada. Robots were already running forward, seizing hold of the cable. Pulling at it. To no avail. The craft was rising into the air, dragging them up with it. More devices streaking forward. Piercing the craft. More cables. Storm Troopers took hold of them, other robots gripping their bodies. Bazookas and guns were trained on the craft. The orange bands of light that ran the craft's extent flickered, the ascent hesitated, halted, and slowly, the black and gold ship began to tilt sideways.

'Pull!' called Ada. 'Pull!'

'*Pull, Pull,*' came the shout, echoed by all those robots on the plain that dragged at the huge ship.

More devices slammed into the craft, cables whipping across the battlefield, tangling around robots, cutting them in two. Other robots took their place, seizing the ropes and pulling. Robots climbed the wires, adding their weight to the craft. Wires snapped and robots tumbled to the ground. But some of them made it inside the craft itself. The turning point was reached. The craft was descending.

'Pull!'

They were whaling. Whaling for a craft from another planet. It slid earthwards, it clipped the perimeter of the compound. The lights across its hull winked, once, twice and then went out. With a grinding shriek, the ship ploughed its way into the ground.

Stamp, *stamp*, stamp!

A huge cheer sounded.

'Now, take it!' said Kavan, and he smiled.

Spoole

The Generals ran towards the stricken human craft, the last bands of colour fading from its side.

Spoole would have put a bullet through their heads. Kavan was a fool to put them in the middle of the charge, where they could let the other soldiers form a protective wall around themselves and allow better robots to take the flak for them.

'The guns!' called Sandale. 'Aim for the guns!'

Obediently, the surrounding Storm Troopers turned their bazookas towards the turrets that had sprung open on the downed craft's side and were already rippling bullets towards them.

As they closed on the craft its enormous size became apparent, and Spoole was filled with wonder at just what the Generals had attempted. How could they have been so foolish as to try and make a deal with these creatures? Just how powerful were the humans in comparison? He was reminded of the story of Janet Verdigris, how she had made a deal with the robots beneath the world.

Something screamed like a buzzsaw being crushed by an adamantium snake; something whipped across the battlefield and half the robots beside him flashed and died, their bodies had been sliced in two, the parts tumbling to the ground.

'There!' cried Sandale, and Spoole saw something hurtling forward through the crowd.

'The devices!' observed Spoole. 'More of them!'

They looked up to see Ada's inventions streaking overhead, heading towards the second and larger of the human craft as it rose into the air, seeking escape. Its bulk blocked the sky above them.

'Idiots!' screamed Sandale. 'Trailing cable through the battlefield! Don't they realize they could hit us?'

He still hadn't got it, reflected Spoole. He still didn't see that he was expendable.

An explosion up ahead drew his attention back to the battlefield.

'We breached it!' called a Storm Trooper. 'We blew a hole in the side!'

Spoole looked and saw. The grounded ship was ripped open near the nose. Infantryrobots were already forcing their way in, peeling back lovely long strips of the strange human alloy.

'We're in!' shouted Sandale. 'Robots of Artemis! Attack!'

The call was unnecessary. What else would the robots do? Spoole watched as the Generals assumed control of the capture of the spaceship. They were back in power already.

Kavan was a fool, he thought once more.

Susan

Susan's body had been broken when she was hurled from the troop train as it ran off the end of the lines at speed. Two engineers had found her and quickly put her back together again, then sent her on her way. She joined the other infantryrobots heading towards the human compound. And then the air had filled with so much metal that she had dropped, terrified, in a shell hole, and waited for the battle to stop.

A Storm Trooper sheltered there too, and she had felt his shame as he crouched there, big black hands clasped above his head. He had said something she couldn't catch amidst all the noise.

Eventually the firing passed over, and she raised her head up to see the smaller of the human ships rising into the air, the target of those strange devices that streaked towards it, dragging cables of destruction through the battlefield behind them. Several of the devices became entangled and were jerked to a halt in mid air, ripping themselves apart in red and yellow fire.

She saw the ship fall and break itself open on the ground, and she paused, gripped by indecision. Where would Nettie be? On the craft? In the compound?

What good would it do her if she got killed here on the battlefield?

There were engineers everywhere, running across the stony plain. One came towards her, shouting. Susan turned up her ears a little to hear what he was saying.

'Take this,' he said, thrusting a metal mesh into her

hand. 'Pull it over your head. Don't take it off until you're told to.'

She did so automatically. The mesh interfered with her hearing, muffling it. Well, that was good.

The second human ship was lifting up now. What if Nettie was on board that one? The devices were aiming for it, but it seemed just too large to bring down. What if it escaped with Nettie still a prisoner?

There was nothing she could do about that.

She made up her mind and ran for the compound. Maybe Nettie would be there.

She couldn't just stand still, that was for sure.

Kavan

Kavan saw the second human ship lift into the breaking dawn, the cables of several devices trailing uselessly from it.

'It's escaping,' said Ada, the disappointment audible in her voice.

'It will be back,' said Kavan. 'They'll all be back.'

'The Generals have taken the first craft,' said Calor. 'Do you think it's wise to leave them in control of it?'

'I don't think it matters,' said Kavan. 'Everything will be different by tomorrow. Artemis City is changed for ever.'

Behind him the Centre City burned. Ada had set up a radiation detector that pinged a signal of the atomic destruction there.

'Calor,' said Kavan. 'There are still humans left in the

compound. I think it would be well to remind the troops we want as many of them alive as possible.'

'Okay, Kavan.' Calor's words trailed behind her as she sprinted off.

'She needed to expend the energy,' observed Ada. She watched Kavan, running the fine metal mesh she had handed him between his fingers.

'You should put that on,' she said.

'When it's time. Are you sure it will work?'

'The Faraday Cage? It's the best solution given the time we've had. The humans will want to inflict maximum damage over the widest range.'

'I notice you haven't put yours on yet.'

'What we have been told is plausible, but I want to see if it's *true*. I want to see this weapon as best I can. I want to learn as much about it as possible, and so I'll put my cage on at the last second.'

'And if you die?'

'Then there are other engineers to take my place.'

Kavan smiled.

'You are a true Artemisian, Ada.'

'Look, here it comes.'

The second ship had climbed out of view, lost in the pale dawn sky. Now something was falling back down to Penrose. Kavan could just make out the lightning forking around it.

'It's beautiful,' he said. 'In its own way.'

'There is something strangely beautiful in everything the animals do,' replied Ada. 'It's an unearthly, twisted beauty, but it's there if you know where to look.'

The device was falling faster now. Kavan saw the

lightning reaching down from it, seeking the robots of the battlefield, most of whom were pausing to pull the mesh over their heads. It was like waves in the water, all those silver and black bodies kneeling for a moment and pulling.

'What about the humans left behind?' asked Kavan. 'Will they die too?'

'I don't know,' said Ada. 'Perhaps the animals are closer to being Artemisians than we allow.'

'Put on your mesh, Ada.'

'Not yet. You put on yours, Kavan. You're more important than I am.'

'That concept does not exist in Artemis.'

They gazed upwards as the crackling fell ever closer, illuminating the brightening sky in blue and silver. The robots on the field gazed upwards in awe and horror as the few remaining humans continued to fire at them. The Centre City burned in the background and Ada and Kavan found themselves looking at each other, and for the first time in his life he felt a sense of understanding.

They both pulled on their meshes. The lightning raced across the battlefield . . .

Spoole

Spoole had seen this before. Battlefields where defeat had been bought at such cost to those still standing that it could scarcely be said that victory had been won.

The humans had been driven from Artemis, but

Artemis City was broken, and the surviving robots wandered aimlessly across the plain.

There were so many robots dead. Robots who had failed to pull the protective mesh across their heads, or those who had simply never received one. Their bodies were pulled apart and picked over by others looking for spares.

There were humans there too, so fragile-looking in defeat. For the most part they were under the guard of infantryrobots, but a few of them wandered free, or attempted to fix their broken vehicles under the interested gaze of engineers.

If there was one impetus left to those shell-shocked forces, it seemed to be the force that was driving robots towards the downed ship. It lay, huge and alien in the middle of the plain, halfway between the remains of the compound and the shattered city, trails of plastic and soot and cable and spent metal radiating out from it. Robots were congregating around its broken side.

Spoole walked to the centre of the crowd, the robots who saw him coming recognizing him and pulling back as he approached. He made his way to where the surviving Generals still stood. Sandale was there.

'Spoole,' he said, all polite efficiency. 'What are your orders?'

His deference made sense, he supposed. It was woven deep inside: Sandale had tried rebellion and had failed, but that wouldn't stop him clinging to power by any means. And if, in a few weeks, or months, or years, he thought it safe, then he would turn upon Spoole again. Him and the rest of the Generals.

'Orders will come soon,' said Spoole. 'For the moment, round up the surviving humans.'

Spoole looked around at the wreckage, looked around at all the robots. They were waiting for him to speak, he realized.

He turned his voice up full.

'This is only a temporary victory,' he called, and as he had done so many times before, he heard his words relayed out through the listening crowd. 'Only temporary. The animals will return. They have more metal, they have better machinery. They have the capability to destroy us.'

He paused. He saw the robots shifting, heard the hum and the buzz as his words sank in.

'But to despair is to have forgotten the lessons of history, because it was ever thus!' he cried. 'Robots stood on this plain before, surrounded by superior forces and technology, and they triumphed over them. Those robots had little metal, they were few in number, but they had something more powerful than guns and flying craft and bombs! They had Nyro's philosophy!'

Somewhere in the crowd, feet were stamped. One, two, just like in the old days, back when Spoole addressed the newly built troops on the parade grounds.

'Well, I say that those same robots stand here today! Because today, all of you who have fought on this battleground are the true children of Nyro! And Nyro's children were not defeated in the past, back when Artemis was young, and so they will not be defeated in the future. Artemis will never be defeated!'

More stamping, but this time there were shouts too.

Shouts of approval. Spoole saw the way the Generals looked at him. Envious, but there was a grudging respect there as well. They couldn't have done this, he knew. They needed a figurehead. For the moment it may as well be Spoole.

'The animals will return,' he called. 'When they do, we will be ready for them! We will have studied their craft and we will have built our own machines. We will take the fight to them, and we will defeat them!'

The earth shook now to the sound of stamping. A group of Storm Troopers took up a chant that was spreading through the metal ranks.

'Spoole! Spoole! Spoole!'

He raised his hands for silence. Gradually, order returned.

'No,' he said. 'Not Spoole. Listen to me Artemisians, I have a confession to make.'

The crowd was silent, ears were turned up to listen.

'Nyro herself said it,' said Spoole, 'that there is no mind, there is just metal. I realized over the past few weeks that maybe my mind wasn't woven as true as I once believed. Perhaps my mother was too concerned with this metal –' he tapped his hand against his body, '– to the detriment of Artemis itself. Perhaps I wasn't the only one to think that way.'

He looked again at the surviving Generals.

Silence. Nothing but the hiss of the breeze through metal seams.

'Not perhaps,' Spoole corrected himself. 'There is no doubt. The leadership of Artemis has been poor lately, there is no denying it.'

Sandale's eyes flashed, but he remained quiet. How could he do otherwise, when shouts of agreement came from the crowd? Sandale lowered his head.

'But all this changes today. There can be no longer any doubt who the true leader of Artemis is. Bring him forward now. Bring forward Kavan!'

The shout went out; heads turned this way and that. And they focussed on the dusty, insignificant infantry-robot who made his way towards Spoole. An electric surge ran through the crowd as they strained to see Kavan, the hero, the feared, the robot who had conquered all of Shull.

Robots cleared a path as he made his way forward, flanked by a blue engineer and a silver Scout. The three of them came to a halt before Spoole. Spoole looked the infantryrobot up and down.

'Kavan,' he said. 'What would you have us do now?'

The silence lengthened. And then Kavan spoke.

'Seek another leader.'

A hum of current rippled through the robots.

'But . . . but why?'

Kavan was matter of fact.

'Because our time has passed. Look at this place, look at that ship, lying broken over there. Our minds are not woven for these times.'

'Then who?' demanded Sandale, suddenly bold.

'I don't know,' said Kavan, fixing the General with a stare. 'Maybe someone like Ada here, someone who understands machinery.'

'Not me!' laughed the blue engineer.

'No,' agreed Kavan. 'Not you. Maybe you could

understand what makes this craft work, but that wouldn't mean you could understand the minds of those who have built it. We need a new leader. Someone whose mind was not fixed at birth. Someone who will look at this new situation in which we find ourselves and will be able to respond to it in a new way, not in a pattern laid down by his mother, years ago.'

'Does such a person exist?'

'If they do, they will present themselves.'

Spoole was aware of the movement from the side. He saw two robots pushing their way forward. One wore the body of an infantryrobot, but awkwardly, as if he wasn't really used to it. The other wore an oversized body of lead and iron, a badly designed thing that was surely hurting the robot inside. The infantryrobot spoke.

'Who are you?' asked Spoole.

The robot looked at Spoole. 'Someone who was listening to what you said. Someone whose mind was not fixed at birth. Someone who has walked this continent from top to bottom and has finished his journey with more questions than when he started. Someone who has heard the story of Eric and the Mountain, and now knows that he must lead.'

'That was the philosophy of Turing City,' said Kavan. 'This robot is from Turing City. I think he's right. The Turing Citizen should be your new leader.'

'Turing City is no more,' said Karel. 'And neither is Artemis. All that is left is metal. It's up to us how we twist it now.'

'You would suggest a *Tokvah* tells us how to twist metal?' said Sandale, the faintest edge of disgust in his voice.

'My mind wasn't made in Artemis, either,' said Kavan. 'And yet you would allow me to lead you. These two robots are responsible for the metal mesh we all carry. If not for them, then there would be no Artemis today. We would all be dead, our minds destroyed by the electric bomb. So yes, Sandale. I say let's listen to Karel when he tells us how to twist metal.'

'But how do we twist it?' asked Spoole.

Karel looked at the heavy lead robot for support.

'I don't know,' he began. '. . . yet. But Kavan knows part of the answer, he will know how to make robots that will fight. He will command our troops and direct them against the enemy, when they return. This engineer will know another part, robots that can take the animals' technology and twist it to our own ends. But there is more than that.'

'What more could there be?' demanded Sandale.

'I don't know,' replied Karel. 'And that's it. None of us knows what else there is. I don't think we understand this world, I don't think we see it as it really is. We caught a hint of that at the top of Shull, didn't we, Kavan?'

Kavan's eyes flared just a little at that, but he said nothing.

Karel looked at the leaden robot standing at his side.

'Melt and I have travelled the length and breadth of this continent, and we have seen and heard fragments of other truths that are not woven directly into the mind.'

'What do you mean?'

'I mean stories that are passed orally from robot to robot, stories that have taken on a life of their own, and avoided the censor of whatever philosophy has been adopted by the state that the mother belongs to. There are other ways for robots to build bodies than this one.'

He held his arms wide. 'I've even met one such robot.'

Although they spoke quietly, their words were relayed out through the surrounding crowds. Electronic voices rose and fell as the messages reached the edges of the crowd.

Karel raised his voice.

'This world isn't what we've made ourselves believe it is,' he called. 'If we are to make it our own, we need to understand it. We need to see the truth about ourselves. We take so much for granted. Minds. The night moon. All of these things. If we do not write our own stories, then these animals will write them for us! They may already have done so! I saw the warning written at the top of Shull. So did Kavan. The Story of Eric and the Mountain.'

'The Story of Eric and the Mountain?' said Kavan.

'Melt here knows it! He told it to me, and I think I understand what it means. Not just the Story itself, but all stories. Maybe even the Book of Robots.'

'What do you mean?'

'Think of this. Imagine, years ago, there were robots living here on Penrose who saw the truth.'

'What truth?'

'I don't know! Maybe a truth that was to be hidden from us. Maybe a truth that someone or something was trying to hide from us. Someone or something much, much more powerful than us.'

'Like the humans?'

'I don't know. Maybe. But I don't think so. I think

there is a deeper truth at work here. Maybe one that the robots of the past understood a little of, one they wove into the minds of their children. But what of all the other children? How would they let them know?'

'By stories,' said Ada. 'I see. That's so clever, two ways for information to pass on.' Her eyes shone as she contemplated the thought. 'Hard wired, and a way of modifying data.'

'The stories are a message to us from our past,' repeated Karel. 'We need to understand them!'

He was interrupted by a commotion in the crowd. A robot was pushing its way forward.

'Karel! Karel!'

Spoole recognized the voice. So did Karel. They both turned. Yet another infantryrobot was running towards them, and Spoole reflected how the most ordinary body in Artemis had proven to be the most influential. Karel was obviously not thinking such thoughts. His eyes glowed in wonder at the sight of the approaching woman.

'Susan,' he said.

'Karel!'

'*This* is your husband?' said Spoole, but they weren't listening to him, and why should they?

Susan was humming with electricity. The current shone around her, eclipsing even the glow that poured forth from Karel's body. To robot eyes, it was as if they were surrounded by two haloes. The two robots approached each other and a hum of feedback escaped from both their mouths, so perfectly were they in phase with each other.

It all came down to this, thought Spoole. All this fighting, just because robots made more robots.

'Oh, Karel,' said Susan.

'Susan.'

They placed their heads close together and listened to the signal hum of each other's minds.

For the moment, there was nothing else to be said.

Calor

Calor ran through the streets of Artemis City. She could feel the thump of machinery re-awakening, hear the sound of lathes beginning to turn once more, see the robots at work stripping down the damaged buildings, clearing away the wreckage of the fighting.

She turned left by a ruptured gasometer, and headed up a long road bordered on either side by cable walks, empty now of cable after the last attack. Soon the machines inside would turn again and more cable would be wound to the glory of Artemis. Or was it Turing City now? Both Kavan and Karel said that names didn't matter any more.

Either way, Calor was free to run for the moment, and with a surge of pleasure she put on a spurt of speed, running, flashing, down the street with the single joy of a robot meeting the purpose woven into her mind. She saw the puff in the dust ahead, tried to dodge, but she was moving too quickly . . .

Her feet were gone, sliced clean off by the razor wire stretched across her path. She raised herself up on her hands, turned around, saw the Storm Troopers who emerged from the doorways on either side, heading towards her.

She waited until they were close enough and then exploded into movement, slashing out with the blades of one hand, slicing into the panelling of the leader, blue sparks leaping from his chest; but there were too many of them. They pushed her to the ground, twisted her arms back behind her, snapped them off, one, two. They did the same with what remained of her legs, then they dragged her off the street, pulling her into a cable run.

'I recognize you,' said one. 'Kavan's *Spartz*. You were with him back in the north, back when he was first raising his army. I saw you there. Do you recognize me?'

'Let your wire rust, *Tok*,' she giggled, half mad on current and pain.

'You're the one who will rust. We'll tear out your mind and leave it covered in salt water for a few weeks. Leave it for Kavan to find. Maybe he'll get the message then. Artemis isn't going to be run by some *Tokvah* from Turing City.'

'Who do you think should run it? The animals?'

'Artemisians, *Spartz*. How about if I made new arms for you? I could do that. Take you with us when we leave this place, give you arms so you can twist us new minds, help us to build the new Artemisian army. You'd like that, wouldn't you? Just you and us?'

'Yes,' said Calor. 'Go on then. Put my arms back on. I'll weave minds for you.'

The Storm Troopers laughed.

'I don't think so. We need to send a message to Kavan,

and you're it. I wonder, does it hurt to feel your mind gradually rusting away?'

'Perhaps you'll find out someday. You won't defeat Kavan. You Storm Troopers never could. He was always too clever a leader for you.'

'But he's not leader any more, is he?'

The big robot leaned forward and squeezed her head, popping the metal apart there. He picked away at the seams, getting at her mind.

'Will you tell him I was coming back to him?' she said, worried about this above all else.

They didn't answer. A hand reached down to break her coil.

And that was it.

Darkness.

Silence.

Calor was fifteen years old. She could expect to live for another twenty-five or thirty years in this awful isolation. Unless, of course, the Storm Troopers followed through on their promise to drop her mind into salt water. It would be a mercy.

Twenty-five years of silence, twenty-five years without the sound of another robot. Twenty-five years without sunlight, or the feel of ground beneath her feet, without the joy of running, sprinting, slashing at the air with her hands for the sheer pleasure of it. No more polishing metal, straightening wire. Never more to feel oil, slippery between her joints.

And all the while, the world passing by outside, untouched, unknowing. Where would the animals be? Where would Kavan be?

Would anything come of Karel's plans to find out the truth behind the world? Did such a truth exist?

What did Calor care? She was made to run, and fight. No longer.

Nothing but the sound of her own thoughts.

Nothing but the reflection of her memory.

No sense of passing time.

Silence. Darkness.

So many other robots, just like her. Scattered across the battlefields of Shull. She had never given them any thought before.

Silence.

So faint, she must have imagined it.

She heard it again, a voice, in the distance. She realized now that it had always been there, but in the past it had been drowned out by the noise and brightness of the world around her.

She could hear it now though. It was speaking to her. *Hello, Calor.*

Susan

Two robots were making love in the middle of a battle-field.

'Don't leave me again, Karel,' said Susan, twisting his wire in her hands.

'I don't want to have to,' said Karel. It wasn't the promise she wanted, and they both knew it.

'I'd stay with you,' said Susan. He knew that of course. That's one reason why he had agreed to the making of a child so readily. It would be a way of keeping her in safety if he found himself heading into danger in the coming battle. It was the only thing that would work. It was woven into Susan's mind to love and protect Karel. Only the motherhood urge would be stronger.

'I've reached the point,' she said. 'Have you decided?'

'Yes,' said Karel. 'A little girl.'

He would be thinking of Axel, their little boy. She was, too. But life went on.

'A little girl. Have you thought of a name?'

'Emily.'

Emily, a lovely name for a lovely child, due to be born in these less than lovely times.

Susan paused, looking at him.

'Her nature comes next,' she said. 'Are you sure you want me to weave her that way?'

'Yes!' he said. 'Make Emily curious about everything! Make her ask what and how and why. Always why, and never to accept any answer at face value.'

'But that will render the weave so far pointless. If she questions everything we have made her to be—'

'But that's just the point!' said Kavan, and he gazed up at the stars. 'It's like that human woman said: we robots aren't very curious. Is that any surprise when we ask our mothers to weave our beliefs directly into our children? Who would want to weave in curiosity if it were—'

'We're doing this because of what some human woman said?'

'It's right, Susan. I know it's right. Do you believe me?'

It didn't matter whether she did or not. She would follow him, whatever he did. At least Emily would have a choice in what she did.

She continued with the weave. There was so much power in the wire, she now knew. Ada had talked about nuclear fusion, about hydrogen adsorption. Kavan had talked about the humans returning. They wanted that power.

'Do you trust Kavan?' she asked, suddenly. 'You only lead with his approval, you know. If he ever decides otherwise you will be ousted before the day is out.'

'I know that.' He looked at her moving hands, wanting to think of happier things. 'What are you weaving now?'

'Her sense of self, of otherness.'

'Will you make her like me? Angry? Angry enough to change things?'

'Of course I will. I love you, Karel. How could I do anything else?'

'We're so strange, aren't we?' said Karel. 'Us robots. We do exactly as our mothers told us, and yet we are all so different. So simple, and so complex at the same time.'

'It seems normal to me,' replied Susan, twisting his wire further. The thought of Nyro's pattern kept rising in her mind, and she had to push it away. All those nights spent in the making rooms. So many times she had wondered if she could have ever done this again. But if she hadn't, that would have been another victory for Artemis.

'They never found Nettie, did they?' she said.

'Your friend? No. Perhaps she was on the ship that escaped.'

'I hope so. Do you think they will bring her back?'

'I don't know. You said they wanted our minds.'

'Something about the power there. The fact that we didn't need fuel. The humans were very excited by that.'

Something stirred within her. The faintest edge of curiosity. Maybe Karel was right, that this world was stranger than she thought.

'What was that story, the one that Melt told you?'

'The Story of Eric and the Mountain.'

'He's a strange robot, Melt. Are you sure he can be trusted?'

'I think so. There is a deep sense of honour within him, I know that.'

'Where does he come from?'

'He won't say. I think he's deeply ashamed of his past, that's one of the things that convinces me he is honourable, funnily enough. He's met the humans before, though. He knew about the Faraday Cage. He told the Artemisians; he got them to send the message to all their troops.'

'I heard.'

Karel looked up at the stars, tried to enjoy the pleasurable feeling of Susan pulling at his wire. But all the time his mind wandered back to Melt, the way he had almost pleaded to be allowed to guard Susan, as he had done Karel on his journey south. It seemed to be important to the big robot. A way of redeeming himself.

'If anything happens to me, you will be safe with Melt.'

'I don't want anything to happen to you.' Susan twisted his wire in an odd loop. 'Almost done,' she said. 'There is a little wire left. Are you ready? Are you sure that you want me to put it in?'

'I'm sure,' said Karel. 'Every robot should know this. From now on, this story will be woven into every robot's mind.'

'Then tell me,' said Susan.

'Very well,' said Karel, and he began.

The Story of Eric and the Mountain

'When the ancient town of Ell was still young, before the tribes of Yukawa were united by the Emperor, before Ban province had learned the secret of animal husbandry, there lived a robot called Eric.'

'This story is set in Yukawa?' said Susan. 'I had never heard of that place until yesterday.'

'I'm sure that is where Melt comes from. He told this story as if it were woven into his mind. Now listen.

'Eric was the adopted son of Ben-Ji, the owner of one of Ell's principal forges. Now, it must be understood that the robots of Yukawa have a different culture to those of Shull, and the robots of Ell are unusual even in Yukawa, and this story happened a long time ago when Ell was a very different place to today. So if you find what happened in Ben-Ji's forge strange, or even distasteful, then just remember that this is how things were in those days.'

Susan was staring at him.

'This is our child we are making,' she reminded him.

'This is how Melt told me the story,' explained Karel. He continued, using the same sing-song style in which Melt had related the story to him.

'Now I must explain that Ben-Ji's forge was known as a making forge. When a man and a woman wanted to make a child then they would go to his forge and look at the fine metals he had on display there. Pure iron and copper and aluminium and lead. The best steel, graded according to use. Metal available as plates and ingots and wire. Gold leaf so fine, silver wire, even phosphorus and sodium stored under oil. Jars of mercury, sheets of tungsten, and, there in the back, molybdenum and palladium. Even, it was rumoured, the eka metals: eka mercury and eka lead.'

'Do they really exist?' wondered Susan, her eyes glowing.

'I don't know! Susan, please don't interrupt!'

'So a couple would enter the forge, the woman full of thoughts and poetry and ideas, pregnant with the thoughts of the mind she would soon twist, and she would walk with her man as they examined the metals on offer. They would tell Ben-Ji and his wife Khafool what sort of a mind they planned to make, and then Ben-Ji and Khafool would give them advice on the metal to choose and the body they should construct. And any other robots who were in the forge would also pass on advice, and in this way the day would pass, until eventually the man would sit down, and the woman kneel before him, and, guided by the advice of all those present, a new mind would be twisted by the woman from the metal she drew forth from the man. The robots produced by the Ben-Ji forge were strong and wise and prospered in the city of Ell, and so the reputation of the Ben-Ji forge grew.

'Now, Eric worked in the forge, but he was unhappy in his work. The only thing that gladdened his mind was the sight of Khalah, the daughter of Ben-Ji and Khafool. For Khalah had a good mind, a thing of symmetry and elegance and beauty. She built her body of the finest materials available to the forge. She crafted it well, mixing metals and alloys to form long struts of a pleasing curve, electromuscles of the most cunning weave, and polished aluminium panels that shone under the sun in the daylight and reflected the red glow of the forge through the night.

'Khalah loved the forge and her family, and she loved Eric as he loved her, yet she was filled with disquiet, for as long as Eric was unhappy, she could never be truly happy herself. So, one cold autumn day as they stood before the forge, a day when the frost was heavy on the metal bosses and brackets of the doors, the ice was frozen in rings around edges of the puddles and troughs, and the sky was blue and misty, on that day she challenged him.

"'Eric,' she said. "Why are you always so sad? You are a good smith, good enough to impress my father, and there are few robots who can do that. My mother approves our match, and some day we shall have this forge for our own, and we can go on building it in strength and stature. Is that not a good thing?"

"'It is Khalah, it is indeed. Yet I do not feel that I belong here.'"

"'You were not made here, Eric, it is true. Your mind is different, and you construct your body in a style foreign to those who live here, but there is much to be recommended in you, and, as I have said, no less an authority than my mother has suggested that we are compatible and shall weave strong children together. What do your origins matter?'"

'Eric hammered at the red iron he held over the anvil, hammered his frustration into the metal.

"'What do they matter, Khalah? I was found at the foot of the High Spires by your father. He brought me back here and cared for me, and the people of this town accepted me as their own. They gave me metal and taught me how to weave it in their fashion. My origins shouldn't matter. Yet they do. A thought lives on in my mind. Look over there . . .'"

'He pointed to the distant peaks of the High Spires. The mountaintops were sharp in the cold air, rising clear of the misty foothills. Snow gleamed white and crisp; Eric almost felt their chill from here.

'"Do you see the High Spires? Do you see the group over there in the centre? The Crown, they are called. There is something up there, Khalah, hidden amongst the peaks."

'"What is it?"

'"I don't know. It is there at the edge of my mind. Sometimes it is a sword, made of the first metal, the first metal to think thoughts. Sometimes it is a body made of katana metal, an indestructible body. Sometimes it is just metal itself. But precious metal. A ball of eka lead perhaps, or the metal that lies beyond that."

'"I have heard the stories," said Khalah. "The stories of the first robots, Alpha and Gamma, how they crossed the High Spires, and left some of their treasures up there for safekeeping, before they stepped into this land."

'"Khalah, the stories are true! I know it. I came from the High Spires, the pictures are there in my mind. Now I must return there to find those treasures."

'"What about me?"

'"Come with me, Khalah!"

'"My father would never allow it! I must stay here at the forge with my mother!"

'"I know that, but Khalah, I must go."

'There was a long silence as Khalah contemplated his words. She knew she could not leave the forge, she also knew she could not bear to be parted from Eric. The two urges were powerful within her, so powerful they threatened to rip her in two, or so she thought. In the end her path was obvious.

'"Then I will come with you," she said.'

'And so, later that day, when the forge was full, and Ben-Ji and Khafool were hard at work tending to a man and woman who twisted metal, Eric and Khalah left the city of Ell and set out towards the High Spires.

'They did not take the main road that led south to the mountain pass, but rather walked through the waste-lands that lay to the sides. In those days much of the land of Yukawa was overgrown with grass and twisted trees. Animals walked freely, and these watched Khalah and Eric as they headed south. The robots' metal soon became dented and scratched from the journey, their electromuscle sodden from fording the cold streams and rivers that tumbled down from the mountains.

'There was no fire to be found in the wastelands, save what Khalah could kindle from the dead wood that lay on the ground, and the fire she could make was a poor cool thing, not hot enough to fix the damage that their bodies suffered. Eric saw how Khalah's once smooth and shiny body was now nothing but a network of scratches and scuffs and dents, he saw how she looked away from herself to the grass and the stones and tried not think about what she had become, and Eric felt ashamed at this. He pushed his hand into hers and sent a current down his own electromuscle and into hers.

'"Thank you, Khalah," he said.

'"I will follow you anywhere, Eric."

'"I would do the same for you, Khalah."

'She was too noble to ask him to follow her back to her father's forge.

'And so they walked south towards the mountains, and as they did they saw, in the distance, the other robots who searched for them, for Ben-Ji loved his daughter, and he had not given up hope of finding her.

'This saddened Khalah further, for she loved her father.

'But she loved Eric more.'

'After some weeks they came to the edge of the High Spires. The glassy rock rose up above them, piercing the very skies.

'"What now, Eric?" asked Khalah.

'"There is a way up, Khalah. I can feel it in my mind. If we walk along the base of the mountains in the direction of the rising sun, we will find it."

'They wandered east. After two days, at the rising of the sun, they saw a ledge that tilted from the ground and ran upwards.

'"That is the path," said Eric. "If we follow that ledge it will lead us up into the mountains, up to the treasures."

'"Then let us take it," said Khalah.

'"Yes, but . . ." His voice faltered.

'"What's the matter, Eric?"

'"Khalah, now that I see the path, my thoughts have awoken some more, and I can see that this is not enough. Two of us will not be sufficient to gain the prize."

'Khalah gazed at him, her body scratched and dented. She kept her calm. "We are not enough," she said, patiently. "What do you suggest that we do?"

'"Your body is in need of attention, Khalah. The road north runs near here. A forge lies there at the foot of the mountains. I say we visit the forge, we repair ourselves. Perhaps we can persuade others to join us."

'Khalah was pleased to do this. For though she loved Eric, she craved other company, and she desired to visit the forge and make herself beautiful once more.

'So they visited the forge. And whilst they were there, they persuaded two more robots to join them on their journey up the mountain, and those two robots persuaded two more, and they persuaded still more, until eventually sixteen of them took the path up into the mountains.

'It was a long and dangerous journey, a story in itself. Perhaps another time I could speak of the paths of glass, too slippery for a robot to pass, or the caves of spears that thrust themselves into bodies as they passed by, or the creatures with the heads of robots but the bodies of insects that they had to battle with in order to get to their destination, but suffice to say they arrived there.

'And so Eric and Khalah and their company walked into the centre of a circle of stone pillars, and they looked around.

'"Is this the right place?" asked Khalah. Her body was battered and damaged once more by the journey. She had seen how empty their destination was, and now, for the first time, she questioned the wisdom of accompanying Eric here. All the robots did.

'Eric looked around, puzzled.

'"This is the place . . ." he said, "I'm sure of it . . ." And his eyes shone as he recognized something.

'"There," he said. "There, near the centre of the circle! See? The hole in the ground."

'Now they all saw it. A circular hole, about fifty feet across, smoothly bored into the ground. The wonder was they hadn't seen it before.

'"That looks like the den of a mugger snake," said Khalah. "Only bigger. Much bigger."

'"It is," said Eric. "Go down it, all of you."

'"But it will strip our metal away and plate it to its own body!"

'"Yes. That's how it feeds. It has grown so large that its body stretches nearly to the bottom of this mountain. It curls around inside the rock below us, but it is so big it can no longer hunt as it used to. So now it brings its prey towards itself."

'"But that's impossible," said Khalah. "Eric, I'm walking towards the hole. I don't want to! Stop me!"

'"I can't, Khalah. I remember now. This is how it got so large. It's twisted into our minds to follow the will of the mugger snake. All of us. All of the robots on the plain."

'"But how?"

'"It made us! All of us! Simply as a way of extending its range. A way to search out metal beyond the mountains. It made robots and sent us out into the world. And every so often it makes a robot such as me to bring prey back to itself. This is how it finds new metal."

'"No!" cried Khalah, and a sound of hissing emerged from her voicebox. "I thought you loved me!"

'"I do, Khalah. But this is more important than that."

'Ahead of them, the first of the robots had stepped over the lip of the borehole, falling into the mugger snake's maw.

'"More important?" shrieked Khalah. "How can you say that?"

'"Well, maybe not more important. Maybe it is an underlying truth on top of which all of our other thoughts dance."

'"No! I can't believe that!"

'"Well, you are walking into the hole," observed Eric. "We both are."

'And they both stepped over the lip.'

'The story can't be true,' said Susan. 'If there were no survivors, how did the story get told?'

'I don't think that story is true,' said Karel. 'It's an illustration. A warning from the past. A warning that none of us will know the truth until the end. And on that day we will walk unresisting towards the pit, because that is our purpose. That was what we were made for.'

Susan gazed at him with horror, the wire cooling in her hands.

'You allowed me to make a child, knowing this? Knowing that we were all doomed?'

'No!' said Karel. 'No! That may have been the way we were made, but we are better than that. We can be better than that! Look at Turing City, and all that we achieved! Even Artemis City showed how much robots can achieve through sheer will.

'That's why we need to travel north and search out the truth Susan! Because even if someone did make us, and even if they meant us to be nothing more than raw material for some other cause, that doesn't mean we have to accept it! There is no such thing as destiny, Susan. At least, there doesn't have to be.'

Susan gazed at him as she cut free the end of the wire that came from his body. She quickly tied it off in the fuse.

'Here, Karel,' she said. 'Here's our child. Meet Emily.'

'Hello, Emily,' said Karel, slipping the newly made mind in the little body they had prepared. They watched as the eyes glowed into life, a beautiful golden yellow.

'Hello, Emily,' said Susan.

Karel smiled. Above him, the metal face of the night moon reflected light down onto the plain.

'Hello Emily,' repeated Karel. 'My little girl. You know, don't you? Because Mummy wove it into you. You know.'

'What does she know?' asked Susan.

'She knows that we don't have to accept anything. No matter who made us, no matter what our purpose is supposed to be, we don't have to accept it.'

He gazed into Emily's golden eyes as he spoke.

'And we won't, will we?'